THE GEORGETOWN HEIST

The Third Book of the Babylon Saga

J.J. Honesty-Bey

Order this book online at www.trafford.com
or email orders@trafford.com

Most Trafford titles are also available at major online book retailers.

Print information available on the last page.

ISBN: 978-1-4907-6196-1 (sc)
ISBN: 978-1-4907-6195-4 (e)

Trafford rev.   09/25/2015

 www.trafford.com

North America & international
toll-free: 1 888 232 4444 (USA & Canada)
fax: 812 355 4082

To The Reader(s)

You have my profound apologies for the way this book turned out. I typed it just like I wrote it several years ago. I couldn't get help in bring this dream of mines to life. My help on the inside was just as non-existing on the outside. I typed this and the other six on a primitive typewriter, so once I hit the return button it was final. I have typos, I have wrong words in the wrong place, I have incomplete sentences do to me trying to rush. I give you, and or you all my word if this book does in fact sells. I will have it re-done immediately. I'll also write the other Babylon stories, and all of them will be done professionally, and that I swear. It pains me that this book wasn't done right the first time, but being incarcerated I had to make a way. I had to get it out there the best way I could. I wanted to give a different read and a different experience coming from a male in my race and my situation. Every male in my race the writes books. Always says that their book is totally different from anything else out there, and it don't. (Except for Mike Harper and Plexx) Well how many more ways can one sell drugs, betray friends and family, get hooked on drugs, kill people, pimp and snitch? I can truly tell you that The Georgetown Heist is one hundred fifty percent different from anything out there, and it won't change if it sells. I once again apologize for the way this book came out. Oh and I have done seven of them I might put out "During The Drought" next. So as of right now you have me and all of my imperfections.

DEDICATION

Always to my Masters, my King and Queen, my Gods!

My Parents

Born

John Honesty-Bey & Dinetha D. Ratcliffe

Johnny Boy and Sunshine, may you two receive all the
happiness in your deaths that you didn't receive in
your lives.

I Love You!

Chapter 1

"Okay here he comes, he's pulling up by himself. He's parking, he's on his way out the car. He's out the car, now he's walking across the street. He's half way, he's on the sidewalk, go now!" The voice from the cheap walkie-talkie shouts.

Out of the alley comes three young men wearing masks, while carrying guns in their hands. They catches an old man before he sticks his key into the padlock to unlock the security gate in front of the building. "I wouldn't do that just yet," says Babylon. "Take them keys and open this bad boy up," he continues.

Bernard snatches the keys from the old man, who tries to put up a fight which is suppressed by a strong elbow to his throat from Babylon. "It's just a robbery old man don't make it a homicide," Babylon says with conviction in his voice.

The old man calms down and Bernard opens up the security gate, and now the front door to the building. They all go in where the old man is tied up immediately.

***

Inside of a parked dark blue Crown Victoria directly across from the building where the old man was just taken inside, a voice yells: "Vat'z zee fok zuzt happenz, iz thziz forz veal?"

***

About eight cars down from the parked Crown Victoria
is a parked black mini van, and a voice cries out from
the inside. "Did you just see that? I can't just sit
here and do nothing," the man behind the wheel of the
mini van says.

"You will do just that, sit and do nothing. This
is great, just keep the cameras rolling and watch for
the response time. This place will be swarming with
agents," one of the passengers explains to the driver.

***

"**Everything is clear,** I see nothing and nobody is
on the street," Teeny-Man says over the cheap walkie-
talkie. Teeny-Man now starts up his black Chevy Capris
and heads around to the back of the building. "I'm at
the back door," he tells them through the radio.

The back door opens up and Teeny-Man is all
smiles, as he is greeted with a smile in return from
Juice-Hop. Both young men go to join the other two
accomplices.

"Teeny-Man, you got the tools?" Asks Babylon.

"Yeah, I got everything," he responds.

"Good because there has been a change of plan,"
Babylon informs them all.

"A change of plan?" Bernard says in a questionable
voice.

"Yeah, a change of plan." Babylon reiterates with
a serious look upon his face. "Look, there's no sense
of us just getting some of this stuff. We will get the
same amount of time if we get caught, so let's take it
all." Babylon looks around at everyone with a steady
eye, along with a wicked smile, that's an invitation
to commit mayhem.

"And that's why the penitentiary is over crowded.
So go tell them mother fuckers to make room, because
Peter Paul said try'em all," Teeny-Man tells the
group.

They all try the different keys to the different
boxes. The thought crosses Juice-Hop's mind, taking an

diamond bank is hard work. He would have preferred kid napping a drug dealer but, here he is in Georgetown robbing a diamond bank with a tied up old Jew watching.

Box after box they open keeping the box contents with itself so the diamonds don't get mixed up. Time passes by considerably and Bernard with a worry in his voice says: "Hey you all, we've been here too, long it may not be wise to over extend out stay. It's not that serious."

They all looks at him in a weird way. "We are going to clean this place out," Babylon tells him. "And it is that serious," he continues.

The time goes by and the four of them just work their tales off to complete the job. "That's it slim we're done, we have cleaned this bad boy out, it's dry. I am going to look for the money in this place. We most definitely are going to need it, and especially for our trip along with our troubles," Babylon tells them.

As the other three begin to load up everything. Babylon goes looking for some money. He spots his goal, and completes his mission and takes it all from the safe with the help of the old man. Now ready to leave, Babylon notices something that looks like a door.

"Where does that door lead to?" Babylon asks the old man.

"To the stairs," the old man answers. Babylon takes out his fifty caliber Desert Eagle and smacks the hell out the old man with it.

"You smart ass, you know what I'm talking about."

"The basement, it leads to the basement."

"Thank you Sir, you should have said it the first time." Babylon goes to the door and down the stairs. Now in the basement he can see a large working table along with tools of the trade. It seems as though its really nothing down here worth taking.

But something is not right he has a feeling. Now he sees it, all four walls are different. Each one is made different from the other and from different

3

material. Now he begins to call up stairs to his crew. "Hey, come down here and bring the old man with y'all."

They all come to the basement with the old man in tow. They are looking at Babylon for some kind of explanation, for calling them down to the basement. "Look at the walls, all four of them. Every last one of them are made from different material. It got's to be some major merchandise down here," he tells them.

"Hey slim, I know damn well you ain't call us down here to steal no damn walls?" Teeny-Man asks.

"No T, it's something behind the walls," Babylon responds. As they all turn to the old man with a look of lust, thirst and desire in their eyes. Babylon takes the lead on questioning him.

"Old man, what's behind the walls and don't lie?"

"There's nothing behind these walls," the old man answers.

"If you are lying and we find something, I am going to put three slugs in your head old man."

"I don't know of a safe or anything of value being down here. And I never had a reason to go behind the walls, the place is all concrete." Babylon looks at the old man coldly.

"You heard what I said old man," he restates his threat with a continuous cold stare. "Hey y'all I can feel it, it's something down here," says Babylon while inspecting the walls.

"Nawl, that's not what you're feeling. What you are feeling is us sliding a couple of levels," Teeny-Man tells him.

"What do you mean, sliding a couple of levels?" Babylon asks.

"We are now entering the life section of the sentencing guidelines," Teeny-Man informs him.

"Damn them guidelines, just help out T."

Babylon goes silent and turns his head sideways and places his right index finger over his lips. "Mr. Goldsmith, are you in here? A woman's voice inquires from up stairs.

"Who is that?" Babylon whispers to the old man.

"It's Maria, she's the bank's geologist. She is no

harm, please don't hurt her," the old man pleads.
"Call her down here and if you try yourself
something I will kill her myself."

"Oh Maria! Oh Maria! I am down here my child, in
the basement," the old man informs her. She's coming
down the stairs talking to the old man.

"What are you doing in the basement? You know it's
off limits," she says to him. She is met at the bottom
of the steps with guns pointed directly at her. "Oh my
God, what is this?" Maria sighs.

"Ah shit Maria, it ain't nothing but an old
fashion robbery that's all. There's no need to be
alarmed by it," Teeny-Man tells her.

"Oh my, I know what you want please don't hurt
me." Maria begs, and without warning she starts taking
off her clothes right in front of everyone.

"Now that's a white bitch for your ass right
there," Teeny-Man says with excitement in his voice.

"What the?" Babylon begins to ask himself. "What
part of the game is this?" Babylon continues to ask
himself. With Babylon now looking around unsure of
what is happening. Teeny-Man starts to move towards
Maria with his gun lowered. Babylon tries to stop him
but, it is too late. Maria uses her straight open flat
hand and chops him in his throat.

It is something from any of the spy movies.
Babylon is watching as it all goes on. Teeny-Man drops
his Desert Eagle forty four magnum on the floor and
grabs his throat. She kicks him in his chest so hard,
that the first thing to hit the floor is the back of
his neck and head.

Bernard makes his move, she kicks him in the
ankle, the ribs and in the face with three consecutive
kicks. As he falls back, Juice-Hop now advances upon
her. She does a one hundred eighty degree spin move
and catches him with an open palm under his chin. As
his body is attempting to fall, she is not letting it.
She has him by his throat just crushing his windpipe.
Babylon is stuck there just in total awe, at this
white woman who has taken out two of South East D.C.'s
best with ease. Even the old man is in total shock of
Maria's performance here today. That

That he looks around to Babylon as to invite him in on it. Babylon has seen enough of this foolishness.

"Stop!" He tells her, but she pays him not one once of attention. "Stop bitch, before I kill your ass," she hears that. Maria stops and turns to Babylon and says:

"You will lay down your weapon, or I will have to disarm you." It is at this point that Babylon knows this woman isn't a regular white woman.

She starts to walk towards Babylon, and talking to him while he has his guns pointed at her. "Can you do it, can you really kill an unarmed woman, a wife, and a mother, can you?"

During Maria's rampage Babylon picked up everybody's weapons. And now he has his fifty caliber in his right hand, Teeny-Man's forty four magnum in his left hand. Juice-Hop's forty four magnum along with Bernard's Sig Sauer nine millimeter is in his front waist band.

Now Maria asks him the same question again: "Can you kill me, a woman that's scared to death that she might not never see her babies again, that her babies will never see their Mommy again?"

Babylon looks down and just shakes his head and takes a deep breath. He looks around and sees his friends and Bernard getting up off the floor and in some serious pain. Maria looks at Babylon and begins to talk once more.

"Do you read the Bible?" she asks him.

"I, I have read it before, but what does that have to do with anything?" Babylon replies.

"Well its a passage in there John 14:1, that says: "Let not your heart be troubled;" you believe in God, believe also in me. Do you believe in God?"

"Yeah."

"Well then believe in me, you can become a hero here today." Babylon finally lowers his guns, and she whispers. "That's it be a hero, that's it. Ask and it shall be given," she continues.

Babylon's guns are all the way down now, on his sides with his head hanging down also. "I'm tired," he says to her. She nods yes to him, she's walking coming

towards him, he says to her with his head still down:
"Can you do me a favor?"

"Yes," she answers. "What is it?" She continues.

"Can you hold these for me?" With his hands slowly moving upwards. Maria has a shit eating grin on her face. "Sure I-," she begins to say.

But she never gets it out, Babylon starts shooting off both Desert Eagles at her. One after the other striking her in the chest, throat, shoulder, stomach and her pelvis. Her body leaves its feet as the bullets from the Desert Eagles knocks her backwards and pins her to the ground.

The dimly lit basement was full of light from the sparks that the big guns produced. He now walks over top of Maria, and places his gun on her forehead, he decides against it. And instead he places it underneath her chin and squeezes off two shots, ripping off the top of her skull.

Even as he watches the fifty caliber bullets rip through her skull, it was the matter of the explosionary display of skull and scalp that blew everywhere, that made the other viewers look in amazement.

"Fuck, it took you long enough to crush the bitch out. You up there shucking and jiving with the bitch," Teeny-Man complains to Babylon.

"Not now Teeny-Man," he pleads. It is, at this time that they all hear a beeping sound. "Hey slim, y'all hear that?" Asks Babylon.

"Where is it coming from?" Juice-Hop asks out loud.

"The wall?" In a questionable voice Babylon answers. They all go to listen and inspect the walls.

"It's right here, over here." Teeny-Man points with his right index finger. "Whatever it is, the shots from the Eagles is what caused it," Teeny-Man explains it. They all can see the bullet holes in the hollowed wall. As the four of them start to tear into the wall, it appears to be a safe of sorts.

"I told you!" Babylon says with delight. As they try to figure out a way to open the safe, Bernard says: "Hey look, we been in here too, damn long we got

7

to fall back and roll up out of here. We have an old man tied up and he has witnessed the robbery, the murder and the buffoonery of us trying to get into a safe and never once asked him what's the combination?"

"I don't think that a combination is going to do us any good. This thing is digital and a slug went straight into it, so that's that," Babylon explains.

"The more reason for us to leave this place," says Bernard.

At that very moment the safe starts to make a buzzing sound, similar to a count down and without warning the safe opens up on it's own. Inside was a black hard looking briefcase of sort. "What's up with all this mother fucken smoke and shit?" Teeny-Man complains.

Once Babylon opens up the case all three of them just stands there with their eyes wide open along with their mouths. "Slim, our shit is serious as a mother fucker," Teeny-Man tells them.

Their eyes are glued to twenty one of the biggest most beautiful diamonds they have ever seen. They were all ready in a case that was made for them. "Let's go y'all, its no sense for us to stay here any longer," Babylon now says.

So Teeny-Man takes the case but, they had no idea that by taking that case it would set off an alarm like no other in the world.

***

Outside in the Crown Victoria, the occupants sit and wonder what is going on inside this brand new diamond bank, that hasn't been open a day yet. But, is the scene of a robbery and brutal murder.

***

The mini van occupants are in the same boat as the Crown Victoria's occupants. They both were here for this new diamond bank. Both may have had the same agenda but, they most definitely are on separate sides of the field.

8

The Georgetown Heist

And this robbery by these young ignorant amateurs places a monkey wrench in their plans. Even if they could not get what they came for, they at lease know who has it. They can identify all of the young men involved in this diamond bank robbery.

***

As they are preparing to leave, Babylon speaks: "Go ahead, I'll be out in a second." He now goes to the old man and just looks at him. He places his Desert Eagle on the right side of the old man's head, closely towards the temple.

Babylon takes a squeeze of his gun letting off three shots to the old man's head. The bullets all go through his head. With the first one exiting through his left ear, the second his lower left jaw and the last through the left side of his neck.

The shot that exited through his jaw, left it barely hanging on to his face. By this time the other three young men come running to see who's shooting and for what?

"You straight Bab?" Teeny-Man asks.

"Why so brutal?" Bernard asks.

"I told him what would happen if we found something in the walls," Babylon answers them both.

"Hey slim, you like, crushed him out like, seventy five to nothing," Juice-Hop tells him. They all just shakes their heads and walk away. As they reach the car Babylon is the last one to get in. He's sitting behind the driver's seat, as he takes a deep breath he begins to speak: "It's off to Miami."

They start their drive home, they stay on the back streets and alleyways. Just as they turn to get on M Street N.W., they see a swarm of police cars and SUV's zooming past them. They all freeze for a moment as the vehicles keep moving by them and they finally laughs at it all.

"Look, I'm going all the way with it, you all have seen what's in the case and in those sacks. I'm willing to die for mines, this stuff belongs to us now point seen money earned," Babylon tells the car.

9

"Now what are you going to do, lay down or lay them pigs down? Because they're coming for what is ours. I don't know for a fact how much this stuff is really worth but, I say thirty million dollars a piece easily. You know I am going to hold court in the street for that kind of money," Babylon continues.

The others agree to hold court in the street, by nodding their heads in agreement with Babylon. As they drive through downtown Washington D.C., everything seems to be going their way.

"Look, we all got to go home to get our stuff together before we leave," explains Babylon. "So Teeny-Man, stop by my house first so we can break down this money," he finishes.

"Okay then, I hear you," Teeny-Man responds.

***

At Babylon's mother's apartment they all have decided to get dressed there to save some time. So Babylon invites them to help themselves to whatever they need from his closet. The agreement is once the money is counted, go and call Ms. Carroll Short, she's a master thief of expensive clothes.

She has perfected her craft so well, that she can dress the Queen of England, if she had to. Once they were all situated they sat and counted up the money from the robbery.

"It's ninety four thousand on the nose y'all. I thought that it would be more there. But then again, it had what it was supposed to have had. So that's like, about hum, it's twenty three five for each of us," Babylon says upon completion.

"Bab, you know it's no guarantee that we all will make it to Miami right? I say let's break down everything now, and nobody tries to get rid of their stones here. Everything goes to Miami and then its whatever," Teeny-Man tells him.

"Slim, I'm cool with that, they belongs to each of us," Babylon replies.

Ms. Carroll Short comes with their orders interrupting their planning.

Chapter 2

The young men handle their purchase quick and go back to their business, splitting up the diamonds. They divide up every small sack that has diamonds in it.

It is a four way split from each bag of diamonds. The same with the rubies, emeralds, and the sapphires. They all just love the different colors of the diamonds. The pink, the blue, the clear, the yellow and the chocolate.

This is for a fact, a robbery made for some Europeans or some well organized individuals with million dollar equipment and the resources. But here they are in the middle of the projects with untold wealth in precious stones.

The Wellington Park apartment complex, would never believe such a story like this one. But on this day in 2555 Elvans Road South East apartment number one zero one, it is true.

"And now for the big boys," states Teeny-Man with a smile on his face. The young men just stare at the big diamonds.

"It's impossible for them to be real," suggests Bernard.

"They are too, big. Maybe, uncut diamonds, maybe that's how they look before they get cut up?" Juice-Hop adds.

What ever the answer is, the truth is that the diamonds have new owners, and Juice-Hop is looking

11

like he is about to say something.

"Hey B, look slim, its twenty one of those big ones in the case. And since you are the one who went the extra mile on this one, and since we can't break them down evenly anyway. I feel as though you should get the last odd one. And I don't think nobody would object to that."

The other two nods with approval, so Teeny-Man, Juice-Hop and Bernard all get five of the huge diamonds each, and Babylon gets the remaining six.

"Bab, you finish in there?" A voice outside his room asks. It's his younger brother so he opens up his door and lets him in.

"Moody, what's up big boy?" He asks his brother. "I got something for you," he continues as he hands his brother a huge amount of money. "Take this and hide it good before Mommy take it from you."

Now handing his brother another large amount of money. "When I leave, give this to Mommy for me."

"Okay I will, thanks Bab I love you."

"I know, I love you too, and thanks for them walkie-talkies they worked good."

As his brother walks out the room, they're still in the act of cleaning up so they can leave. "Boom!" Babylon's mother bursts through his bedroom door.

"Get me! I know you mother fuckers hit good as a mother fucker. And I'm not trying to hear that bullshit either. You mother fuckers all up in this bitch taking showers and shit, like you mother fuckers are a bunch of bitches. I know y'all ain't up in my mother fucken house swapping out with each other-"

"What, fuck type shit you on Bunny?" Teeny-Man interrupts and asks her, and she pays him no mind.

"You nasty, freak body mother fuckers, break a bitch off," she continues. And it is at this point that she realizes what she is surrounded by. She sees the four piles of money along with velvety bags, indicating that they belong to four different people.

She notices the diamonds as they are being placed in the sacks, and she notice a lot of sacks. Babylon just can't hold it back any longer.

The Georgetown Heist

"Ma, what are you doing? You see I have company and you still come up in here like this is a joke. Get out my room," he says while looking very angry at her.

She knows that her son is out in the streets doing all sorts of stuff including killing but, she also knows that he will not hurt her. So she doesn't take him seriously.

"You ain't got no mother fucken room," she responds to him.

"And that's why I'm not coming back here."

"Mother fucker, what you waiting for? You can get the fuck on now!"

"Let's go y'all," he tells his crew. They all leave the apartment to go up to the car. "Hold on for a minute I'll be right back, I forgot something." Babylon tells them as they are now at the car.

He goes back down to the apartment and go to his room to get the black case that the big diamonds came in. He says good bye to his younger siblings. He got more hugs and kisses than he could handle. As he is leaving going through the front door, Bunny starts.

"I know good goddamn well you ain't going to leave without giving me some money for this house and these babies?"

"Ma, I got it covered."

"What cha mean, covered?" He's playing with her to make her more mad than she already is.

"I got Ayanna and Karen coming over to bring you all everything that you need. Just call one of them and they will bring it over here," he tells her.

"I don't need no mother fucken bitches, taking care of me. Like you, putting a mother fucker in charge of me and my mother fucken babies.

"Fuck Ayanna and Karen, I'm not going to call them for a mother fucken thing." Without even answering Babylon just starts to leave, and yells to his younger brother.

"Moody, you can have my room I'm moving out, everything in there is yours now." His mother is in full rage and begins to talk.

"Your room? You ain't got no mother fucken room. And his little pissy ass ain't going in there for what

13

just so he can piss the mother fucker up? Pissy mother fucken bastard, I should take your mother fucken pissy ass sheets, write your mother fucken name on them and hang them right on the mother fucken fence surrounding the trash can. And show them little bitches that your mother fucken ass be pissing in the mother fucken bed.

"Trifling mother fucker you, you lay your funky ass down in all that piss and filth, with them stinking damp ass sheets. Them mother fuckers so goddamn dingy, filthy and black. Them mother fuckers look like big ass used tea bags."

She's so loud that Babylon can still hear her from the top of the stairs and can't help but laugh to himself, as he shakes his head. Finally in the car he takes a deep breath.

"Let's go Teeny-Man, we have a long ride ahead of us."

***

Inside of the Homeland Security Headquarters, a woman is walking extremely fast down the hall. She gets to the office of her destination. "Excuse me Mr. Sears, we have a situation that needs your attention," she informs him while handing him a piece of paper.

"Okay, now that's bad, real bad," he says to himself as he's finished reading the paper. Suddenly his phone rings, he's hesitant to answer it.

"Yeah, who is it?" Mr. Sears asks.

"Darryl Rowe," the caller replies.

"Give it to me, D.R."

"Some time this morning Ronald, Operation Candy Shop was compromised an agent along with an civilian was killed in the process. And on top of that, the football has been intercepted."

"D.R., I just got the data on it no more than two minutes ago."

"I see, so where are we right now?"

"We do have video surveilence, so identification confirmation will be done within the hour."

"Send a copy of the feed here, and everything else that you get. Do I take it that you have nothing to go on either?"

"No D.R., nothing." As Ronald Sears become silent, Darryl Rowe knows that Ronald will have to make that phone call. As much as he hate to do it, it must be done.

"Ronald, I would like to come there with you. While this is being sought out, and if need be take to the field. Are you going to make the call yourself?"

"Yeah, I'll take care of it, I just ask that you make sure that any and all intel that comes in, comes to me. And to also keep Jimmy out the game."

"Ron, what makes you think that he won't find out about this? The entire government will know in ten minutes from now. And then every government in the world, and next every criminal, and then every terrorist and mercenary, that weapons of mass destruction are loose in the United States of America."

"Not if I contain it first, and recover the football."

"I wish you all the luck in the world but, if this gets ugly. They will call him in and they will put him in charge of the situation.

"They couldn't care less, who does it just as long as it gets done. But if you go any other route, don't let them know you talked to me. I'll catch it all on the six o'clock news." Darryl Rowe finishes. Now the phones disconnects and Ronald Sears is on his way to the command room.

***

In the command room of the Homeland Security Headquarters, he stands on the platform and begins to speak to his employees. "Listen up everyone," he says in a loud and sturdy voice. He has the attention of the entire room with all eyes on him now. "As of right now, we are a code red throughout the entire country. All F.E.M.A. regional offices will be on high alert."

***

She places a call from Morocco to her counter terrorist agency in the United States.

"Have you heard about what happened at the Candy Shop? I know Ron is one mad somebody," she says.

"Tonya, what is it with you? You are out at God knows where, just spending the agency's money recklessly. And I am here trying to hold together what's left of this agency."

"You worry to much, maybe you need to get yourself a young boy to work the kinks out your back."

"Bye Tonya."

"Not yet, I will be monitoring this situation with Ron." And with that, they both hangs up.

***

"Since the hurricane Katrina mess-up, the Federal Emergency Management Agency was reassigned under us, Homeland Security. So now, I have them at my disposal. The country is in great danger and millions, and I mean millions of American lives are at risk.

"This morning Operation Candy Shop was for a fact compromised. An agent was killed along with an civilian, and on top of that the football was intercepted. We all know what the football really is? But at this agency, the term football is used in terms, of something that can't be lost or talked about." Ronald Sears tells them as he watches over the room.

"We have the fate of millions in our hands and this is not a drill. I will have the intel for you in a matter of minutes. This is what I need done, yesterday. I want a vulnerability analyses which is done to determine and identify the worst hazards and threats.

"Along with the worst case scenario, I want pre-disaster recovery posts throughout the country. I want every emergency manager in the country on full alert. I need for the Emergency Operations Center in all states and cities fully operable.

"As you all know the E.O.C. has several functions. It serves as the command center and as such it must contain the necessary communications equipment so that we can direct the units out in the field.

"It serves as an operations center for local government officials our E.O.C. staff and selected emergency volunteers. It provides a center of operations and information for government officials that's away from the disaster scene.

"Inform the Centers for Disease Control and Prevention to alert all of their offices country wide. Activate the Incident Command System at the Operation Candy Shop west side entrance.

"For those of you who do not know, the Incident Command System was developed in the nineteen seventies in response to a series of major wild land fires in southern California. At that time municipal, county, State and Federal fire authorities collaborated to form the Firefighting Resources of California Organized for Potential Emergencies, which acronym is F-I-R-E-S-C-O-P-E.

"Having identified several recurring problems involving multiagency responses, such as nonstandard and non-intergrated communications, lack of consolidated action plans, lack of designated facilities.

"Efforts to address these difficulties resulted in the development of the original Incident Command System model for effective incident management. Now although originally developed in response to wildfires.

"The Incident Command System has evolved into an all risk system that is appropriate for all types of fire and nonfire emergencies. Much of the success of the I-C-S had resulted directly from applying a common organizational structure, key management. Also I-C-S is a model tool for command, control and coordination of a response.

"And provides a means to coordinate the efforts of individual agencies as they work towards the common goal of stabilizing the incident and protecting life, property and the environment.

"But it can be used for, hazardous materials incidents, planned events, celebrations, parades, and concerts, official visits etc. Response to natural hazards, single and multiagency law enforcement incidents.

"Like fires, incidents involving multiple casualties, multijurisdictional and multiagency incidents, air, rail, or ground transportation accidents, wide area search and rescue missions and pest eradication programs.

"I want the EPA, DOT, DOE, FBI, ATF, DEA, and the Nuclear Regulatory Commission all put on full alert and also sent the intel, all city and states S.W.A.T. teams on alert.

"Let the F.A.A. know, that nothing leaves D.C., Maryland and Virginia, nor comes in. If it's in the air, it better have feathers. I see that we finally have the surveilence feed from the Candy Shop. Take all we have and run analysis on them. That would mean now, people." Mr. Sears says as he finishes.

As people start to scramble to their assigned jobs. Ronald Sears is a wreck, he knows that if he doesn't find the football and contain this situation million of lives will be lost. By the wicked country that secretly created them behind it's citizens back.

"Weapons of mass destruction, to die by that in which your own country has made is one hell of a fate," Ronald Sears says to himself.

***

"Hello, I'm Detective Victor Williams, I am with the Metropolitan Police Department." People could hear as he is conducting interviews about the double homicide that has occurred this morning. This is a business area that's really besides itself right now. He could not believe all of the information, or better yet the cooperation he's getting.

He is so accustom to the South East section of Washington D.C., where all he ever got was, "Fuck you!" or "Get the fuck on!" But here, he's getting help from this community, but then again, he's now in the Georgetown section of the city.

"Vic, come here and check this out."

The Georgetown Heist

"What is it Darren?"

"The Suits came and took the woman's body from the crime scene but, they left the old man's. Detective Vic Williams and his partner Darren, goes back to the crime scene. They both see that the woman's body is missing but, also that the old man's body had been moved from it's original spot. So Detective Williams leaves to go see the Suits about his crime scene.

"You know we never identified her," Detective Williams says. "The girl huh?" He continues.

"No, a woman about five foot ten one hundred thirty pounds, black hair, well dressed and in excellent shape."

"How the hell you know she was is excellent shape, Darren?"

"Because of those calves of hers and that' ripped mid section she got."

"Where are the Suits now?"

"They're over there, by that fancy meat wagon. But let me warn you Vic, these are not your regular Suits, they're different, like super Suits or something." Detective Williams walks over to the ambulance, he's cut off and is met by two of the agents wearing suits.

"I'm Detective Williams, Victor Williams homicide. I was told that you all took the body of the woman from my crime scene. I would truly like to know why?"

"Detective, is it?" One of the agents asks.

"It is."

"I was going to let you down easy but, since you got the whole Metropolitan Police thing going, here it go. This one here is above your pay grade, Vicki. Above you and anybody that you think you know."

"This is a murder we are talking about. I'm not in any competition with you or any agents or agencies. I just wish to find who's responsible for the death of those two victims."

"That was real heart felt but, I don't have the time to entertain you today, so if you would excuse us we have work to do."

"I'm afraid I can't do that. You see, when you all took that body you corrupted my crime scene. And by doing both acts you all broke the law, and the charge is-"

"Don't make me have to say it, because if I do I swear when you get back to your little station your Captain is going to chew your little ass out."

"I wish to hear this one, I'm all ears." Detective Williams tells the agent. At this time, his partner Darren has finally joins him. "I'm glad to see you Darren, you and I are about to hear why he's not going to be arrested for destroying evidence at my crime scene."

"Okay, you asked for it Vicki, by the power of Executive Order 12699 I am ordered by the President of the United States of America to produce no such property, evidence information, physical or other that may hinder or interfere with the orderly fashion of the President of the United States of America safety, life, liberty or property."

"And that's it?" Vic asks him.

"Yes Vicki, unless you just want to hear my oath. You know the one that talks about me up holding the Constitution of the United States of America, and also the Constitution of each state in the United States of America. And also defending the United States of America against all enemies foreign and domestic so help me God. Which is ususally my favorite part."

And with that one, Darren has seen this rodeo too, many times. But he has never heard it in his face like this. He know his counter part is beaten but, still determined.

"Never heard of it, Sir, please place your hands behind your-"

"Vic enough, he's not being arrested not today anyway." Darren cuts him off to tell him.

"You pulls this jurisdictional bullshit on me? I'm not finished with you yet!" Vic yells. The agent reaches inside of his jacket pocket and pulls out his credentials.

"You see this Vicki? This is something that you will never in your life have. Look at it, its called a level five clearance. The look in your eyes tells me all I need to know, you have heard of this, so you also know the only people who carries them." And with that Vic is defeated.

"And you call yourself a detective?" The agent asks Vic.

"I'm the best detective in my station if not the city."

"Yeah but, you couldn't detect this coming?" Cracking up with laughter, the other agents join in with laughter as Vic and Darren walks off.

"Darren, what would a level five government agent be doing with the body of a woman who was killed in a jewelry heist?"

"I don't know Vic."

"I'm going to find out, this here is too strange."

"Let it go Vic."

"I can't do that Darren."

"And why not?"

"O.J. baby!"

"What, what are you talking about?"

"This is my white bronco."

***

"I am going to have to remember all of the codes so I can recite them from the top of my head like you," a rookie agent says.

"No need, everything I told him was a lie."

"What?"

"Yeah, Executive Order one two six nine nine is

for disaster relief. I believe its earthquakes." They all look at him in shock.

***

Inside of the Homeland Security Headquarters a video conference is taking place. "Mr. Sears, I am wondering just how bad it is, that you would call the Joint Chiefs of Staff personally?"

"Good morning, to you all I have some disturbing news to report to you all. This morning Operation Candy Shop was compromised and an agent and an civilian was killed. And also the football has been intercepted."

"Mr. Sears, don't you think it's a little early for a drill. I thought that we were supposed to have a memo before a drill?" Another one asks.

Ronald Sears takes a deep breath and begins to speak: "To the Joint Chiefs of Staff, this is not and I repeat, this is not a drill, a joke or a hoax. This morning Operation Candy Shop was for a fact compromised and an agent along with an civilian was killed. And on top of that the football has been intercepted."

With the entire Joint Chiefs of Staff watching him, he can truly feel the weight of the guillotine about to come down upon him, even through the screen. Everything is quiet now and then a voice speaks:

"Mr. Sears, you need to come in for a debriefing, now!"

***

Detective Williams looks over the crime scene and he notice that everything has been taken and whoever it was, did not leave a thing except two dead bodies.

He further looks around in the basement he notice the wall. "What the hell was in here?" He asks himself. Whatever is was, it could not have been jewelry, he believes this to be true. Now if he can just put it all together he would be fine.

"Hello Ms. Alexandria, come here sweetheart and

22

take some pictures of this for me please. Inside and outside of it, and have them sent to me immediately, thank you darling." He thinks that he may be on to something, so he take another swing at it.

"Maureen," he yells out. "Ms. Maureen Canter, I need to see you my pretty," he jokes. Now she appears before him looking as evil as ever and watching him the entire time.

"Maureen I need for you to get samples from this safe." Being that she's the best forensic tech in the metropolitan area.

"When the results come in, please have them sent to me, thank you Maureen."

***

"**Are you telling** me that this happened right in front of you all?"

"Yez." Now the voice is laughing away in the distance.

"Doez I amuze yooh?" The Frenchman asks.

"This county, we plan to go take a place and somebody else takes it right in front of you all. It's too, much crime in this country. The only thing about it, is that we don't have to worry about being exposed." Mr. Titus Wright tells them.

"Szo vat za-bout thzee ziamondz?"

"That's not a problem to me. Once we run their faces through our contacts. We'll go and take back the stones."

"Szo INTERPOL, howz vee getz pozz thzem?"

"Oh my French friend, have you forgotten that we. I mean you, did not take them from the bank?"

"I vish tzoo vee prezent vhen it iz tzime tzoo getz ziamondz bok."

"My dear Frenchman, I see that you forget your place here."

"Vhat dzoo yooh meanz, mi plaze?"

"We had a deal and you failed to deliver the goods so however we salvage this is our keep, and you gets nothing."

"I dzid not leave Fronze forz vacation. I came for

jzob, and no dzamn Yankz vill tzake it fromz mi." As
the Frenchman finishes his words sudden unpleasantness
fills the room.

"Is that how you feel about us?" Mr. Titus Wright
asks him.

"Fuckzah yooh allz."

Now the men in the room with him all make their
move against him. Jaquiel, sensing danger earlier
planned his get away prior to the last two question.
As the American men start to pull out their weapons.

Jaquiel knows he can't win this fight at the most
he could kill, would be seven out of the thirteen. So
if he couldn't kill them all, then the hell with them
all, for now.

So with the odds against him, Jaquiel makes a
quick and powerful jolt and dives out of a window.
After falling three stories, he still manages to get
up and run around the corner of the house. Knowing the
men will not shoot in or around the house, he makes
his escape.

"Let's go get him," one of the men shouts.

"Leave him be," Titus tells them all.

"We should take him out, instead of letting him
run loose in the city. He will be looking for us, you
do know this, don't you?"

"Let him come he's just one sad ass Frenchman.
What can one little sad ass Frenchman do against us?
You got the faces of those lucky bastards from the
heist, so go and run them by our contacts. And let's
get some names and addresses by those faces."

The men return to their seats all of them are in
agreement that the hard part is over with. The job has
been done by somebody else but, the wait is hectic and
the unknown is worst. Who is it that have them. And
what are they willing to do to keep them? Who are
they, really? They all wonder, will they be willing to
die for them, or each other?

The thought never entered their minds that maybe
since they were beaten to the punch, they should just
go and find another job. But no that's too, much like
right to look for another score to take. Besides this
one is the best one ever.

The Georgetown Heist

***

Holding his shoulder leaning to the side, he is still able to flag down a cab. "Pleaze Szir, tzake mi tzoo," he catches his breath so his english won't sound too, bad. "Twzoo-threez-fourz Kenzucty Avenue, Szouth Eazt."

As he replays the night over in his mind. He is already plotting his revenge but, before he puts his plan into action. He must find out where the stones are.

He tries to think of ways to track them down. But the pain from his fall interferes with his thoughts. He's sure of one thing, that he will have his revenge on those who betrayed him.

The cab pulls up in front of his house, he pays the driver and goes into the house. Prior to his arrival to Washington D.C., his assistant made arrangements for a few safe houses for him.

Finally inside the house, he goes straight for the shower, while inside, the hot water and steam takes whatever strength he had left. Now out the shower the cool air wakes him back up. He fixes himself a drink, finishes it immediately and walks over to his bed.

He's over top of the nicest bed, and takes his hand and slides it between the mattress and the box spring and with one heap of a pull snatches the mattress off the bed.

The tossed mattress now reveals the hardware of weapons. Two Heckler and Koch Mark Twenty Fives with silencers, one phone, one Vector nine millimeter, one tactical knife, one M.P.-Five (a) with silencer. Lots of ammunition and four hand grenades.

He loads up to carry out his will, he takes a breath that is met with a sigh of pain from his fall but, he still manages to get his words out. "Vive les Fronze, here comez thzee Frenchmon."

***

While night has fallen upon the city of Washington D.C., Detective Victor Williams is turning in early. For he knows that come tomorrow he begins his quest of looking for the murderers of the diamond bank slaying's.

As he prepares himself for bed, one of the few joys in his life, his son V.J., comes to him and gives him a much needed hug.

"Hey V.J.," Vic says to his son. "It's past my bed time, so I know its past yours," he continues.

"I wait up for you."

"You wasn't scared?"

"No, I big boy!"

"Yeah you're a big boy, let's get you to bed." His son agrees tonight but, doesn't like it one bit. And he sees it but, Vic is mentally drained tonight.

Taking his son to his own room Vic tucks in his son, gives him a kiss on the forehead and goes to his own room. As he enters his bedroom, he sees that his wife has that look in her eyes.

"Not tonight," he says to himself. He's beginning to undress and just now decides to forego the shower, and just take one in the morning. His wife is looking for a little loving. The phone rings and she answers it.

"Hello?" She answers it. It's for Vic and she hands him the phone, he's saved by the bell.

"Yeah Vic," he's listening to the other end. "What! I don't fucking believe it. I'll see you in the morning." He has just been told that the diamond bank had exploded.

"That was for me, and that's why I act with the quickness."

***

Somewhere in an undisclosed area a meeting is being held at 2:17 a.m. Inside this think tank are the minds that play God with the lives of the country and the world.

"My name is-"

"This is no time for introductions, where are we with this situation?" A voice cuts him off and asks.

"As of right now, I have the command room working over time on this. And also at this time we have no

26

The Georgetown Heist

sure leads as to the perpetrators only a hunch at this time." Mr. Ronald Sears says to the group.

"Have there been a ransom, a claimed responsibility?"

"We wish to know, what you know, now," another voice commands. Ronald Sears readies himself in front of the big wigs.

"Some time this morning Operation Candy Shop was compromised. Two were killed, an agent and an civilian and the football has been intercepted. And that's were we are right now gentlemen. And I took all the necessary steps with all the agencies." Ronald Sears got a little bit of confidence with the words that he had spoke.

"So you mean to tell me that all of the candy is gone?" A faceless man asks.

"No, not all of it is missing." As silence fall in the room, Ronald knows his behind is grass, he just don't know how its going to be cut. He is the man responsible for protecting these highly designed weapons of mass destuction.

Now he can't even tell his superiors where they are but, only who has them. What are they going to do with them, he hasn't a clue. But more importantly he can't tell them what went wrong. As the men still sit in silence one of them speaks:

"Let me see if I got this right, there are highly made weapons of mass destruction, that can fit in the palm of your hand, to a cavity in your mouth, on American soil? And you know who has them but, don't know their whereabouts? Or more important where they have them at, or better yet what plans they have for them, is that correct?"

"Yes Sir, that's correct," he answers but, he recognizes the voice. It's Senator Walt James.

"I can deal with the fact that you don't know what they're going to do with them. I can deal with the fact you don't know why they did it. The part I'm most disturbed is that you don't know the location of them.

"So I can get my family and a couple of my personal secretaries to safety. I miss the good old days, when shit like this happened, you were told ahead of time. When that anthrax shit hit after nine eleven, shit we were all conveniently on trips. That's why its so important to keep fucking Republicans in office."

"I can assure you all, that I have the best of the best working on this," Ronald tells them all.

"Is Jimmy on your staff?" Asks one of the men present.

"No he is not, this is my operation Sir. And I will find the football and recover all of the candy as well."

"You may need his help on this."

"With all due respect Sir, he's a butcher and this sort of mission calls for a more, how can I put it? A finesse approach, Jimmy the Butcher and the men he commands are not typical for a job this delicate. One of his lackeys shoots and hits one of those stones and all our asses will be gone." As they think it over, he sees a chance to take charge of the situation.

"I am going to leave you all now and go back to the command room but, I will keep you all fully informed of all progress." His phone goes off and he answers it. "Yeah, its me. What! I knew it, I knew you could do it," he says into the phone.

"What is it Sears, did they recover the football and the stones?" The Senator asks.

"No but, all involved have been identified and teams are being mobilized as we speak. So if you all don't mind, I would like to hurry up to the command center."

"Debrief here, so we can hear it first hand," one of the Joint Chiefs of Staff says.

"Sure why not, we have the monitor ready anyway. Put it on the jumbo screen and start the video conference procedures," says the Senator.

***

At the Homeland Security Headquarters a middle aged woman by the name of Jean Culp is about to take the lead on a video conference with her boss and the Joint Chiefs of Staff.

She knows that her boss is in a tight bind. But as a veteran she understands taking one for the team, its part of being a team player, and a heads up person.

***

Ronald Sears makes the call so they can start the debriefing. Before they go online for the video conference, he takes a deep breath.

"Are you all ready?" Mr. Sears asks.

"Yes we are," the Senator tells him.

"Commence the briefing." Ronald Sears orders.

"My data shows clearly who were involved and-"

"Who am I talking to?" Asks Mr. Sears as he cuts her off.

"Sir it's me, Jean Culp. On the screen now you are seeing who went inside the Candy Shop."

"Is this it?" Asks the Senator.

"Surveilence also show targets on the outside of the structure as well," she continues. It seems as though things are worst off now than before.

"We were told that they where identified. Do you have the identities of those involved?" Senator Walt James asks.

"Yes we have positively identified them all."

"I don't understand the delay then?" The Senator continues.

"Please see the screen, for Bernard Jones,

29

date of birth is four-twenty one-ninety eight. His juvenile record reads: Drugs, guns, assaults, assault while armed, robbery, armed robbery. But the funniest thing about his record is, that it reads new."

"What do you mean, it reads new?" Mr. Sears asks her.

"It has no time line, no dates of events. It's as if he committed all this in one day. It has no history."

"In the District of Columbia, just be lucky to have that. You know how lazy and unprofessional they are," says the Senator.

"Okaaaaaay, this is Neil Green, A.K.A. Juice-Hop his date of birth is five-five-ninety eight. And his Juvenile record reads: Drugs, assault with intent to kill. He's recently released from the Department of Human Services, by way of a residential placement.

"This is Maurice Barnes, A.K.A. Teeny-Man his date of birth is three-twenty six-ninety eight, and his juvenile record reads: Drugs, guns, burglary, murder, armed robbery, thief over a thousand, forgery and indecent exposure-"

"Indecent exposure, good lord what did he do?" Asks the Senator.

"Well he apparently pulled out his penis and began to masturbate in front of this woman, or on her. But she wasn't the one who reported it. It was another civilian, a man called authorities. He told the police what happened-"

"What did he say?"

"The man reported that, the young man had his hand on his penis masturbating in front of this woman and was talking to her-"

"Talking to her?" The Senator interrupts with another question.

"Yes, according to his statement the young man was saying and I quote: "Eat it up bitch, I know you're hungry. You're starving for it, go ahead and eat you share." And then he released himself onto the woman and she did not go to court."

"I wish to know-"

"Enough with the details," one of the Joint Chiefs

of Staff says, cutting off the Senator.

Everybody in the room believe that the Senator is getting turned on by the information. Or getting some new ideas for his personal life.

"Please continue Mrs. Culp," asks Mr. Sears.

"And the last one is Nimrod Hannibal Mohammed, A.K.A. Babylon his date of birth is twelve-twenty five-ninety eight. And he seems to have only one kind of crime and he has beaten it every time at trail."

"And what might that be?" Asks Mr. Sears.

"Murder, just murder charges is all that he has. Seven in all, a triple, a double and two singles."

The men ponder on this new information. They have the video feed and sees it quite plainly. And these juveniles fit the bill to perfection, not to mention all of their faces are seen plainly also. The pondering is interrupted by Mrs. Culp.

"We have also identified the occupants in the other two vehicles as well," she informs them.

"The other two vehicles?" Mr. Sears asks.

"Yes, I believe that the juveniles beat them to the robbery."

"If there were two other vehicles and you are saying that they wasn't together, this could prove to be fatal for the youths as well as the country," one of the Joint Chiefs of Staff says.

"Who were in these other vehicles Mrs. Culp?" Mr. Sears asks her.

"The mini van was occupied by Earnest E. Simpson, Keith Brooks, Tracy Jackson and Howard R. Southern. They're all mercenaries, a bunch of pure brainless cut throats," she tells them.

"Now the Crown Victoria was carrying Timothy Moss, James Hamilton, Calvin Stevens and Raymond Reed. They are all rogue agents, working in a underground network of other rogues. Some to rival the government and if not the world. Their goal is to do something so phenomenal that they would be accepted back in the government, or use it as a bargaining chip.

"And also in the vehicle was a Jaquiel Froscois. A Frenchman that INTERPOL has as an international hitman and a master thief." The room is silent once more and

31

once more Mrs. Culp interrupts that silence.

"Mr. Sears, I must also report at this time, that I was wrong in my assessment of the other weapons of mass destruction being secured. It's been confirmed that all of the weapons have been taken. And you have my apology for the inaccurate information."

Ronald Sears knows it was really his fault. And picks right up on what she's trying to do for him. They both know that he will reward her for this one, she has freed him, for now anyway.

"You mean to tell me that on top of having nerve agents, blister agents, blood agents, choking agents and irritating agents loose inside the city. We also have nuclear weapons loose also. My God, that's enough to take out the entire country ten times." The Senator says.

"Sir, I think I can track the weapons," Mrs. Culp tells Ronald Sears.

"Mrs. Culp?" Sears calls her.

"Yes Sir."

"You're fired clean out your desk, now!"

"Bullshit, she stays on," says the Senator. "Mrs. Culp, this is Senator Walt James, can you track down the whereabouts of those weapons?"

"Yes, I think I can Sir," she answers him.

"And just how will you go about doing that?" Asks one of the Joint Chiefs of Staff.

"Well since they were stored at such freezing temperatures. I truly believe that the weapons will give off a thermal reading." They all look around at each other and now her. Without them having to say anything to her, she gets right on her computer.

"I think this is them, um, here heading south on ninety five in North Carolina."

"I must get back to the command center to over see this situation gentlemen," says Mr. Sears. All of the men in the room nod in agreement with Mr. Sears. But before he leaves them he gives an order to the command room.

"Deploy strike teams to that location and await my orders, and do not shoot, I repeat do not shoot."

***

The Georgetown Heist

The car rides through the little town as the sounds of
Supah Sug goes off. Now the car is silent awaiting for
the next song to come on.

***

"**I see that** they have the identities of those who
they claim to have broken into the Candy Shop. But
they are going to have to do better than this here, if
they think I'm going to believe that these young black
boys did this one." Ms. LaShonne Williams says.

"I don't know its something about one of them. I
think it might just be his name. I know that it don't
suppose to happen. But maybe, this one time some young
black men out did the government. And everyone but
them knows what they really took.

"They got heart anyway you look at it, and that's
what we need around here. Some new young men with
heart. They would fit right in, and give us that spark
that we so desperately need right now to keep us
afloat," Tonya responds.

"Oh please Tonya, they won't see night fall,"
LaShonne tells her.

***

"**Did y'all see** that?" Babylon asks the car.

"See what?" Teeny-Man asks in responding.

"All those cars and SUV's that just came out of
nowhere."

"Hey slim, don't spook yourself, we're going to
see a whole lot-"

"Pull over now!" The driver of a SUV yells through
his microphone.

"Hit it!" Babylon tells Teeny-Man in a loud voice.
As Teeny-Man begins speeding off, Babylon pulls out
his Desert Eagle with one hand while rolling down the
window with the other. Just as they were about to pass
one of the cars, Babylon is face to face with its
passenger.

They make eye contact, that's when Babylon places
his gun out the window and let off seven carefully

aimed shots. With four hitting the passenger in the body, and striking the driver once in the right leg.

That one from the fifty caliber is enough to make the driver stop the vehicle. But it is too late for the passenger of the car. "We got action," Babylon yells to everyone. At this time they are getting surrounded by cars and SUV"s.

Teeny-Man now sees that this is the real thing and goes into action, pulling out his own gun and rolling down his window. "Oh, I have something for your ass," he yells at his persuers.

"Teeny-Man, just drive we'll take care of it," Babylon tells him. With Juice-Hop and Bernard now following suit rolling down their windows, they're about to hold court.

"Push it Teeny-Man," Juice-Hop yells to him.

With Bernard, Juice-Hop and Babylon all now with their guns hanging out of windows. The young men begin to open fire on all vehicles following them. Juice-Hop sees his target and just unloads into the driver side of the car. He can see the red, and knows that the driver is hit.

Now that the car is swirling off the road he knows the driver has been shot bad. Behind him Bernard is just unloading on the driver's side of a car. He can see the driver slumped over and the passenger is reaching over steering the car now.

Babylon is working from behind Teeny-Man, he is shooting into a SUV but, has to stand up all the way out of the window to make sure that he hits something.

At this time Supah Sug C.D. is playing "Don't Run Now." and its loud. And Teeny-Man is driving with a force, bouncing to the music. As a SUV, pulls up next to the car trying to knock them off the road Bernard now stands up out the window.

He sees the SUV trying to ram them so he's trying to time his shot as the SUV goes back and forth he see his opportunity. The SUV now is coming back for a ram but, Bernard moves quickly out the window, and begins to fire into the SUV striking the driver in the body with slugs.

Two of them passes through the driver right into

the passenger. As all of three of them shoot and reload. The most shooting action is on Babylon and Teeny-Man's side and they are running low on ammunition.

"Hey I got to reload my magazines, I'm out of everything," Babylon yells in the car.

"Switch with me," Bernard tells him. They switch places and Babylon begins to load up his magazines with Juice-Hop in the front seat firing away.

"Push this bitch Teeny-Man." Bernard yell.

"You just keep firing that mother fucker, that's what the fuck you do," Teeny-Man yells back. As a SUV begins to ram their car Juice-Hop, by accident fires and hits the front tire of the SUV and the vehicle turns away from them violently and starts to flip over and over.

"Hey y'all, aim for the tires," he tells the car.

"Maaaan, fuck them tires bust their mother fucken asses," Teeny-Man yells. All of them sensing what's about to happen. "Crush them bitches out y'all," he continues.

"We got it Teeny-Man," Babylon tells him. Babylon tries but, its to late.

"Don't run now, mother fuckers." Teeny-Man sings along with Supah Sug. At which time he switches hands on the steering wheel. Placing his right hand on the wheel and holding his gun in his left.

"Don't stop bumping, no don't stop now mother fuckers come on." Teeny-Man still going on. A car is pulling up beside him they were not ready for what they are about to get. Teeny-Man opens up his door and places his foot on the arm rest and starts shooting into the vehicle striking the passenger in the face.

All can see that it is a loss cause for him. The driver tries to drive away with his wounded but, Teeny-Man follows him still shooting. He reloads while looking at the road and back at the car. "Got your ass mother fuckers, got your ass," he whispers to himself.

Teeny-Man fires into the car and the driver let it be known early that he is hit. When both his hands comes off the steering wheel. "Don't run now," he raps.

Babylon is reloaded and did not remember Juice-Hop's advice about the tires. A car pulls up this time and Babylon can see the driver plainly as the car tries to ram them off the road. Babylon takes a good aim at the driver and squeezes twice.

He can see that the windows have all turned burgundy, the car by default rams into them. The passenger is to late to get to the steering wheel of the car. "I see you, push this bitch T," Juice-Hop proudly tells him.

Teeny-Man tries to make his move another car comes and sandwich them in. Bernard and Teeny-Man unloads into the car sandwiching them in, Teeny-Man shots goes in the passenger. Positioning a good angle Bernard takes out the driver of the car on his side.

The car swirls off, Juice-Hop is having a hard time with the passenger, so Babylon takes a good angle on the passenger and just rips him apart. Teeny-Man slams on the brakes and the car keeps on going taking off with it the bumper.

A SUV pulls up but, this time behind the driver someone has a shotgun firing it. The first shot takes off the right fender, the second shot takes a chunk out the hood of the car. "Bab, crush'em," Teeny-Man yells out in duress.

Babylon is waiting for the SUV to approach once more. It does and Babylon goes for the driver. The Desert Eagle rips through the driver's leg and strikes the passenger's leg, the SUV is swirling off.

Babylon with the passenger behind the driver in his sights lets off his entire magazine into the door of the SUV. By looking at a figure beside the man with the shotgun. Babylon knows that he has indeed hit his mark.

"Ain't no fun when the rabbit got the gun," sings Teeny-Man. "Hold on y'all," he continues. He slams on the brakes of the car and snatches the steering wheel to the right, the entire car spins around. He now places the car in reverse, as he's now driving backward.

"What the fuck you doing?" Juice-Hop yells.

"Just follow my lead," he replies. Teeny-Man

sticks his gun out the window and begins to shoot at the cars and SUV's. They all do it a little different now. But all of the cars and SUV's are in front of them now. So all of them start to fire upon the vehicles in front of them. In this awkward position, they try their best to go on an offensive. But they can't seem to make the adjustment of it. It's too odd to them, to shoot while the vehicles are advancing on them.

Bullets are flying through windshields into the faces, bodies and limbs of these would be assassins. As they begin to fall off one by one, Teeny-Man now is about to turn the car back around. He slams on the brakes and snatches the steering wheel to the left and puts the car back in drive and never breaks his stride. "Okay then, freak this bitch Teeny-Man," an excited Juice-Hop yells out.

Now the Crown Victorias are pulling up on both sides of them, they see the cars approaching. They are reloaded and awaiting them. As the Crown Victoria's occupants begin to pull out M-4's but, they are too late the young men already have their minds made up.

Juice-Hop, Bernard and Babylon start to open fire on the approaching vehicles occupants, as the vehicles are easing off the road. Here comes a new convoy of vehicles. "Shit, they want it that damn bad?" Asks Juice-Hop.

All of the young men reload their weapons and get ready for the onslaught they're about to bring. So as they ready themselves, it will be business as usual taking out the new drivers.

As the cars and SUV's are directly behind them, the vehicles never come up beside them. "That's right fuck boys, respect these mother fucken South Eastmen," Teeny-Man yells at them.

"Hey y'all, they threw something," yells Juice-Hop.

It is a perfectly thrown hand grenade, that explodes when it was supposed to have, right in front of the driver. Teeny-Man is already down ducking away. With metal fragments flying everywhere, the windshield and the hood of the car tells the full

Chapter 5

story.

Watching the way their car is swerving on the road. The pursuers watch them preparing for a crash or to pull over. "Talk to me T," asks Babylon. "Hey, everybody alright?" He continues to asks.

"I'm straight Bab," answers Juice-Hop.

"I'm okay," Bernard tells him. With still no answer from Teeny-Man and the car still not yet under control he speaks: "Yeah, I'm straight Bab, here we go," he says as he's forcing the car back under control. Now his back is against his seat.

He's regained control of the car their pursuers have notice and also see that this is far from over. So the pursuers decides to go in for the kill. With another hand grenade ready for the throwing. He begins to pull out the pin. "Hey y'all, here comes another one, here it comes!" Teeny-Man shouts.

The nineteen ninety five Chevy Capris is at it's top speed. The Corvette engine along with the chips are doing their job. Teeny-Man is itching for something, they all can see his fingers twitching on the steering wheel. So they all brace themselves for whatever he's about to do.

"Hey y'all, me and Juice gonna stay low. Y'all back there hit 'em high," Teeny-Man instructs the car. Now he once again slams on the brakes and yanks the steering wheel to the right and begins to make the car spin around. As the car becomes fully backwards, all

The Georgetown Heist

four doors open at the same time.

Teeny-Man and Juice-Hop have a foot on their doors, while Babylon and Bernard are standing up between the door and the car itself. Using their elbows to hold on to their door and keep their balance on the roof of the car, while shooting.

The full assault takes their pursuers by surprise. With bullets hitting the windshields going through to find their intended targets. Slugs are hitting bodies, faces, arms, throats, necks, hands and heads. Teeny-Man has his left arm resting between the door and car while shooting, he's looking straight ahead and periodically checking the rear view mirror.

The passenger of the Crown Victoria is struck in the arm and drops the hand grenade inside the vehicle as it goes down the highway on route seventeen just past Wilmington, North Carolina. The car begins swerving off the road but, before it could hit anything, the hand grenade explodes inside the car.

The SUV is hanging on for dear life. Before they could reload and start another assault, another grenade explodes in a the SUV. As they all look at what they have left. They're down to six vehicles, four SUV's and two cars. "We can't shake 'em, we might have to split up," suggests Bernard.

"No, we move as one for now," answers Babylon.

They can see that the vehicles are advancing upon them. In a spread out formation, covering all of the lanes. The two cars and just two of the SUV's are leading the charge this time. While still driving backwards, Teeny-Man almost losses control of the car.

"Hold her steady Teeny=Man," Juice-Hop pleads.

"I got her slim," he replies. In the same thought and the same tactical mind set. The young men begin to fire upon the vehicles with a flurry of bullets. As before two from the bottom and two from the top.

But this time Babylon decides to shoot at the engines of the SUV's, while the others are shooting to hit humans, he takes his aim at the grills. Now shooting he strikes the SUV's grill and what a hit it is.

He immediately sees some steam with that he starts

on the next one. Another direct hit, steam and liquid
seeps from its grill. All three of the other young men
dismantles the two cars. Killing it's passengers with
ease. As the last two SUV's keep their distance. "Oh
no, don't do that, please don't do that," begs Teeny-
Man.

The SUV's now get into an I formation. The second
truck is invisible to them. With the young men already
reloaded. The leading SUV swirls off the road racing
fast, they all fall for the bait.

It's a ploy to draw their attention for a split
second. The second SUV has a M-16 and a Heckler & Koch
G-3, that's already in the double digits of firing. By
the time they look up, they are under extremely heavy
fire.

The array of three o' eight battle ammunition just
eats up their car. Chopping away their hood and roof.
With all of them in full duck mode, their grill is
shot out. The windshield is Swiss cheese. They notice
that the shooting have stopped.

They all begin to raise up and take their
positions. With two up front hitting them low. And the
two in the back, hitting them high. But without
warning the second SUV appears out of nowhere and
starts shooting a Bennelli tactical shotgun.

The semi automatic shotgun in its full tactical
mode, is firing rapidly upon the young men. It seems
that the shooter would elect to shoot at the tires.

A move that will prove to be vital to him as the
shooter. The bullets from the Desert Eagles just rips
up the occupants in the front of the SUV. Also the
occupants inside an unrelated vehicle. It seems as
though the assault rifles have lost this battle
against the Desert Eagles.

"Hey, its one more y'all," yells Teeny-Man.
Reloading themselves along with the last SUV they
watch eagerly as the SUV now gets in front of them.
With the shotgun blasting away at them, they can see
those are not regular shotgun shells.

As they duck down to take cover, they can see what
appears to be fire, real fire spitting out of the
shotgun barrel. When the blast hits the windshield it

literally blows it off. Once again with the hood of the engine flying off onto the road as it too is hit by the shotgun blast. It seems that the momentum has shift a little.

"Man! Won't y'all do something," Teeny-Man yells.

"Hold on T, I got it," says Babylon. Babylon begins to go into action, he turns his head and sees a sign that says: "Long Beach." At this time he thinks that he may be dying. Because he knows for a fact that Long Beach is in California.

The young man doesn't know that there is a Long Beach, North Carolina. With that in mind his thinking is not to die in his own piss. But to die fighting the good fight, or at lease shooting back at whoever it is trying to kill him and his friends.

"T, when I give you the word, I want you to hit the brakes hard on her, you got me?"

"Yeah slim, I got you." The young man tries to get himself together. His mind is clear, of what he must do to get this over with. And at this time the car is sounding like its about to give out, so time is of essence.

***

Inside of the SUV, one of the agents cell phone is ringing. "Don't answer it, we're in the field," the driver tell the passenger.

"I have to its command," the passenger explains. he brings the shotgun back inside the SUV, so he can talk to his superiors on the phone.

"Goddamn it, I said no shooting. Stop all shooting now," yells an angry Mr. Sears over the phone.

"Yes Sir, no more shooting, Sir." He turns to the driver and states: "Mr. Sears just ordered a cease fire."

"Where are the youths now?"

"They're in front of us driving backwards."

"In front of you driving backwards?" Mr. Sears asks himself and the agent.

"Inform Mr. Sears, that the targets are shooting at us," the driver tells the passenger. Mr. Sears can hear him loud and clear.

"I don't care, you have a direct order to cease firing now!" The driver heard it through the phone crystal clear.

***

With Babylon now climbing into the front row of the car. He takes Juice-Hop's Desert Eagle out his hand. Now places his palm ends on the dashboard, still clutching on the two Desert Eagles in each hand, bracing himself, he yells: "Now T!"

Teeny-Man slams on the brakes, the car is now sliding backwards, the SUV is still coming at them full speed. The agents sees it but, its nothing they can do to stop the collision. "Whaaaaam!"

The SUV slams into the car. On impact, Babylon is thrust through the opening where the windshield used to be, and is now standing on the firewall.

He jumps on top of the carburetor and makes another quick jump. This time on top of the fender walls. With his legs spread apart, he takes one last leap of faith onto the core support on top of the radiator.

He now just steps up onto the SUV and with both guns in hands, standing on top of the hood of the engine. Babylon opens fire with both guns blazing. Hitting both occupants while both vehicles are stuck and still moving as one at very high speeds.

In his right hand is his fifty caliber and in his left is Juice-Hop's forty four magnum. He's blasting away, releasing the fifty caliber into the driver and the forty four magnum into the passenger.

He strikes the driver with a center mass shot that freezes him. A center mass shot is the same fate for the passenger. "No shooting!" Is being screamed though the cellular phone.

The driver tries to turn his body and his head some how thinking it will prevent him from getting shot. His attempt fails terribly as the young man lets off a carefully aimed shot that catches the driver on the side of his head.

The Georgetown Heist

It rips through the right side of his head just taking a chunk out as it scrapes it deep. As the blood from his head wound squirts on the passenger. The driver does not feel it, nor does he knows that he's been shot in the head.

Another shot from the fifty caliber catches the driver in his chin on his left side, only to exit on the right side. The passenger has been in shock since the initial center mass shot. And just stares at the young man standing on top of the hood of his SUV.

Babylon is especially pissed off at the passenger. He's the one that has the shotgun. Still firing at the passenger the last shot to strike him, is directly on his hairline.

The forty four magnum bullets enters between his hairline and his forehead. The force of it jerks his head back into the headrest. The entire top of his head explodes. It's a bloody mess, from the passenger's side window to the headrest, to the ceiling of the SUV.

Finally empty the young man is pleased at the result of his work. He sees that the shotgun welding man, has been turned into pulp. "It's about time you stopped shooting, now tell me what the youths are doing now?" Asks Mr. Sears.

The SUV, along with the car is beginning to swerve a little off the road. Babylon takes his cue and goes back into the car with his friends. As he goes through the same motions that got him out, he's back in the car. He hands Juice-Hop back his gun and climbs back in his seat behind Teeny-Man. "Shit, that's how you feel huh?" Teeny-Man asks him.

Teeny-Man spins the steering wheel all the way to his left. As the back of the car begins to fishtail. this maneuver allows him to free the car from the SUV and also snatches the front bumper from the car, and grill off the SUV. He places the car in drive and hits the gas. Teeny-Man straightens out the car to drive and they all watch as the SUV leaves off the road.

***

"**What's happening now**, can any agents hear me?
This is Mr. Ronald Sears, do anyone read me?" As he
stays on the line he finally hears the SUV crash on
the side of the road.

***

Babylon and the rest of them are watching from a
distance as the SUV, finally crashes. They are not
impressed. They know that they were lucky against the
law enforcement they just killed off.

***

"**I like this** young boy Nimrod."
"You like anything that's sour, or you can sour,
Tonya."
"You know they just got past an entire strike team
of agents? That's never happened before. I got my eye
on him, he might prove worthy."
"Worthy of what?"
"We need to up grade around here. We need new
young fresh blood in here."
"Please, you will not embarrass me with a bunch of
uneducated street thugs."
"LaShonne, you have lost your vision. You can't
see the big picture anymore. This place is crumbling
down around us and when there is a chance to save us,
you go back in the box. I am going to be monitoring
this situation very closely now. Nimrod might be a
natural at this, I'm talking about raw unharnessed
talent."
They're two women who sees life totally different.
But must work together for their own survival, and yet
most of the time they can't get along. Their jobs are
about to be taken from them, after that their lives.
Yet, only one of them truly knows the reality of
their future, the other is naive. But they need each
other. And on top of that, they need to make a huge
splash in their field of work.

***

The Georgetown Heist

"**Get Vic in** here now," the Captain yells from his office.

"Vic, the Captain wants you in his office," a voice informs him from across the room.

"Shit, what is it now?" He says to himself. "You called for me Cap?" Detective Williams asks.

"You damn right I did, I need to know what were you doing trying to arrest an National Security Agent yesterday?"

"Cap, the agents tampered with the crime scene of my double homicide case." As the Captain looks at him, Vic continues. "There were two bodies in that diamond bank, as you know. Those agents took one of the bodies-" "What!" The Captain yells in shock.

"Yeah, the female, and in the process they destroyed any and all evidence relating to this case."

"Vic, why do you think they took the body?"

"Cap, I'm leaning on, they had their hands in this, or did it. Or maybe they know who did it, or better yet Cap, she may be one of theirs. Either way I need to get to the bottom of this."

"Vic, I don't know about this one, I am thinking about pulling you on this one."

"Cap, that old man as well as that woman, deserves to have their killer or killers caught. Even if that might be some government agents also. And-"

"Stop right there," the Captain says as he cuts him off. "This ain't no time for your I'm the best detective shit. Vic this shit could get ugly, very fucking ugly. Let me see, was she dressed as if she belonged there or better yet did she look to be a fit there?"

"No Cap, she looked totally out of place. Extremely well groomed, extremely well fit, I know for a fact that they know something, why else would a level five agent be at a robbery and murder crime scene?"

"Not only that but, when they called me about you. They asked for anything that we might have on four juveniles."

"That's my first big lead Cap, what's the names of these juveniles?"

45

"I don't know about this one Vic, I'm getting a bad vibe about this one. These juveniles either did it or they saw something they didn't supposed to. Either way they may be in danger, and any one close to this case."

"Cap, its what we do, its our job we owe it to those murdered and their families to find out who did this and why?"

"I'm going to hand this over to the F.B.I. Vic, it may prove to be too dangerous."

"No Cap, I need only a little time with it, and if I can't find anything or, if its over my head, then yeah, give it to the Feds."

"How much time are we talking about Vic?"

"Two weeks maximum and if I catch fire leave me on the case."

"That's fair enough you got it, now follow my lead," the Captain gets up and cracks his office door open. Just enough so his voice can be heard. "Vic, this one you do off the grid and on your own, you ready?" Detective Victor Williams nods in agreement.

"That's it Vic, your ass is in the street for two fucking days!" The Captain yells at the top of his lungs, as both men are leaving out his office.

"Two days, why don't you make it a fucking week for me?"

"Your ass is in the street for a week!"

"Well hell, since you're finally granting requests, why don't you make it two weeks so I can have that vacation you won't sign off on?"

"That's the one right there Vic, you're suspended for two weeks without pay. Turn in my badge and piece." Detective Williams hands over his badge and his gun and turns to leave his Captain. On his way out the office he stops at the Captain's secretary desk.

"How are you today Ms. Jones?"

"I'm fine Detective Williams, how about you?"

"I'll make it, I am working on a double homicide, and I have four juveniles on the list for questioning."

"Me myself I was given four juveniles names but, only found three with physical records for the Captain

46

not too long ago."

"I wish it was my four that I needed to make my case." As he begins to walk away she looks up at him.

"Detective Williams, do you know the names of the juveniles that you're looking for?"

"No, no I don't."

"Well sorry, if I can help you let me know okay?"

"If I had a name of a juvenile that's on record with us, that's known for robberies and murders. Maybe I could get him to help me out on this double homicide case."

"Good lord that fits the profiles of the juveniles that I just pulled for the Captain."

"Who are they?"

"Let me see here, oh, shucks why don't you just take the jackets and bring them back once you get through with them," she hands him the records to take with him.

"Thank you Ms. Jones, I see you when I get through with them."

"As he goes through the records he sees all that he needs to see. At this time he gets an idea into is head. He goes back around to Ms. Jones's desk to drop off the records.

"Ms. Jones here, I'm finished and thank you for your help," he tells her.

"Any time Detective Williams."

Now he's leaving the station, he gets in his car

and his mind is already made up where he's going. The first house will be the strangely, data entered one, and try to figure out what's his roll might be in this mess.

***

Pulling up in front of Bernard's house he sees that it is quiet. So he gets out and goes to the door and is met by a young lady.

"May I help you?" Asks the young lady.

"I'm Detective Williams, and I'm looking for Bernard Jones, is he home?"

"No he is not here, what do you want with him?"

"I just would like to ask him a couple of questions."

"He has not been here all day."

"And you are?"

"I'm his sister."

"So you know when he'll be back?"

"No, I do not."

"Can you tell me if he's been acting strange lately?"

"Strange, what do you mean strange?"

"Well like he got something big going on, with his friends. Or maybe his friends are acting strange lately. Like shopping sprees or something, flashing large amounts of cash?"

"No, I haven't seen him or his friends with anything, no money, no shopping sprees and nothing else that you're looking for." At this time she is getting tired of all the questions. "Look I don't know where he is and I don't think talking to you is such a good idea."

"Now why would you say something like that for?"

"Because its the truth you come here looking for my brother. So why are you still talking to me? You claim that you just want to talk to him but, you're asking me all about him and his friends."

"No, its not like that I'"

"Look you are here to see if you can get some information on my brother, to lock him up. It's time

48

for you to go, happy hunting somewhere else." He looks on, he knows that he can't get nothing out of her. And on the other hand he doesn't care so he leaves.

***

Now at the home of Maurice Barnes, he pulls up to the apartment building. He has not been around the Stone Lake Projects in awhile. He parks beside the little swimming pool, that's right in front of eight forty Barnaby Street.

He gets out and goes all the way to the basement to apartment number one zero two and knocks on the door.

"Who is it?" A voice asks.

"Detective Williams, Metropolitan Police Department." Someone looks through the peephole and now the door is opening up.

"Hello, how may I help you Detective?" A woman asks.

"I'm looking for Maurice Barnes, A.K.A. Teeny-Man, is he home?"

"No, he isn't. But may I ask why you're looking for my son?"

"I just wish to ask him a couple of questions."

"Is he in some sort of trouble?"

"Who is it at the door?" A man's voice inquires, and he can see that the man is approaching the door.

"What can I help you with?"

"I'm Detective Williams, and I was just talking to the mother of Maurice Barnes."

"Now you're talking to his father. What can we do for you?" Vic is just now notices the wedding bands. It's a shame that in his mind, a marred couple in the projects is just a unseen sight but, nonetheless he's surprised.

"I just need to ask him a couple of questions that's all."

"You still have not told me what for?" The father says. Vic, trying his best not to upset them.

"I can't lie to you all, I think that your son might be in some really big trouble," the mother

49

places her hand over her mouth in shock.

"Shaunda, y'all go in the room," the mother instructs her young.

"Okay, what kind of really big trouble," the father continues.

"Well it was a heist and two people were killed, and there may be a chance that your son may know something about it. Or may have been involved in it."

"How did you come up with my son's name?" The father asks.

"Well that's confidential information Sir."

"You show up here at my home and tell me that my son may be in really big trouble, that it was a robbery and some people got killed. I asks you how did you come up with my son's name, and you pulls a, its confidential information on me. You can leave now Detective, my son is not here."

"Sir, a diamond bank was robbed and two people were killed during the robbery. The place was cleaned out, one of the people murdered, we believe was a National Security Agent.

"Who's body was taken from the crime scene by her coworkers. Now you all know that nobody moves a body from a crime scene. But I myself have seen this done yesterday, and when I got back to the precinct.

"I was told that the National Security Agents requested any and all records of a few juveniles, and your son was one of the juveniles. Here is the paper that I am going off." He now hands the parents his work sheet, hoping that they will help him. Vic is impatient and he knows that time is not on his side.

"Mr. and Mrs. Barnes, I fear for the worst. Why would the National Security Agency be looking for four black juveniles in such a high profile case?" The parents both are now watching Vic.

"I don't think that he and his friends did this, its too, sophisticated for anyone around here to do. And I also believe that there is something else going on," he continues.

"It would take a crazy man to make this up. But I did see this on the news yesterday and today," the father says.

The Georgetown Heist

"I'm truly trying to find them before anybody else does, and I am trying to get to the bottom of this case."

The parents look on they can't help but to not believe this man, with his delivery and his eagerness. They can sense that he is telling the truth. But they both also can tell that it hurts him to even tell them what he has so far.

"Detective, I do not know where my son is, and do not know when he will come back to see us," the mother explains.

"Is there anything that you all can think of that might help me, like call him over here?"

"Hell no!" The father says angrily. "I'll never set my son up, nor will I ever lead him to the slaughterhouse," the father now stares downs Vic. Vic knows that his time here has run its course. The parents are sicken to their stomachs with the notion, not to mention having the detective in their home.

But now being told that their son's life may be in danger. The straight laced couple would do all that they could to save their son. And in the process try not to hurt his situation any further.

"Detective maybe it's time for you to go," suggests the mother. "Lord, we do not know where he can be at, and we have never been to his place," she continues to tell him.

"That would be nice to have his address."

"I bet it would," the father replies. "And by the way, are they or my son being charged with anything?" The father continues and asks.

"No, not right now but, there might be charges in the future."

"So you don't have nothing on them right now, just my son's name as a potential suspect. Is that right?"

"Yes, that's correct."

"Well like you stated earlier, we know a little about how this goes. You wouldn't be here if you had whoever was responsible for this. And if it was my son for a fact, you would have had my front door knocked down.

"With your guns all in my wife's and children's

51

faces and cursing us out and the whole nine. But now you're trying diplomacy because you don't know, and the so called higher ups, government agents gave you the cold shoulder and pulled rank on you all.

"And now you come in here trying to scare the working folks about their son being charged with murder. Just so you can have an advantage over us. And the sad part is, you never once talked about the robbery part to us. You just used the murder to talk to us about," the father continues.

Vic, looks at the father, he knows that he's right. And remembers why con men never try to run a con on a real working stiff. Because hard working people know you can't get something for nothing. And he knows that he can never recover for this one.

"Well Sir, I have to agree to disagree on that one,"

"Is that the best you can come up with?" The father asks Vic. Mr. Barnes shakes his head in disgust at the detective's reply. "If that's it, you can go now Detective, we're having family dinner here."

"Okay Sir, I will just leave you all my card. And if you all feel the need to call, please don't hesitate to do so."

He leaves the apartment truly believing that these people will not call him. Hell, why would they, they don't trust him now. They are not as naive as he had thought that they would be. And he just knocked himself out of favor with them.

"Okay just two more stops and I can call it a day," he tells himself. He goes to the home of Neil Green but, no one is home so he leaves.

Trying to go through some papers while still driving is giving him a fit. So he pulls over for a moment to find a sheet of paper, he has it. "Twenty five fifty five Elvans Road South East, apartment number one zero one," he says out loud.

***

He goes to the address he can't but to wonder, what did he do to misread those working folks? Now arriving at the address, he gets out and takes a look around, and sees nothing but potential suspects just crawling through out the complex.

He goes down the stairs and knocks on the door. His mind is made up that this interview will go as smooth as wood grain interior. He knocks once more.

"Who is it?" A child voice asks.

"It's Detective Williams," he responds. The child runs away, Vic can hear and feel the little one's feet hitting the floor as the child runs away.

"Yeah, who is it?" The voice of a woman asks.

"It's Detective Williams, I'm-"

"Who the fuck is it?" The woman voice yells out.

"Um, um, Ma'am I am Detective Victor Williams. I'm with the Metropolitan Police Department. And I am looking for Nimrod Hannibal Moham-"

"Hey!" She yells through the door cutting him off.

"Yes," he answers.

"Fuck, you the police?"

"Yes, I am Detective Williams."

"Oh, a detective?"

"Yes Ma'am, I am a detective." He's thinking that with her repeating that he was a detective meant something. Or has an affect on the woman. Out of nowhere the woman's voice gets loud as a shot being fired.

With people standing around in the apartment building hallway. They all watch as they know that something is about to happen, so they all stop to see it all unfold.

"Maaaaan, if you don't get your bitch ass away from my mother fucken door. What the fuck I care about you being a mother fucken detective? Let me up out this bitch, to see your monkey ass," the woman says from behind the door. The door is now open and she steps out of it.

"Excuse me Ma'am, are you Fatima Mohammed, mother of Nimrod Hannibal Mohammed?" He asks.

"Fuck no! I am the Queen of Sheba, mother of Melelik I, mother fucker," she answers him. Now her facial expression changes, and she looks calmer.

"Oh, shit I didn't know it was you out here," she

says in a smooth voice. "I haven't seen you in a minute baby, please forgive me," she continues.

'Miss you don't know me but, I'm working a case and I-"

"I'm hip to you bitch, I know what you really want. Plus I just got a new one too, I call it the big gun. That mother fucker is like fifteen inches long, it's black and that mother fucker shoots."

'Ma'am, I think there's a mistake."

"Hell nawl, ain't no mother fucken mistake, Bunny knows when a bitch is in heat."

"Ms. Mohammed, I am a detective," she looks at him with a cleaver smile on her face. He's wondering when will this all be over. She's wondering if her son has taken care of his business with those diamonds. Sensing that its time to make his move, he decides to swell up on her.

"Bitch, you ain't gonna throw me off the scent that damn easily. I'm hip to your ass. What's your name?"

'My name is Detective Victor Williams."

"What's your punk name.?"

"I don't know what you're talking about."

"Okay baby doll, what's your stage name?" He looks puzzled about the question being asked to him. "I'm going to take a guess at it. I am going to say it's Vikki, no you're a sophisticated bitch, your name is Victoria but, it must roll off your tongue." He can't think do to all the people in the hallway laughing at him.

"You came all the way down here just so I could knock your mother fucken back pockets off."

"No, I came down here to talk to you about your son."

"That boy ain't on ass, I am," now in a soothing voice she begins to talk to him. "Oooohhh, baby, I want to put this dick in you so bad." He can't believe what he's hearing from this woman.

'Miss, I am married with a child," he tells her.

"And that's a good cover too, Miss thang."

"I'm not gay."

"Who said something about being gay?" He looks

Chapter 7

around and the people are laughing even harder now. "Whatcha wanna do baby doll?" He now sees that this is a losing battle. So he goes into his inside jacket pocket to get one of his cards.

"Ms. Fatima Mohammed, if you hear from your son can you please give me a call?"

"Oh, just fuck what I'm saying huh?" He walks over to hand her his card. She grabs him by the hand and pulls him towards her. She kisses him on the cheek, he nod's and begins to walk away.

She now walks up behinds him and grabs him by the waist and begins to hump on his buttocks. His eyes become as big as golf balls. He spins around in a flash to see her.

"Miss what are you doing?"

"Just letting you know that I'm in love with, I'm I'm in love with," she sings to him and winks.

He turns to walk up the stairs she goes and squeezes him on the backside and blows him a kiss. With that one the entire hallway erupts into a roar of laughter.

Detective Williams tries to jolt out the scene immediately, by running up the stairs. Now everybody is cracking up laughing as the detective hauls tail up the stairs. "Bunny, you're terrible," a voice from the hallway yells out. Finally in his car he can barely get it to start. He's in such a frenzy about what just happen to him.

"I can't believe this, why would she actually do something like that?" He asks himself. But it wasn't really him, he just came at a time that she was bored. And on top of it, he was law enforcement. So somebody had to get it and once she had her audience it was a wrap. Its not personal with Bunny, its just how she is.

A strong black woman in her own right, a woman's woman. Who also has had a very strong upbringing in the Nation of Islam. She has a hair trigger of a temper and total package to go with it.

Vic begins to drive off, still shaken from his ordeal with Bunny, his phone rings.

"Yeah, Vic," he answers.

"Hey Vic, its me Maureen."

"Finally a woman with a nice voice and mouth," he says to himself.

"I'm sending you the lab results now," she e-mails him the results from the crime scene that he had requested for her to analyze. Checking on his car computer, he's in quickly.

"Okay I have it, can you give me a little help here with all the chemistry?"

"All right, the first one they're all in the same group. Sarin (GB), Soman (GD), Tabun (GA), and V-Agent (VX). These materials are liquids that typically are sprayed as an aerosol for dissemination.

"In the case of GA, GB, GD, the first letter G, refers to the country Germany, that developed the agent. Now the second letter indicates the order of development. In the case VX, the V stands for venom.

"While the X, represents one of the many chemicals in the specific compound. And this group is called nerve agents."

"Are you sure about this, Maureen?" He asks her in an playful unbelievable voice.

"Am I sure?" She asks him and then goes silent.

"Please go on Maureen."

"By the way, in twenty years of this I have never had an opportunity to put my skills to full work like this. And I never came across anything like this. So I

checked it several times myself, after the rookies
told me what it was they found."

"Is there more?"

"The next one is Mustard (H,HD), and Lewisite (L).
They are very toxic much less so then nerve agents. A
few drops on the skin can cause severe injury. And
three grams absorbed through the skin can be fatal.

"Clinical symptoms may not appear for hours or
days. And this group are called blister agents," he
can't understand what she's saying she found,
especially where she's saying she found it at.

"Now the next one, heyfrogen cyanide (AC), and
cyanogen chloride (CK). Cyanide and its compounds are
common industrial chemicals which deals with rapid
death, and this group are called blood agents," he
doesn't believe what he's hearing.

"Up next is chlorine and phosgene which are common
industrial chemicals. This one causes edema, that's
fluid in the lungs. And this group are called choking
agents.

"Now we have chloropicdrin, mace, (CN), tear gas
(SC), capsicum and pepper spray, and dibenzoxazepine
(CR). And this group is called irritating agents."

He sense something in her voice, he thinks she's
holding something back from him.

"Come on Maureen, what are you keeping from me?"

"Vic the reads that I just gave you, do you know
where they came from?"

"Yes, the safe down stairs in the basement."

"No, they were from the entire up stairs Vic,"
with a sense of sadness in her voice she continues.
"Vic, I got a nuclear reading from that safe in the
basement. Vic something bad is going on here."

"What do you mean nuclear, that can't be right?"
He insist.

"I ran the tests myself, after they all came back
positive for all of the substances. Vic, what I'm
trying to say is that entire place was hot."

After she said that, they both fall silent. It is
no way for her to be wrong on this and he knows it.
But how can he find all of the answers that he needs.

"Thanks you Maureen, look go in and see the

Captain and speak only with him about the findings and put a gag order on your lab."

***

As they come to this little town they go behind some warehouses to ditch the car. They all get out to stretch their legs and quickly get out of sight from the vehicle. Juice-Hop sees the sign that reads: "North Myrtle Beach."

This is a place that they have never heard of before but, here they are all wrecked and ready to go again.

"Teeny-Man, Juice-Hop y'all straight?" Asks Babylon.

"I'm straight Bab," Teeny-Man replies.

"I'm okay B," Juice-Hop answers.

"What about you, are you okay Bernard?" Babylon finally gets around to ask him.

"I think I can make it but, I got to see a doctor whenever we get settled," Bernard explains.

"Slim, that doctor idea is dead. As soon as you go inside with a scratch on you, them people are going to be right there on our asses. And you should know this," Babylon tells him.

"Yeah, you're right," Bernard agrees and the other three looks at him strangely. "But I'm going to have to go and get some medical supplies for myself."

"I hear you Rambo," Teeny-Man tells him.

"And lets not act like we just come from a shoot out. But instead act like we are just passing through town," Babylon tells them.

As he talk, he turns around and sees a bus station across the street. "I'll be right back men," he tells them. He begins a light jog across the street to the bus station.

"Man, maybe we made a mistake, what you two think?" Bernard asks Juice-Hop and Teeny-Man.

"Mistake, where at!" Teeny-Man fires back.

"This whole thing."

"Shid, you done bumped your mother fucken head." Teeny-Man tells him.

The Georgetown Heist

"I mean the way things are going right now. Don't you think its a bit too much?"

"Slim, the only thing that's too much is all that damn talking you're doing." Teeny-Man and Juice-Hop watch as Babylon comes back from the bus station.

"Look, there's a bus that just left for Atlanta, Georgia. So that's the bus we missed and are waiting for the next one so we can leave. The reason we are going to Atlanta is to break into the entertainment business," Babylon explains to them.

"You just couldn't let us walk around telling four different stories huh?" Asks Teeny-Man.

The entertainment business was the best story line Babylon could come up with and it is a nice one to. The other three thought it over to themselves the smile on their faces shows that they all were in agreement with the cover.

"We have to find a gun shop and fast," says Babylon.

They all glance at their empty magazines and shake their heads. They go on about their way to either a gun shop or find an individual who can get them some ammunition. Babylon feels that the worst has not happen yet. And wants to be in the best shape possible to defend himself.

And hope that his crew wishes for the same thing. For the life of him he can't understand where them people come from and what they truly wanted.

In North Myrtle Beach, it's not like anything the three young men had ever seen before. With red bricks on the sidewalk, whereas at home the sidewalks are all concrete.

But that is the least of their worry. They see a lot of old looking flags hanging everywhere but, pays them no attention.

"Hey slim, ain't that the same one that's on the Dukes of Hazzard car?" Asks Juice-Hop as he's pointing up at the flags.

They all nod their heads in agreement, not knowing the flag name, and goes up to a hardware store. Inside of the store they can see and feel all the funny looks that they are getting, from those who work in the store as well as the customers.

"Look, y'all we are going to try and buy some bullets and get out of here without any infractions," Babylon tells them all and they agree.

"You know that in some of these small ass hick towns they are still on that southern comfort thing, and hate us with a passion. So don't do nothing to provoke them to act crazy or go and put the dogs on us. I would hate to have to kill Cleofus, Billy Bob, Jim Bob, Clint and Beauford," Teeny-Man tells them, and they laughs at his remark.

"What's so funny boy?" One of the customers asks.

"Ain't nothing just a joke that slim shot at us," Juice-Hop answers and the man hasn't clue to what he said.

"You boys must be lost," the same customer asks.

"No we're not, we are just waiting for our bus to come through town again so we can leave here," explains Juice-Hop.

"And what bus are yous waiting on?" Asks the man behind the counter.

"The Atlanta, Georgia bus Sir," Babylon tells him.

"We were waiting on the bus but, we missed it. So now we're stuck until the next one comes in," Juice-Hop explains.

Without a hint the man behind the counter picks up the phone and places a call. The man on the phone heard all that was being said and began to talk to someone on the other end. When he got off the phone he gives a head nod to the whites in the store.

Babylon catches the jester between them, that's when he goes into action. "Well I'm looking for some tools and supplies. You see we are in the music business and we're going to Atlanta to start up. So I wish to start getting all of the equipment that we need now. Since we have to wait on another bus to come."

The man behind the counter shake his head no to someone behind Babylon as if to call something or somebody off. "So Sir, can you help me?" Babylon asks.

"Well how much are you trying to spend boy?" The boy remark does not sit well with Babylon, and that just placed the nails in his coffin.

"I'm trying to spend around five grand."

"Well go on over there and get it your damn self, and don't you steal any damn thing either." Babylon is pleased that his spending money with this man is easing the mood around the store.

"This is all that I need Sir," Babylon tells him once he returns. The man rings it all up, its over the five thousand and Babylon pays him his money. The five grand plus is the most his store has made in almost three months.

"We will be looking for some rooms to rent later, do you recommend a good hotel Sir?" Babylon asks him.

"Well since you said it, I just so happen to have some rooms in my house that I'm renting. But it's not cheap, then again I don't know you boys. Yeah, just go down the street here until you reach the Rebel Inn, just tell them Luke sent yous."

"How do they feed there?"

"It's a place across town if yous want to eat something." This place has it all guns, machine guns, hunting riffles, shotguns, knives and ammunition, all inside a hardware store. So they all are leaving the place but, in the back of their minds they will be back in this store again.

As they go on their way to the hotel, its hot as hell in the little town. They finally reach the hotel and they all goes inside to get their rooms.

"Hello, we would like to rent four rooms until tomorrow, and by the way Luke sent us," Babylon can see how the desk clerk facial expressions changed from excitement about the four rooms to a blank after he stated Luke sent them.

"Sorry, we don't have any rooms available," the clerk informs them. And it is at this time that Babylon understands what's going on and just smiles at the hustle.

"What are you smiling at Bab?" Asks Teeny-Man.

"I just seen the move they're bringing us," he answers. They look at him with questionable eyes but, he keeps smiling at them and takes them to the side for some privacy.

61

J.J. Honesty-Bey

"Pay attention everybody, we are going to see old Luke again. And when we do, the prices of his rooms will be sky high. Plus with us having no place to go and being hungry in all, he'll think we'll have no choice but to take his offer," Babylon explains to them.

He now turns away from his friends to speak with the clerk. "Thank you Sir but, do you recommend another hotel or motel?"

"They're all over town just keep walking in any direction you will walk straight into one. "Okay, lets walk," Babylon tells them. They depart the hotel and notice that the desk clerk is acting like he's pissed off about something but, they all know what it is. But Babylon says it out loud anyway. "He's mad that he couldn't rent us them rooms."

Bernard seems a little slow on the subject, and they sees it so Babylon takes it a little further for him.

"Look, you know how we do with girls, if you see her first she's yours? Well Luke seen us first and we are his. And since he want us, he shall have us all to himself," Babylon tells them.

Now they just wastes the day going from place to place asking about hotels and motels, and buying little snacks to eat on. They stop to take a break on the corner.

"You boys still here? I thought for sure that you all be getting some much needed rest for yous trip tomorrow," he slyly says to them.

Its Luke and Babylon refuse to give in to him too, fast. He wants him to have to go through the motions. With Bernard really wanting to get this over with so he can get his wounds cleaned and patched up.

"I tell you boys what I'll do for yous. I will let yous in my home for one hundred fifty dollars each," he tells them. They look at each other and then huddle up and begin acting as if they're really talking about whether they should take the deal or not.

"Mr. Luke Sir, what all comes with the rooms, for a hundred and fifty dollars?" Babylon asks.

"Why hell yous only need one nights sleep right?"

The Georgetown Heist

"Yes, but we would like to get a hot meal also." Teeny-Man tells him. Now Luke is thinking how can he get out of feeding them. He can't think of anything, so he agrees to the hot meal.

"And also hot showers," adds Juice-Hop. He also agrees to the hot showers for the youths.

"Yous come with me," he tells them while beckoning them to get into his old pick up truck. "Get in," he orders them inside the old rough looking truck. Teeny-Man, Juice-Hop and Bernard hops in the back of the truck. Babylon is on his way to sit up front with Luke. "Oh hell no boy, you get in the back with the rest." Babylon goes to the back of the pick up, and hops in with the rest of them.

"Oh, you thought you were special or something?" Teeny-Man playfully asks Babylon. They takes off for Luke's house, its a very long and dusty ride to his house. But they think they can see it now and can't wait to get something to eat, and their tails washed. As Luke is pulling up in front of his house.

Four of the meanest and ugliest dogs you could ever find, comes running up to the truck. Not to greet their master but, to attack the youths in the back of the truck.

"Get the fuck!" Teeny-Man shouts at the canines, while cocking his leg as to be readying himself to kick one of them. "These mother fuckers ain't like them strays in South East, once you say "get the fuck." them bastards haul ass," Teeny-Man continues.

"Down boys, down." Luke commands the dogs. The dogs come to Luke as he smacks his hand against his thigh. The front door opens and a white woman with some very thick thighs comes out and towards the truck.

"Hey Sue, where's Tammy?" Luke asks the woman.

"She's out back taking down the laundry from off the line," she answers.

"Is this your wife, Mr. Luke?" Teeny-Man asks him. She smiles at the question and then mumbles something under her breath.

"No she's my sister in law, she stays here with us," Luke answers. They all go into the house where they are met by five small children who are calling out to Luke.

"Hi Paw," one of the young boys says.

"Hi Paw," one of his little girls yells to him but, Luke looks at her and totally ignores her and her sisters.

"Your Paw done brought home some goodies for you and your brother," he goes into a bag that he had with him and pulls out fishing tackle. They seem to love it as the girls looks around sad.

"What did you bring us Paw?" The oldest of the three little girls asks. He looks at her with the meanest set of eyes, goes over to the little girl and smacks the hell out his daughter. The smack hurts so bad, that the poor little girl can't get her cry out.

"You will stay in a woman's place as long as you are under this roof," he yells at her. "If that whore of a mother of yours could ever teach you anything," he continues.

The four of them are just watching like spectators. "White men still treat his children and women like dogs," says Teeny-Man. "I got that one from the Natives, they said that back in the Western days. Well to correct the Natives, the white man treats his dogs kind of better," he finally finishes.

The mother finally hears the child's cries, she tries to come to her care but, Luke stops her. "Tammy, we have guests for the night and they are hungry for a hot meal," he tells her.

"I reckon I can do it Luke."

"You bet your fat ass you reckon, woman." The guests are truly entertain by this ugly display of red neck etiquettes at its best. They all follow Luke into the dining room area and sit down. His wife and her sister comes in also.

"Is there anything yous prefer to eat?" Tammy asks them.

"We don't have no water melon and fried chicken, ha, ha, ha, ha," says Luke as he's laughing.

"Will chicken or turkey be okay with you?" Asks Teeny-Man as he's looking her over.

"Turkey is good, I have some already carved up,"

she replies.

"Then turkey it is," says Teeny-Man. Now all of them are in the dining area as Babylon goes into his pocket to give Luke six one hundred dollar bills for the rooms, with his wife and her sister looking on. They already knew what time it was when they first came through the door with Luke but, this is the most ever.

And just for a night, Sue had a certain reaction to the six hundred dollars. That led all of the young men to believe that she would be getting a cut of the money some how.

"Here's the money Mr. Luke."

"It took you long enough to give it to me, boy." At that time Luke and Sue gets up and leaves out the dining room. A little time later his wife comes in the food.

"I hope this will satisfy yous?"

"Oh, it will Tammy," insists Teeny-Man with a sinister look upon his face.

Now Tammy leaves their view and after a while they hear yelling then a rumbling noise. "Someone is getting their ass beat," says Teeny-Man. A few moments later Tammy emerges. Okay, it was her she has just been found guilty of getting her ass beat with the physical bruises on her.

"Man, cracker Luke be putting down the big hand up in this bitch, Teeny-Man tells the group.

"Tammy we would like to go to our rooms now, if you don't mind," asks Babylon.

"Sure, come with me," she says as she tries to conceal her face. They all get up from the table and the strangest thing happen after. All of the children just start attacking the left over food. like starving animals in the wild.

She shows them their rooms, Teeny-Man is the last one up the stairs, so he gets the last room, she's showing him the room.

"Can you roll back the covers for me please?" She starts to roll back the covers on his bed, while slightly bending over.

"Is this far enough for you?"

"Yes that's all right, right there." Now Tammy turns around and she catches Teeny-Man watching her ass and he wasn't even trying to hide it, nor did he turn away after she seen him.

"If I need something can I call you Tammy?"

"Yes you can." Tammy goes back down stairs to be with her children. And you can now hear the voice of Luke's through out the house. Bernard is the first to take a shower, while he's in the shower.

Babylon tells Juice-Hop and Teeny-Man of his plan for Luke, they love the plan to the fullest. Now it is Juice-Hop turn to take a shower because Teeny-Man did not want to go. Babylon takes the next shower and once out of the shower he goes to Teeny-Man.

"Slim, everything straight with you?"

"Yeah slim, everything straight, I just want to be on point that's all big boy." And Teeny-Man goes in to take his shower. He gets to the door and calls out for Tammy.

"Tammay," she hears him and goes up the stairs t se what is it that he wants.

"Yes," she answers him.

"Tammay, could you please bring me a towel." She leaves and gets him a towel.

"Are you decent in there?" She asks Teeny-Man through the door.

"Yeah, I'm straight," he answers back. She walks into the bathroom and there he is standing in his boxers. While he was calling her earlier, he was priming up for her. So by the time Tammy makes it back with the towel. His penis would be rock hard for it and it is. Her eyes are glued to his boxers.

She is now looking at him the way he was looking at her earlier. She has never in her life seen a bulge that big before, and she is truly recording it.

She can see, hear and feel the pulse coming off that huge bulge in his boxers. And he knows that he now has her and he knows that she's an eater. Not even the voice of Luke can snap her up out the trance that she's in.

"Hey T, you straight in there?" Babylon asks not knowing what's going on inside.

"Yeah slim, I'm straight," he yells back. "Tammay, leave now before he comes in or something," he finishes. She begins to leave out the bathroom. "Hey Tammay, I am not a print man, the timing is off right now," he tries to explain.

She has no idea what the hell he's talking about but, she agrees with him and goes on. "I can't even hit the bitch head without interference," Teeny-Man says to himself.

Now that she's gone Teeny-Man smiles and takes his shower. After Teeny-Man's shower all of the young men are fully aware to what's supposed to go down is a matter of hours.

"Look, it might come down to us just taking the whole house," Babylon tells them.

"It don't make a difference to me one way or another," says Teeny-Man. The young men all go to their own room to have a little rest, before they pull their move. They all know that tomorrow will bring something new.

And Teeny-Man hearts something going on in the backyard. He looks and its Luke and Sue, they're going into the shed. As he watches, he now see Luke comes out with no shirt or pants on.

It's just as he had thought it was, Luke is sleeping with Tammy's sister, and Tammy knows it. "That's how them Rednecks are," he tells himself. Teeny-Man gets up and goes downstairs, he sees Tammy at the dining room table by herself.

"Hey Tammy, what are you doing up so late?" She doesn't answer him, she just stars off in time as if she's in a daze. "Well I'm about to go out back for a moment if you don't mind?" He says to her knowing she will say something now.

"No, don't go out there," she tells him.

"Why not?"

"Because there's nothing out there."

"Well I'm fine with that."

"Okay, go ahead and the dogs will eat you alive."

"I can't stand that one, you win. I won't go out back."

"Good." They both smile at each other.

"You have a beautiful smile Tammy."

"Nobody has ever told me that before."

"Well you do and I don't believe that no one never told you that before."

"You don't have to be nice to me."

"I'm not being nice to you, its the truth Tammy."

"In that case, thank you."

"You have a nice smile and a nice body."

"Now, I doubt that one very seriously."

"No, you most definitely have a nice body."

"There you go being nice again."

"No not really, all I say is true. You know I comes from a different ethnic background and area. In my culture thickness is very accepted, and in fact it is preferred."

"Well thank you the same but, I'm married with children, I have a family." He's furious but he doesn't show it. He can't believe that she's trying him like this.

"Well I'm going back up stairs now, I'll see you in the morning." Teeny-Man tells her. He get's up to go up stairs, going through the kitchen. She is truly hurting over her husband and sister's affair. And the last thing she really wanted was to be alone. But before she knows it, Teeny-Man is on his way back down the stairs. She hears somebody but, she's not sure who it is.

"Who's there?" She asks.

The Georgetown Heist

"It's me Teeny-Man," he answers her.

"Oh, are you staying down or going back up?"

"I'm going to stay down just until I finish working." It's taking him a minute to come out the kitchen.

"Finish working on what?" As he enters the dining room from the kitchen, he's raw ass naked. He goes over to the dining table mildly stroking himself, and reaching on top of the table he takes the top off the butter container.

He switches hands on his fully erect penis and now with his right hand digs deep into the butter container using a circular motion. Teeny-Man takes his hand out the container, with his hand now is a cup like position, just cradling it in his hand.

He squashes it between his fingers in front of her. He takes his other hand and begins to gently message it into his palms. Now taking both his hands, he's placing the warm butter on his rock hard manhood, right in front of Tammy and begins to message it all around his pulsating member.

It is taking no time for the butter to melt away. Chunks of it falls to the floor, as if he's using Lava hand cleaner to get car oil or grease off his hands. It's still a good amount left in his hand and him.

His rod is good and shined up now and looking like a brand new perm. She can not believe her eyes, she has to look around to make sure no one is watching her watch him and it. Teeny-Man has his shaft in his hand stroking it ever so gently, as though his hand is just gliding back and forth.

As she looks on she has never felt that much meat between her thighs before, in her life. She sits there watching him just stroke away, and now he begins to talk to her.

"Eat bitch, eat it up. Bitch I know you're a eater," he tells her. She, not knowing what to do, just sits there in watches.

"Open your legs bitch," he demands, not knowing she opens up her legs. "Poke it out bitch, poke it out." She scoots up to the edge of the chair and pokes her mound out from behind that old house coat of hers, to expose her no panties covering mound.

"Let me see that tongue bitch, slow bitch, I want to see it glide slow." She's scared to death of what she's doing. If Luke catches her, she knows he will beat her snseless.

"That tongue bitch, I've got to see it," he eagerly expresses. She nervously slides her tongue across her lips, going back and forth in a slow motion.

"Yeah, yeah, oh yeah itch, you're working now. That's it baby slide that tongue on this dick," he tells her. "You can taste it, can't you?"

"UM-hum," she agrees.

"That pussy on fire ain't it?"

"Yessss."

"Rub it, rub on that hot pussy Tammy."

"I rub," her voice trails off. She put's her hand between her thighs and begins to rub on herself.

"That pussy trembling ain't it?"

"Yes!" She answers with excitement in her voice. She starts to feeling too good. She inserts her fingers inside herself. And starts to fingering her love nest. She closes and opens her legs repeatedly, and closes them and arches her back while her head is all the way back.

"No bitch, open your legs bitch. It ain't for you its for me, stupid country ass bitch, now open up!" She reopens her legs for him while still fingering herself. It is at this time that he smells her, and the scent is strong coming from her love box.

"It's got to be morning, I smell that coffee percolating bitch. It's the best part of waking up bitch. Look at this big mother fucker Tammy, its ready to spit."

He takes a couple of steps towards her still stroking violently in front of her. He got his throbbing tool two to three inches from her face. He's pulling long strokes in front of her, that's causing his fist to hit her in the face, almost every other stroke.

He breathing is now more like the panting of a dog and she's sweating extremely bad. He's still in front of her stroking that huge black dick in her face.

"Oh yeah, Tammy breakfast is about t be served, bitch." Tammy is so into the dick that's in front of her, that she never sees her daughter who looks in on and then steps back into the kitchen. The daughter is in disbelief, she has seen ding-dings in he life. But not one this big, and not in front of her mother.

Seeing how her mother has her hands between her legs. The little girl, already in her own little nightgown goes straight for her won little honey pot and start playing with herself.

"you hear this mother fucker Tammy?" He asks her.

"Yesssss," she sighs. Inside of the dining room all one can hear is a popping sound. "Pop, pop, pop, pop, pop, pop, pop!" That's the sound of his foreskin smacking the head of his member. It sounds like a nine millimeter shooting off in that room.

He take his dick and with a flick of his wrist, smacks her across the face with it. She opens up her mouth inviting him to place it in there but, instead of placing it there, he smacks her with it once more.

"Oooohhhh, huuuummmmm," she moans. Teeny-Man hears somebody else's moan, and don't even care about it. Since the smack she can smell it, she couldn't at first but, now she can. His hand and dick has that butter cooking. It smells like hot, freshly popped popcorn with extra butter, and that buttery aroma fills the air.

"Its here bitch, it-is-here," he informs her. He takes one last step towards her as he continues to stroke, he's humping his fist and moving his hips all in perfect rhythm. "Oh yeah!" He sighs. "Oh, its your birthday," he sings. "Splat!"

The hot man glue hits her tight between the eyes, and the secondary splash catches her on the nose and upper lip, it totally covers her entire face. She thinks he's either a heavy comer or he hasn't released himself in months.

The heat from the blast is like nothing she has had on her before. His young body temperature is one hundred and two easily. As he now takes his hand to the base of it and squeezes it to the tip.

After wiping her eyes off not only can she see the chunkiness of his fluids but, she also sees the biggest vain on the of it just bulging out as he shakes the last of his juices on her.

He makes sure it gets all on her face. He now puts up and turns to go back through the kitchen. Once in the kitchen he discovers the daughter laid out in the middle of the floor with her hand still on her stuff.

With her little body exposed from the waist down. He steps over her to go back up the stairs, now he stops and goes back down. He walks back over the top of her face and whips out his penis again.

And he's still rock hard, he kneels down over top of the little girl, and with a flick of his wrist he smacks the little girl across her face with his dick. "That's for stealing your mother's food, you little nasty bitch you," he tells her. He now returns back upstairs and here comes Tammy in a faint voice:

"I'm ready, I'm ready for it. Come and put it in me," she begs.

"Bitch, I just feed, I don't handle the need."

"Please!"

"Look bitch, I done fed four country ass, that's all I am going to do for you." He goes to his room and get's his wash rag so he can wash himself off. But it seems that his crew has other plans.

"What's up y'all?" Teeny-Man asks them.

"Its time," Babylon tells him. He goes to the bathroom only to find Tammy in there playing with herself. "Damn!" He says to himself as he leaves out.

"I'm going to the master bedroom to get Luke's ass, then we're out of here," says Babylon.

"He's not in the bedroom slim, he's out back in the shed fucking Sue," Teeny-Man informs him. So they all go down stairs to get Luke and Juice-Hop goes into the bathroom to piss and is looking crazy.

"What the fuck is this?" He asks himself.

Tammy is straddled over the toilet with her back arched playing with herself. "Damn, them some nasty mother fuckers," Juice-Hop continues.

They makes their way down stairs going through the kitchen and see the little girl just smiling her ass

off. They go to the backyard and walk up to the shed.
"Hey, start shooting I'm going to crush his ass, and
just take the keys." Babylon tells them.

Now at the door they can see between the cracks of
the wood that they are still having sex, Babylon says
a silent count. "One, two, go!" And Teeny-Man kicks
open the door. The young men comes in with guns drawn
on the unfaithful couple.

"What the fuck are you boys doing?" Says Luke. "Do
you know who I am boy?" He continues. At this time
Teeny-Man smacks the mess out of Luke with his gun.

"Don't nobody give fuck about who you are, as you
can see you're no mother fucken body," Teeny-Man tells
him. "Sue we are here just for him not you sexy,"
Teeny-Man tells her. Looking at Sue's body Teeny-Man
is wondering if he can fed her real fast or not but,
he knows that his friends will not understand and the
will be in his way. "Come on let's go," Teeny-Man
tells Luke.

"Go where?" Luke asks violently.

"Back to work where do you think?" Teeny-Man tells
him out the shack and his tin box in on a stand.

"Let me get my box?" Luke asks.

"I got that Lukey boy," Teeny-Man tells him.
Babylon takes and opens the box he sees that its full
of money.

"I'm going to take out what I gave you today,"
Babylon informs him.

"Juice, hold this cracker for me," Teeny-Man asks.
They switch places and them Teeny-Man gets the box
from Babylon. Tammy is down stairs by this time and
couldn't believe it. She done had more excitement
tonight than her entire life. Juice-Hop takes Luke
outside now and Teeny-Man goes over to Tammy.

"Look here, this is all his money, minus what we
took out. You need to save it for a rainy day, for you
and the girls," he tells her. She look at him and
can't understand why he's doing this?

"I don't know about this?" She says.

"What do you mean, you don't know about this? Them
damn boys ain't around to see it and tell on you. Luke
didn't see me give it to you. So you're okay, I just

want you to be all right."

So finally she takes the money from him. "Now make sure you hide it real good, cause one day you might have to leave this hell hole, and you'll have to start from fresh."

She begins to walk away, she stops turns back around. She gives him a kiss on his cheek and walks on. Now he turns to Sue, who's in the dining room.

"Alright Sue, I am only going to give you five grand, I hope that's enough for your keep quiet fee?"

"She looks surprised and then just hunches her shoulders. "And I am going to tie up everybody, so it will look like nobody had anything to do with it."

She agrees to it, it isn't like she cares for Luke anyway. She's putting the money into her pocket, when Tammy walks into the dining room with a sinister look on her face.

"Girls go up stairs now," Tammy tells the girls. "Teeny-Man?" Tammy calls for him he's a little chocked that she called him like that.

"Yeah Tammy," he replies.

"Yous on the run huh?"

"Yeah, something like that."

"That was yous on the highway shooting with the law?"

"I don't know what you're talking about."

"That's the answer I'm looking for." She begins to reach down to his waist trying to get his gun out.

"What the fuck you doing?" He asks her as he smacks her hand away.

"I just need to see it for a second, I'll give it right back and I'll help you and your friends." He looks at her for a moment and gives her the Desert Eagle.

"Be careful with that, that's a man's gun."

"I'll try my best not to." Teeny-Man knows in the end he will have to kill Tammy, she knows his name and everything. She takes the gun and starts towards her sister. Now Tammy has a different look about herself, she look dead serious.

"Bitch, I let you in my home and you turn around and fuck my no good ass husband," she tells Sue.

Chapter 9

"Tammy bitch please, go sit your fat ass down some fucking where," Sue coldly says to her.

With Tammy's face now expressionless she turns her head to the side as to think about something. And without warning she gets a firm grip on the gun, now releases her grip while still in her right hand.

Tammy rolls her shoulder while raising the gun up, she twirls the gun around on her finger, when she stops the gun is pointed right in Sue's face. She cocks back the hammer and fires three shots into her sister's face.

The three blasts literally blows the back of Sue's head off. A red haze of blood fills the air and as it moves, Teeny-Man can smell and taste it.

"Don't worry about the shots won't nobody come, now bring his ass to me," she orders Teeny-Man.

As Teeny-Man goes through the house to get to the front door. He still can't believe what he just saw. As many times as he himself tried to twirl that gun, he could never do it but, some white woman just totally out did him.

"Hey y'all bring him in here," Teeny-Man yells outside to them.

"What's up? You know the rule T, nobody lives to tell about it," Babylon reminding Teeny-Man of the law, after seeing the dead woman on the floor.

"Hell nawl slim, you need to watch this shit unfold," Teeny-Man tells Babylon. At this time Babylon realizes, Tammy has Teeny-Man's gun he thought it was Teeny-Man who killed the woman.

"This is how you treat me after all I've done for you?" Tammy asks Luke.

"Woman I'm going to give you a real good whipping after this is over," Luke tells Tammy. They all are just watching the couple. "I'll teach you to sass me woman," he contnues.

Luke turns around and sees something on the floor. It looks like pieces of brains but, it can't be. He sees it quite clearly now and he also sees the body of Sue.

"Oh my gracious, you fuckers run please don't get caught. If I catch your black asses I will hang every last one you son bitches," Luke promises them. As he continues to look at the corpse of his dead lover's .

"They didn't do it, I killed the bitch," Tammy tells Luke. Luke stares at Tammy with the look of a mad man. "That's right I killed her, just like I'm going to kill your ass," she continues. Now walking up towards Luke, she's smiling at him.

"Hold him for me would you?" She asks. Juice-Hop and Teeny-Man holds Luke by his arms. Babylon walks behind them and strikes Luke with a blow to the back of his right leg. The blow is more than enough to bring him to his knees. And Tammy now places the gun to his forehead.

"Bitch, you really showing your ass. You better be leaving with them, because I'm going to skin your fat ass alive bitch. You worthless fucking cunt," Luke yells.

Just one shot brings about silence in the dining room as they look at Luke's head leaking like a spilled can of tomato juice. It is plain to see that this woman has had enough and this is her way out.

They're about to leave to go to Luke's store to rob it. Tammy goes through her sister's pocket and takes the money from it.

"Don't be alarmed nobody will come," she tells them. They all know that they still have to go and they have been here too long anyway.

"I have something that might be useful to yous."

The Georgetown Heist

Tammy tells them. They just look at her. "Everything I think, yous will need should be downstairs," she continues.

"Well we're going to tie you all up first," Babylon tells her.

"And also take the old Pontiac, the keys are down stairs too." They tie up everybody in the house who's not dead.

"Let's go down in this basement to see what she's talking about?" Babylon says.

They all go down into the basement once there Teeny-Man turns on the lights they could not believe their eyes. This is a hardware store for their tails. They have never seen this many guns in one place in their entire young street lives.

The basement is full of A.K.-47's, S.K.S.'s, M-4's, M-16's, A.R.-10's, A.R.-15's, G-3's, FAL's, MAC-10's, MAC-11's, MP-5's and all the hand guns in the world in plain sight, with ammunitions to go with everything in there.

The night vision goggles, the scopes, threat level five bullet proof vests. Pipe bombs along with hand grenades. This place is straight out a movie, with backpacks already in place along with duffel bags. Each young man gets what he likes along with his brand of ammunition.

Once they're loaded up they head for the garage to find this Pontiac. She neglected to tell them that its a classic nineteen sixty eight super charged G.T.O. But it wouldn't have made a deference. They wouldn't have known what it was anyway. They get their fill and load up in the car.

They begin to ride out to their destination, as they pulls out onto the street. "Damn, this bitch got a little pull with her," Teeny-Man says.

***

As he slowly creeps through the hallway inside of its master's house all is sound asleep. At the master bedroom he quietly lets himself in, looking at his prey. He decides to go to the side of his victim's wife just in case he's packing a surprise for him.

Once over the woman he believes that he has him.
He gently pulls the cover off him from his wife's side
of the bed, now his mark is fully exposed.

This is when he goes into action and moves over to
him and plucks his nose. As the man wakes up he sees
the intruder over top of him with his left index
finger over his lips. While his right hand holds a
silenced gun.

Once the awaken man sees the intruder he
immediately looks over to his still sleeping wife. The
man with the gun makes a jester for him to get up and
move. The sleepy man realizes that his family might
live though this night, even if he doesn't.

"Aide-toi, le ciel t'ai-dera," ("Help yourself and
heaven will help you.") The Frenchman says as he's
watching him pull on a cigarette. The sleepy man
begins to talk but is cut off.

"Gallice!" ("In French!")

"I don't know what you want but, the safe is in
the pantry. And I can't speak French," the awaken man
says.

"Homme d'affairs." ("Man of business.")

"Just take the money and leave, do with me as you
wish."

"Homme d'asprit." ("Man of wit.") The Frenchman is
ready to start now. "Whoo hozz thzee ziamondz?"

"What?" He responds, and the Frenchman looks at
him tiresomely and takes a deep breath.

"Whoo hozz thzee ziamondz?"

"Some young boys."

"I knowz thzat, I wvaz thzere vemembah?" Jaquiel
is getting extremely impatient with him.

"All I know is they are out looking for them with
everything we got."

"Namez, I'z need namez."

"I don't know any names, Q knows all their names."

"Whvere dzoez Q vee-zidez?"

"Man why don't you just kill me?" He says and then
pause for a second and looks at Jaquiel.

"Aussitot dit aussitot fait." ("No sooner said
than done.") Now Jaquiel looks around as to see if any

78

one is up or watching.

"Okay, okay! Just don't hurt my family. He stays off Sixtenth Street. No wait he moved, that's right. He stays at that old elementary school Bryant or Brian, it's on Independence Avenue, right off Kentucky Avenue." Jaquiel shakes his head at the information being told to him and sighs.

"Hiz veal name iz?"

"Quinton Norris."

"Okay ovah tzoo thzee valcony."

"What's over there?"

"Yooh," he tells him with a serious look upon his face. Jaquiel marches the man over to the balcony.

"Nowz zump ovah like mi didz."

"Are you for real? I told you the truth."

"Yooh zump yez? Or I'z vill tzake out jorw fambahly, yez?" He knows he has no choice in this matter. What man would not give his family a chance at living. So he jumps six stories down and the Frenchman leaves from the dwelling. As he's leaving the scene he passes the fallen man and sees the pain he's in. "A votre sant'e." ("To your health.")

***

As he now approaches the back door of the condominium building he sees a couple at the back entrance. No doubt a late night session of some teenage love. The two love birds goes inside the building.

The door is not closing as fast as it should be. The Frenchman quickly extend his arm to catch the door. He has it and lets himself into th building.

Once inside he goes straight to the directory and looks for his man. He's got his suite C-7. He start his way towards the back stairs and he already has his mind made about Q.

He remembers all too well how Q was the one with the gun. Jaquiel knew who was who in that outfit. And Q is indeed a top prize for him. As he walks through the hallway he begins to size up the condos.

And trying to figure out the best way possible to attack. He believes he has found the focal point. He goes to suite C-8 and pushes the doorbell several times.

"Yeah, who the hell is it at this hour?" That's what he wants to hear, not the man's voice but the sound of the dog barking. "Yeah who is it?" The man yells through the door once more.

"Szir, vee got za-call za-bout za dzog varking. Szo I hadz tzoo come up here andz check thzingz out Szir," he explains.

When the man opens the door he's met by silenced forty five slugs that hits him in his chest. As he is falling he also catches the rest of the magazine. The Frenchman let's himself into the man's home and immediately drags the man further inside before he starts to bleed everywhere.

"Shhhhhh, dzown bvoy," he tries to whisper to hush up the dog. The little pooch is not barking for its master, he's just barking out of being playful. Jaquiel tries to quiet the little fellow but, it not happening. He immediately goes to the kitchen and gets some dog food. The dog is now quiet and the Frenchman scans the house. The spouse is now getting up and will be on her way to see what's happening.

So he goes straight into action again he takes the dog in the hallway. He runs back into the apartment grabs a bottle of Edmond's hot sauce from the counter and runs back to the pooch in the hallway.

He now picks up the dog from the back of its neck and places his hand underneath it to secure his grip on the dog. Now using his mouth he takes off the top to the hot sauce, spits it out as far as possible on the floor.

He takes the bottle and jams it in the poor pooch's rectum. He now turns the dog upside down and squeezes the entire bottle in the dog's rectum while squeezing hard on the bottle.

The pooch gives off one hell of a cry. As the dog cries in the hallway the spouse is coming to the front door. Its open, so she goes right out into the hallway. With the man's body hidden the spouse never sees it. Jaquiel is behind the front door the entire time as she ran passed.

The Georgetown Heist

As she goes out into the hallway in her frantic
state Jaquiel closes the door behind her, locking her
out her own home. He's now staring at the living room
wall. His mind is on, this used to be a school so
figuring it was made with the cheapest materials.

He calculates a spot on the wall inside suite C-
8's living room, that should be suite's C-7's bedroom.
So he waits knowing Q, being a professional will be on
high alert. And will not come out until he knows for a
for a fact what's going on.

He now thinks that Q, should be about to look
through his peephole. He's wrong, Q is now in the hall
so, Jaquiel makes his move. Taking a few paces
backwards. The Frenchman charges towards the wall and
push kicks and manages to put a hole through it.

But needs to make it much bigger so he repeats the
act. He takes his place and goes through the motion
again and this time he's successful. Now he's inside
of Q's bedroom he sees that he's fully covered in
white chalky debris.

He knows that he must act fast because Q will not
be entertained by this ruckus. He goes and closes Q's
bedroom door and awaits his return. It does not take
him long to return.

Q is locking his front door back while the
Frenchman is raising his silenced gun towards him.
"Pssshhh, pssshhh," two shots in the dark whisk
through the air. The silenced shots from the Mark 25
hits their target with ease.

Q knows immediately what is going on but, the two
slugs feel like the heaviest weights in the world
penning him to the floor.

"A bon chat, bon rat." (To a good cat, a good
rat.")

"Are you mad at me French toast?" Q manages to say
while ignoring the pain.

"Au con trair." ("On the contrary.")

"I couldn't care less about your French ass and
whatever you got in mind for me just do it." Jaquiel
has already search Q, and disarmed him and Q knows
he's at the mercy of the Frenchman.

"I vish tzoo know thzee namez of thzee youthz whoo

hozz thzee ziamondz?"

"I'm not telling your faggot ass nothing."

"N'importe." ("It's no matter.") Jaquiel sees the paperwork on the dining table. He looks through it and sees what he's been looking for he now turns towards Q. "Howz dzoo yooh vish tzoo goh?"

"Brutal!" Q tells him proudly.

"Dieu vous garde." ("God keep you.") He walks over top of Q and pulls out another silenced gun and softly says: "Bon nuit," ("Good night.") he now positions himself at an angle with both guns aimed at Q.

"You faggot ass French mother fucker, you're going to get what you got coming to you."

"C'est la vie." ("That's life.")

"Fuck you and that whore of a mother of yours. My father used to fuck her for loaves of bread, you honorable faggot."

"De mal an pis." ("From bad to worst.") He now begins to unload both silenced guns into the face of Q, "Pssshhh, pssshhh, pssshhh, pssshhh, pssshhh!" The only sound in the condo is that of the weapons softly taking Q's life.

He ejects both magazines and begins to insert new ones. He looks down at what used to be Q's face. The matter looks burgundy, stringy and syrupy along with the gunpowder fills the room. The Frenchman goes inside his trench coat and pulls out a mini French flag and places it on Q's corpse.

Making sure the coast is clear he makes his move to the back stairs as the door closes he can hear the dead man's spouse with the concierge, who's about to let her into her suite. After the door to the back stairs close he just glides down them without breaking his stride or making noise where he just disappears into the night. Now that he has the info on the youths he can trail and surveilence them for his own purpose. His phone vibrate with a caller.

"Yez," he answers. This is not an American voice on the other end telling him something of grave importance. "No!" He says out loud. The caller finished telling him. "Thzey veally arz youthz?"

The caller is still talking to him but, for some

reason he's not trying to hear what the caller is
trying to say. Somehow the news of the caller changes
the complexion of him and changes his mind set towards
the youths.
"Thzey arz allz szeventzeen yearz old?" He asks
the caller. He's a bit confused right now and have to
pull over and talk to the caller. "I can'tz velieve
it," he says. "Dzoo yooh know vat thzey arz up
againzt?" He asks the caller. "Thzey hozz no military
training, szo thzey arz szitting dzuckz and needz
help," he continues.
The caller is telling him that the youths had a
shoot out with agents, rogues and official ones along
with mercenaries and luck upped and escaped with their
lives and killed a lot of their pursuers in the
process.
"Hourra!, vive!" He applauds the youths. The
caller not at all amused at the reaction of the
Frenchman. "Szo now thzey hozz everythzing, allz of
thzem?" The caller informs him that the youths had
everything prior.
"Oh my," he says. Jaquiel Froscios, has made up
his mind he will find these youths himself and help
them. "Thzey arz alone out thzere and dzon't evenz
know vat thzey hozz." The caller just stops talking
for a minute and Jaquiel begins to speak: "Get'z
vuyers nowz!" He tells the caller in a demanding
voice.
If the Frenchman pulls this one off here he
believes that he would become a underworld legend not
just in France but, the world. Even if he's just a
middle man who helped broker the deal. He would be a
very big man in the international crime lure for
eternity.
He would never have to do a single crime again.
All over the world they would pay homage to him and
have feasts in his honor. Just so he could tell the
story over and over again about how he helped the
American youths who stole weapons of mass destruction
from the American government.
"Vill yooh put out thzat I, Jaquiel Froscois may
vee ablez tzoo szell szome preshuzz ziamondz forz a

handzome price. And give thzem thzee catalog of
goodz, firzt come firzt szerved. And putting a
little szomethzing up frontz forz consziteratshon
vould not hurt. Nor vill it vee forgotten ven
szurpliez arz low," he continues.

And with that he disconnects the phone. Jaquiel
Froscios is thinking that if he can just talk with
the youths they might see things his way and allow
him to help them get rid of the stones for them.

Before he could get the thought into his mind
good the phone lights up. "Yez," he answers. It's
the previous caller bringing news of buyers wishing
to pre-order. "I dzoo not hozz anythzing availavle
yet vut, I vill not forget jorw promptnezz," he
assures the caller by way of conference call.

At that time he does nothing but smile at what
has just happen. And in such short amount of time
he sees the light shining once more. "Yez," he
answers. The caller is letting him know that
another buyer is requesting a test. "I dzoo not
hozz nothzing yet, tzell thzem thzat I vill notzify
thzem wonze I dzoo," he informs the caller.

He knows that everybody knows of the youths
precious cargo and that they are in danger. Once
more his phone beacons, this time he won't answer
it, he decides to play if you want me you can wait.
He was told that the youths were spotted in North
Carolina and South Carolina.

The Georgetown Heist

So its a good chance that they are on the move but, to where? While his phone still goes on he just scans through them taking none of them. Then the caller number shows and he takes his assistant call.

"Yez Ponc'e vat'z izzit?" He asks him.

"Intzel stzatez thzat thzey arz going tzoo Flo-reedah, Miami, Flo-reedah."

"Arz yooh szure Ponc'e?"

"Thzee dzata feed vas intzercepted from thzee air vavez, everyone iz on thzeir vay tzoo Miami, Flo-reedah law enforzement and jorw rivals alszo."

"Ponc'e make preparazionz forz mi az szoon az pozzivle."

"How dzoo yooh vizh tzoo travel Monsieur?"

"Par avion," ("By airplane,") he answers back to his assistant. Feeling the need to finish what he has started. "Ponc'e I vill call yooh ven I am veady tzoo goh." Ponc'e already knows that he has to get a charted flight for his boss.

The Frenchman has unfinished business and is about to go and finish it. He drives to the same house in which he had previously jumped out the window to escape death. He just rides pass the house to see what the scenery is over there.

It seems as though all are asleep so he decides to go over to Kieth Brooks's house first to see him in the flesh just like the first house. It seems as though all are asleep the Frenchman walks around the back of the house.

He now stops in his tracks it seems as though he made the right decision to come to Mr. Brooks house first. He sees that Brooks has a little late night action going on. He watches Brooks get into a car and he follows them. Once the car comes to a stop, the driver gets out and goes into a house. Sensing he only has a few minutes before the driver comes back.

Jaquiel tries to seize the moment but falls short, the driver comes back too quickly. He follows once again from a far distance he could barely keep them in his sight.

He looks up and they have vanished, how could this be? His facial expression says, he's not worried, just concerned. He turns around and goes past an alley. He sees a flash of headlights so he goes to park on the next block and walks over.

He sneaks his way around to the alley he sees what appears to be a burglary in progress. "Thzey arz vreaking intzo szomevoby'z houze?" Jaquiel asks himself. "Vhy not?" He asks himself again in a low voice.

He goes the same way the first burglars went he can see that this is an inside job. Whoever lives here has a little wealth. With his guns out and drawn the Frenchman is casing the place himself, he hears something in front of him.

It's Brooks driver he's cutting around the edges of a wall painting. "Pssshhh, pssshhh, pssshhh, pssshhh." That sound is like no other with the first going into his body he knows it will put him down. The second one strikes him directly in the right eye, snatching out everything on the left side of his head.

Even in the dark you can see the splatter of his blood. As it explodes from his head and shoots a bloody mist through the air. The third tears off his jaw and keeps going until it hits the wall and rips apart some electrical wiring.

The wiring is now shooting off sparks from the wall, that's lighting up the dark living room. With most of his jaw missing the fourth strikes him in the nape of his neck which exits on the opposite side, it just blows out his throat.

With the leakage from this one, he might not have any blood left once he's discovered. Jaquiel now sits and patiently waiting for Brooks. It takes him a good little while before he reappears.

"Eddie," he whispers out. "Hey Eddie, where are you?" He asks softly in the night. Not sure where his companion is, Keith Brooks takes a look around for himself. He bends the corner and enters the living room area he sees something on the floor.

"Pour acquit," ("Received payment.") the Frenchman says in the dark in a low and surprised voice. "Pssshhh!" And shoots Brooks in the right thigh, just to bring him to his knees.

The Georgetown Heist

"Ooooooowww, aaaaahhhhh!" he screams out loud in the empty house.

"Pssshhh!" Another silenced forty five slug just to shut him up from all that yelling.

"Please don't kill me," Brooks cries in a low voice. "You can have all this shit in the house, take it all," he continues in a begging attempt to save his life which the Frenchman despises.

"Est perdu hors l'honeur," ("All is lost save honor,") the Frenchman firmly says to him. Jaquiel starts walking towards him, Brooks begs for his life.

"Oh, please don't kill me." At this point Jaquiel decides that Brooks is not worthy of being killed by his Mark 25's, so he holsters them both and walk past Brooks.

"Thank you, thank you," Brooks say faintly. The Frenchman is looking for something more fitting for a man who whines like a woman. He returns from the bathroom with something in his hand. He sticks one end of it inside Brooks mouth, and with the rest of its length he wraps it around his throat and begins to strangle him with it.

Brooks can't even fight off the death hold. His lifeless body can not put up a worthy fight for its existence Jaquiel holds on tight until he's sure that Brooks is dead in his book.

He lets go of the hose like contraption at the end of it's hose is a rubbery bag that the Frenchman leaves covering his face. He's leaving this place, he has one more house to visit before his trip. He decides to forgo the others at this point, due to the time restraint and how far down they are in the ranks.

Before he walks out the house he places a small French flag on both corpse when one would have done just fine leaving one's mark is serious work. The last thing you would want is for somebody else to come along and claim your work.

It is so rude, he believes to claim someone else's work, and also truly unbefitting of a gentleman. Looking at his phone he can see that he have too many people trying to talk to him. He scans it for his assistant number and finds it and places the call.

"Ponc'e yooh hozz szome newz forz mi yez?" Jaquiel asks.

"Yez, yooh hozz a flight vith za new carrier szervize and thzey hozz allz jorw favoritez, andza thzey hozzah Greek stzewardezz," Ponc'e pauses after telling him that.

"Greek, vat'z szo good za-bout a Greek woman?" He asks, and they both begins to laugh at their private joke.

"I'm szending yooh thzee intzel now," Ponc'e tells him.

He's pulling around to the back of Titus Wright's home and his phone has just confirmed what Ponc'e have previously told him. He has just received his intel and directions about his flight and safe houses in Miami. And his regular arms he uses on an search and rescue trip like this one but, this one has the most danger of them all.

***

Now at Titus's, house he is just concentrating on him. He goes through the backyard he can't wait to see his face when Wright find's him standing over top of him. As he goes to work on the patio door, it takes him no time at all to get in.

Once inside he already knows the place having been in it several times prior. Now he's in it as an enemy. He creeps through the house and sees Wright lying fast asleep on his couch with a blanket that someone placed over him.

This is a great opportunity for him to get Wright up and out the house without being seen by anyone. Jaquiel draws back his hand and smacks the daylights out of the sleeping man with his gun. As he wakes up he can't quite understand things yet. But his head is bleeding and he doesn't knows it and the pain really isn't there yet. As his eyes adjust he sees the Frenchman standing over top of him.

"Where you come from?" Titus asks.

"Outre mer," ("Over seas,") he replies. By the time Titus Wright fully awaken, it's to late Jaquiel

The Georgetown Heist

Froscios has his gun.

"Getz up let'z goh," Jaquiel orders him.

"I ain't going no fucking where with you, so what ever you're going to do to me just do it and get it over with. You faggot ass French whore."

"Voila tout." ("That's all.") Titus refuses to cower and makes his move towards Jaquiel. The Frenchman is not having it in no shape form or fashion. The silenced forty five, that hits Titus in his chest. Makes it seems as though he had a rope tied around his body and on cue, had it yanked. Titus goes backwards so fast and violently that his feet almost kicks the gun out of Jaquiel's hand.

As he lays on his back looking at the Frenchman he speaks: "Fuck you whore," he tells Jaquiel in a faint voice but, the Frenchman hears him clearly.

"Ventr's a' terre." (Belly to the ground quickly.")

"Sorry, I don't speak fag." Jaquiel refuses to waste time on him, so he flips him over on his belly and positions both guns at an angle and fires both silenced guns until they're empty. The blood is everywhere the fragments are more evident. The gel of the cerebellum is all over the place.

Both guns are a mess now and in a freak of nature act. Titus's body takes and rolls over on its back. The Frenchman's eyes are wide open. And by the body rolling itself over. He can now see where all the bullets that went through Titus's head, and are now lodged in the expensive wood flooring.

***

As they drive along the highway the sirens are hit so Teeny-Man pulls over. He believes that Tammy would not call the cops on them, or at lease he thinks not. "Can I see some I-denti-fah-cate-shon," the officer asks.

"Sure officer give me a second," Teeny-Man replies. And at this exact moment Teeny-Man discovers that his bag is not tied up all the way. While he fumbles around with the bag of stones he's not trying to give a hint that his bag is open.

He pulls out his wallet and is handing it to the officer, just as Babylon fires center mass at the officer. The armored piercing projectile goes through the officer's vest.

It leaves such a hole that you can see traces of blood on his uniform shirt. "Don't nobody get out the car they got those damn cameras mounted on them. T, back up and then turn to block the cameras." Babylon instruct him. Teeny-Man backs up and cuts the steering wheel to the left totally cutting off any cameras view.

Babylon goes and gets Teeny-Man's credentials off the ground, once he has it, he picks back up the riffle and fires five more times into the fallen State Trooper.

"Okay slim, roll out," Babylon tells him. It is a good kill the Trooper recognized the GTO and knew it belonged to Luke. And he has already called for back up and now they're on their way. The GTO is going at a good pace they are moving fast away from the dead Trooper's body.

***

With all the Sheriffs and State Troopers at the house. They decides its a good idea for Tammy and the girls to leave. Luke's brother, a deputy feels his nephews should be here since they are now the men of the house.

As Tammy and the girls are getting ready to leave to go over to Luke's brother's house. One of the little girls finds a pretty diamond on the floor, she picks it up and its her favorite color, pink.

One of her brothers sees this and go takes it from the little girl. She starts to cry but, its nothing Tammy can do, especially with Luke's brother there cheering the boy on. In her mind this is her chance to leave for good anyway.

So she packs a nice one for the road she also takes all the money with her, and also money that Luke had stashed, she and the girls leave.

The Georgetown Heist

***

Flashing lights only mean one thing, that the young men are in trouble again. The cop car pulls up beside the GTO. Babylon takes a good aim at the car and releases a bombardment of the mighty three o'eight riffle shells.

The cop's car turns off the road and crashes. Teeny-Man not yet aware of what the GTO can do but, is very pleased at the old vehicle. As more cop cars are coming Juice-Hop and Bernard ready their weapons.

With all windows rolled down they get sandwiched in by two cops cars and Juice-Hop let loose his M-4. He places thirteen rounds into the door hitting the cop in the legs.

The cop hits his emergency brakes without any warning and the domino effect collision is a blow to the police but, not like the one they will soon get.

***

"**Let me see** that boy?" One of the deputies asks Luke's son. The boy hands it over and the deputy looks at it very carefully. In his mind it is a one hundred percent fake.

Because nobody in this town would buy it and even if somebody around here could afford it, there's no place in town to buy something like that.

"Hey Skeeter, you know that they say if you take a hammer to a diamond and it shatters it's a real diamond," another deputy tells the boy.

Now the deputy goes and gets a hammer with two dead bodies in front of him. Never mind that this is supposed to be a friend of his, now with hammer in hand.

"Dang gone Skeeter, since it's your diamond you do the honors of telling us if it's real or not," he tells the boy.

The boy takes the hammer from him and draws it back. He comes down with a force to much to be his own. They never even got a chance to see it break or shatter, the explosion from the stone made people in

Chapter 11

Virginia feels it.

And as far away as Maryland sees it in the skies. It just destroys a ten block radius, but that is not the worst to come.

***

"**Goddamn, did y'all** feel that shit?" Asks Teeny-Man.

"Fuck did y'all feel that did y'all hear that mother fucker?" Juice-Hops asks in responding.

"Slim I don't know what the hell that was, but I do know we wasn't around for it and that's a good thing," says Teeny-Man.

"Get ready here they come again everybody." Babylon informs them.

On Babylon's side a K-9 Unit is closing in on them. Babylon takes the riffle and just points it towards the back and let off a couple of rounds to that part of the van. He hits the dog, blowing the Shepherd's head off. The driver of the van sees the dog's headless body and goes into a frenzy over it.

"You son bitch, you killed my dog," he cries.

"Hey B, that mother fucker is thirty eight hot at you for something," Teeny-Man tells him.

***

The Georgetown Heist

Her phone rings and she answers it. "Hello Tonya, what is it?"

"It was an explosion."

"Purposely or accidental?"

"I don't know yet but, I'll keep you posted."

***

The K-9 Unit driver continues to curse out the young man. He starts shooting at them from the driver's side of the van trying his best to shoot out the passenger window at them.

"Lean back," Juice-Hop tells Teeny-Man. Now he's firing his M-4 into the side door of the van. His estimated aim is right on target. Hitting the driver several times from the hip to the upper body.

Teeny-Man notices that this car is getting up in speed. "Both sides, both sides, they're all around us y'all. Let's crank these bitches up and go," Teeny-Man tells them.

***

"**Ohhh my God!** We have a, we have a detonation," screams Mrs. Culp.

"Where at?" Asks Mr. Sears.

"It's, it's in North Carolina, Myrtle Beach."

"Are you sure its a detonation?"

"It's emitting now." The entire command center is waiting for the official read. "It's toxic Sir, it shows the possibility of chloropiicdrin, capsicum and dibenzoxazepine. That means the its positive for irritation agents Sir. And it has an blast affect of twenty kilometers.

"But its the fallout from the blast that's going to kill all them people down there," she says in a sad voice.

"Okay, listen up people, Mrs. Culp please never use the word detonation unless it is a detonation. A detonation refers to one thing and one thing only. And that is the detonation of something nuclear by way of purposely or accidently, is that understood?" Mr.

Sears asks her.

"Sir we have shooting going on in North Carolina around the Myrtle Beach area. It appears that the local authorities are in pursuit of four young black males," Mrs. Culp informs him.

"Activate agents in the field down there to protect the football at all costs," Mr. Sears orders.

"Sir all units in that area have been activated."

"Okay Mrs. Culp give me an up link to all agents in the field at this time there."

"You're linked to talk Sir."

"To all agents, this is Ronald Sears please be advised that an chemical explosion has occurred. This is not a test or a drill, a real live explosion involving a weapon of mass destruction has just exploded on American soil.

"All agents will have their person protection equipment in place if you are in the hot zone or zones. And remember, your P.P.E's which protect you from whatever hazards you are to encounter, must be worn if you're in these hot zones," he informs them.

He disconnects with the field agents and now turns his focus to the command room. "I want a crisis management and a consequence management done yesterday." Mr. Sears orders the group.

"A crisis analysis?" Mrs. Guillory ask.

"No, a crisis management because it is the law enforcement response, and focus on the criminal aspects of the incident. Specific components of crisis management includes activities to anticipate, prevent and or resolve, a threat or incident, identify, locate and apprehend the perpetrators.

"And investigate and gather evidence to support persecution. Crisis management also, involves local, State and Federal law enforcment agencies with the F.B.I. having the lead role."

"So who does the response functions then?" Mrs. Guillory asks.

"The consequence management is the response to the disaster and focuses on alleviation damage, loss, hardship or suffering. Specific components of consequence management including, activities to

The Georgetown Heist

protect health and safety.

"It restores essential government services and provide emergency assistance to effected Government, business and individuals.

"Now last but not lease, consequence management includes Federal, State, and local volunteer and the private agencies," Mr. Sears finally finishes.

As all the workers in the Homeland Security building are busy running around. Mr. Sears is a nervous wreck, he knows that, that call is on its way to him. And the F.B.I. is going to be crawling all over the place.

"Do we have a visual on the young men?" He asks.

"No, not yet Sir." Mrs. Guillory answers.

***

As the young men brace themselves for another shoot out. They're still at the top speed of one hundred eighty five miles per hour.

"Here they come, let's go," Babylon says. The first car on Babylon's side is the first to get it. He sticks the M-16 out the window and let the cop car have it. The bullets are so damn hot, that they're sparking off the security bars of the cop car, back into the GTO.

The cop in the car is scared to death and with good reason, these young men are not playing around today. Juice-Hop is still working his M-4 as he shoots he is noticing how the gunpowder is getting kind of thick in his face.

But it doesn't stop him from shooting this cop in his head and spraying his brain matter all over the place. Babylon goes and reloads with a new magazine. He can see that the cops are now trying to double up so that they can shoot and drive like they are doing.

"Hey y'all they about to be coming up beside us with a passenger shooting, be ready for their asses. Hey, we shooting off the break," Teeny-Man tells them.

The cop cars come rolling up and they have officers hanging out the side of them. Babylon is the first to let loose on them. He hits the windshield and

95

the bullets go straight through to hit the officer riding shotgun.

"Got'em," Babylon says th himself. Another one takes his place but, this time he starts shooting behind him.

"Oh shit, they're shooting from the back," Teeny-Man says. Babylon starts shooting out the back window. Taking the stock of his M-16 and knocking out all the loose glass. Now he start to shooting it out with them. With a full assault upon the squad cars they are out manned but, not out gunned.

Babylon continues to fire he can see the results of his dead on assault, so he keeps it up. Babylon reloads again and goes back to the window for the onslaught he's giving these officers but, what he sees he can't believe.

"Hey they done called in everybody on us!" At this time Babylon takes all the magazines out the bag by dumping them on the car seat. He is getting ready to throw down with these officers today, he takes aim at one to get the party started.

He takes and fires away at its windshield he places the entire clip through it. He watches the squad car turns off the road and then start tumbling. He know he can not be stopped with the M-16 now. He has a new magazine in and the cops are still firing at them.

***

"**Go to their** channel and get them to stop shooting," a voice from inside a Crown Victoria says.

"This is the Department of Homeland Security, I am ordered to order you all to cease firing at once. I repeat stop your firing upon that vehicle, it is a matter of national security."

"You hear that Beau?" One of the deputies asks another one over the radio.

"Yeah, I hear it and don't give a rat's ass bout it. Them son bitches killed Luke and Sue, and by God they fixen to pay for it," the other responds.

There are Deputies and State Troopers all in

pursuit of the young men who all refuse to stop shooting at them.

"You are being called to stand down I am talking to all county, state, local law enforcement along with the State Troopers. I am advising you all to do so now," the voice warns them all.

"This here is Beau, Beau Snyder and I ain't gonna let some paper pusher from Washington D.C. come down here and tell me shit. We run our house down here boy. Do you hear that Mr. Homeland Security?" He states boldly over the radio.

"Hot dangit, you sure did tell'em Beau."

"This is a matter of national security, please stand down," the agent asks once more.

"Stand down deputies, this is a matter of national security," Beau mocks him using a little girl's voice. And all of the deputies are laughing through their radios.

"All agents switch back to secured channel," the voice instructs. Now is a crisp clear voice: "We have our orders and now we will commence protocol. Now Blue Team, we should be in your visual in about four kilometers. Red Team commence evasive maneuvers and secure a path for the football," the voice orders.

***

"Mr. Sears, the teams have made contact and are about to engage protocol dealing with the local law enforcement there who refuse to stand down," Mrs. Culp informs him.

"Protocol huh? Mrs. Guillory since they are going to protocol on the locals, can you get me housekeeping down there immediately?" Mr. Sears asks.

"Housekeeping is in route," she informs him.

***

The cops run out and are about to reload Babylon comes up from taking cover and begins to chop down the squad cars one by one. He's hitting nothing but grills and vehicle parts.

His aim and his confidence is up since all he has
to do is just point the weapon in the right direction.
"Hey we are handling everything back here," Bernard
boasts. But at that time the State Troopers and the
deputies are bringing a full assault to the young men.

"All shit here they come again, Teeny-Man push
this bitch," Juice-Hop yells out.

Babylon fires and so does everybody else. He's a
natural with the weapon he set his sights on one and
just chops him down. A squad car is firing at them
Babylon takes cover. The cop is hanging out the
passenger side window.

He goes to reload and Babylon catches him in mid
magazine switch and knocks sparks from this badge. The
M-16 strikes the officer in the throat, chin, and
several times in his body just ripping apart the thin
body armor the cop has on.

"Hey T, keep your eyes open for them road blocks
up ahead just in case they called in for one," Babylon
tells him.

***

"Red Team is in position team leader," the Red
Team lead man informs.

"This is team leader, fire at will you have a go."
The Homeland Security cars and SUV's move out and
about, through the highway. Their windows are rolled
down. A agent has his target in sight and squeezed his
trigger on his silenced M.P.-5 riffle.

It is a shot directly in the back of the head. The
deputy's squad car starts to drift off at top speed.
Nobody seems to even notice him. The same fate is
given to other deputies, State Troopers who refused to
stop shooting.

The Red Team is taking out everything in the far
rear. The young men are taking out everything behind
and on the side of them. The deputies and State
Troopers are sandwiched between the young men and the
Homeland Security agents.

And its a slaughter everywhere you look cars are
swirling off the road. Officers that was shooting out

of their windows are now dead on the highway by way of gunshots or being run over by vehicles.

***

"**Blue Team, they** should be in your zone in a matter of seconds. The first vehicle is the running back, lets give him some blocking shall we. All sirens and marked cars are yours to block, I want no trailers. You have a go," the team leader instructs.

The young men continues to fight it out so does the agents behind them. This is the most gun fighting any of the agents have seen in their lives, the young men also. The car carrying the young men comes zooming pass the four kilometers mark. Once all the law enforcement pursuers, cross the mark.

They are being slaughtered by the Blue Team who was dispatched to be there waiting on them to pass by. The Blue Team are in the woods and some are in the trees, and other are in vehicles firing at all pursuers.

The Troopers and Deputies never stood a chance they all runs right into it. The two, three car collisions are a constant. Crash after crash with cars tumbling over one another the Blue Team never thought about stop firing.

With cars exploding in the air after continuously being shot, they can't even get out of the way of it. With the Red Team already slowed down. Following these young men is a life hazzard.

With the young men still firing they are down to a mere three cars. Convinced after seeing first hand what the young men can do. The team leader calls off the attack and let the young men take care of the last of them, in which they do in grand fashion.

"Sir, the State Troopers and Sheriff's Department along with the locals all put out their S.O.S's, what do you want us to do with the distress signal Sir?" Mrs. Culp asks.

"Mrs. Culp?" He calls out to her, but still not saying anything and everybody's awaiting his words.

"Yes Sir," she replies to him.

"What do you tell a man with two black eyes?"
"I don't know, Sir."
"Nothing, his ass been told twice."

***

As a convoy of huge trucks go pass the highway no one knows their true purpose, with an amount of people to fill a small event.

They begin to take their places with siren after siren and ambulance after ambulance. Cell phone towers are rerouted to send out signals to an disclosed location. And to intercept all calls which are being jammed and to take all photos taken and then being inserted with viruses, and all wireless.

They load up the dead law enforcement personnel and stack them in to meat wagons. They takes the vehicles of these dead lawmen, and place them on huge trucks and some on tow trucks.

Those ones that can not be placed in the trucks. Are stacked up on to an eighteen wheeler carrier. All of the Troopers and Deputies that are placed into ambulances. There's dump trucks being loaded with their vehicles and truck debris along with ammunition shells, magazines, unfired ammunitions and everything too small to go into the trucks.

Now as the sanitation tankers roll in, all ready to load up and go. It's only the last of a few tires left. The big tankers full of chemicals to rid the ground of blood and DNA. The first four tankers are used to kill the blood and DNA evidence using disinfectants made to dissolve it.

The next four are street sweeping trucks using sterile water and bleach to wash and sweep all that may remain. This entire process takes less than three hours. "It's a new record for us," one of the workers says proudly.

Without so much of a who are you, these people are gone. The civilians looking on are truly impressed with the speed of the cleaning up that took place. Some believes that the state did a good job.

None will believe that a higher power of

government just cleaned up its mess. And has gotten rid of any and all evidence that would have or could have linked them to the slaughter of all those law enforcement men, women and civilians.

***

"**Mr. Sears, housekeeping just** cleared Sir," Mrs. Culp informs him.

"Good, good," he replies.

"Mr. Sears what about the people of that town?"

"Mrs. Culp they're just a bunch of rednecks."

"Sir, the exposure rate is extremely high and the death toll will be at lease in the thousands."

"Okay, since you put it that way, tells F.E.M.A. to get their asses down their now."

"Mr. Sears we have agents down there now who can evacuate the area and save a lot of lives."

"Oh, thanks for reminding me. Am I still linked to the field operatives?"

"Yes." He grabs the microphone and pushes the speak activation button.

"All agents, if you are not with housekeeping you should be trailing the football," he tells them. The entire room goes silent he can see that his decision has shocked them all so he addresses them.

"This is a go straight to hell job, that I have. And a lot of times my decisions are ones that I can never take back. I hope that you all can take what I am doing and remember how I am making some of these decisions because one of you will be in this position. Do I save twenty five thousand, and let twenty five million die? Or do you do what Ronald Sears would do, let twenty five thousand die to save twenty five million.

"I will at lease try and teach you all something here and besides who's going to miss some jug blowing, banjo plucking, rubber band yanking, spoon shaking, washboard tapping, corn pipe smoking ass rednecks?"

***

Chapter 12

"**Owwww! Hey slim**, our shit is serious as-e-mother fucker," Teeny-Man says.

"I don't know Teeny-Man," Babylon answers him.

"B, how many pigs do you think was on our ass back there?"

"T I don't know, but I do know that something isn't right with this picture."

"Bab, slim we are going to shoot the moon on this one. All we have to do now is go straight down to Florida and we're home free." Juice-Hop tells Babylon.

"Slim, it ain't as easy as it sounds," Babylon tells him.

"Bab don't do this to me right now slim, with your better safe than sorry theories. Just help me do one thing baby." Teeny-Man asks.

"What?"

"Help me enjoy Myrtle Beach for the first time, baby boy." Do to the big wreckage on the highway the Homeland Security agents was unable to follow them or anybody else for that matter. They immediately ditched the GTO and head towards the hotels. Babylon has the biggest bags as they casually walk to their destination.

***

"**The two women** sit at their conference table and just stare at one another. The power sharing between the two is taking its toll on the both of them.

"They're going to kill us, you know? Put us both in abeyance Tonya, and that will be the end of us," LaShonne tells her.

"Please if they kill anyone it will be your tired ass."

"We're in this together so both heads are going to roll."

"If we're both in this together, why are you going against me on this one? When all I am trying to do is make us relevant again, so we won't be expendable."

"I am going to ask for a transfer and then I'm going to make a proposal to them for a new agency, that I am to be the Director."

"If you do, you are surely putting your neck in a noose, not to mention mines as well. And a rival agency, please what you think they are going to just let you out and start fresh? You know better than that. What we need is to get back in the game.

"What we need is something big, just to let them know that we are still here and still major players in the field. And I believe I have found the one to bring us back to the forefront. You know the young boys got away without even a scratch on them and I've read the file on that Nimrod Mohammed one. He's the one to get us over the hump for years to come," Tonya tells her.

"I'm leaving now and I already sent my request in. You can do as you please with the agency, Washington is on notice that, from this date forward you are the sole Director. Any actions from this date on is on you and not I. I love you, but I don't have the stomach for this any more."

***

As the young men find their way to the hotel of their liking. They are wowed to see the sight of all the beautiful women around. This is their first time away from home, this far anyway, by themselves. And it couldn't have come at a better time for them.

"Hey B, I'm going to get two rooms for myself," Teeny-Man tells him.

"What the hell you need with two rooms?"

"Because with all the girls I'm planning to be hitting. I am going to need to change up on them, I don't need them doubling back on me."

"Mmm, mmm, mmm," Babylon sighs while shaking his head at Teeny-Man. With all the young men finally settled in, all but Babylon has decided to hit the stroll.

"Hey Bab, don't start that," Teeny-Man tells him.

"T, I got to stay and get my head right because things are not what they appear to be."

"Slim you think too, hard. You should just relax and take a load off your mind and go get some freaks."

"I'm cool Teeny, you all go ahead if y'all want, but I prefer if you all didn't, but I'll be right here if you need me."

With that they leaves his room and go on their way. Teeny-Man can't believe that his main man is going to pass up a time like this, not with all these fine women down here.

***

As he sits and wonder to himself he knows that something is wrong with this picture, but he has to figure it out. In his mind the thought of all that shooting couldn't have been just them. He's disappointed that they all went outside, but he know he would have gotten a fight out of Teeny-Man.

"What am I missing?" He asks himself as he begins to pace the room watching and counting his steps. In hopes of coming up with the answer in his mind, this feeling is tearing him apart it doesn't sit well with him. So he just prepares himself for the worst, he puts all his weapons on top of his bed along with the ammunition.

With everything spread out across his bed he just sits and thinks his next move.

***

"Man I feel bad that slim ain't here with us,"

104

The Georgetown Heist

Teeny-Man says.

"He said that he was cool with it, so just keep going." Bernard states.

"Slim you might got something." Juice-Hop tells Teeny-Man.

"Well I am going to get myself another room, because I am going to get my freak on for shizzle." Bernard tells them.

"Slim, you ain't from the city originally are you?" Teeny-Man asks Bernard.

"Yes."

"Oh hell nawl, you moved here from somewhere slim." Teeny-Man continues.

"I am born and raised right in the Nation's Capital."

"The Nation's Capital, huh?" Teeny-Man finishes and he and Juice-Hop give each other the eye. "Anyway I'm going back to the hotel to see Bab. I'll see y'all two later."

"Look slim, I'll be up a little later," Juice-Hop tells Teeny-Man.

"Teeny-Man, you don't like pussy?" Bernard asks him in a slick voice.

"Do a bear shit in the woods and wipes his ass with a fury rabbit?" He responds, and Juice-Hop laughs at his reply.

"You got that Teeny-Man, I just want to enjoy it before its gone."

"I can dig it slim, but I got to go and check on my homie," Teeny-Man tells him. They start to turn around and head back towards the hotel. They walk up on a conversation about oral sex. And a female police officer in uniform is also present.

But not too, far from them are rogue agents watching their every move. Teeny-Man goes and enter the conversation with the women and begin to tell them about his moves. Other women are beside him as well as the policewoman.

The women are shocked at how explicit Teeny-Man is and how he's explaining the reaction of his female companions during certain moves of his.

"And when she's about to get her nut off, that's

when I speed up it up because that's what she likes. But don't get it twisted, no two women are alike," he finishes. With that, and all that he said before the women know he's the real thing. But only the policewoman has the heart to say something to him as the other women watch her.

"I was listening to what you were saying and I can tell that you know exactly what you're talking about. And I would have no problem with you putting your face between my legs and letting you go for what you know," she tells him.

The woman cop just stand there waiting for him to answer her. She's eager to hear what he has to say to her. But Teeny-Man is truly offended by the officer's invitation. "Well I'm waiting for an answer," she reminds him.

But of course the only person standing around out there that felt it coming was Juice-Hop. With Teeny-Man looking straight at the policewoman he begins to speak: "With all due respect, Teeny-Man don't eat pork."

The other women stand there with their mouths wide open. This is indeed a bad chess move by Teeny-Man. Every black man in the world knows that you don't try to one up a black woman in front of no one, especially other black women. Their pride is just as big as black men if not bigger.

With the other women now laughing at her, after catching on the pork joke, referring that she's a pig. That really makes her blood boil.

"You lame ass mother fucker, that's the only thing your black ass good for. Just eating a-"

"Bitch fall back, you came fucking with me. I was minding my mother fucken business," he interrupts her to tell her.

"You verbally assaulted a police officer you are under arrest," with Juice-Hop now by his side he pretty much know how this is going to end. And at the same time the rogue agents are moving in on cue.

"Hey Pig bitch, I don't feel like getting arrested today."

He pulls out his Desert Eagle, in the sun the big

gun seems to shine like as if he has a mirror in his
hand. The chrome cannon starts to spark up the area
where they're standing. Watching the gun empty out
shells it seems as though the gun is stretching out as
much as fifteen inches long.

The first slug strikes the cop in her face it
exits out her back. The second hits her in the throat
that passes through just a few inches where the first
one exited from.

The last shot causes the entire area to just
explode and the back of her head just oozes with
blood. The young men are already in the wind, making a
run for it.

With gunshots now being fired they wonder who's
shooting they did not see any other cops around. They
run towards the hotel it seems as though the shots are
getting closer to them. They have to stop and take a
stand as they take cover behind a car.

They start to return fire on whoever it is firing
at them. Teeny-Man couldn't help, but to think about
Babylon's words. Well that's water over the bridge
now. As they lay down fire they now hear the sirens.

So it is not time to be playing around, but they
have no way out. They got themselves pinned down and
at no time are they not returning fire. As the rogue
agents fire they're behind them.

The sparks shoots off the car that covers them. In
a bold attempt, Teeny-Man makes a run for it. So he
can get an better angle on the people shooting at
them. He's rewarded with a great view of his would be
killers.

He gets in position and can now see his targets.
He begins to fire off shots with the cannon. The
agents takes their attention off the car for a second
to concentrate on Teeny-Man who's firing at them from
a new position.

Now all hears the sound of a machine gun in the
air and become nervous. Thinking that they are truly
out gunned it is Babylon coming from behind the
agents. They never stood a chance the agents were
never trying to hurt them, but only to hold them until
they had used up all their ammunition. And then

just walk up to them and take the stones.

But their backup has not come in time to stop Babylon from chopping them down. Its another slaughter to the young man's credit. Now they come up for air and are on the move.

As he runs Teeny-Man is putting in the last clip to his Desert Eagle. As they run its a man using his phone to video them. Teeny-Man stops and goes back a couple of feet and takes a swing at he man's phone. The man refuses to give Teeny-Man his phone and tries to put up a fight and takes a swing at Teeny-Man.

And now, Teeny-Man shoots the man in the face at point blank range. The man dies immediately they are taking the back stairs to get to their rooms. Now hauling ass up their floor and rushing to their rooms to retrieve their belongings.

Teeny-Man is rushing so bad he drops his bag of stones and some falls out, but he manages to pick them up.

But not before one of them gets away from him. With all of their stuff ready they get on the elevator and straight out the front door. Once out in front of the hotel they see a young man around their age.

"Hey slim, look we need some help, let us get that car from you," Babylon asks him while handing him some money.

"Go ahead, handle your business Brah," the young man tells him.

As they take the car they are happy to be getting away. The Ford Mustang will do for now, but their main concern is to get away from Myrtle Beach in one piece. They drive on and Teeny-Man sees that they have company behind them.

"Hey y'all we got a trailer on our ass," he informs them as he drives by a gated town home community.

"Pull in there T, hurry up," Babylon tells him.

"That's a dead end," Teeny-Man informs him.

"I know, hurry up."

Teeny-Man goes through with his friends's request. The rogue agents are in a black Chevy Tahoe, and think they are fools for turning onto a dead end road.

Just as they are going down the winding road, there's a blind spot a billboard that's too low to the ground. As Babylon taps Teeny-Man's shoulder he brings the car to a halt. "Make sure that you drive slow so they can see the car," Babylon tells him as he's getting out the car.

Now fully out the car he start to run going behind the big billboard sign. He's in position now and Teeny-Man is already in action.

He sees the SUV in the intersection turning on to the road. So he start to act like he's driving to one of the town homes. The SUV continue to go along the road and Babylon is still hiding from them.

He can now hear the SUV's motor he is looking around and can see the freshly cut blades of grass in front of him. Along with the empty bottles and wrappers. The SUV nears him and he readies himself for his attack.

Just as the Tahoe lines up in front of the billboard sign he readies his weapon. The sun is shining down on the drivers side of the SUV. It's moving so slow that he can see the shadow of the truck.

With the M-16 in his hands the young man leaps out from behind the billboard sign and start his assault. The passenger as well as the driver never sees him come from behind the billboard sign releasing shots.

The first shot just shatters the glass on its way through the right shoulder of the passenger. It goes in and passes through the windshield. The second hit's the passenger in the back of his neck, that explodes his throat.

The projectile just keeps going through the windshield. With a shower of blood that completely covers the windshield. The third one hits him in the left shoulder just like the first two it explodes his shoulder.

This time blood gets in the driver's eye and he slams on the brakes. The entire time Teeny-Man is watching while moving towards his friend. The SUV comes to a complete stop and Babylon goes and snatches

the driver's side door open with M-16 in hands pointed
at the driver.

"Get out now!" Babylon yells at him. The driver
still unable to see has a hard time seeing and is a
little slow.

So Babylon establishes dominance as he jabs the
driver in the face with the barrel of the M-16, with a
strong force that makes the driver head snap to the
side.

"Okay, okay, give me some time," the driver cries.

"No time, get out now!" Babylon shouts as his
accomplices are now out of their car with guns in
hands. "T, see what's in the back," Babylon asks.

The driver is now out and is laying face down on
the ground. Teeny-Man has a lot of things that were in
the front seats of the Tahoe. He has a lap-top
computer and two cell phones that are in hard metal
cases.

Teeny-Man is amazed to have found a bundle of
plexi cuffs and Babylon sees the plastic ties. "Hey,
get his hands and feet and put him in the trunk,"
Babylon tells them. As they search him they discover a
Sig Sauer nine millimeter and takes it immediately.
Teeny-Man takes and smacks the hell out of him with
his own gun.

"What the fuck was that for?" The driver yells at
him.

"My bad, its that South East shit in me," Teeny-
Man tells him in an apologetic voice.

As they attempt to place the driver into the
trunk, he tries to put up a fight. But his fight is
met with an full scale assault. They put pistols on
his head now that he is in the trunk they all get back
in the car. Teeny-Man now throws Babylon a walkie-
talkie radio he found.

"T, find a good place where we can talk to our
friend back there," Babylon asks him. Babylon cuts on
the radio and the first thing he hears is: "Yeah,
that's correct a white Ford Mustang with rental tags.
I have the hotel employee with me right here," the
voice says over the radio.

The young men can not believe what they are

hearing. It could not be maybe it was another employee that made the statement to the authorities. It is evident that they didn't pay any attention to their home boys in the Federal system.

Who on many occasions stated how the males from North Carolina was majority stool pigeons. "We have to get off the road and fast, they made us," Babylon tells Teeny-Man.

Teeny-Man continues to drive until he sees what looks to be a trailer park. So he pulls over through some woods a little ways from the trailer park, but in nice walking distance. Once they all get out the car they pops the trunk to get the agent out.

"Who are you, and who do you work for?" Teeny-Man asks him.

"He's not answering," Juice-Hop says.

"What is this case for?" Babylon asks him while holding the phone. The driver looks up at the young man and begins to talk.

"Its a special metal case that once it is placed over the phone the Government can't track you or your movements." Babylon goes and picks up the lap top.

"Activate this," he tells him.

"My eye." Babylon brings the lap-top across his face so he can get his eye scanned. Babylon attempts to log on and the agent watches him. "Password!" Babylon says firmly. He pauses for a moment and just looks at Babylon and puts his head down.

"Tell me how you want it?" Babylon asks him.

"Are you going to kill me Nimrod?" He's a little shocked that he knows his name. And looks at the agent, he knows now that he's in something bigger than he could have ever known.

"Hey slim, let me just kill his bitch ass," Teeny-Man asks. "Off the strength of that secret squirrel shit he pulled, so the government can't track you," he continues.

"No, I'm not going to kill you I only do it when I am forced to," Babylon tells him.

"Number one maneater." [#1maneater$]

"What?" Babylon asks.

"Number one maneater, dollar sign, man eater is one word. First, the pound sign and the number one, maneater and last a dollar sign." Teeny-Man is looking at him sideways, with his face making deferent expressions.

"Man, what the fuck kind shit you on?" Teeny-Man asks him. Juice-Hop is laughing he can't hold it. Bernard turns his back and starts to walk away shaking his head, Babylon refuses to laugh.

Babylon tries the password and he's in. "Okay we're in," he tells them. As his head is down in the lap-top.

"What part of the mother fucken game is this?" Teeny-Man asks as the same three are still laughing their asses of the agent. "Man eater, what type of freak ass mother fucker is he? Slim, this shit is crazy, mother fucker on that hannah," Teeny-Man states.

"How many of you are out there?" Babylon asks.

"I really don't know I was with my team, you killed them all, but they are some that are all around."

"Now?"

"No, I mean in the town for you each team is called in when another is finished of killed off. So I don't know how many more are out there. I would say around a hundred for you Nimrod."

The young man doesn't like what he's hearing not one bit of it. Especially him saying his name and no one else's. But what can he do? He's not the only one to take notice in it either. Teeny-Man is building up a rage inside of himself for some ungodly reason.

"Hey nail biter, I mean man eater who do you work for and who are you?" Teeny-Man asks. He refuses to answer Teeny-Man question and its a bad move on his part.

"Oh! You don't hear me huh? You gonna respect my gangster." Teeny-Man walks closer to the agent. Babylon knows he can't stop him he's in his feelings that the agent was answering Babylon's questions and not his. He places his forty four magnum on the agent's forehead.

The agent shakes his head as to get the weapon away from his head. A shot rings out and goes into the distance. The bullet enters the forehead and exits the left side of his neck. And once more entering his shoulder and exiting his shoulder.

His lifeless body falls to the ground the young men all looks like they all had seen nothing out of the ordinary. The freshly pour of blood spills out the body of the agent. The dirt and grassy land begins to soak it up, but it still manages to make pools of blood in a couple of spots.

"Well I guess its no reason to stay here any more y'all," Teeny-Man tells them.

"But of course not," Bernard responds.

"I have never in my life witness such savagery. The South East Butcher in the flesh," jokes Juice-Hop.

All of the young men start to walk towards the trailer park, they reach the area site. Babylon is looking at the lap-top and the phone. Juice-Hop has to use the rest room so he asks this woman could he use hers.

She has no problem with it as he enters the trailer he takes a close look at it. Being that he's never been inside one before it's small, but cozy. He goes into the bathroom he sees that this is a real trailer park.

He would never see anything like this D.C. In the bathroom he can't help but to open his bag of diamonds, they are calling him. He looks at them and is once again reminded why him being shot at is worth it.

"Are you alright in there?" The lady asks, her voice shocks him and he drops his bag on the floor. He hurries to pick them up and he breaks a piece off one of the big diamonds.

"Yes I'm okay," he tells her. As he gets ready to leave he can't seem to find the handle to the toilet, he's looking all over for a handle.

"Hey Hon, there's no handle if you're looking for one," she tells him.

"Thank you."

It's been over three hours now as they walk, they see a farm. And they also see that there is an old man and woman on the farm. Since they're black the young men feel as though they could go to them for some help. But Babylon is hard at work on the lap-top and periodically on the phone.

"Let me see that for a second," Bernard asks. Babylon hands it to him, he inspects it and looks at the screen.

"This shit is worthless we can't get no money with this." Now he lifts it up over his head and before Babylon could say stop he slams it to the ground totally destroying it.

"Damn, that could have been useful," Babylon tells him.

"My bad Babylon, I thought it was nothing." Babylon is still messing around with the cell phone, and his eyes gets big.

"Hey y'all go ahead to the farm I'll be back in a little while. And stay out of sight until I get back," he tells them. As he walks off Bernard is watching him like a hawk. And then he smiles wickedly and nods his head in agreement.

"You alright B?" Teeny-Man asks him.

"Yeah Teeny-Man I am okay y'all lay low until I get back."

"You straight main man?"

"Yes, I'm fine," Bernard answers Teeny-Man, as Teeny-Man watches the way he's watching Babylon leave.

***

The Georgetown Heist

As Babylon walks alone, he thinks of how it was a good move to give all his stuff to his friends. So lugging all that stuff will not be a problem for him. Looking at the phone he sees the red dots on it.

In his mind the dots are the coworkers of the captured driver from earlier. He stays on with the map on the phone and sees that all of the red dots are not far from where he is.

He's hoping that his guess work will be a hit for him he's getting closer to his first stop. He looks around and sees a SUV, that could be one of those Governmental given trucks.

The Chevy Suburban is black with tinted windows, now the plates is what says no, civilian. He begins to take a look around the house. He's trying to enter it the old fashion way, through the patio window.

He places his hands on the glass and start to press hard against the glass with his palms while going in an upwards motion making the door come off it's track. The stick that is laid in the track slider to prevent the door from being opened was of no use in a weak effort to stop someone from opening the patio door.

He sees that the house is fully furnished so he begins to walk lightly through the living room. He pulls out his gun when he hears someone coming down stairs.

"Joanne, I'm going to the store do you want anything? a voice asks while coming down the stairs.

"Stan, bring me back some peach tea," a woman's voice answers.

The male leaves the house, Babylon still looks around the house since the woman is still in the shower. He takes his time to survey the entire house and it proves that he is alone with the woman.

The shower cuts off he knows it's about to be show time. But how it will go down is the part that he don't know, so he just hides behind the door of the master's bedroom since it has women clothing spread out over the bed.

He is in position and the woman is on her way. Once in, the woman closes the door is such a rush, that she doesn't see him standing behind it. Now she's

115

turning around and sees him standing there with gun in hand.

She knows exactly who he is her eyes shows it and how scared she is. "What do you want? The money is in my purse," she says to him. He's not here to play around so he just looks at the woman. Basically the look means to try it again.

"I don't know what you want, but the money is in my purse and my husband is at work and won't be home until late. So please just take the money and go. Please!"

Once again he says nothing to her and decides to give her one last chance at it. "Oh my, please don't, no!" She says while clutching her bathrobe tightly.

Now he's in his feelings because she knows what time it is and he knows that she knows. So Babylon begins to walk towards the woman in a mad dash she runs for her purse. He lets her go to it knowing what she is really going for. As she get's the purse in her hand her facial expression changes.

"I got your fucking money right here," she says. Her face shows that she is let down. He had already been through the purse and took out the Sig Sauer nine millimeter handgun. Her face now looking stupid she knows that he has it.

"I need to know why you all are really chasing us?"

"Sir, I don't know what you are talking about."

"I don't have time to be playing around with you Miss."

"Sir, if you need some help I will make sure personally that you get some help." He has his gun pointed at her at this time and pulls back the hammer on that cannon of his.

"The time has come to put you out your lying ass misery."

The first shot from the gun strikes the woman in the chest dead center of it going through her body and exiting out her back. Placing a hole in the wall behind her. The second shot strikes her in the right breast.

The second one it too goes through and hits the wall. As she falls he walks up on her slowly. She's slumped over, but very much alive and breathing.

"I have kids a, a, a, boy and a gir, ah, girls," she managed to get out while coughing up blood and crying.

"You should have thought about that before you started playing stupid," he tells her. He looks at her and shakes his head. "You look bad," he continues.

She closes her eyes just for a second. "My husband will," she fades off.

"Your husband what?" he coldly asks her while watching her on the floor.

"Will kill you," she says in a soft voice. That makes him feel good about himself for some weird reason.

"Well you won't be around to find out."

As the woman continues to cough and cry he just looks at her. In her mind she sees that they have truly under estimated this young man. It is no way she thought that any civilian could watch a woman die. He can hear the door open and close the make is back.

"Joanne?"

"Your husband is back you're about to find out after all."

"Joanne?" He calls out to her, but there is no answer. "Joanne I put your peach tea in the frig for you," he tells her. As he goes about his business down stairs he also checks in with some of the other agents in the area and gives an everything is good on his end report.

Hoping that the male comes up stairs Babylon takes his position behind the door again. After propping the woman's body up against the opposite wall. Now placing her barely living body against he wall in a better position. He notices that her body is identical to that of an eight year old boy's.

"Hey Jo." This may be proof that he's not her husband after all because he stopped to knock on the door And is waiting on a reply from her. Now he's knocking on the door a little harder.

"Joanne!" He calls out with authority in his voice

Babylon just looks down at him he's in no shape to answer any questions from the young man. So he start searching the agent's pockets for anything he can find. Now looking for the vehicle keys they're not on him, so he goes down stairs to look around.

They are on the table stand in front of the door, so he leaves the house and heads for the Suburban. He gets inside and takes a look at the phone and sees where the next set of red dots are located and he's on his way to that location.

***

Babylon pulls up to the apartment complex and cuts off the engine. He now gets out and walks towards the building. Once at the building he takes a look around and sees that this is an open community with a little wealth.

He also sees how kids are coming in and out of their apartments. He tries to pinpoint the location of the apartment, the right one. He takes a look at the phone while he's inside of the apartment building.

"I know your friends," says a little girl with a smile on her face as he looks at her for a moment.

"You don't know my friends," he tells her. While hoping she would go on somewhere.

"I know Tony and Jeff," she tells him.

"I don't know anyone by those names, Tony and Jeff," he replies back to her.

"You know them they got a phone just like you do. And I know because they got the same phone case like that one," she says while pointing at the phone case. "All of their friends that come over here has the same case on their phones too," she continues.

"If you know them then where do they stay?"

"In apartment number one o' two down stairs," his mind is racing he knows that its two of them, but he needs to pull off a miracle to get them both. He looks at the little girl he has no choice.

"Do you want to help me play a trick on my friends?"

"I thought you didn't know them?"

"Don't get smart."

118

Chapter 14

"Okay tell me what you want me to do," she asks him while looking at him in a funny way as if she's remembering something. "But first you got to let me see your gun," she continues. He looks at her in pure shock over her request.

"Tony and Jeff along with their other friends let me see their guns," she tells him. This is an opportunity he can't pass up and its still sunlight outside. So he takes her down stairs one landing above the basement and shows her his Desert Eagle.

"Woooooow! Look at yours it's the biggest I've every seen," she tells him.

That doesn't sound right coming from a little white girl in a apartment building with a black man. After he shows her his gun he tells her what he needs for her to do, so he can play the trick on his friends.

He goes and lay under the last row of stairs to hide from them. The little girl comes running down the stairs to the apartment knocking on the door hectically. And in a frantic state she begins: "Tony, Jeff, Tony, Jeff come quick I need help," she cries.

"What's the matter Jenna?" Jeff asks her.

"There's a man in the parking lot he tried to grab me, but I got free," and that's all it takes to get him hooked.

"Tony hurry up there's a predator in the parking lot the fucker tried to grab Jenna, lets go,"

Jeff hauls ass out the door with it slowly closing Babylon lets himself into the apartment. Now with gun in hand he has the drop on Tony while he's still lacing up his shoes.

"What's the chances of you coming out on top?" Babylon asks him. The mean looks they exchange to each other is a sure indication that have the agent had his gun it would have been a shoot out. And have the agent had his gun he would be dead in the eyes of the young man.

"Go ahead and try it, I dare you," he tells the agent.

The agent begins to place his hands above his head and the young man beckons the agent to move over towards him.

"Turn around and keep your hands up." He turns around and Babylon snatches the phone cord out the wall and ties up Tony and does it extremely tight.

"My hands," Tony cries.

"Now you know how people in those damn black boxes feel after your counter parts put my counter parts in them."

"Black boxes?"

"Yeah especially during transportation." The young man begins to gag Tony's mouth he now sets him up on top the bed in the master bedroom.

"Do you want to really see what's coming to you today or do you want the blind fold?" He asks Tony.

Not being able to talk Tony just moans out of control. Sensing that the little girl would play her part to the letter and Babylon begins to take his place. So once Jeff comes back he wants to be in position to get the drop on him. It takes a little while, but he finally comes back in.

"Tony where the hell are you?" Jeff yells through out the apartment. "Hey Tony," he continues.

Laying in the second bedroom with his body turned sideways waiting for Jeff. The man walks pass the bedroom, and Babylon leaps out on Jeff.

"You know you done fucked up right?" The young man tells Jeff with his cannon still in his hand. Jeff did not bother to turn around. "Go ahead I dare you to try me." Jeff is thinking that this is a robbery.

"I'm broke and the country is in a recession I don't carry cash on me," he tells him.

"Put your hand in the air or I'll kill your ass from the back you all been doing it to us for years." Jeff feels as though this person can not be talked out of robbing him.

"Where is my friend?"

"He's a little tied up at the moment."

"Is he alive?"

"Yeah, he's alive, but if you make a move I'll kill your ass and them go kill his ass." With his hands still above his head Jeff realize that he's not in control of this situation.

"Oh yeah I am also going to tell his family that you were the one that got him killed."

Jeff is being talked down like he's trained to do to others.

"Get on the ground now. " Jeff does as he is told. Babylon starts to check him for weapons. After finding his Sig Sauer nine millimeter he shakes his head at Jeff.

"I'm not finished with you yet," Babylon continues to search Jeff and finds his secondary weapon on his ankle. A mini Sig Sauer nine millimeter its his break glass in case of an emergency gun. After searching him further he's clean.

And now just like his partner before him. Jeff is tied and gagged and brought into the master bedroom with his partner. Babylon pulls out Tony's gag and looks at him with a funny stare.

"I want to know who you two work for, I need a name?" Babylon asks. The two men just looks at each other and smiles at him. "Oh! I see its funny huh?"

Babylon leaves out and goes into the kitchen and pulls open the silverware drawer and withdraws a huge butcher's knife that has a wooden handle on it. He now returns to the master bedroom and their eyes gets big.

But they think that the young man is a joke. "That's nothing," says Jeff and now he and Tony start laughing.

Babylon gets up and leave again to the kitchen and

returns with a bag of apples and now in a loud scared
voice Jeff says: "Oh no! Not the apples courses," he
and Tony are in stitches.

Babylon eats one of the apples using the knife to
slice the apple. Now finished eating it he looks up at
Jeff from the side just cutting his eyes in his
direction.

"You're my duck," he informs Jeff. Babylon walks
over to Jeff while grabbing a pillow from off the bed.
He wraps it nicely around the cannon. And shoots Jeff
in the head three times at an angle that he takes on
purpose. While Tony looks on all three bullets goes
through Jeff's head.

All hit the wall behind him the blood mist is
still visible from the initial blast the blood from
his lifeless body leaks on.

"So you see that haze of blood floating around
this place?" Babylon asks Tony. Tony eyes are wide
open and alert now and he's acting like he wish to say
something to Babylon.

"Man I just done killed that wall with those slugs
going through Jeff's sorry ass." Babylon begins to
walk towards him. Tony has been breathing heavy after
the gag was taken out his mouth.

"Calm down Tony I just want to talk to you and ask
you a couple of questions that's all." Tony eyeballs
Babylon he knows that he can not tell him anything
about his job or who he works for.

"Tony I'm tired and I don't want to be here. Who
do you work for and what do you all want with us?"

"I don't know what you are talking about you must
be crazy," Tony tells him. Babylon look on he sees
that this man just wishes to play hard ball, so he
picks back up the large knife, and turns in the
directions of the man.

"This knife is not for you." Babylon goes and
picks up Tony's cell phone after awhile of going
through some numbers he's satisfied.

"Tina, yeah I will use this knife on Tina. As soon
as I get back home for this crap you're pulling."

"I don't care about that bitch go ahead do as you
well may please."

The Georgetown Heist

"Stop, I know she's your daughter." Babylon is fed up with Tony's antics that he decides that its time that he dies. He pulls out his cannon again leaves the room to go to the kitchen. He comes back with a honey dew melon, Tony looks at him.

He thinks to himself that his young man can not be this smart and so cruel. He now goes over to the dresser and takes a towel from the top of it. He wraps the towel around the barrel of the gun and tightly he places it to Tony's head Tony hoping its a hoax to get him to talk.

Tony holds fast and refuses to even look scared this really pisses the young man off. He was going to kill him at first, but now he will suffer. Babylon gets a good angle on Tony's head and purposely shoots him on a bad angle.

The shot takes a nice chunk out his head to make him die slow and painfully. "I was going to kill you fast, but that's for not playing fair, so go slow."

The one shot fired has his head bleeding badly onto the bed and floor. His eyes are moving with excitement all over the place Babylon looks at him coldly.

And start to walk for the door on his way out he sees a recharger for the phone and takes it with him. He opens the front door and jumps out his skin after seeing the little white girl standing right in front of the door.

"Hey little girl I'm about to leave now and my friends are tired so I guess I'll see you some other time," he tells her and she's not buying it.

"Cut the bullshit you off them, didn't you?" She asks him with both her eyes looking straight into Babylon's.

"No my God no they are my friends."

"Come on Bro, I'm no rat. I watch the internet its not cool to be a snitch." He decides its time to take out the little white girl now. "Bro, let me see the dead bodies?"

He can't believe what he's hearing. "Come on Bro, and don't get any ideas of offing me next I just want to see the dead bodies. Come on Bro its the only form

123

of fucking education I'll ever get," she begs.

"I have to go back inside if you wish to come in with me you can." He turns around and starts to go back into the apartment and she follows him.

"Wait Bro, isn't that theirs?" She asks him. She's talking about the recharger. She breaks out running to the kitchen and blows out all the pilots on top of the stove, and in the oven and cuts on all the gas.

"We have time before she blows you might have touched too much stuff. And plus it will help you get all the way free. The explosion will take away all the evidence and just fucken cream those bodies. Yeah! It will be a huge explosion."

No one in the world at this point can tell him that this little white girl isn't crazy.

"Hey Bro, where are the bodies?"

"Master bedroom."

"Cool."

She goes to the bedroom by herself and sees the bodies its the highlight of her life. "Look at all that fucking blood." She looks like a child seeing something magical for the first time.

She's glued to the scene she has a smile on her face and is nodding her head yes. Now taking the lighter from her pocket she begins to set the sheets on fire along with the bottom of the bed.

"This girl has done this somewhere before," he tells himself.

Now she goes for the dresser drawers and tosses the clothes everywhere. "It will need to keep burning until the gas builds up," she informs him.

"This little girl is a natural at this stuff," he mumbles.

"Okay Bro, we got to leave I got to get my shit out my parents apartment, fuck all the rest of it and anybody else." She set fire to the other room as well and closes and stuff both doors so no air can escape.

The thought of killing her completely leaves his mind as they walkout the front door. "Wait, let me see if the coast is clear," she motions for him to come out and they walk up the stairs.

"Hey Bro we homies now, right?" He just keeps

walking out towards the Crown Victoria he just commandeered from Tony and Jeff, but as he's pulling off. The little white girl comes running up to the car.

"Hey Bro wait my name is Jenna, Jenna Nixon, but call me Jenx. I spell it J-E-N-X just in case you might want to look me up to put in some work with you," she tells him. She winks and smiles at him and says: "Bye Babylon."

He thinks that he's hearing things, until she tells him: "I hacked their phone yesterday." And with that he goes on about his business. He checks the phone and sees that there are too many of them, so he decides on just one more for the night. He hope he can choose one that will get some kind of results.

***

As she hums her new favorite tune she's finishing up her linen folding duties. She just got through pulling for this room with her bright white uniform on she's about to be done with this room.

All she has to do now is vacuum the floor and it will be ready for somebody else to use. The hotel will not have a problem with renting the room out for sure. She continues to hum her tune. She's in the mid thirties five foot three inches tall about one hundred thirty pounds.

Her shape is thick all in the right places, brown hair red lipstick, eye liner, arched eyebrows. She is of Latina decent and a proud mother trying to make a way for her and her children. She continues to vacuum the hotel room.

She hears the particles of debris like she has heard a million times before.

She now goes to a different area of the room and can hear and feel a big piece of debris in her vacuum cleaner. She never feels, hear or sees the explosion that claimes her life not even her brain can say what happened.

People walking by the hotel hears and feels the explosion and when they all look up they sees nothing

but debris coming down towards them. People across the
street watches and see what might look like pieces of
human body parts that comes flying out the windows
from above them.

Pure pandemonium is at hand people running
screaming and yelling. A stampede breaks out in the
hotel lobby. Out side of the hotel a shower of glass
masonry and other debris fall upon the heads of those
underneath.

"Terrorists," a voice cries out.

"Oh my God its Al Qadea," yells another voice. The
shower of glass and debris coming from the explosion
above is still raining down on the people below.

***

"**Okay give me** the satisfactory report on this
one?" Mr. Sears asks.

"It's another irritation explosion Sir." Mrs. Culp
answers him.

"Well now, get a housekeeping team over there to
handle it and tell F.E.M.A., the official report, is
it was a gas pipe line that erupted due to it being
old. Get public relations on top if it now. Run the
same specs as before. The same precautions as the last
agent released, P.P.E's etc." Mr. Sears orders.

Their jumbo screen shows that the explosion is in
Myrtle Beach. "Where are you going my busy Bees?" Mr.
Sears whispers to himself about the young men.

***

As Babylon drives to his next destination he thinks
about the hard hours of hostility he and his friends
endured, but anything worth having is worth dying for
or at lease he thinks so.

He come upon a gated community of nice rows of
town houses. He now checks the cell phone to pinpoint
his targets. He looks around its easier said than
done. It's dark now and there's really nobody left
outside.

So he backs into a parking space its a little ways

from the cell phone directions, but its striking distance. He can see that a car is pulling up and going in the directions of the cell phone's map.

But he just watches the vehicle and slumps down to avoid being seen by the on coming car. He can see two men getting out of the vehicle now.

***

"**You know it** was another explosion?" Tonya informs her friend.

"Where at?"

"Myrtle Beach."

"And this is the one you took a liking to? And that's another reason why I'm gone. Good bye Tonya and thanks for the update."

***

Babylon stays low to keep his head position hidden from the on comers. He looks from a new position, but sees that both men exit the car and one stays out to smoke a cigarette. Wasting no time at all he quickly gets out the car.

He's now pursuing the man who's smoking the cigarette. He starts to get into character at this time and his mind is revving on all cylinders. He begins to walk towards the man smoking and can start to see the features in his face.

He's a black man in his mid thirties, tall with a short haircut, clean shaven. With the cheapest suit he's ever seen.

"Hey can I bum one of those from you?" Babylon asks.

"Here you go Buddy," the agent says then hands Babylon the cigarette. The entire time Babylon has his hand on his gun ready to fire if it should arise.

"Thank you, light?" He finish getting his light he begins to walk off and at the best time to. The agent is getting suspicious of him.

"I haven't seen you around here are you new?" The agent asks him.

Chapter 15

"No I date the crazy blonde who lives in the house with the hedges, Amber," Babylon answers.

"Oh okay I've seen her around." Babylon starts walking towards the house in which the blonde lives when the agent yells out to him.

"Hey you want a drink?" Not knowing how to play it yet he decides he will decline the offer.

"No, I'll hear her mouth the rest of the night." Its bad enough with that filthy cigarette he has to put up to his lips he hates that he did it. Babylon does not smoke or drink. He now goes up to the house and knocks on the door. When it opens he says something to the person who opens up the door.

And just like that the agent's suspicion is gone, but once inside the house Babylon asks: "Do any of you have a cell phone charger that I can use?" He asks with a sense of urgency in his voice.

"Yes I do you can use our house phone until your phone is recharged if you like?" the woman of the house tells him.

"Only white people would let somebody in their home talking about a damn cell phone charger," he says to himself. "I'm parked just a couple of cars down," he says while pointing with his right index finger.

The Georgetown Heist

They offers refreshments to him until his phone is recharged and with the young blonde now a friend of his. He decides to try his hand with the house he came for.

"Well I truly appreciate what you all have done for me here and I will never forget it. Just so nice of people helping people I tried every door on the other side you all were the only ones to help me, and I thank you." And with that he begins to walk out the door.

"Walk him to his car Britney," the mother says as he looks at her. Now as the two are walking towards his car he leans in for a nice hug. In front of the man who appears to be a chain smoker. That's might be why he's outside smoking in the first place.

"If you don't mind I had an offer earlier and wish to accept it now if you are okay with it?" He asks.

"No, not at all," she answers. Babylon starts to walk towards the man smoking the man sees him.

"How's it going, you're leaving now?"

"Yes, but I'll have that beer now if the offer is still open?"

"Always Brah." At this time the man yells in the house. "Hey Todd bring a beer out would you?"

"Come get it yourself you human ashtray," the voice yells back at him.

"Look go and get it yourself its in the frig just go straight to the rear of the house." Babylon goes into the house he does not see the other man inside nowhere yet, so he walks light and yells:

"Hey anybody in here? I'm here for the beer." The second man bends the corner to an unpleasant surprise.

"Who's here for the beer? Oh shit!" He says once he sees the length of the Desert Eagle that's pointed right at him.

"What's the chances of you coming out on top? Turn around and get on the floor and don't make a sound in here." Babylon instructs him.

Todd does as he's told the young man snatches the phone cord out the socket and begins to tie up Todd with it. Now as the first man is still outside smoking Babylon has Todd tied up extremely tight.

"The dude outside what's his name?"

"Starks, his name is Starks."

"Thank you." Babylon says, and now gags Todd's mouth and goes halfway through the house and yells out:

"Hey Starks, Starks its your friend in here he won't let me get the beer out the frig." He sees the man enter the house he points at Todd lying on the floor.

"You know you done fucked up right?" He tells Starks. Starks is shocked and stunned by what he is seeing he is powerless. The young man holds the cannon like he knows exactly how to use it. So trying to get it is out the question.

"Put your hands up high," he orders Starks. "Now turn around slow I don't want to kill you but I will to get what I want," he continues.

It is all just a lie for Babylon hoping that it will release their fear. "Get on the floor and spread them."

Starks complies with the order he searches him and now disarms him like his partner. And now he to is tied and gagged. And the young man just looks at both of them with a real bad facial expression.

"By looking at your faces now I see that the both of your know who I am. You done slipped up and let me get the drop on you. Rest to sure you two will die here tonight just like the others I've killed today."

The two tied up men looks at the young man. They can't relate to what he is talking about because none of their friends have been killed that they know of.

"I got a dude and a woman, and then I got two dudes," he tells them. He calls good money, but is he right? They both wonders, but if he's right then he killed Starks's wife.

"I am going to start with you first Todd since you were here first. Tell me who do you work for and what do you want with us?" He goes and removes the gag from his mouth and just stares at him with scorn.

"Let's hear it Todd who's your boss, who do you work for and what are you chasing us for?"

"I don't know what you're talking about, but the

money is in my wallet," Todd tells him.

"You know something I had this same exact conversation with the first sets of y'all. And you sound just like the female. I think her name is or was Joanne. She had a body like a eight year old boy. It's a sad sight to see a black woman with a body like that. Now she's not here any more because of that exact same answer."

With that remark he sees a reaction out of Starks. So he decides that Todd is no longer needed. So he goes to the living room to get a sofa cushion, and comes back to Todd and places the gun inside the cushion. He positions the cushion on top of Todd's head.

Todd looks at Starks as if to say, do something. But he does nothing but just watch the young man fire one shot into his head. Todd lay there with blood squirting out his head, but still very much alive.

Babylon turns his attention to Starks. "So, you got something to say to me or am I going to have to punish you too?" He asks Starks.

"How do you really know about Joanne?" A scared and nervous Starks asks.

"You knew her, Starks?"

"My wife's name is Joanne."

"Well if she was with this dude inside a house and she drinks peach tea, yeah I killed her."

"Aaaaahhhhh! You piece of shit you black son of a bitch." Starks is overly upset and his voice is loud as he talks to the young man.

"You will pay for this you know this don't you? You will pay with your worthless life." Todd gasp's for air bedside Starks. The both of them sees that he's fighting for his life on the floor.

"He needs a doctor he can be saved," Starks tells him.

"I don't care about saving his life I didn't shoot him to save him. I want to know why y'all are chasing us, and who do you all work for?"

"Who do we work for?" He says in a disgusting voice.

"Yeah, who do you all work for what's the

letters?"

"You want to know, I'll tell your black ass something. We work for ourselves, we don't have a name because we don't exist. It's our game our rules and we rigs the game so we will always win—"

"That's not what I really wanted to hear. I wanted names, and addresses, can you provide me with them?"

"You are stupid, you're the stupidest black bastard on earth. Now go and get my fucking cushion you black bastard." Babylon honors Starks's request and now returns to him.

"And remember you black bastard, we are the things that go bump in the night," he yells at Babylon. Babylon does away with the cushion, and places his gun underneath the chin of Starks and looks him straight in the eyes.

"I bump's back," he boldly states. He now releases five shots from his gun that rips through the top and back of Starks head. The shots that comes out the top of his head. Reminds one of a trapdoor spider, jumping out on it's prey.

All five shots goes completely through his cranium and into the wall. As the burgundy syrupy juice flows, Starks eyes are still open wide. With the smell of blood an gun powder in his nose. Babylon rises to leave out the house.

"Pah, paaaahhhh, paaaaahhhhh," is the sound that Todd is making. He looks at him with a bit of confusion, with his face a little bald up. He can see Todd's eyes watching him. His eyes begs for Babylon to help save his life, or at lease give him a mercy killing.

"Damn, you're not dead yet? Well that's one thing I can say about you, you're a fighter," he tells Todd as he's walking out the door and leaves him as he is.

***

The command center employees are working to their full capacity. They have been here since the incident first occurred. They are tired and restless, but leaving or going home is not an option, not here, not today.

"Give me a full update Mrs. Culp if that's not to

much to bear?" Mr. Sears asks.

"People are experiencing burning and also irritation, tearing of the eyes, respiratory distress, coughing, choking and a difficulty with breathing, nausea and vomiting," Mrs. Culp reports.

"Of course, its an irritation agent that was released on them, they're supposed to feel what they're feeling. The only good point is that the weapons work." Mr. Sears coldly states.

His team watches him from far and near, they're beginning to see him as a insensitive bastard who cares nothing about the people he supposed to protect.

Others now see him just as guilty as the individuals who are releasing these deadly agents on American soil.

"I thought that I had taught you all a lesson the last time you all felt so, so blue. But I guess I was wrong about it. So here we go again," Ronald Sears says to them.

Now with all eyes focus directly on him he begins: "Ladies and gentlemen, do any of you know the definition for these terms: biological agents, chemical agents, terrorist incident and weapons of mass destruction?" Mr. Sears asks curiously.

With silence through out the room he paces and observes their faces. "No? You? Nobody knows huh? Then I, your head honcho will tell you." They're like a bunch of school kids waiting for the teacher to teach them something. But not all, some are looking like they are calling his bluff.

"What did I say first, was it biological agents? Yeah, I think that it was. Okay here we go people the F.B.I. lists this definition, but make no mistake it comes from this very room in which you are now standing in.

"They define biological agents as microorganisms or toxins from living organisms that have infectious or nonifectious properties that produce lethal or serious effects in all living things. You can get this from what is called the F.B.I. W.M.D. incident contingency plan."

Everybody is just looking at him to see him say

something to the effect that he is playing and is making this up. The way he always jokes, but not today his face is as steady as a surgeon's hand.

"Now chemical agents the same as before you can get this from the same place. But are defined as solids, liquids, or gasses that have chemical properties that produce lethal or serious effects in all living things." He says still watching their faces.

"Okay next one up is terrorist incident. A terrorist incident is defined as a violent act or and act dangerous to human life.

"In violation of the criminal laws of the United States or of any State, to intimidate or coerce a government, the civilian population or political or social adjectives." Looking like he's hurting or something is wrong, he takes a deep breath and begins to continue.

"Now people for those of us who actually knows a little about the law, Title eighteen United States Code twenty three thirty two (a)m defines a weapon of mass destruction as one, any destructive device as defined in the section nine twenty one of that title.

"Which reads, any explosive, incendiary, or poison gas, bomb, grenade, rocket having a propellent charge of more than one quarter once, mine or device similar to the above.

"Now two, is any poison gas, and three is, any weapon involving a disease organism. And four says, any weapon that is designed to release radiation or radioactivity at a level dangerous to human life."

Most in the room have already begun to get on their computers to see if he's lying to them. Checking all that he has said to them, and especially the title eighteen law.

"Oh I'm not done yet, you all are going to stop doubting me up in here one way or another. Now who can tell me what is P.D.D.-39?" Nobody dare say anything right now they know by the sound of his voice he's on a roll and no one is about to get in his way, not today anyway.

"Well boys and girls, this P.D.D.-39 in which I

speak of is what gives us the luxury to love the life
that we are now living. And the mere fact that nobody
in this room can tell me what it is.

"Well, its a damn shame, but yet I'm the bad one.
At lease I know my fucking job description. P.D.D.-39
is basically out charter people its the reason for my
work, your work.

"P.D.D.-39 stands for Presidential Decision
Directive-39. And this is the United States policy on
counterterrorism, it is dated June twenty first
nineteen ninety five. And if you didn't have your head
up your ass at that time you would have known that
Slick Willy signed that one into effect."

"Who the hell is Slick Willy?" A white woman asks
a black woman.

"That's Bill Clinton girl," she answers.

"And that's what this country goes by not how you
feel about my job decisions. The full text of P.D.D.-
39 is a classified document. State and local officials
however has learned that P.D.D.-39 essentially gives
the responsibility of response to terrorist attacks to
the F.B.I. for crisis management and F.E.M.A. for
consequence management.

"And just to give you a few of the policy
objectives, here we go. Measure to combat terrorism,
to ensure that the United States is prepared to combat
terrorism in all its forms, a number of measures have
been directed.

"These include reducing vulnerabilities to
terrorism, deterring and responding to terrorist acts.
And having capabilities to prevent and manage the
consequences of terrorist use of nuclear, biological,
and chemical weapons and those are included in the
weapons of mass destruction.

"And you should know what the acronym N.B.C.
stands for nuclear, biological and chemical? Next is
reduce vulnerabilities, in order to reduce our
vulnerabilities to terrorism, both at home and abroad.
All department and agency heads have been directed to
ensure that their personnel and facilities are fully
protected against terrorism.

"And deter terrorism, to deter terrorism it is

necessary to provide a clear public position that our policies will not be affective by terrorist acts and we will rigorously deal with terrorist and sponsors to reduce terrorist capabilities and support.

"And I will not go into the rest of it, by now you all should have it in your heads that I know my job inside out, and I'm qualified."

At this time his entire staff are beginning to feel like heels, realizing that their own feelings about this situation may be in fact the wrong way of thinking about this situation, and that's why he's their boss in the first place.

"Someone get my wife on the phone for me, or on this com." Mr. Sears asks.

"She's on, Sir."

"Hey Martina?"

"Who is this?"

"Just that piece of shit you married a long time ago."

"Good Lord Ronald, do you have to use that language?"

"Yeah I do, it makes me sound cool and hip. I need for you to do something for me today."

"Oh yeah, and what might that be?"

"I need for you asks at lease five prime location owners in Myrtle Beach if they would like to sell."

"Bye Ronald."

"Martina damn it I'm serious, find the properties that I ask for."

"My guy would have told me had there been something available."

"I got something your guy don't have now get that ass to it." they all are in agreement that Ronald Sears is a very cold man all over again.

"Don't look at me like that its just me being heads up on some properties that's all. I have a feeling the somebody or bodies might want to sell their property soon, I think."

The can't believe him he don't either. So he tries to break up the salty looks he's getting from everybody. "Let me tell you all a true story, it involves myself and your Madame President. When I was

136

being nominated for this job she said let's talk salary over lunch.

"She tells me that she's going to write down my salary on a piece of paper and pass it to me. And if I don't like it just pass it back to her. So she writes down a figure and passes it over to me. And I stated to her very loudly, hey I'm responsible for the safety of the country your family included.

"So she looks at me funny and pulls back the paper again. She writes another figure on it and passes it back over to me. I again pushes it back to her. She's like you're killing me Ron how much is enough?

"I tells her, the entire country. So she again pulls it back, but this time she's nodding her head up and down like she knows for a fact I'm going to accept the offer this time.

"So she pushes it over to me and says: "Don't tell the rest of the Cabinet members I'm paying you this much." Me sensing that this was the end of our little salary game, so I just went for my guns. I looks at the offer and says to her. I promise not to tell anybody, I'm just as embarrassed about this shit as you are."

His entire staff starts laughing their tails off at what he just told them. And that's the Ronald Sears they know.

"I hope I'm not interrupting anything?" A voice asks coming through the doors of the command room.

"So its you," says Mr. Sears.

"Spare me all the goddamn pleasantries Ron. You know why I'm here, and its not to meet the press."

"Jimmy-Boy, how are you? I hope your plane ride over here was the worst ever, was it?"

"The Joint Chiefs sent me in Ron."

"No, they didn't. They sent your crying ass over here to watch, and if it gets worst and feel the need to use you, you will be already in position."

"Ron you're out of your league with this one."

"Well what ever I am, I am running it, and running it by myself. So I'll keep you informed of any and all activities that involves this matter, Jimmy The Butcher." Knowing that would totally piss the man off he still calls him by that name.

"I'm not here to play Ron, I am here in my full capacity."

"Well then I better go and get you your butcher's apron because the butcher is in."

"Ron I need a briefing now please."

"Well to sum it all up to you Jimmy. We know who these young kids are, and we know that they do not know what they truly have. We do know that we are not the only ones out looking for them.

"We now know for a fact that there are international intercepters that are looking for them along with rogue agents trying to get right and come home. Then there's the various mercenary groups, and every terrorist group with enough money to fund an operation this size. To put it in a nut shell everybody is looking for them."

"So you forgot to tell me about why you haven't captured them yet? A group of street punks with no education or nothing else for that matter."

"Well Jimmy it might have something to do with them having all that weaponry and the fact that they are teens."

"I read the profiles its not like they are savable Ron, they're past the point of no return. Plus we can save the tax payers money by killing them now instead of them going off to jail in the future."

"To you that's your thinking, but to me they will

be processed accordingly. Who knows I might even go and put the hand cuffs on them myself."

"Put the handcuffs on them? You got to be playing its no way in the world that you me or anybody are going to bring them in alive and breathing."

"They will face the law for the murders of our agent and the civilian and for stealing jewelry."

"And that's why you're out of your league with this one Ron. Its impossible to bring them in on anything at this point. Once you failed containment, you squandered the entire operation.

"You lack of leadership made cause for this whole mess, and you tell me that they will face the law? On murder charges, please even the worst of public defenders will eat the fucking case up.

"Not to mention the heavy hitters that will be lining up just to represent them for free. You have no eye witness, no motive, no physical evidence. You have nothing to link them to the murders of those damn dead officers and Troopers down in North Carolina.

"And you are going to lose and lose royally, and further more bringing them to court will be a big risk. If they find out what it is they're truly carrying, and then the Government will be not only at fault, but imbeciles.

"And all because you want to bring in the young boys who foiled your Candy Shop? That will never happen Ron," he finishes.

"Jimmy I have no problem with alerting the media and letting them know who the suspect are and what they have done. And if need be place all of the blame on them, but what if we're wrong about them? And the explosions are not them or their fault? I just want to make sure before I bring the hammer down on them."

"So you would go to the media huh?"

"Yeah, why not?" he says sarcastically.

"You would tell the media that four young black boys from the ghetto robbed a secret Government weapons stockade, and then made off with trillions of dollars worth of weapons of mass destruction."

"Now exactly like that you know we have personal relations in place."

"Ron let me have a word with you outside for a moment." The two men walk out into the hallway. Jimmy takes an open hand chop to Mr. Sears throat causing him to gag awfully hard. As he begins to grab his throat, Jimmy start to speak: "You are relieved of your post effective immediately."

At that time a few of Jimmy's men start to carry Mr. Sears away by way of his underarms. Just dragging him down the hall as it seems with just the tip of his shoes dragging on the floor. Jimmy goes back into the command room.

"Listen up people there has been a change in command here, I am now in command, you already know my name, don't get to know my bad side."

The entire room is quiet as hell just waiting to see what he will say next and he does just that. And they could not believe it.

"Go to Def-Con Five!" Jimmy orders them. This is enough to ensure that they will not be leaving any time soon.

"Sir with all due respect Def-Con Five is a litle harsh don't you think? It is the highest alert status for the U.S. military. The numeral system start out at one and five being the maximum readiness," Mrs. Culp tells him.

"Thank you for that brief history of Def-Con Five, but we are a go. I want a complete status update on all the fugitives.

"The Nimrod one bring me his file and I also want a location on them. And a calculated improvision on where they may be going. But I want it to be as close as one can possibly be for assault teams can intercept and neutralize."

He begins to read their profiles now, but Nimrod is holding his attention. He sees in full detail of the account of havoc the young man has caused and is amazed at his evasiveness and ruthlessness.

"But can he hold his own or will he bitch up and surrender if he's by himself?" Jimmy asks himself about Babylon.

He finishes reading the young man's file he sees that the intel has come from a field source about the young man's gun fights.

"This young boy might be worth me catching myself," he says under his breath. As he reads on he sees something that freezes him. "I want to see just how good this young boy is since you all think so much of him. I will break him down the way I break down all the so called though Tony's.

"And when I do I want all of you cowardly men and women to see real government power at its best," he says to the room. "And not sitting on their asses behind a fucking desk," he continues.

The entire command center just turned against him, every last one of them hates him.

"Now go, and bring me his dear Mommy," Jimmy orders his men.

Chapter 17

As she walks around in her bedroom looking for
something to wear tonight her phone rings. "Yeah who
the fuck is it? Oh shit girl Bab gave me some money
the dirty mother fucker, so shit I'm going out
tonight. I sent Moody and them over to their
grandmother's. Shit I might not be back for two or
three days.

"Fuck it carry it like a Bitch seventeen again
just drop them mother fuckers off and keep getting
up," Bunny says while talking to her friend Juanita
Short.

"Look Juanita just meet me at the Velvet Banana
tonight, and bring your sister Carroll with you. I
haven't seen her in a good while," she continues.

She finds herself something to wear, but before
she goes out tonight she's going to stop by an old
friend of her's first. She gets all the stuff that she
needs.

Her phone rings again, but this time she doesn't
answers it she just goes on out the door. She gets to
the top of the stairs in her building, and there are
four men coming in to the apartment building. As she
passes them one just so happen to see her facial
features.

"Excuse me Miss, but are you Ms. Fatima Mohammed,
and do you have a son by the name of Nimrod Hannibal
Mohammed?" One of them asks her.

Sensing that these are no regular suits in front

of her she decides to play it her way. "Nawl mother fuckers, I'm Dragon Fly Turner mother of Nat Turner," she coldly tells them.

The men looks on they felt it wasn't nothing that they can't handle, so they all take deep breaths. "Ma'am we're here on official government business," another one of the men tells her.

"So I take it you want me to go with you?"

"Yes ma'am we do."

She begins to light up a cigarette as they all are walking back towards their car. She sits down and starts smoking her cigarette. She now takes out her phone and takes pictures of each of the men the license plate along with an text message and sends it off to somebody.

She's through using the phone and now she drops and stomps on it while still sitting down. She did too, good of a job on it. One of the four men goes over to retrieve it, but it's a lost cause.

She finishes her smoke and goes and get in to the car. She looks over the whole complex its like she never truly seen the place before.

"Who did you send that to?" One of the men asks.

"My son, I sent it to my baby."

"And what did you tell him?"

"To do one thing for me."

"And that is?"

"To kill all you mother fuckers on sight. Now where the fuck are you taking my ass?"

"Well since you asked like that your ass and you are going for a ride because you son is an asshole." Now he injects her with something that knocks her unconscience.

***

As the moans leaves her mouth her head is spinning like a top. She's in the fetus position and she's cold. She tries to open her eyes, but the lights are too bright for her. She can smell the stench of the slobber from the side of her mouth.

It makes her frown with disapproval she now tries

to move her arm so her hand can wipe away the smelly sleek substance from the corner of her mouth. Her faculties are coming back around to her.

"Oh yeah a bitch is going to pay for this foul ass shit here," she whispers.

As she comes to her feet she sees that the room is a smooth room it has no lines on the walls, and you can't tell where the door is at. It is however one of those spongy sofas in the room like in a crazy house padded room and it matches the wall.

She takes a seat on the sofa, and holds her head in her hands while shaking her head from side to side. She feels that this here might just be it for her. "Why would these Bitches come get me like this, what the fuck did Bab do? Ah shit them fucking diamonds," she tells herself.

The door opens its to her left and a tall older black man enters the room. He looks like the old sergeant killed by Denzell in that movie. His face looks cold, but his eyes is like that of a servant.

"Ma'am my name is not important, but what I need from you is information, that is important. I need to know any and all information and or the whereabouts of your son Nimrod Hannibal Mohammed A.K.A Babylon, and I'm talking about right now!"

"I don't know where he is and if I did you already know I wouldn't tell you a mother fucking thing. So why waste your time and mines?" She answers.

"We thought-"

"We? We? Malcolm X said that the slave and the master are one. We sick today Massah? We goin fishing today Massah?"

"Miss I do not play games at all."

"Mother fucker I don't play no mother fucken games on no mother fucken levels at all." She looks at him for a moment. "I know you got your hands in this mother fucken shit with these bitches. Your people had that mother fucken whip on their asses just like mines did," she continues.

"That black brother shit don't work on me," Jimmy tells her.

"That's what I'm trying to tell your boot licking

ass.

She watches him closely and sees that he's about to do something, but she doesn't care one way or another.

"I see that you have to be taught a lesson in manners."

"Manners? You need a lesson in Blackness you bojangling mother fucker, you good jeffin mother fucker you step and fetch it mother fucker. Ole dancing ass, soft shoeing mother fucker. I don't have to sprinkle any sand on the floor do I?" He just stares at her.

"What you say Sammy?" He waste's no time with his decision to bring in a female to teach this woman to respect his authority. In comes a white female who's tall and has a nice size advantage over Bunny. The white woman should have no problem with Bunny.

"You like to disrespect authority do you? I've been sent here to teach you some manners, and I promise it won't hurt, that much," the white woman sarcastically tells Bunny.

"I hope not."

The white woman start making her move towards Bunny. She is getting into her stance Bunny sees well what she's doing. But pays very little attention to her hand motions. The woman jolts towards Bunny with trained awareness.

"It's what you don't know that will get you fucked up," Bunny informs her coldly.

The women are at a stand off they're moving in a circular motion. When the woman jumps up and tries to kick Bunny she weaves the kick and shoots a hard fast open palm to the woman's face that snaps her head back.

The hit from Bunny surprises the white woman Bunny smiles and winks at her. Now in her feelings the woman attacks Bunny in a rage. Bunny standing in her stance blocks the woman's chops and blows to her head and with lighting speed.

Bunny stoops down with a violent sweeping of her foot the woman is leveled in the air. When she hits the floor the first part of her to hit was her tail bone. The fall that she has sends volts of itching nerves through out her body. Bunny now in full attack mode jumps up in the air over top the woman and comes down on top of her chest with a driving knee that has plenty of force behind it.

The blow to the woman's chest made her gasp for air, but Bunny isn't done with her just yet. Bunny picks the woman up by her hair and slams her face into the floor while still holding on to her hair. With seeing the blood that comes from it.

Bunny decides to take the woman out, she starts to stomp the life out the woman. In a violently way she's stomping and at times jumps and comes down with both feet on top of the woman.

The white woman now lay lifeless on the floor, while Bunny takes time to go through her pockets. Just getting items from them, she finally finishes and goes to sit down to smoke a cigarette. Now the door is opening and it's Jimmy who just shakes his head in disappointment.

"Bring in the next Bitch," she tells him. Jimmy watches her, and a very distasteful look comes over his face. He now approaches her, and with a closed fist he strikes her in the face. She goes down to one knee and stays there for a few seconds.

"I know that's not all your bitch ass got?" Bunny asks while grunting.

Now she begins to pull herself off the floor while grunting in the process. He can see her face, but can't really read it as he should had. She comes off the floor with the force of an iron horse bringing with her a haymaker that knocks him on his bottom.

He can't believe it he's shocked to the utmost. He quickly gets off his tail and begins to strike her everywhere. She can not properly defend herself against him. His skill set is too much for her, and his strength.

But she refuses to go down her Nation of Islam days serves her well as a former Vanguard and she continues to fight back. She strikes him, but he's about to tire out and she knows it, and he knows she knows it.

"Stop! Before I kill your ignorant ass," he yells

at her.

"You dancing mother fucker you got to kill me. I'm going to try my best to kill your ass," she responds back.

He looks in her eyes and sees something that he has never in his life seen before. A strong black woman that's happen to be in full attack mode and is not afraid of him.

"I'm going to spare your ignorant ass this time," he tells her.

"Before I die you will pay for putting your mother fucken hands on me, and my son is going to kill your ass, you can bet your life on that one."

He just watches her as he backs out the room. He never felt her take his keys from out his pocket. Now with him out the room with her he decides that it's time for her to talk to her son.

***

"**Have you located** the boy yet?" Jimmy asks.

"No not yet Sir we are not picking up anything from the field agents." Mrs. Culp answers.

"Well people I am about to upgrade you all to incompetent poor excuses for Americans," he informs the command center. They all wish that he would just go to places.

"Hey you!" Jimmy yells.

"Who me?" Mrs. Culp answers.

"Yeah you I have an idea why don't you try to at lease act like you're doing your job."

"Yes Sir I will do my best Sir."

"I need to know who's this field agent and where the hell is he with new information?"

"Well we don't know he just gives us the information that's all." Mrs. Culp feels as though she knows where he's trying to go with this, but she refuses to go along.

"Okay I see where you all are I know that its a rogue sector out there looking for them. I also know that Ron has a plant inside that rogue cell. I want to talk to that plant. To ask them how do they keep up with the young punks?" Jimmy asks.

"Only Mr. Sears can call out we wait for the intel
to be sent." Mrs. Culp informs him. At this time one
of him men comes into the room and hands him a piece
of paper.

"And that's why you are on this team you are the
best of the best," Jimmy tells him. They all just
looks at him with regret. Now it seems as if his own
team are mobilizing for some sort of mission.

"I just need one alive do what you wish with the
others," he orders.

With their orders the men leaves, now his goal is
to get the mother of Babylon to make a call. But he
knows it will be impossible to do it. He gets up to go
and see her to try and ease her pain a litte.

"Fatima are you hungry? I think that you are," he
turns and looks at one of his men on guard watching
the door. "Hey you out there go and get her something
to eat. No wait, you ask her what she wants to eat,
she will not talk to me." Jimmy orders his subordinate
and goes back to the command room.

***

"**Well I guess** I'll just have to wait until they
catch something," he says to the room.

He just sits in Mr. Sears big soft chair and
watches the giant screen in front of him. After about
an hour and a half he gets a phone call from one of
the men who left out earlier.

"Hey boys what you got for me?" That's not bad now
finish up there and get back here because there might
be a plane that you all may have to take."

The caller informs him that they have one of the
rogue agents and that a lot of the rogue agents has
been taken out by somebody. And one of their agent's
phone is missing from his person.

And he gave the men that phone number to the
missing cell phone. Now they can track that cell phone
anywhere in the world. But they know that they don't
need the world. Who they are looking for is right down
in North Carolina and on the move.

The Georgetown Heist

"I need a fix on this cell phone," Jimmy tells Mrs. Culp. She does as she's told, and the entire room is looking up at the giant screen to see if there are any hits, but the screen is blank.

"Go to the U.S. satellite," he tells her. The screen is still blank, but there are funny lines. "So he has the phone covered up, but I can see where he's been I can see the footprints," Jimmy says. He's thinking of something and now comes to his conclusion.

"Upload these coordinates and send them to my team," he orders. Mrs. Culp is in the process of doing just that and now he grabs his phone.

"Yeah look I'm sending you the intel that you all will need. I'm empty on suggestions, but I do have the coordinates for the last known whereabouts of them. You can handle the rest of it, and go straight to the jet, and shake the tree gentlemen, let's see what falls out."

***

With a feeling of a victory he goes to see Bunny and once he get's there his face goes blank. He sees that his subordinate assigned to feed her is lying in a pool of blood. "She's loose inside the building!" he yells into his radio.

Now men are running through out the building looking for Bunny. Mrs. Culp gets up to go to the ladies room, and when she gets in there she's greeted by Bunny.

"I will kill bitch how do I get out of here?" Bunny asks her.

"Don't be alarmed the keys in your hand will get you out of here all you need are some directions. Just stay on this side of the building and use the back stairs and go down to the floor that says G-Five, and go out that door. It will lead you to an alley and you'll be okay from there.

"Oh you are actually in Washington D.C. the South East section, and your son is still alive. And good luck to the both of you." Mrs. Culp tells Bunny next its a hard knock on the ladies room door.

"Who's in there?" A man's voice shouts.

"It's me Mrs. Culp," she answers.

"Are you alone Mrs. Culp?"

"Yes I am and wish to keep that way." As she start to leave the ladies room she looks back at Bunny and knows that she has her hands full already. There's no sense of turning her in.

"Excuse me gentlemen," Mrs. Culp says to the men as she's trying to get pass them. They watch her leaving trying to see if she is hiding something. It's very bad to enter a ladies rest room, so they leave off, sensing that the coast is clear Bunny takes off into the wind.

Following the directions that she was given. She goes straight for the stairs, but is met by accident by Jimmy himself. She wants so badly to see him again anyway, as he reaches for his side arm.

She's reaching for the straight razor that's always been between her cleavage. She beats him to the draw, and he never sees or feels it. She takes it downward on the left side of his face, from hairline to jaw line.

Now twisting her body leaning on the right side. She's now taking the razor back up on the right side of his face from his jaw line to his temple while arching her wrist.

"Go get her," Jimmy orders his men he doesn't know that he's been sliced extremely bad around his face.

"Sir your face," one of his men tries to tell him, but he would hear none of it. He turns his head fast to the side, and sees something come from his face, he now touches his face.

The blood on his hand along with a dripping clot of blood caught between his fingers. He goes into an all out shooting frenzy. He looses total control of himself. He shoots Bunny in the left shoulder, as she spins around from the impact of his nineteen eleven.

He continues in his shooting frenzy out of fear or desperation she is able to grab one of the men who has been shot and uses him as a human shield, while she tries different keys to unlock the stairwell door.

The Georgetown Heist

With shot after shot being fired she is peeping around her shield from time to time and sees men lying in the floor. With every body she sees a pool of blood it lays in, and the bodies still moving, with five of them and her.

"Got it, got his ass," she says as she finds the right key.

She unloads her human shield and starts to go through the door, when she's hit once more by one of the new men coming to help. This time she is hit in the right thigh and she falls through the door with the key breaking off in the keyhole.

Now on the other side of the door the next thing happens is that the lights goes out in the entire building for a full minute. Now they cut back on for a full minute, and then back off, and then back on all in one minute cycles.

As she goes down the stairs she goes too far. She ends up in the basement, but sensing that she went past her floor. She remembers G, something? She's in pain and sees some blankets and takes one for herself and heads back up the steps she sees G-Five.

"Oh G-Five!" She says to herself. Now she's going out the door once she steps out she is met by an awaiting car with men standing around it. They rush her into the car and she's taken away.

Hours later after Jimmy has retaken control of himself. He is then fully briefed of the entire situation that occurred when he had blanked out. With no time to worry about his own embarrassment over the affair. Or the fact that he shot some of his own men and the fact that he was seen by others when he zapped out.

He just stares into time and whispers to himself. "It was M.O.T.H.E.R., damn you Tonya."

***

As he walks up to the farm he is met by the old man. "Hey how ya doing?" the old man asks him. Babylon looks the old man over he doesn't sense any bad vibes from him.

151

"**Hello to you** Sir," Babylon replies to the old man while extending his hand. Babylon is one who truly respects his elders.

"My name is Edward, Edward Honesty and that's my wife up there," he says while pointing with his finger towards what looks to be the main house.

Babylon looks in that direction he notices that they have a lot of land. But he also can tell that Teeny-Man and the other two are not here. Because its too, quiet and the old man is not scared or nervous.

"Oh my wife's name is Arabella, well I guess you are ready to see your friends?" He asks Babylon and his eyes actually gets big seeing that Teeny-Man didn't mess up nothing here. As they walk they come up to a shed type dwelling.

"They're in there," he tells Babylon and goes on about his way. He goes into the barn he's reaching for his gun once he gets in he sees everyone laying down on blankets.

Once they all finally sees him Teeny-Man and Juice-Hop get up and rushes him.

"Slim where the fuck you been at?" Teeny-Man asks him.

"I've been out and about," he answers. Teeny-Man is just so happy to see his friend he doesn't ask any more questions about his long absence.

"Man I need to know why every time we go somewhere them people are on our tails like that?" Babylon asks his friends. "Its like somebody is telling them people our every move."

They just look at each other and now looks at him. And it is at this time that Babylon hears what sounds like a bell being rung.

"What the hell is that?" He asks.

"Its the old lady letting us know its time for breakfast." Teeny-Man informs him.

He almost forgot about that, but he had other matters to talk about when they would get back to this barn. So for now he will go and eat with the elderly couple. Once they get into the main house of the couple.

Babylon immediately speaks to the husband and wife.

"Good morning Mr. and Mrs. Honesty?"

"Good morning to you," the wife says and the husband just nods.

"My name is Nimrod Mohammed."

"Now that's a name we don't get every day around here," the wife states.

"I don't know how long we can be here or how long we will be here. But I would sure like to help you all out around here if I can? There's a lot of land here that you have and I would not mind. Plus it would help me to think." Babylon tells them.

They both just looks at the young man and smile. "It would be free labor of course," he finishes.

"Young man if you think you can work as a hand on a farm, you can be my guess. I can sure enough use the help," Mr. Honesty tells him.

"I wish to help you with everything that I can help you with around here." Knowing that he's a city boy the old man feels in his heart that the young man is just trying to be nice. So once they finished eating Babylon is shown all his duties by the old man.

Mr. Honesty thought that Babylon was going to have something to say about it, but he did not complain nay time and just begins to work.

***

153

"Mrs. Culp?" Jimmy yells.

"Yes Sir," she answers.

"Send this text message, are you ready?"

"Yes Sir."

"Babylon when you get this message it would be in your best interest to call me back. So we can talk about what you have in your possession. And to talk about Bunny, I've got her, and her straight razor."

"It has been sent Sir."

"Well then, you're good for something."

***

Hours has passed and Babylon has yet to stop. Even after Mr. Honesty insisted that he do so. He truly believe that the young man will tire out and will not be of no shape come tomorrow.

Dinner has come and the young man still refuses to come in and eat. Time has passed by drastically and the young man is still outside working. This lasting until the a.m. hours, and the old man sees this with his own eyes.

Its breakfast time and he is the first one in the kitchen. When Mrs. Honesty shows up to cook breakfast he startles her a little.

"I'm trying to get a little jump on the work this morning. It's plenty to do around here and you all are by yourselves," he tells her.

"You don't have to work yourself too hard. You just started to work," she tells him.

"Yes I do, it's a lot of work to be done around here," She just looks at the young man and with a smile and says:

"Oh well suit yourself."

He grabs ten big apples from out a basket, and goes back to working around the farm. When the rest of his friends reaches the kitchen they asks each other has the other seen him.

As the old man sits at the table he can't help but to notice that Babylon is not in attendance this morning. And starts smiling at his wife, she knows what he's smiling about, but she still wants to have a little fun with him.

"What are you smiling at?" She asks him.

"I knew that old city boy wasn't going to make it out of bed today," he says with surety i his voice.

"I wonder which one you're talking about? It can't be the one who was working yesterday? Because he grabbed himself some apples and high tailed it out of here to start working, that's what he told me." Mrs. Arabella Honesty says to her husband with a gleam in her eye.

Because she knew what everybody else did not know. That in over fifty years no one has never beaten her husband to work. As the old man get's up to see for himself.

"Well I be damned, I don't believe it and to think it would be a young city boy," the old man says to himself.

Just like the day before Babylon refuse to come and eat lunch. Dinner came he refuse that also, working into the wee hours of the night. But at breakfast he begins to talk to the wife.

"I bet he thought I would quit by now?"

"You need to put something in your belly Nimrod."

"I will tomorrow at breakfast." He again takes some apples and leaves her alone in the kitchen, but this time he comes back to ask her a question.

"Do you have a jug that I can put some water in?" She gives him what he's looking for and he leaves to go to work. The morning is like the day before as is lunch and dinner. And he stopped in the wee hours of the night. But Mr. Honesty could most definitely see the results of the young man's labor.

At breakfast Babylon is still the first one in the kitchen. But he stays and waits for every one else. At the table he begins to talk with the old man.

"We need to get that fence behind the barn fixed before one of them bulls gets out of there," he tells him.

Mr. Honesty knows that he's right, that fence should have been fixed by now. But it would have taken more than him to fix it, so this is as good of time than any to fix it.

"Just tell me how to do it and I will fix it." Babylon tells him.

"We have to go into town to pick up some supplies for the fence and some other stuff also." Mr. Honesty explains.

As Mrs. Honesty starts to pass out the food, she first start serving her husband and next Babylon. Teeny-Man is usually the second to get his food, and he notice this change.

The same goes for everything that is passed out during the meal. It is evident that the first to eat were the working men of the house. Everybody else get in, where they fit in. As they get ready to leave to go into town.

"Mrs. Honesty is there anything you wish for me to bring back for you?" Babylon asks her.

"Oh my! I have a list of things," she tells him.

"Don't start Arabella," the husband says. Babylon turns to leave out with the husband. But holds out his hand from the back to the wife, so she could give him the list with her stuff on it. She sees it, and the transaction is smooth the husband never sees the hand off.

***

They leave the other young men behind to watch the farm and the old man's wife. Now in town the old man goes straight for the supplies that he came for, Babylon helps him with everything. Now he puts the old man on hold for a second while he himself goes to buy some things.

Once he returns the old man just starts to shake his head. He knew that the young man got the stuff that his wife wanted. Mostly sewing materials, and a lot of scratch offs and some homemade butter pecan ice cream along with some twizzlers for himself.

"You just had to get it for her?" Mr. Honesty asks. They both laugh and start their way back home to the farm.

***

156

The Georgetown Heist

As Teeny-Man looks from side to side to see if the coast is clear. He doesn't see the old lady so he thinks its a go for him. But the woman is looking directly at him through the window. And he never sees her he already has stolen a red and white checkered table clothe.

Now he jumps over the gate where the bulls are, but only one bull is out in the pen. He now starts challenging the bull.

"Toro, toro mother fucker!" He yells at the bull. Now with the bull in full charge mode Teeny-Man being the good coward he hauls tails back across the fence. The bull in a rage charges at him from behind the fence. He starts swatting the table clothe at the bull and this takes the bull rage further.

He twirls the table clothe up and pops the bull square on it's behind. Mrs. Honesty hears the smack she looking at this in pure amazement never have she seen an inexperience person play around with a bull like this.

She just looks on as the young men laughs at Teeny-Man. It all seems funny right now to them. In a not so good move, Teeny-Man after tiring himself out decides to take a seat on the same fence that is holding the bull.

He never sees the bull kick up the dirt with his right foreleg. The bull charges towards the fence and didn't stop until he hit the spot where Teeny-Man is sitting. "Whaaammm!"

Teeny-Man goes flying through the air right as the pick up truck is pulling up and they see the entire event. Now on the ground in what seems like severe pain everybody goes to his aid.

Only the wife doesn't go because she's too busy laughing her tail off at the event. She is on the floor, and she is loud. So loud that Babylon and the husband runs to see if she's all right.

After seeing what's wrong with her they had to stay inside themselves to hide their laughter. Knowing that Teeny-Man is not too stable. Babylon has to go to him before he does something stupid. He gets off the ground and is going to kill the bull, and Babylon knows it.

"Slim you can't kill the people bull," he tells him. Teeny-Man just starts walking towards the town. With that, Babylon and Mr. Honesty begins to fix the fence. By the time Teeny-Man get's back they are finished. As they all goes to sleep Teeny-Man is the last one to enter the barn.

"Where you been Teeny-Man?" Bernard asks.

"Getting back," he answers. As they all looks at him they did not hear a gun shot. So they all figured that he couldn't have done nothing too bad. All night they hear a bull whining.

Morning has come and Mrs. Honesty is feeding all their animals. She is coming from the stalls, so she is finished feeding the bulls there. Now she's about to go and feed the one bull that's out. Once she gets around to the front of the pen.

She has never in her life seen anything like what she seeing. It truly scares her to death the bulls entire head is raw. It's covered in a pink reddish skin of its own.

It's not a piece of fur anywhere on the bull's entire head. The old woman just breaks out running towards the main house. Once inside she tries to explain it to her husband, but she can't.

Babylon himself runs up to the main house to see what is wrong. Mr. Honesty and he both goes down to see the bull. What Mr. Honesty sees is something he has never seen in his entire life of farming, and his mind is made up he has to put the bull down.

"It must be killed immediately before it spreads whatever is has to the other bulls and animals on the farm," he tells Babylon.

As he leaves Babylon is looking at the bull. But there's something that's not right with this picture. As Mr. Honesty comes back with his riffle.

"Hold on!" Babylon shouts to the old man. As he takes his final looks at the bull. "There's nothing wrong with the bull Sir," he continues.

"You need to take another look at him son."

"No he's fine just a little sore trust me on this one. I know for a fact that there's nothing wrong with

the bull Sir." He just looks at Babylon for a moment.
"I hope you're right about this son."
"I'm positive about it Sir."
"Well I'll wait and see then." Babylon don't have
the heart to tell the old man the truth of the matter.
So he goes straight to Teeny-Man to talk to him.
"T, slim you're wrong as hell for that. Supposed
them people would have put us out for that? The old
man don't know what could have done that to his bull."
"What he do B?" Juice-Hop asks.
"Threw magic shave on the damn bull's head." They
all start laughing at his act of vengeance, but
Babylon is the first to stop the laughing.
"We have been through a lot y'all and I truly feel
like we have not seen the last of it yet. But I am not
stopping for nothing or nobody. I feel as though
somebody is letting them people know where we are.
"Its crazy every time we hit the street we are
being shot at. And why are you always on the phone
Juice?"
"I didn't know I had to explain myself?"
"Slim I didn't say nothing about explaining
yourself. I just asked you a question that's all
slim."
"Look Bab I took my test and I've been checking to
see if my results have been posted online yet."
"Oh shit, slim Black Hazel gave you that shit
didn't she? I'm going to kill that black bitch as soon
as I get back home, right after I feed her ass,"
Teeny-Man tells Juice-Hop.
"Hell no I took my C.D.L." He now shows them on
his phone where he can check his results. They're
relieved with that, but not Babylon.
"Man I wish I could get this shit over with slim,"
Juice-Hop says.
"Why what's the hurry?" Babylon asks.
"Today is grandma birthday."
"You talking about grandma Edna?"
"Yeah its been a full year now."
"Man I even miss her she was off the chain for
real."
"Man I knew her my whole life she smoked coke

before I was even born and after. When she died I was
fucked up myself. But man that was the best that bitch
ever looked in my life time, laying in that mother
fucken coffin," Teeny-Man tells him. Babylon eyes get
as big as golf balls he knows its coming.

"What the fuck you say?" Juice-Hop asks.

"Man I am talking about how peaceful she looked in
the coffin slim, damn." Teeny-Man answers him. As they
looks at one another all three burst out laughing.
Juice-Hop knows that Teeny-Man is telling the truth
about his grandmother.

Babylon gets up to use the bathroom, while he's
there. He decides to check up on those people through
the phone. So he cracks it open and takes a look at
the map, but first sees a text message for him. He
goes back to the others to show them what the text is
saying.

"Hey come and look at this here," Babylon tells
them. They all come to see, so he starts to read the
text message to them.

"Babylon when you get this message it would be in
your best interest to call me back. So we can talk
about what you have in your possession. And to talk
about Bunny, I've got her and her straight razor." He
now gives them the phone to see it for themselves.

"Damn! Hey we got to give this shit up. We got to
give it back to them," Bernard tells them. Babylon's
face frowns up with distaste, and in his eyes there's
a rage.

"Where the hell they do that at?" Babylon asks
Bernard.

"Man that's your mother."

"Slim we're like Navy, full speed ahead." Bernard
looks at Babylon likes he's out of his mind. Bernard
now looks at Teeny-Man as to ask him for help. "Man
don't look at me Bab is a mother fucker with his shit.
Mother fucker is as rough as number four sandpaper."

"We have to go now, but we must split up no more
cars or trucks. They tracks us too fast that way. Look
we will meet up in Miami the spot is called Little
River," Babylon tells them.

Chapter 19

"Little Creek," asks Teeny-Man, Babylon looks at him. "Small Pond? Tiny Ocean? Baby Lake?"

"Come on T."

"I got you Baby."

"Hey look hit my cousin and tell her where you are, so we can keep contact with everybody." Babylon tells them.

"Which one?" Juice-Hop asks.

"My cousin Gloria."

"Whoa! Little Gloria, fine red mother fucker there," Teeny-Man says as Babylon looks at him and shakes his head.

***

"Sir we got a hit for the phone," Mrs. Culp informs Jimmy.

"Send the team the coordinates," he replies.

***

"Let's say good bye and go," Babylon tells them. They go and say their good byes, and now they head out. The husband and wife wish them all the best they both can sense that they need it. Babylon has a quick one on one with Mr. Honesty. He shakes his head in agreement with the young man, and now the young man leaves.

The young men start their journey they are going into town to the bus station. At lease they can start there travel off right. Once they get in town they all see the local gun shop.

"Slim let's get proper before we roll out of here," Teeny-Man suggests to Babylon.

"T this is a country gun shop they ain't got our type of stuff in there," Babylon tells him.

Knowing that he's not going to change Teeny-Man's mind. Babylon gets ready for the break in Teeny-Man is about to bring the gun shop, as he looks the building over. He sees that this place doesn't have any visible security system.

"Oh this bitch is too sweet," Teeny-Man rejoice to the others. He takes his place at the lead, and now at the last moment he changes his mind. "Let's hit the back way," he suggests.

They all go around to the back and Teeny-Man goes to work on the door. It takes no time before he's in. They take a real good look around the place and to their surprise this country gun shop has it all.

"Man these hillbillies got it all slim," says Juice-Hop.

"Hell I was wrong about this one here," Babylon informs everyone. They go for their brand of ammunition and all of the magazines they can carry. Babylon looks and sees something that takes his breath away.

"I know you," he says in a low voice. He has in his view an identical fifty caliber Desert Eagle like the one he already has. Juice-Hop and Teeny-Man both knows that he's been trying to get another one for months now.

"Now I really don't like to brag, but damn can I pick'em or what?" Teeny-Man says to the group.

Everyone just watch how Babylon's face lights up after picking up the weapon. It's been over three months this weapon is not one to easily float through the inner cities, but he finally has it.

With a over sized duffel bag Babylon loads up to

the maximum. With a new M-16 plenty of loaded magazines for the Desert Eagles. He just spots some one hundred round drums for the M-16, and loads ten of them up as well.

"Shit slim you got enough?" Teeny-Man asks him. They all looks and laughs at him he finishes with his loading and spots a nice light material trench coat. And the night is getting cool so after they all are content they leave. Bernard and Juice-Hop wait for buses. While Babylon and Teeny-Man are leaving walking off. They all embrace before they depart from each other. And Babylon gives his last instructions to them.

"And once you get there ask for my family his name is Tootie, and wait for me with him."

***

As the little girl readies her E-Z Bake Oven to begin baking her mother a cake. She goes to the bathroom of the trailer. After she finishes using the toilet she washes her hands on her way out something catches her eye.

It is beautiful to her and she just has to have it to place it on top of the cake she's baking for her mother. So she carefully places it on top of the cake batter. She starts baking it after two minutes of baking she goes over to look into the E-Z Oven's window to catch a glance of the pretty stone.

She never sees or hears the explosion that takes her little life along with her mother's and the entire trailer park. The trailer park is in the sky on its way back down turned into debris. Not yet seen, but the ground where the trailer park once stood will look like a meteor crash site.

***

"Oh my God it happen, it happen. It's a detonation." Mrs. Culp yells. They all are just looking up at Jimmy for instruction, but he does not know what to do in a situation like this. So he just looks back at them.

"Sir with all due respect you must go and get Mr. Sears," Mrs. Culp tells him.

"With all due respect Mr. Sears has been relieved of his command here," he boldly states. She now looks around at the command room and can see all the worried faces. So she just takes control of the situation at hand.

"Attention all available field agents this is Mrs. Jean Culp, I need a analysis done and I need a civilian count of loss of life, and I need plume direction and management. I need immediate evacuation of the outer areas," she relays.

"Why not evac the immediate area?" Jimmy asks her.

"This is a nuclear detonation anything that's within the area is already dead," she replies. Now coldly looking at him knowing that his inexperience may cause more loss of life.

"I want to know the direction the plume will be moving and I want hand held survey instruments down there," Mrs. Culp says over the com.

"The plume?" Jimmy asks.

"A plume Sir is an airborne cloud of radioactive gasses, particles and or vapors released from a power plant or in this case nuclear explosion. And you already know that radiological survey instruments is what is used to determine the exposure rates," she explains to him.

"Okay now we must consider the seven ten rule of thumb I will do this myself," she continues.

"This seven rule-"

"The seven ten rule of thumb is a method that states that for every seven fold increase in time after detonation. There is a ten fold decrease in the exposure rates. Where the rate is the same unit as the time increase of seven days, R/day.

"For an example Sir between the initial measurement taking one hour after detonation and the future time interest, three hundred forty three hours after detonation, there are three seven fold increases in time after detonation. Five hours, times seven equals thirty five hours Sir," she explains to Jimmy after cutting him off.

The Georgetown Heist

"Now do we have the analysis on the shock effects?" Mrs. Culp asks. "The fallout alone will do major damage. What all did the blast take out? Never mind that, what did the electromagnetic pulse take out?" She asks agin.

As the room scrambles about doing their jobs on over drive Jimmy looks on.

"Call F.E.M.A.'s spokes person and tell them to say it's another pipeline that bursted into flames. And to get those people down there ready for radiation treatment. Prep the entire area hospitals," Mrs. Culp orders.

As the room looks on Mrs. Culp is about to pick up the red phone.

"What are you about to do?" Jimmy asks her.

"I'm about to call Madame President," she answers him.

"No you're not," the entire room is stunned.

***

As the two young men stop for a breather one of them reaches for something in his pocket.

"I know you're not about to pop them damn things right in front of me?" Babylon asks Teeny-Man.

"Slim this is my thing." Teeny-Man tells him. Now he shakes like three pills from the bottle and swallows them all.

"Goddamn Teeny-Man you don't have to take them all like that do you?"

"Yeah I do."

"That's bull crap."

"Only to you baby."

"I don't know who in the hell got you started on that foolishness, but enough is enough."

"Bab you just have to see their eyes. When their eyes gloss up after swallowing that big ass load. It's like something you have never seen before."

"Man you're going to blow a girl brains out one day, and end up dried out yourself."

"It's worth it slim they look like they just swallowed a spoon of castor oil."

"Castor oil?"

"Yeah castor oil most people can't keep it down when they swallow it."

"Hey T, you're gone."

"Yeah I know, and I love being gone."

"You are going to need medical help the way you be eating those nut-a-bunch pills. You eat them like they're candy."

"Please! They're called ejaculents, my friend." As the two young men prepare to leave one another. They know that it's not guaranteed that they will see each other again. They know that they are up against something big. But the look they give each other is a look that says, they will try their best to make it.

***

He's taking a back road like he was told to do by Babylon. His bus pulled off without him and Juice-Hop didn't even say nothing. Something is happening in this town, the cops are running all around looking for something or somebody.

***

As Bernard looks at some woods he thinks that they are a good place to go in. To give himself some cover, so he makes his way to the wooded area.

"All these fucking bugs," he says. Once inside the woods he start his way. He stops and begins to listen to something. He thinks he hears something in the distance coming towards him. It's getting closer, he can hear it clearly now.

Out of nowhere comes a wild boar the beast damn near rams him, but it's squealing gives it away. He now starts to run like hell. While he runs through the woods he looses tract of the direction he supposed to be keeping up with.

He jumps up into a tree, and tries to shoo the boar away. It's not working he's afraid to shoot at it. For fear that it might bring some unwanted company he has no choice in this matter.

"Okay you asked for it," he tells the boar. As the first shot misses the boar, it does not flee as he had hoped that it would. The second shot hit's the beast on the top of it's back. The bullet goes straight through the boar.

"Go ahead now I don't want to kill your ass." The boar just starts squealing and breaks out running through the woods. Now he's a little more relieved that the boar is gone. And gets down out the tree and starts to walk on his way.

He gets through the woods at the end of the trail. It is a clearing just ahead of him he can see it clearly. So he start towards that way, but once there he notices that it is too quiet to be the woods.

He can feel something in his gut, but by the time he can react, its too late. The lights cut on and he's completely surrounded. It is nothing he can do he just looks at all the vehicles.

Its all over for him he just walks over to the closest car and places his bags and hands on the hood of the car and completely surrenders.

"Where's the rest of your friends?" A voice asks Bernard.

"We split up."

"Is that right?" The man points gun directly at Bernard's head. He sees it, and don't even flinch or closes his eyes. The man cocks back the hammer on his gun and pulls the trigger. The squealing of a pig is heard in the distance.

***

Its been a nice little while since he has departed with his friend and now he hopes that Teeny-Man will make it to Miami in one piece. But he himself knows that its a long shot.

Do to the fact that somebody wants them dead. He stops and looks up to the skies. "I hope y'all make it," Babylon whispers to himself.

He wishes it also for himself, but he knows that the only way for him to make it will be for him to keep bringing his sanguinary assaults on all who stands in his way.

He wish he knew for a fact who it is that's trying to kill them. Or even if they are not trying to kill him and his friends. Either way he will not stop trying to figure this puzzle out.

***

Its been awhile since he and Babylon has parted their ways, but his mind set is to meet back up with his friend in Miami. He comes upon a gathering of some sort he sees that it might be a vigil. But he too, just founded out about an explosion that occurred in the town that he and his friends were just in.

As he approaches the church he sees that there is no shortage of women here. And he sees that there's an old white lady with a hunched back walking around looking lost.

"Okay everybody listen up we will like to welcome you all. My name is Earl, and I am the Pastor here. This will be a night of remembrance and of study. So while we send out our prayers to those who lost their lives in this disaster we also send our prayers to their loved ones."

Teeny-Man just looks around at all the women, he doesn't even care what's going on. "We can also educate ourselves and learn new things as well as study the good book," the Pastor continues. Teeny-Man sees that the women out numbers the men damn near twenty to one. He see that they are going into groups.

"Hello Sir, how are you? My name is Pearl would you like to lead one of the groups, perhaps one of the children groups?" She asks Teeny-Man. The fool that he is he can't turn this down. And on top of it a children's group how can he pass this one up?

"So will this be a Bible study or more like a life skills group?" He asks her.

"Oh wow! You have experience in this huh? Well that's great just great. Hold on for a minute," she asks him, and now she leaves to go somewhere else.

Chapter 20

He can see that she's talking to an older lady.

***

"**Momma I found** someone to lead the children's
study group. I asked him would he like to lead one of
the study groups for the children. And he asked me
will it be a study group of a life skills group. I
think we found someone to lead the children's Bible
Study group."

"Okay that sounds like a winner to me. Let me see
the young man who you are talking about Pearl." They
both go over to Teeny-Man he sees them on their way
straight for him.

"Hello my name is Mother Catherine, and I was told
by my daughter that you would like to instruct our
youth Bible study class is the right?"

"No ma'am, that's incorrect. I was asked by a
young lady if I would like to lead one of the groups.
And then she said perhaps one of the children groups
and I asked her would it be Bible or life skills. She
told me her name was Pearl."

"Well that in its self lets me know that you're
not short of common sense. What is your roots young
man?"

"Southern Baptist ma'am."

"Well, its not a problem for you to hold a group
for the children. When you are through rejoin us up

stairs in the assembly."

"Thank you I'll do just that."

"And if you have any problems just as for Mother Catherine."

"Who's C.B. Honesty?" Teeny-Man asks.

"What? Oh that's mines," Mother Catherine tells him.

"I know a old couple with that name, Mr. Edward and Mrs. Arabella."

"Who are you? I don't know if you're playing or not, but those are my parents names."

"I just met them and stayed with them for a few days. Whenever you talk to them again tell them you met Teeny-Man. I'm the one the bull attacked."

"Oh wait, you're one of the young men that stayed with them for a few days."

"Yeah, I'm one of them."

"Well you are family they spoke highly of you all, and especially one of you, so enjoy you stay here with us." Now all of the children are being sent to the basement.

***

"**All right y'all** what would you like to do first the Bible or life skills?" Teeny-Man asks the children.

"We just started over in the Bible we are in Genesis now," a little girl informs him.

"Okay then its Genesis," he replies. They all looks at him he's new and they don't know him, so the class is hesitant.

"I am going to teach you all just a little bit deferent than what you're used to learning it. Now you all have to understand that in the beginning it was some wild ass shit going on."

"All he said shit," a little girl says out loud.

"Shut up and stop snitching," Teeny-Man tells her.

That fast the children are stunned by their new teacher.

"Now look, go to G-one verse eighteen," he

The Georgetown Heist

instructs.

"What is G-one verse eighteen?" A little boy asks.

"That's Genesis one eighteen baby boy, everybody got it now?" The class nods their heads in agreement. "Good, now right quick who was the first man and woman an the planet?"

"It was Adam and Eve," answers a little boy.

"Did God make any more people after them?"

"No!"

"Okay lets go to G one verse twenty six y'all got that? Then God said, "let us make man in our image, according to our likeness," the children just watches him now.

"Now verse twenty seven goes, God made him in his own image, and that image was of the spirit kind-"

"We are past this part we're on Cain and Abel. And Cain just killed his brother," a little girl informs him.

"I'll go to there for y'all then. Now when God told Cain that he had to go, but said that he was going to place a mark on him. Do anybody know what that mark was?" None of the children answered him.

"I'll tell you he made Cain a black man. He took his white skin away and turned him black." They look at him with a look of true uncertainty on their faces.

"I got y'all little asses with that one, didn't I? I'm going to give y'all the real not that bullshit them Preachers be given y'all."

"He said bullshit," come from the back rows.

"Now look at G four verse sixteen, then Cain went out from the presence of the Lord and dwelt in the land of Nod on the east of Eden." The children actually are into it, and he knows it also, but just can't help himself.

"Now verse seventeen says, and Cain knew his wife and she conceived and bore Enoch." He watches their little faces for a minute.

"Do anyone knows what it means when it says that he knew his wife?"

"Yes. It mean that he knows who she is when he sees her," a little boy answers.

"No, that's not what it means. What it means is

he fucked her, that's right he put that mother fucken dick right on her ass." The kids are shocked beyond repair. The class is majority eight to thirteen year old children. "Alllll-"

"What I tell your little ass about that mother fucken snitching?" He asks the little girl, but she doesn't like it one bit.

"Now y'all told me that Adam and Eve was the only two people on the planet. So that means it was only them two and their children right? So how did Cain leave and get a wife then? The children looks puzzled, he saves them.

"Lets go back to G one verse twenty seven. See the part where it says, he created him, male and female he created them? The them part you get it? He made more than one, and Adam really means man and that's the truth.

"Just like in Ezekiel, y'all go to Ezekiel and read from verse one to twenty two. And once you all get through tell me what it is that he is seeing?"

So as the children starts to read he just paces through the aisle and watches them. Now it seems as though their are all finished with their reading. "Well?" He asks them. Not a hand goes up he's not happy about it, and he's ready to leave anyway.

"Not one of you?" No one still hasn't answered.

"I'll tell you what he saw, it was a flying saucer or should I say a U.F.O." They start laughing at him.

"Man you're crazy they didn't even have those back then," a little boy tells him.

"What you're saying is one hundred percent right, and its one hundred percent wrong. You see how you got X-Box and Play Station? Well twenty years ago could any body call it X-Box or Play Station?

"No because the words were not invented yet." They all are looking at each other trying to figure out whether this is acceptable information or some foolishness. "Did y'all know that you can call your mothers, woman, when she call you for something, and be like Jesus?

"That's how Jesus used to talk to his mother Miss Mary. I guess y'all don't believe that one either?

The Georgetown Heist

Turn to John two verse four and read it for yourselves. You little girl, right there you read it for us," he asks her while pointing at her.

"Jesus said to her, woman what does your concern have to do with me. My hour has not yet come," she reads.

"Now if y'all read just above that y'all see that it was Miss Mary that he's talking to," he tells them. They seem to be in agreement with him on what he told them.

"See when people talk about the Bible they don't teach y'all what y'all should be taught."

"My father didn't teach me this," a little boy tells him.

"That's because your father is on the hammah. He's a cold blooded faggot, and the freaked out mother fucker be making videos of himself sucking his own dick. The nasty freak body mother fucker." All the children start laughing at the little boy.

"You're not like President Obama," the little boy says to him.

"Let me tell you something about Obama-"

"You can't tell me nothing about President Obama, my daddy voted for President Obama."

"You think your daddy help put Obama in the White House?"

"He did my daddy said we put Obama in the White House."

"Okay class write this down for me, the electoral college. This is who, no, they are the ones who decides who will be the President, not the people who vote. The people vote don't mean shit, the fore father, meaning them old mother fucken crackers.

"Actions states that this country is to damn stupid to elect a leader of this country. Americans are so ignorant they would have elected Michael Jackson for President, um, in the eighties that is. Now look that up children.

"Now back to you fuck boy when Obama first became President. Do you remember what happened right after, within a sixty day swing? And the situation was just swept under the rug?" He asks the little boy.

"Yeah it was the officer and Mr. Gates, and they later had a beer at the White House."

"No slut boy you are wrong that wasn't the biggest story that was swept under the rug."

"That was the biggest story."

"No it wasn't, the biggest story was the fact that a dark skinned President wasn't in office a hot ninety days and a black man was killed in Texas by racists white men, and the so called black President didnt' even acknowledge it.

"He never spoke of it as if they told him not to address it, not a word of it out his mouth. But he's your President huh? He's not black anyway, he's a halfbreed and they gave it to his white side." With the class total attention he gets to end this and get on his way. He almost forgets about his journey.

"Hey fuck boy can you tell me who was the first American President?"

"That's too easy dummy it was George Washington."

"Who all agrees with him?" The class is quiet, but only a few of them raises their hands. "You all who agree with him are one hundred percent wrong. America's first President was a mother fucker from Maryland and his name was John Hanson-"

"No it wasn't it was George Washington," the boy argues.

"Write down his name and find out for yourself then. The President seal that is used today was made by him. And I think his title was, The President of the United States in Congress Assembled, this was in seventeen eighty one." The children don't believe him, so they writes down everything he just told them, but he knows that he has them on this one for sure.

"Hey that's it for this group shit Teeny-Man got's to roll. I'll see y'all later, you monkey mother fuckers you."

He leaves the basement and goes up stairs so he can go. But to his surprise the grown ups are just starting their own Bible study group now.

"Oh my, Teeny-Man where are you going?" Asks Mother Catherine.

"Momma, I'm about to leave," he answers her.

The Georgetown Heist

"I would love for you to stay until we finished up our Bible study session. We have a new resident in our church for the first time and she doesn't have a partner to read the Bible with," she explains.

"Okay, I'll do it for you Momma." He doesn't want to do it at all, but he knows her parents. And the fact that they're good people who took him and his friends in. So he begins to walk with her towards this new resident she was talking about.

And to his surprise it is the old white lady he had seen when he first showed up.

"Ms. Wanger, this is a very nice young man, his name in Teeny-Man, he'll be your Bible study partner for tonight," Mother Catherine tells her. She leaves them to themselves, they're on the very last row of the pews by themselves everyone else is up front.

"It looks like we're going to have to share my Bible," the old lady says.

"Yeah, it looks that way," he responds. As the pastor calls out the page where they will be reading from, Teeny-Man pays none of it any mind. He just has thoughts of his own going through his mind and then speaks them.

"This old bitch pussy probably raggedy as a mango seed. Or look like chitlins with a whole lot of hot sauce," he say under his breath.

Being old fashioned she finds the page and now passes the Bible to Teeny-Man, so he can hold it being that he is the man. The poor old lady has no idea what she's in for as the Pastor talks and people asks questions.

Teeny-Man goes into action, he lifts the Bible up to let her see it more clearer. His other hand is underneath the book massaging himself for her. By the time she looks up at the Pastor and looks back down at the Bible.

He done struck he ups on the old white lady. The young man has place the biggest, blackest, hardest dick in front of her right in the middle of the Bible. She has never in her life seen a dick like this, and he's stroking it right in front of her.

Her face is beet red the old lady looks like Santa

175

Clause in the cheeks. She is so nervous that she looks
all around the church while the young man steadily
strokes himself. She can not believe this is happening
to her, in a church of all places.

Teeny-Man seems to have at lease eleven inches on
him, as he continues to stroke it she just watches.
"You got some cocoa butter?" He asks her. She shakes
her head no, but goes into her purse and finds some
lubricant and hands it to him. "Myyyy girlllll," he
drags.

As he apply the lubricant his member has now
become super shiny. She watches it with a hungry
steady eye he knows that she's into in now.

"That's right get your share, the lioness share.
You're a lioness eat it up. Eat bitch, you're a eater
from back in the days. A veteran eater, bitch been
eating since Martin Luther King."

With a firm grip on his rock hard erection he's
now humps is hand and grinds his hips. The old lady
just stops looks around and keeps her eyes on the dick
in front of her. Now her eyes are getting watery and
he sees this, and it makes him go into freak mode.

"You love it, look at you, nasty old mother fucken
buzzard you, eat it up."

At this time he notices that the old lady is just
a tapping one of her feet with quick taps. He starts
back grinding his hips in his seat. She acts like she
can't take it any more and he's showing her long
strokes.

She slips out of her right shoe and with her foot
arched she begins to bounce her knee off the ball of
her foot. Her mouth seems to be only sucking air in
and not out. He can hear the Pastor telling them to
turn the page.

And now takes the base on his rod and with a flick
of his wrist, smacks down on the right side of the
Bible in a circular motion going from the right side
trying to smack the right side page left.

But the page just stands straight up in the Bible
still holding his dick by it's base. He flicks his
wrist once more and smacks the page to the left side
of the Bible. With that move she gasps for some air

after seeing her gasp he wish to reward her.

"Hold it," he tells her and she does as she's told
and places her small hand around the big black cock of
his.

"Squeeze it, and squeeze it tight," he tells her
again. As she squeezes the dick in her hand she's in
another world and he sex her hand, just humping away.

"Okay, that's it you're in the way now," he tells
her while pulling her hand off it. She acts like she
don't want to let the dick go. While she bounces her
knee in her seat he continues to grind his hips again,
but this time he will not last.

"Get me some tissue, Momma," Sensing that the
young man is at his peak she wants to look for some
tissue, but something is happening to her, something
that hasn't happen in a very long time.

"Ahhh, haaaaa!" The old lady sighs while she
squirms about with her back arched.

"Ah shit, you need to get that mother fucken
tissue for me. Don't even worry about it I'm going to
paint the inside of this damn Bible," he tells her.

"My mother gave me this Bible," she says in a
faint voice.

She is moving awfully fast now with all of her
teeth showing she's straining to keep down the noise.
She shakes and squirms all over the place, and he's
steadily stroking. She's rubbing her knees and thighs
together.

"That old pussy trying to muster up enough juice
so you can get a nut off huh?" He asks her. She's
going through her climax cycles. It seems as though
she will get her one off as she goes down the stretch.

She has that arch in her back along with the hump
her teeth are gritting hard. "MMMMhhhhhhhhh!" She
moans. "Mastifallah!" He says. It is apparent that she
just got off one of the best climaxes of her life.

"Alright here it comes bitch it's my turn I'ma
show you how to shoot, bitch."

She can't find anything to catch it with. Looking
around trying to see what's available or better yet,
within her reach.

"Here it comes bitch, eat," he tells her while he's shooting his massive load. She rushes to catch his release with her scarf as she snatches it from around her neck, just in time. She can feel the warmth of his huge load he has just sprayed. She has her hands in a cup like position its been awhile since she been around an active dick.

With the ejaculent pills working its magic she will never forger this night. She has never felt a batch this damn hot and so damn much in her entire life.

As he shakes and squeezes the last of it out he flicks his wrist once more to smack the old lady's hand, she looks at him and smiles.

"Nasty buzzard you," he tells her. She gets up to go to the lady's room. But once she gets back the young man is gone. She's feeling useful again, she just sat down and finishes her Bible study. Now it is over, the old lady stands up.

"I would like to become a member of this fine church."

"Amen!" Some one says in the church followed by several Amen's. The membership applauds, and are pleased to hear this announcement. The old lady listens to all the applauds coming her way. But her mind is on what she had just seen, and now she looks off into time. "My God, he came everywhere," she whispers.

***

Night has fallen again and he finds himself alone and walking in the woods deep in Georgia. His mind is on getting to Miami to meet his friends, so they can have a good chance to sale their merchandise.

He's walking at a fast pace and doesn't see the brightly lit torches right above him fifteen feet in the air from him. He doesn't look up to notice them. At the rate he is going he will meet up with the group of torches in no time at all.

Up ahead of him the path that he's on will soon come to a point and connect. He will run directly into them and they him. For now the trees and bushes

Chapter 21

separate them.

Before either of them knows it they walk right into each other. When he sees what's going on its too late. The torches seems with a quick burst, to just surround him. He watches and sees that they are all together.

Now totally surrounded and out numbered he watches them all while slowly turning around so none of them can sneak up on him.

"Yeeeeeee-Haaaaawwww! Lookah here Yahweh has sent us a nigger," a voice yells and informs the group. This is not a dream this is the real deal. Babylon has walked straight into a Klu-Klux-Klan ceremony, an a couple of the hooded men begin to come closer to him.

"Keep still boy and don't you run," another voice tells him.

"Run, why would I run?" The young man responds. At this time he pulls back the trench coat with his right hand and before it can close back he pulls up the M-16 riffle, and takes the safety off it.

Babylon begins to let freedom ring he releases an array of hellish fire. He has to take a knee and just aim for all of their bodies at center mass. This is the only way to get the best results.

As he chops down the hooded racists he hears one of them yelling. "Get down the nigger has a weapon!" Never one to let anything go, but he sees no sense on trying to kill all of them. He needs to make his way on, so he can get to Miami.

He start running in the way he truly think is South it didn't care really as long as he is out of the area with those good old boys. He see some of them still lying on the ground. All of them he see now are crying in pure agony.

It is music to his ears, but he can not stay there and finish them all off. One of the men lying on the ground reaches up to him for help, but he think its to catch him. He points the M-16 down at the face of the hooded man and pulls his trigger twice. And even in the dark he can see or think he sees the blood splatter mist in the air. He did not see any before when he was shooting them center mass.

The entire hood is red with the Klansman blood and that seems to get the young man started on yet, another assault.

As he continues to run to get out the area. He reaches another set of woods and he's running on all cylinders. He has his big duffel bag over his left shoulder and he reloads and places the M-16 back on his right shoulder.

He thinks that he might have gotten away from them. It is at this moment that he hears, "Pop!" and the next thing he knows the entire night sky is lit up.

"A flare?" he asks himself. Now he knows for a fact that they are coming for him. He puts more pep into his step. He has a nice lead on them or at lease he thought he did.

He hears the sounds of vehicles all around him, and he knows that it will be just a matter of time before its all going to go down. But he know that this is their back yard and he's hell bent on not giving them any more advantages than they already have. He shoots back up deep into the woods and almost like clockwork another flare is shot up into the night sky.

"There, he's over there," a voice cries out. He now knows that he has been made so he starts to haul tail out the area he's in. They are coming from all over the place.

He sees that he's going to have to make his stand

and make it soon. For they are coming at him real
fast. He decides it will be here, at this spot. He has
no choice, but to hold court now. They are all over
him and closing.

He takes out the M-16, and heads out to meet them.
He sees pick up trucks all over the place. It's one
coming towards him. He takes his aim as the truck gets
a little closer he readies himself its now in his
sights. He fires into the pick up truck, and see the
sparks shoot up off the truck.

He know that he has hit the occupants of the
truck. So he gets ready for the next one and goes out
to meet him also.

At his point of attack he has a nice side angle on
the truck, and takes what he's given. The driver of
the truck never sees him, and still don't know who
killed him. The M-16 shoots though the window without
breaking it out.

It goes through and kills the driver and keeps
going and kills the passenger also. But he doesn't
know, so he keeps firing into the truck. It crashes
into a tree, and begins to smoke up the night.

He begins to hear gun fire someone is taking shots
at him from a distance. Babylon takes aim himself and
start to fire upon him. He can now see light flashes
from the muzzle of a shotgun. So he takes cover behind
the crashed truck.

He now knows that the shooter is firing slugs at
him from the shotgun. One he can't hear any buckshots
ricochetting and two, he can now see the big holes in
the truck. Babylon shoots as straight as he can, but
still hasn't hit him yet.

"I got'em, I got'em penned down," one of the
hoodsmen yells. Now all of the trucks are coming in
his direction he reloads and come from behind the
truck and start firing his riffle like its going out
of style.

"Uuuggghhhh! I'm hit, I'm hit damn it!" a voice
yells out in extreme pain over the C.B. radio. Babylon
keeps on making his advancement in that direction with
the M-16 just tearing up everything in it's path.

He just wants to get in the wind, as he reloads

again he totally destroys a truck and it explodes into
flames that brightens up the dark night. He can see
exactly what he is up against in numbers, and he's
still out manned.

As he makes a dash for it he comes across a paved
road. This indicates that civilization is not far away
since he is in the back woods he just needs a sign to
go off.

The road he's on leads him to the back of a
building. He takes to the window, and lets himself in.
Once inside it doesn't take long to find out that he's
not alone. He hears singing from a man inside the
building.

Time goes by and Babylon is hoping for a sign that
he can move on again. So he finds himself a spot to
hide for the moment. But his mind is made that first
chance he gets he will leave from this place.

The singing gets loud and then fades off again. So
the man is very active inside of this building. So he
will have to be on point when his time comes to make
his move. Babylon hears something it's somebody at the
door of the building the man inside goes to answer it.

"Hey Skip did you let anybody in here within the
last ten minutes or so?" The voice asks.

"Hell no Connor why would I let somebody in here
that I don't know?"

"Well Skip just to let you know its a killer on
the loose. He done killed six brothers during
tonight's ceremony, and he's a nigger."

"Holly shit, a nigger in these parts? He's not
from around here. Who did he kill?"

"Chuck, Bobby Lee, Bret, Cooper, Tommy and Jess'e
and he shot over seventeen others."

"Holly shit I know Clint is one mad son bitch bout
Cooper. That's his youngest boy, he had no reason
being there anyway he's just twelve years old."

"Make no never mind when we catch him we going to
have ourselves a real good old fashion lynching."
Babylon hears this information he knows he has to get
away from these rednecks. So he takes it upon himself
to find another spot within the building to hide.

He can hear that Connor is leaving the building

behind Skip. Who wanted to catch a glimpse of what is happening on the streets for himself. And now Babylon takes and surveys the place to his surprise he has broken into a morgue.

"Out of all the places to break into I breaks in a damn morgue," he whispers to himself.

He goes from room to room looking for a nice enough hiding space for himself. In one room he sees the body of a woman. She is young and she's the thickest deadest white girl he has ever seen. He can see purple marks on parts of her body he sees that her private is extra fury.

Her legs are spread apart so that anyone who looks can see it all. It's no doubt that she had some kind of accident. He hears something, somebody's coming so he has no choice but to hide inside of this room he's now in.

"Yeah Skip just let me take a quick look around. Just to make sure he didn't come in here no kind of way," Connor says.

As Connor looks around for the young man. He comes across the body of the dead woman and just looses it. He starts to break down right in front of Babylon. Going through the motions and now he starts crying and sobbing all over the place.

Skip comes into the room he see that the man is crying, and takes him out the room with the body. Seeing the body is just too much for him to bear.

"And he say he's looking for me?" Babylon whispers to himself.

Both men goes back outside together, and once again Babylon is on the move to find a new spot in which to hide until his time comes.

As he see the body of the white woman its kind of a new experience for him. Being around a dead body this long.

Just looking at it he can not tell how old she is. He's not good with woman ages, especially a dead white one. He believes if you seen one you seen them all. Now Skip is coming back, and he's alone.

"Okay Reba, I'm sorry about that, but it seems as though a nigger is loose in the town. And done killed some decent folk. But don't you never mind that because it's just you and yours truly," he tells the corpse.

"I know this man ain't crazy?" Babylon asks himself.

"What you say? I'm fixen to do it right now," he continues to tell the corpse.

Skip leaves the room and comes back with some kind of machine hook up that has large hoses that's connected to it. Babylon in hiding can see that whatever is in those tubes is hot as hell. Skip continues to work on this woman's body. He sticks the long needles inside her body in different places.

Babylon finally know what it is. "He's pumping the embalming fluid into her." Babylon tells himself. It is that simple to figure out, but no. Babylon eyes betrays him he now sinks lower to the floor from being detected by the man working in the room. Skip once again leaves the room and Babylon gets up and goes to another location in the room.

This time on the floor right in front of the body. He slides all the way down to the floor up against the wall underneath a table. Skip returns to the room this time he has a jar in his right hand.

A big blue jar with no label on it to identify its contents. Babylon looks on from a bottom view. He sees that Skip is taking the top off the jar that he brought in. He sticks like four fingers inside the jar, and pulls out a petroleum jelly like substance, Babylon believes.

He now puts the substance between the dead woman's legs, and keeps on packing it with the substance. Skip now goes over to the window and takes a good look out of it.

Now he's taking off his clothes, and Babylon looks as confused as one can look. Seeing what he's seeing now, Skip is kissing the dead woman's lips soft, as he takes out all the needles and tubes.

It finally hits Babylon, Skip wasn't just placing that stuff between her legs, but he was also packing it inside of her as well. He's on top of her, and is motioning his hips while on top of her.

184

The Georgetown Heist

"My God you're too hot, its that damn one hundred ninety degree water," he tells the corpse. Skip is humping her now he's really into it as if he's dug in, and is about to do some deep digging. "Yeah Reba I told you I was going to lay you one day," he says.

Babylon is a little slow to the situation due to him not knowing the true nature of this necrophiliastic act.

He just figuring out that was some kind of lubricant that Skip put between her legs. As Babylon watches this sick act he still hears the sirens and trucks outside. So he stays put and places his head down to the floor.

Skip is now starting to bang this poor woman's corpse. Babylon can't even stare at the floor its so much noise. "Flop, flop, flop, flop!"

He's slamming himself into the corpse of the woman he's pulling out of her for the moment. Skip looks up above the table they are on, and reaches for something. Babylon is puzzled now, he doesn't know what he can be reaching for.

As he stands up on the table, Babylon turns his head not wanting to look at Skip's little pink willie. "Damn he's trying to gun me out." Babylon whispers low.

He reaches the object, and pulls it down to the table. Babylon sees it, but don't know what it is. The lines of sort falls onto the table. He goes to the table and starts to place her arms through the lines, Babylon can't really see it clearly.

The body is strapped under the shoulders and around the high thighs. He now goes around to what appears to be a control panel of sort, and start to operate it, and the chains higher up starts pulling.

The next thing Babylon knows, the woman's body just jumps up. It's in a sitting position suspended in the air just bouncing up and down. The body is in some kind of harness contraption.

Skip now goes and lays down under the body, and measure the body length in the air. It's to much lag, he gets up and readjust the chains, and goes back over to the table and lays down one more.

Now he puts himself back inside the woman's corpse. The corpse is riding him with the help of the spring coils. He's pulling the body down using her body and the coils lifts her up.

The recoil is so great that he has a rhythm. With the body bouncing up and down on him. He purposely lets go and the body goes too high, and completely off him. He has to lean up to bring it back down on him.

he's having the time of his life with this corpse. He spins it around, so it can be in a reverse cowgirl position, now the body rides him backwards. Babylon shakes his head in disbelief. He takes one of the legs and with a hard pull, he spins the body a full three hundred and sixty degrees while still on him.

Skip stops and just squeezes the corpse ass and now he releases it from the harness. The corpse falls down to the table he gets behind it and props it. He folds the arms across each other, and begins to take the corpse from behind.

"Oh yea! Reba it's good," he tells the corpse while he is delivering powerful thrusts into it. At one point he smacks the backside of the corpse.

As he humps her lifeless body like a true barbarian, the arms give way to their position. He stills humps the body unmercifully. Some air escapes her lifeless body while he ravages the corpse.

"Oh no Reba, bitch you gonna take all this dick." Babylon just can't take it any more he comes up from behind the tables with his Desert Eagle cocked. He slides his bag on the floor with his foot, while looking at Skip.

"Don't move sicko," Babylon tells him. With Skip looking directly at Babylon he can't believe that someone is here with him. He comes closer to Skip so he can get a good look at him, and he him.

"You that nigger?" Skip asks him.

"No, but I will be," he answers with the Desert Eagle pointed right at Skip.

"What boy, you want some too? Well you can't get none she's mines."

"I'll pass."

The Georgetown Heist

Babylon begins to walk up on Skip, during the whole ordeal Skip never misses a stroke the nasty bastard. Babylon has his position on him, and now shoots him in the head twice. With the fan blowing in there the blood haze flies back in Babylon's face.

Both bullets goes through Skip's head, and hits some glass jars bursting them. Skip never had enough time to pull out the woman's corpse. Now he's slumped over her body with his member still inside her.

Babylon looks for Skip's keys to a vehicle. He remember seeing a pick up truck outside when he first came. He looks no further than his pants pockets. He sees Skip slumped body over top of her's, and see how his blood is now flowing down her back just running off the side of her neck.

With his little pink willie still inside her, they're stuck like dogs. Babylon picks up his bag and heads for the door.

*****

His phone rings, but he's slow to answer it. "Hello, who's this?" He asks.

"Detective Victor Williams, don't say a word, or I'll hang up. The youths you're looking for are going to Miami to sell their precious cargo. You can believe me or not, either way you owe me for this valuable information," the caller tells him and the phone line goes dead.

*****

As he drives along the road he's feeling pretty good about himself right now. "I made it," he says to himself.

His destination is not far now, not far at all. Now his personal phone rings, and its his friend Teeny-Man on the other end.

"Yeah! I'm on my way now I'll be there in a minute slim. I'm turning off the ninety fifth street exit now. I'll be just a hot second," he tells him.

*****

187

Chapter 22

"**Now that we** know for a fact where they are lets
put this in motion shall we? Its like I'm working in
here by myself. Mrs. Culp I need for you to get my men
on this com," Jimmy tells her.

"Yes Sir, you're linked."

"Look set up the buy, go through all available
channels. Once you have secured the package finish off
the bastards and anybody that's with them."

"Sir, yes Sir," the voice over the com responds.

***

He pulls up and he sees his friend and some of his
family members. So he's about to park and get out the
pick up truck.

Out of the truck he now sees everybody in view and
some faces he can't remember. "Hey aunt Shelly how you
doing?" Babylon asks her. He's taking his time on the
rest of them he doesn't want to call somebody by the
wrong name.

"What's buzzin cousin?" Tootie asks Babylon. Now
his mind is putting the faces together as he's
pointing. "Barbara, Stacy, Lacy, Vicki? Aunt Hazel,"
he's all named out and receives hugs from them all.

"Juice-Hop, hey big boy I didn't know you made it
here, and Bernard?" Babylon asks.

"B, Bernard is a no show," Juice-Hop informs him.
After all the hugs and kisses he takes his friend

to the side.

"Look we're going shopping and wait to see if Bernard and T show up. But the whole while we'll be trying to get rid of the stones, as fast as we can."

"B, Teeny-Man is in the house, he said he's feeding one of your cousin's friends. Babylon doesn't has a clue, but is relieved that he's already here.

"Hey Bab, what's up with this very important shit, you got to see me about?" Tootie asks.

"Tootie first find us a good hotel we can stay in and I'll talk to you about it."

"That's not a problem there, but I'm glad to see you. It's been too, long since the last time I saw you."

"Tootie we're trying to go shopping take us to y'all mall or something."

"Okay Cuzzo, I'ma take y'all to Aventura Mall I see y'all pockets are fat, but not fat enough for Bel Harbour in Miami Beach. It's on Collins Avenue, that's some exclusive shit over there, you even pay for the damn parking," he tells them.

"Hey Tootie on the movies every time the scene goes to Miami. It's always some of that Spanish music playing in the background. Man I don't hear none of that shit playing now." Teeny-Man tells him.

Tootie looks at him for a moment not knowing how to take Teeny-Man only his family calls him Tootie. But sensing that his cousin told him, he must be cool people.

"Man that's what you'll hear if you go to certain parts, the city if full of Latin people. And that's what them movie people prefer to show the world," he answerrs.

They pulls up to the mall they see all kinds of girls lined up in every flavor in the shop. They first walk past some white girls. One of them is watching Teeny-Man with the look of a hungry animal she's making sex faces at him.

He doesn't say anything to her he just keeps on going pass them and her, so they begin to shop. This mall is one hundred percent different from the malls up their end. It has too, much   space   and   too, many stores. They don't want to over do it, they just want to get a few things and get some toiletries for themselves.

"Please remember that this is Miami, and not D.C., with that being said don't get nothing too, countrified," Tootie tells them.

"Countrified?" Teeny-Man repeats him.

"Yeah, countrified, you know how you up North jokers are." The young men shops until their needs are met now as they head back out the mall. Teeny-Man sees the white girl from earlier and she's still eyeing him. He sees the white girl coming towards him. He has never in his life talked to one before. He has never came across one before in South East D.C. Plus it is truly taboo to be messing with one.

"Hey what's your name?" The white girl asks him.

"Teeny-Man," he tells her while looking around.

"You got a girl or something?"

"Nawl."

"So why are you looking all over the place then?"

"I'm just checking out my surroundings."

"That's a good answer, but that's not the reason. You're looking like you stole something. You never dated outside your race before, have you?"

"Yeah." Now his friends are watching him smiling at him. They both know he is lying, he never been with nothing but his own kind.

"Well you need to relax a little, are you good with your history?" She asks teeny-Man. At this moment Babylon is all ears.

"Yeah, I'm pretty nice with it," he answers.

"Well if you know your history then you should know that we have a history together."

"A history together?"

"Yeah a history from eighteen sixty one to eighteen sixty five, the black man and the white woman. We showed our asses all over the place, and we're still doing it right now today. But we did it best in the eighteen hundreds during the Civil War.

"When Master wouldn't let the black man fight in the war. A few did, but the majority did not. But all who didn't go off for whatever reason stayed behind,

or got killed. But during this time period the
halfbreed population shot up one thousand percent.

"Now if all the white men were gone off to fight
in the war. Who in the hell was making all those damn
mixed babies? I'll tell you, it was us.

"Some escaped from being killed because their
Master refused to allow them to stay back without a
white male presence around. Others had no choice in
the matter. Without their big black bucks, their crops
and fields would be wasted and their family lives
destroyed.

"Some were castrated, some were killed and some
just left and once the war started returned to help
the women.

"So they had to let old Sambo come back or they'd
starve to death, and he and Miss Anne fucked up a
storm. And that storm is still raging inside us right
now. You just don't know it, back then we got back at
Master and Kizzy's black ass. For all those times they
fucked in front of us and laughed in our faces.

"It was nothing we could do about it, but we had
our day, well our four years, and we made up plenty
for it. If and when Master came back we put the babies
on deserters who raped Kizzy black ass.

"And Miss Anne told Kizzy if she told it. Right
after Master kills Sambo, her black ass would be next,
and Kizzy kept her fucking mouth shut. And if one was
lucky, and Master didn't come back, shit we just kept
it rolling babe."

Babylon is truly impressed with what he's hearing.
This white girl is on dot with her history. And Teeny-
Man doesn't have a clue what to say about the whole
ordeal.

"And now you need me more than ever, for your
son," she goes again. Teeny-Man looks at her in a
puzzled way. Do to the fact that he has no babies, let
alone a son.

"That's right I said it your son. I know you've
been seeing the signs? They are all around us, and now
is the time to get the best of us. So I'm offering you
the best with me."

"Is that right?" Teeny-Man asks her. It's the best

he can do, he's really not one for a lot of words plus
he has no game.

"Yeah that's right, if you just open your eyes to
the signs. You will see it for yourself that's, if you
love your son. If so then you really need me, because
that's the only way he's going to be President of the
United States of America, is if he comes out a white
pussy.

"Moesha, Laqueisha, Rolexia and Moelexus, none of
them can put him in the White House only Miss Anne and
Miss Charlotte. Look light skinned and brown skinned
sisters are seasonal. And the dark skinned sisters
only get play during black history month. Asian and
Latino women are also seasonal, and seasons come and
go. But, the almighty white woman is always in seaon."

After that they all burst out in laughter, at what
the white girl has just said. It is the most craziest
thing they've heard from a white girl.

"Just get her number Teeny-Man, so we can go."
Babylon tells him. So they exchange numbers and leaves
it at that. Now they are driving around doing some
sight seeing.

"Hey Tootie, y'all let white girls talk like that
down here?" Teeny-Man asks.

"Hell nawl, she knew y'all wasn't from down here,
and tried y'all asses."

"Tootie that's one for the books, cousin." Babylon
tells Tootie.

As they continue to drive along they come up on a
pack of girls and Babylon's cousin pulls over. He
himself is trying to catch, so they all get out trying
to shoot their shots at the girls. Once out the car
Teeny-Man again has caught some action.

"What cho name is?" A girl asks Teeny-Man.

"Where y'all from?" Another one asks.

"Goddamn, all their asses sound like Trina,"
Teeny-Man says out loud.

"Oh hell nawl you didn't," one of the girls says
in protest.

"He didn't mean no harm by it, he meant to say
y'all have that Miami voice," Babylon tries to
intervene.

The Georgetown Heist

"Bullshit, you got your meaning and I got my meaning. All of them got that high pitch country ass voice." Teeny-Man reiterates.

Now all hell breaks loose the girls are in straight attack mode. They are outraged over the remark that Teeny-Man said. Babylon just looks at Teeny-Man for a second and gives that look. In a way he's right, they can't understand nothing the girls are saying.

"I though y'all supposed to be nice down here? I'm going back home and tell everybody that y'all are just like sisters everywhere else, just hateful and mean. Y'all need to take us somewhere," Babylon suggests.

"We'll take y'all, but his ass can stay," one of the girls says while pointing at Teeny-Man.

"Ain't nobody going if I don't go. Plus I wasn't talking to you, you don't sound like Trina," he says with a smile on his face.

"Oh, okay then clean it up."

"You sound like Lil Boosie."

"Stupid ass up north nig-"

"Hey!" Teeny-Man yells out loud. "What's your name anyway," he asks while cutting her off.

"Annette why?"

"Annette what?"

"Annette, Annette."

"What's your last name?"

"What are you the police or something?"

"Nawl, I just wanted to know my baby mother's maiden name that's all," he says with a straight face that everybody catches.

"Annette Downing," she tells him and all the other girls give one another a look. So Babylon takes it as the girl told Teeny-Man her real name.

"Hey Tootie we got action so take me back to the house so I can get proper, and we will get a hotel with help from them." Babylon tells his cousin.

So Tootie agrees with his cousin's request. Babylon goes back to his family house and Teeny-Man and Juice-Hop goes with the girls to get the hotel rooms.

Once at his family house they go inside and Tootie

193

begins to speak. "Cuzzo don't get all personal with those hoes, Cuzzo," he tells him. "And as soon as y'all are through with them go and get some more rooms somewhere else, so they can't bring nobody to y'all afterwards," he continues.

Babylon gets his duffel bag and his friends stuff and leaves without saying any good byes to his other family members.

Once he's told by phone what hotel to go to he is gone. His bag is still heavy as he had remembered. But he will not tell the girl about it's contents or any thing else about him or them.

As he goes up and knock on the door he can hear laughter inside the room. He's pleased that Teeny-Man is not messing up like always, so they let him in and introduces him to the girl that's for him. Lenore is her name, or at lease that's what they tells him.

Teeny-Man gives Babylon his room key he goes to his room to put his duffel bag up. He sees all his clothes from the mall and they hit the town. Babylon not one to be out partying all night, so it's no surprise he's the first one to call it a night.

Teeny-Man and Annette refuse to end the night, but everybody is ready to go. "Y'all are a bunch of killjoys," Annette tells the group.

They head back to the hotel with Teeny-Man and Annette mad as hell. Now back at the hotel they stayed paired up. The girls say their good nights to one another and head to their own rooms.

"Hey slim, I'm tired I'm going to get some sleep," Babylon tells Lenore. Earlier in the night she had been watching where he was placing is money, and noticed that he kept it in an envelope at lease ten grand. Right after he takes his shower he lays down. But gets back up and goes into the bathroom one last time he finishes up there and returns to bed.

***

In the middle of the night all three of the girls are in the hallway of the hotel. "Come on Annette, shit girl," Lenore whines.

The Georgetown Heist

"Look y'all go ahead I'm staying with him for a minute," she responds.

"Girl I've hit and you up here bullshitting, fuck that love shit Annette. It's about this paper bitch, or have you forgotten?" Lenore asks her while holding Babylon's envelope. Annette recognizes the envelope she know's it belongs to Babylon.

"Damn these mother fuckers are cool as fuck. We might can do something with these dudes, shit start over or something I don't know. But what I do know is that they're some good mother fuckers."

"Look you start over, but you know how this shit goes girl. You can't stay, and we gone with these tricks money."

"I'm not gonna tell them nothing, I'm not some rotten ass bitch. I'll take my chances with Teeny-Man crazy ass."

"Look we gone girl, you better come," Lenore tells her.

"Nawl y'all go ahead," at this point Mona, the girl that's with Juice-Hoop speaks up.

"Annette might got something, Juice ain't no bad dude either."

"Fuck y'all I'm gone," she says and spins on her heels and leaves. As she walks through the hallway she makes a swiping motion with her right index finger and places it in her mouth.

"Sweeeeeet!" She says with a smile on her face as she's leaving. Annette and Mona goes back to their rooms and go to sleep. Inside Babylon's room he's wide awake just looking up at the ceiling.

"That's crazy all over the world sisters are the same." He says to himself and then turns over and goes to sleep.

***

As the cab drops her off in front of her house. She pays him from out her purse she goes into the house and up to her room. Now taking off her clothes she goes straight into the shower after taking care of herself.

Chapter 23

She put's a man's button up long sleeve shirt.
Before she goes to sleep she decides to count her
nights take from the out of towner. As she opens up
the envelope she looks inside of it, and her mouth and
eyes are wide open.

She reaches for the paper on top to read what it
says. "I am from South East D.C., and this is called
the pigeon drop, bitch." She looks back down into the
envelope and sees nothing but hotel coupons.

***

He get's into his house he sees that his new phone has
messages on it. So he checks them all and discovers
that he still doesn't have the information that he
wishes for. But he still puts out his prices for the
products he still doesn't have yet, if he even get's
it.

The temporarily home is elegant all around. With
white walls, white wall to wall carpeting and matching
white furniture. The long wall in the living room is a
full mirror. It also has a one hundred twenty five
inch flat screen mounted on the wall surrounded by an
entertainment system.

With ceiling fans above in the living room and in
the dining room areas. He just looks into the dining
room, but doesn't goes in. He turns to check out the
kitchen. The new Maytag refrigerator, with ice and

water dispenser along with a T.V. monitor on it's face.

Everything in it is also white, so he just looks through the rest of the house to make sure all is well. "Vhere arz yooh mi young vrave comradez? Jaquiel Froscios iz looking forz yoohs," he says to himself in a soft questionable voice.

***

After leaving their hotel the young men heads over to Babylon's cousin house. Once there he already knows what to do.

"Hey Cuz we have an appointment well to be truthful we have two of them," Tootie tells Babylon. As they head out the house Tootie sees that they still have two of the girls from last night, and they have gotten themselves a rental car also. But Babylon still rides with his cousin.

"Hey Cuz what's up with your men, they never had pussy before?" Tootie asks in the most sarcastic tone.

"I can't speak for what another man has had or has not. I don't do any watching." Babylon responds.

Tootie still looking at his family member as they are followed by Teeny-Man and Juice-Hop with the two girls in tow, and Tootie refuse to let it go.

"Cuz when you up North jokers come down here and get that sand between y'all toes you mother fuckers don't know how to leave, and end up all in love and shit."

"Slim I couldn't care less about love, but if they are feeling them girls then so be it. I'm here for the stones Tootie. And as far as me staying down here, I love all the four seasons."

They smile at one another as they are now on Seventy Ninth Street and turns into this place called Flea Market U.S.A., they all gets out. But Tootie gives a motion with his hands for the girls to stay put, they act like they don't appreciate the hand waving.

Once inside the building they heads to one of the shops a jewelry shop and they're met by an

Arab looking man.

"Tootie my man what can I do for you?" The Arab ask.

"You know what I talked to you about," Tootie answers the Arab. He takes them towards the counter and a woman buzzes them into the back. Once in the back Babylon pulls out one of the small stones so the Arab can take a look at it. "What's this?" The Arab asks uncertainly.

"That's what we're trying to find out," Babylon replies sarcastically he already knows what he's got, he thinks.

The Arab goes and places his apparatus on his eye, and start to examine the stone. His face is squashed up they know its a hit.

"This isn't worth anything," the Arab tells them.

"Look Habeeb! We know this shit is worth millions, you're trying to pull a stunt. That shit ain't gonna work on us, that Afghan shit you're trying to pull," Teeny-Man tells him.

"I'm Iranian, and this stone is worthless, it's so poorly made it could never pass for a diamond, only from far far away."

"Okay thanks Ark," says Tootie. And they all leave out the store and heads for the cars.

"I got one more set up for you Cuzzo." Tootie informs Babylon. As they ride through Miami Babylon is numb right now at the thought of some Arab trying to play him out his stones.

"Tootie you and this Arab, are you close?" Babylon asks his cousin.

"He's just a dude that sells jewelry." The young man's mind is made from that point. They're not that far now from their destination.

"Cuzo this is The Carol Mart, it's old name was One Hundred Eighty Third Street Flea Market." Tootie informs him. Once out the same procedure happens with the girls now they are met by an Asian man.

"Popa Sawn! What's happening with you?" Tootie asks the old man.

"It's been slow," the old man replies.

"I'm here on that business we talked about. I'm

trying to go into the back and talk to you." Tootie
tells him.

"You come, they stay," he tells Tootie. As Babylon
now hands over the one stone he has on him. A little
time later Tootie and the old Asian man both come out,
and now the young men and Tootie all head out the
store. Now at their cars they huddle up.

"Cuz the man said this here ain't nothing. It's
not even a stone, its something else and he says that
its man made also. But whoever made this spent a nice
piece of money to have it made. Because he doesn't
know what it is he can't do nothing for you." They all
just look at each other for the moment.

"You gave up the numbers to both of them?" Babylon
asks his cousin.

"Yeah."

"They will call watch." Babylon assures them all.
They all now get into their own cars and go their
separate ways.

***

His cell phone rings he answers it he is given the
information he needs and leaps into action. He has
gotten the break that he needed.

"Thzey gave yooh thzee numbah alszo? Yez givezit
tzoo mi it'z like thzey arz looking forz mi insztead.
I'm coming comradez," says Jaquiel.

***

Since the explosion there has been silence in the
command center.

"Sir we have a hit on them, they are trying to
sell the stones in Miami," Mrs. Culp tells Jimmy.

"Okay get a buyer on them and bring me my
weapons," Jimmy tells them. Now the command center is
in full swing their main objective is to set up a buy
with the young men and retrieve the weapons back.

***

199

Babylon leans his head up against the window of the car he's confident that one of the jewelry shops will call back and asks to see the stones again. His new throw away phone rings.

"Yeah who's this?" Babylon answers.

"Canz yooh zuzt hear mi out pleaze? I vish tzoo vuy allz of jorw merchandize, or helpz yooh tzoo get vid of thzem," the caller tells him.

"How did you get this number?"

"Vith hoom dzid yooh leave it?"

"Hold on for a second," Babylon tells the unidentified caller. Now motioning his hand at Teeny-Man to pull over. "Hey pull over slim." Babylon tells him. As the car pulls over Babylon gets out the car and waves to his friends to do the same.

"Yeah I'm back where would you like to meet?"

"Anyvhere yooh feel comfortable," he responds.

"Okay meet me at the One Hundred Eighty Street Market in one hour."

"I'm on mi vay," they both hangs up their phones and Babylon looks at both Juice-Hop and Teeny-Man.

"Look we got action on the stones, shake the girls we have to get proper. And go meet whoever this is trying to buy the stones," he continues.

As they get ready to see what's up with this buyer the young men are arming themselves to the teeth. And Babylon takes one of the stones with them for a tester.

"Let's hurry up over there and try to beat them to the punch," says Babylon.

They reach the destination they see nothing out the ordinary in plain view. So they all get out the car and begin to watch. But it's as if they are just watching everybody in the parking lot. Now Juice-Hop sees a man who's looking at them or at lease in their direction.

"Hey y'all." Juice-Hop says while tilting his head in the man's direction.

At this time Babylon opens up the other phone to see if any of the people are around, they are not. What he did find out is just as bad. He sees that a message has been left for him and he sees there are a lot more dots in the immediate and outside areas.

"I'm a potential buyer I've been trying to buy since you got it. Call 202-440-4894," is what the message says as he scans through the rest of the text messages he comes across another one. "I'm a buyer, who wish to buy all sixteen of the big ones, and all the little ones." He now turns to his friends.

"Damn y'all, Bernard is dead he got caught or something they got his five big stones and the rest of his small ones," he informs them. Before they knew it a pair of headlights are flashing on and off at them.

"We're on y'all anything looks funny crush it." Babylon instructs them.

They all start to walk when Babylon nods his head to tell Teeny-Man to go out wide and the same for Juice-Hop. They split up, but all paying close attention to their surroundings. Babylon reaches the vehicle he sees that there's only one person that's in plain view, so he beckons for him to get out the car.

Once out the car the man is sharply dressed. The young men are watching him like a hawk.

"Mi name iz Jaquiel Froscios," he introduces himself. Babylon and the other two remain silent. "And yooh arz Bab-boo-lawn, yez?" He asks. Babylon just stares at him after hearing him call his name. "Or dzoo yooh pre-fairh, Nimrod?" He continues.

"I'm here to do business," the young man tells the Frenchman.

"Yez, and vee szhall."

"I have one on me now," Babylon informs him and now hands him the one stone. He's met by a smile from the foreigner and it's a real smile upon his face. As he checks the stone out he knows that this is what he's been looking for. But right then and there, Jaquiel phone rings, and he answers it in front of them.

"Yez? Vhat? Okay thzen vee goh now," he says and hangs up the phone. "Vee have tzoo goh now people arz coming forz uz, yez? I vill follow yooh," he finishes as he's handing Babylon back the stone.

"No we'll follow you," says Babylon. They're getting into their vehicles its too late, vehicles galore are pulling up to a screeching halt. And they are not friendly they tries to block them in. The Frenchman looks back at the young men and see that they are getting out the vehicle.

The young men opens fire upon the cars blocking the entrance. The Frenchman follows their suit they light up the cars with ease. As if they thought they were going to come along easily.

The Frenchman is shooting away also Babylon sees that he's not playing either. Babylon is trying to go out through the back way, but the firing is too, heavy. But they have to go forward with their assault plus the Frenchman.

Babylon is reloading he sees that Jaquiel has two guns firing and have silencers on them also. He can see that he's firing the both of them. He can't see what kind they are from his distance, but he's working with them.

As the Frenchman advances pass some parked cars Babylon sees him and begins to lay down heavy fire on their enemy. Babylon and the other two lay down fire while the Frenchman sneaks up on them from the side. The silenced fire keeps his position hid from their enemy. By the time they look up the Frenchman had done killed six men.

But their numbers are too great for them to keep their ground. They are trying to surround them they can escape, but Babylon refuses to leave this black Frenchman. For one he's helping them put up a fight, and two he believes the man can help get rid of the stones, and three Babylon will never leave a man for dead.

Babylon and Jaquiel make eye contact once more. This time it's Jaquiel who's pointing at the back entrance for Babylon and them to go. The enemy is slowly coming around to surround them. Babylon refuses to leave, Jaquiel gives the signal again, and again Babylon refuses. Jaquiel respects the young man's decision. "Ah! Nouveau honneur." ("Ah! Young honor.") But he can't get caught, he's the one with the stones.

"Ils ne passeront pas," ("They shall not pass,") Jaquiel tells Babylon about the agents.

With a nod of his head the Frenchman shows a smile

smile. Babylon Juice-Hop and Teeny-Man get to going
out the back way to leave the parking lot. Babylon
can't help but to look back at Jaquiel, and he's
putting up a fight.

As they are leaving Babylon reloads and sticks his
gun out the window. Juice-Hop follows suit they lay
down fires that finally frees the Frenchman. As
Jaquiel runs to his vehicle he knows that it was the
firing from the young men that freed him.

***

"**Sir, they got** away and so have Jaquiel Froscios."
Mrs. Culp informs Jimmy.

This was supposed to have been a trap for he young
men, but they once again escapes unharmed. Underneath
Jimmy nose the entire command room is just won over by
these young men beating the odds this long. They have
seen trained operatives die within hours of a
termination order on their lives.

But these young men had defied the United States
government, and thus the command room has just became
their biggest fans now.

***

So as time goes by the young men are waiting for the
Frenchman to call them back, but he doesn't Babylon
decides to call him up.

"Hey, is this Jack?"

"Comrade, I'm glad tzoo hear fromz yooh. Let'z
meet onze more szhall vee?" Jaquiel asks.

"How do you pronounce your name?" Babylon asks the
Frenchman.

"Jack-kwee-ale, Fros-swah."

"Would it be all right if I just called you
Frenchy?"

"I vould vee honored."

After getting the instructions to get to his
house. Babylon and the other two young men goes
straight over there. Once there they go up to the door
and rings the door bell and he lets them in.

"Hello Comradez I hope jorw trip hear vaz nize, yez?" Jaquiel asks.

They all just shake their heads in agreement and looking around his house.

"Hey Frenchy, whoever those people are they been all over us for awhile now. I say we go and get them before we do anything else. Because as long as they are out there they will try to find us again," Babylon explains.

"Dzoo yooh know howz tzoo locates thzeze inzivizualz?

"Yeah I know how."

"Aux arms." ("To arms.") The Frenchman tells them. They are inside one of Jaquiel's safe houses and he goes and get some more of his gear. They are just looking at him go and get all this stuff of his.

"Man, this mother fucker goes hard as shit in the paint," Teeny-Man tells Juice-Hop and Babylon.

Watching Jaquiel they almost forgot their own stuff. They have to make a run themselves for their assault. Jaquiel tries to give them some if his stuff, but they refuses it. They want their own stuff, so they leave Jaquiel and go on the their hotel to get their tools.

While they are getting ready, Teeny-Man take Annette to the side and hands her a lot of money gives her a kiss along with his family's number. On the drive back over to Jaquiel's they all know its an all out battle.

"Hey y'all I don't know how it's going to play out, but push come to shove knock down everything in your way," says Babylon.

Now at the Frenchman house they get out to meet him. Jaquiel is standing out front and Babylon goes to the trunk, and gets out his M-16 and his duffel bag. All of the young men had already reloaded back at the hotel and is ready for war.

"Once I cut this phone on I'll be able to see where they all are. And then we can go and get them all." Babylon tells them. He cuts on the phone's screen. "I got'em."

"Entre nous dieu defend le droit." ("Between us,

The Georgetown Heist

God defends the right.") Jaquiel tells them.

***

After getting off his plane he catches a cab straight
for the Dade County Police Department Headquarters.
He's going to see an old friend of his from the
Marines. As he enters the building he sees that this
is one clean establishment.

The Metropolitan Police Department Headquarters in
D.C. is a real stink hole compared to this place. He
walks up to the receptionist desk and sees a young
lady sitting behind it.

"Yes I'm here to see Detective Joseph F. Mercury,"
he tells her.

"Is he expecting you, Sir?"

"He's always expecting me."

"What's your name Sir?"

"It's Vic Williams, Detective Vic Williams," she
gets on the phone and makes a call.

"Yes, who is this? Oh hi girl, this is Harmony let
Mr. Mercury know that a Detective Vic Williams is here
to see him. She hangs up the phone and returns to what
she was doing. A few minutes later the phone rings on
her desk, and she answers it.

"Yeah, he's right here okay then, will do." With
the phone still in her hand she looks at Vic and tells
him: "Sir, you can go right up he's waiting for you."

He gets on the elevator and goes on up to the
fifth floor. He has seen which floor he's on from the
directory. Now he exits the elevator and starts
looking for his friend when he hears a voice.

"Vic Williams, you ain't got a lot, but until you
get what you need baby hold what you got." He knows
the voice, it's his friend and with no time to waste
he gets straight to the point.

"Can we go somewhere and talk, Joe?" He asks.
Sensing that this is no vacation visit, Detective
Mercury says: "Sure Vic come with me," as he leads him
to his office.

"Look Joe, I have a major problem that might just
become your problem. Last week a diamond bank was hit

205

Chapter 24

and two people were killed in the heist. But the strangest thing happened, national security agents with level five security clearance came and took one of the bodies out. A female, and now these same agents are looking for these young boys who supposed to have done it, or know who done it or seen something they had no business seeing.

"I received a phone call stating that they are down here trying to get the ice off. A tip that came from a female I need all you got so I can find these young boys. And try to figure out why the suits really want them so badly. It just don't add up Joe," he tells his friend.

"Okay get settled in and I will give you everything I got on fencers, pawn shops, mob and mob ties the works," he informs Vic.

And with that the two men gets up and goes for the door. This is no social visit from Vic. But a job that has brought him from Washington D.C. to Miami, Florida for the sole purpose of finding these young men.

***

As they get ready to leave Jaquiel get's a phone call. That he takes in front of the young men. The look on his face all but says that its good news for him. He sees that they are watching him and gives them all a nod.

The Georgetown Heist

"He looks too, damn happy," Teeny-Man says. They can see that he is really into this phone call. But they watch and monitors his body language and listens to what he is saying to the person on the other end.

"Yez, yez, tzell mi whooz allz on voard andz whooz vowed conziteration tzoo thzee cauze?" He asks Ponc'e. As Ponc'e is about to start he gathers his thoughts and papers together.

"Monsieur, I'm gohing tzoo runz off thzee namez tzoo yooh and whoo pre-payed. And yooh tzell mi whooz tzoo scratch off and whooz tzoo contzact."

"That'z good enough forz mi Ponc'e."

"Morenzanist Patriotic Front, thzey arz fromz Honduras."

"Scratch thzem."

"Mujahedin-e Khalq Organization, thzey arz fromz Iran."

"Scratch thzem, thzee Jooz vill vee allz ovah mi azz."

"National Liberation Front of Corsica, vut of courze yooh knowz thzem."

"Scratch thzem, thzey vill vee upzet, but szell it tzoo thzem now and thzey vill veleaze it vere I'll vee wun dzay."

"National Liberation Army, thzey arz fromz Columbia."

"Scratch thzem."

"Nestor Paz Zamore Commission, thzey arz fromz Bolivia. Hmmm! Holdz thzem forz a szecond, got it. New People's Army, thzey arz fromz thzee Philippines."

"Scratch thzem."

"Palestine Liberation Front, thziz iz thzee wun fromz Iraq." He goes through some papers for a second. "And thzey szent a dzonation of twzoo hundred fifty million dzarlarz, just forz conziteration," Ponc'e continues.

"Szend thzem flowerz and tzell thzem thzey vill vee conzitered."

"Palestine Islamic Jihad, thzey arz fromz Palestine."

"Scratch thzem."

"Party of Democratic Kampuchea, thzey arz fromz Cambodia."

"Scratch thzem."

"Popular Front For The Liberation of Palestine, thzey arz fromz Syria, and thzey szent a dzonation of wun hundred million dzarlarz juzt forz conziteration."

"Szend thzem flowerz."

"Qibla and People Against Gangsterism and Drugs, thzey arz fromz South Africa."

"I could vuy a nize pieze of land if thzey ever arz tzaken szeriously, and szome influence alzo. Szee how much thzey can come up vith forz a dzonation?"

"Red Army Factor, thzey arz fromz old Germany."

"Never again vill thzey vee onz tzop, scratch thzem."

"Red Brigades, thzey arz fromz Italy."

"Scratch thzem."

"Revolutionary Armed Forces of Columbia, thzey szent a dzonation of wun million dzarlarz."

"Szend thzem tzen million dzarlarz pluz thzeir wun million bock and thzen scratch thzem."

"Next up is thzee Revolutionary Organization, thzey arz fromz Greece and thzey szent a dzonation of wun billion dzarlarz. And all in Euro, I might add and thzey vant vhat ever vee can szend."

"Yez, yez, tzell thzem thzey vill vee conzitered and szend thzem flowerz."

"Revolutionary People's Struggle, thzey arz fromz Greece."

"Scratch thzem."

"Sendero Luminoso, thzey arz fromz Peru."

"Scratch thzem."

"Sipah-e-Shahaba Pakistan, thzey vish tzoo szee a dzemonsztration. And thzey szent twzoo hundred fifty million dzarlarz."

"Tzell thzem, thzey allz veady hozz dzemonsztraion, it hoppened in America and I'm vith thzee young men now."

"Tupac Amaru Revolutionary Movement, thzey arz fromz Peru, and thzey vish tzoo vork on consignment."

"Scratch thzem, whoo thzee hell thzey thzink I am,

Pablo Escobar? Consignment!"

"Abu Sayyaf Group, thzey arz fromz thzee Philippines."

"Scratch thzem."

"Al Gam'a al Islamiyya, thzey arz fromz Egypt and szent wun hundred fifty million dzarlarz."

"Szend thzem flowerz."

"Al Qaeda contact hozz veen on uz all dzay. Thzey vant all thzat vee hov and thzey vant it now. Vut vill pay uz at a later dzate."

"Szo greedy, tzell thzem tzoo stzop playing and tzoo tzell thzeir American bockerz tzoo hurry up and szend thzem thzeir allowanze."

"Armata Corse, I know thzat yooh arz not gohing tzoo give thzem szomethzing?"

"No, vut thzey arz stzill Frenchmen, scratch thzem."

"Armed Islamic Group, thzey arz fromz Algeria."

"Scratch thzem."

"Aum Shiri Kyo, thzey arz fromz Japan, and thzey szent five hundred million dzarlarz."

"Szend thzem flowerz."

"Basque Homeland and Freedom, thzey arz fromz Spain."

"Scratch thzem."

"Chukahu-Ha, thzey arz fromz Japan."

"Scratch thzem."

"Democratic Front For the Liberation of Palestine-

"Howz many terrorzt groupz dzoo thzey hozz in Palestine? Thzey need szomethzing in Palestine, yez? Scratch thzem."

"Fatah Revolutionary Council, thzey arz fromz Lebanon, and thzey szent wun hundred million dzarlarz for conziteration."

"Szend thzem flowerz." Ponc'e is hesitant and now begins:

"Fatah Tanzim, thzey arz fromz Palestine."

"Scratch thzem."

"Force 17, thzey arz fromz Palestine."

"Thzey need another Prophet in Palestine, goh ahead and scratch thzem."

"Hamas szent wun point five billion dzarlarz," as

Ponc'e's voice trails off.

"Szend thzem szome green and vhite flowerz, vut scratch thzem and keep thzee money."

"Harakat ul-Mujahad, thzey arz fromz Pakistan and thzey szent twzoo hundred fifty million dzarlarz."

"Szend thzem flowerz."

"Hizbollah Lebanon Party of God."

"Scratch thzem."

"Hizb-ul Mujehideen, thzey arz fromz Pakistan."

"Scratch thzem."

"Irish Republic Army, thzey szent wun hundred fifty million dzarlarz in Euro."

"In Euro?"

"Yez, pluz thziz iz thzee veal I-R-A."

"Thzey szay thzat thzey dzon't need it now, vut may need it in thzee future. Thzey szaid thzat thzey arz vetired fromz active dzuty. Vut szometimez shzit happenz."

"Yez, I luv thzem," he stops to gather his thoughts for a moment, and finishes. "Tzell thzem thzat vhen shzit happenz, I vill hov szomethzing forz thzee shzit."

"Jamaat ul-Faqura, thzey arz fromz Pakistan."

"Scratch thzem."

"Japanese Red Army."

"Scratch thzem."

"Jihad Group, thzey arz fromz Egypt."

"Scratch thzem."

"Kach and Kahane Chai, thzey arz fromz Israel."

"Not on mi vatch vill thzey get anythzing, scratch thzem."

"Kurdish Workers Party, thzey arz fromz Turkey."

"Scratch thzem."

"Lashkar-e-Toiba, thzey arz fromz Pakistan."

"Scratch thzem."

"Lautoaro Youth Movement, thzey arz fromz Chile."

"Scratch thzem."

"Liberation Tigers Tamil Edlan, thzey arz fromz Sri Lanka and thzey szent wun hundred million dzarlraz for conziteration."

"Scratch thzem, thzee children vill suffah thzee mozt, vut keep thzee money."

"Loyalist Volunteer Force, thzey arz fromz Ireland."

"Nobodies, scratch thzem."

"Manuel Rodriquez Patriotic Front, thzey arz fromz Chile."

"Scratch thzem, I vacationed thzere before." As the young men takes a real close noticed of what is taking place before them. This Frenchman has totally forgotten them, they continue to watch him.

"Abu Nidal Organization alzo known as Fatah The Revolutionary council, thzey arz fromz Palestine."

"Scratch thzem."

"Al-Aqsa Martyrs Brigade, thzey arz fromz Israel and thzey szent five billion dzarlarz for veal conziteration."

"I juzt gave thzem veal conziteration, scratch thzem."

"Ansar al-Islam, thzey arz fromz Iraq."

"Scratch thzem."

"Asbat-al-Ansar, thzey arz fromz Lebanon."

"Scratch thzem."

"Islamic Movement of Uzbekistan, thzey szent wun hundred million dzarlarz."

"Szend flowerz."

"Jaish-e-Mohammed, thzey arz fromz Pakistan."

"Scratch thzem."

"Hey French man, what's the business slim?" Teeny-Man asks him. The Frenchman places one finger in the air towards them.

"Ponc'e yooh hozz a good enough idea of vhat I vant. I vill call yooh if I need more forz tranzferz," he hangs up the phone and now turns towards the young men. "My apologiez gentlemen, thzat vaz forz all of uz, tzoo szecure thzee fundz for thzee merchandize."

So at this time they all heads for the door and leaves one after another. They get into different cars and the Frenchman follows them. Once at a fast food place they pulls into it's parking lot. Babylon gets out with the cell phone in his hand.

"Once I cut this phone on I can look at the GPS map to locate the people. So let's get ready because they can locate me too."

As he cuts on the phone they are now looking at the red icons on the phone, but Juice-Hop and Teeny-Man can't make anything out. Babylon and Jaquiel know what they're looking at. Babylon along with Jaquiel Froscois sees that they're in a place that has a lot of them present.

So Babylon get's the address to that location. It is a house, but just as they were about to close the phone. A red icon rolls by right in front of them, as the Frenchman and Babylon looks around they see many vehicles.

"A bientot," ("I'll see you later,") the Frenchman tells them as he's about to eliminate someone.

"No! We might can use them." Babylon tells him. As they all get back into their cars, Jaquiel follows the young men as they weave their way through traffic. The Frenchman seems to have lost sight of the target. But Babylon is dead on the case the young man scans the area until he sees a white woman in a black M-3 BMW.

So he watches her, but all the time he's remembering Maria from the diamond bank. Now he put forth the effort to see something himself. He watches her with an steady eye, and sees what he's been waiting for, a sign.

She's watching her mirrors and her surroundings like she has been taught to do so the young man jumps into action.

"Teeny-Man, we got to get into that Beamer," he says while pointing at it. Juice-Hop goes to the helm of the action, but Babylon stops him in his tracks and now points to a car with another white woman in it.

"Go and take her car and drive it into hers very lightly. And Teeny-Man you go and take care the rest," he instructs them.

The plan goes into motion and the young men are executing it to the fullest. Juice-Hop goes and snatches up the white woman and pulls her out the car. Once he has her outside he folds her up like lawn furniture, wiht a hard blow to her mid section that knocks the wind out her.

He takes the car and gets in position and lightly rams into the BMW. He now gets out to check on the woman.

"Are you okay Miss?" Juice-Hop asks the woman.

"Yes I'm okay," she answers him. Now there's a lot of people that's watching the accident scene. This is what Babylon is hoping for. Knowing that the woman wouldn't want to draw any attention to herself.

"Look Sir, I'm okay there's no reason to be concern about me. I'm fine and the car is not damaged."

At that exact time Teeny-Man is getting in position in the back seat of the car. He's already in it, and nobody seen him. They are too busy watching the two people talk. Babylon is now looking from the driver's seat of the car and sees it all unfold right before his eyes.

As Juice-Hop and her approaches her car he makes sure that she don't have a chance to see Teeny-Man in the back seat of the car.

"Ma'am are you sure you're okay?" He asks. All the time he has his hand on her shoulder making her pay attention to him. She get's into the car looking around to make sure that nobody has made her or no one is taking pictures of her.

Now she's pulling off and checking her rear view mirror to see if she's being followed by anyone. About two miles later she gets the scare of her life once she hears a man's voice.

"Turn off here to the right."

"Who the hell are you?" She asks him while looking in her rear view mirror. "And what are you doing in my car?" She continues to ask.

"Shut up bitch and pull the fuck over." She's acting as if she's doing as told. "Bitch don't try nothing stupid to make me kill you ass in this car."

She's not taking him seriously and decides to speed up and go the opposite direction. She zigzags through traffic to get him off balance. But it doesn't work, he now places his gun in the back of her seat and yells to her:

"Stop bitch! Stop bitch before I bust your simple ass."

She didn't and he does, he presses his gun against

the back of her seat. The seat acts damn near as a
mini silencer for the big gun. The shot goes through
the seat, her and the dashboard, coming out the hood
of the car.

As he scrambles to grab the steering wheel of the
car, she is still driving it. With both hands on the
steering wheel she is now feeling the effects of dying
in the car and pulls over and begins to talk.

"Please help me," she begs him.

"Nawl bitch I told your simple ass to pull the
fuck over didn't I?"

"I can still make if you take me to a hospital."
At this point he is watching her every move. Knowing
that this woman might be carrying a weapon, but the
slug from the Desert Eagle has taken it's toll on the
woman's frame. He can now see the blood coming from
her mouth.

"Bitch it don't look good for you."

"Please help me, I won't go to the police." he
looks at her with a blank stare on his face. Waiting
for the others to catch up with him. As he looks
around for his crew he reaches over her to open the
driver's side door.

Just as she's reaching for something inside her
purse. He sees her the entire time and is waiting on
her to make her move. And she does it, but its useless
as she attempts to pull her gun.

He goes between the driver's and passenger's seats
and fires two shots into the woman's chest. With the
driver's side door still open the two bullets goes
through her, the seat and the trunk leaving out to hit
the side of the building.

Her blood now flows down her clothes and body. He
can smell it in the air he now gets up in the
passenger's seat and places his back up against the
door and raises his foot and kicks the woman out the
car.

As her body lay half way on the ground. He can see
the gun burns from the gun being so close up on her
when it was fired. He hears the cars coming behind him
they are now pulling up beside him.

"What happened?" Juice-Hop asks him.

Chapter 25

"The bitch tried me," Teeny-Man answers him.

"Shit I see you had no problem in getting her attention." Juice-Hop continues.

"Fuck her, crazy bitch." They all looks at the mess Teeny-Man has made of this woman.

"This was not part of the plan, the plan was to keep her alive to take back to the house. Slim, how are we going to use this woman now?" Babylon asks him.

"I will improvise with plan B," Teeny-Man answers him.

At this time Teeny-Man jumps in the car and slides the driver's seat all the way back and takes the woman's body and places it back in the car. He now drives to an nearby alleyway. They all follows him there where he pushes the woman out the car once more. He gets out and places her body into a big dumpster.

"Hey get me some towels and stuff y'all," he asks them. They brings him what he asks for and he wipes down everything, he even wipes down the entire inside of the car. As Teeny-Man looks up he sees a UPS truck. At this time he gets an idea so he goes back into the big dumpster to retrieve the woman's body.

"Man what the fuck you doing?" Juice-Hop asks.

"I'm about to put this monster plan in motion, if the fuck you don't mind," he was about to go up to the UPS truck, when he spots an Ashton Trucking Inc.® straight truck and stops in his tracks.

"That's the one right there," Teeny-Man tells

himself. He know that the independent trucking giant, straight truck does air freight and curb side deliveries. He's hoping its some blank delivery forms in the truck.

***

It is a African American male driving the truck and Teeny-Man decides to have a talk with the man first. He had his talk with him and now gives him a large amount of money for himself.

"Okay, I need a volunteer for this one," he tells everyone, nobody says a word.

"So I don't have any volunteers for this one huh? Well let me see here, okay French man it's you." Now they all gather around Teeny-Man to hear his plan.

"I vouldn't hozz velieved it hod it not veen forz mi veing here. It iz thzeze ignorant, stzupid and unconventional methodz along vith thzere azzaultz thzat keep thzem alive." Jaquiel says to himself.

As they continue to hear Teeny-Man's plan the worst its sounding. Nobody likes the idea that he comes up with especially the Frenchman.

"I'm telling y'all this will work, it has to work," he pleads his case. They all stares him down for a few moments. Babylon shakes his head, and looks up at Teeny-Man with a look of uncertainty.

"Hey slim, if this is your best plan, lets hear your worst," Juice-Hop asks him.

"This will work if its done right we have to start thinking a little better than what we've been thinking around here. Or we are going to loose one of these battles, and it's going to cost us heavy," he tells them all.

"Okay slim you got it tell us the plan one more time and we're going to roll with it. I say no to it, but if you think this will work then I'm all for it." Babylon assures him.

As they gather once more Teeny-Man's plan is explained once more. This time it is listened to more carefully. Once he's finishes with his debriefing, it is time to put it into motion.

The Georgetown Heist

When Babylon and Juice-Hop pass the house they don't have a visual on who is there. So Babylon phones the others to tell them about their find.

"We're still a go," says Teeny-Man. In front of the house is a gate, and one must be let into the drive way. As the truck move into position it drives right up to the gate. With its horn blowing finally someone comes out the house.

"Yeah! What you want?" The man who comes out asks.

"I have a delivery for a Ms. L. Tucker," the truck driver tells him.

Before the drive over Teeny-Man took the liberties to check to see who's name the house was in. As soon as he tries to radio back into the house. He sees the black BMW drives up and wave.

As he see its the woman whom he had been waiting for. He now tells the truck driver to go ahead with his load inside the gate. As the truck drives through the M-3 now turns in extremely fast through the driveway.

With the man not paying any attention to the woman. He sees the gate closes and goes to unload the huge boxes. Using the dolly he and another man takes the heavy boxes into the back of the house, he signs for the washer and dryer and tips the driver, and sees him out.

One of the men goes to let the truck out. While the other goes to check on the woman. Soon as the truck is halfway out the gate, in comes Babylon and Juice-Hop with their guns drawn on the man. The other man is still walking towards the BMW.

"Kelly! Kelly, do you hear me? Come on I know you're not still mad with me are you?" The man asks. Before he can get his words out again he is met by an Desert Eagle forty four magnum. His eyes tells the story, he does not believe what is happening to him.

"Don't make me," Teeny-Man tells him. Sensing that he's about to make a move first. The shot rings out like a real cannon in the quiet that was kept. The second, third and fourth shots were all the same.

Striking the man in the stomach, chest and shoulder. The young man barely see anything, but he

did see the splatter from his shoulder. As the man
falls to the ground he sees the young man get out the
car. With the car door still open he can see the woman
who looks to be dead is lying inside the car.

Babylon now turns to his prisoner and takes aim at
him without warning fires two shots at him. One in the
chest to put him down and another in his head, so he
won't have to see him again.

Juice-Hop looks and shrugs his shoulders at it.
They both see Teeny-Man, he's pointing to the back of
the house. As if to say he wants them to go around to
the rear of the house, they go.

They're met by heavy fire they both fall to the
ground to protect themselves, and they start to return
fire. They both are hiding behind the large heating
and cooling system, it gives them cover from the fire.

The rogue agents now are trying to advance upon
the young men. When they hear different fire, it is
Teeny-Man coming up from the rear. He see his friends
are pinned down and goes into action. All of his shots
hit the men in the back or back legs and that's all
that Babylon and Juice-Hop needs.

They both spring back into action with Teeny-Man
ducking back behind the house they have the green
light. Babylon and Juice-Hop starts to shoot their way
back in the game.

All one can see is the men leaving their feet and
landing on their backs. Teeny-Man goes back around to
the front of the house. He lets himself in the front
door. He takes his time he can see bullets on the
floor like somebody was in a rush to load up.

As he walks slow through the house he tries to
listen for some footsteps or heavy breathing coming
from someone. He doesn't, but continues to walk in
silence through out the living room.

Out of nowhere he hears it, shots ring out at him.
With picture frames in front of him shattering and
chunks of the plaster exploding. He fires back without
looking at where he's shooting, and doesn't hit
anything.

Now in a corner of the house he has a little bit
more room to breath. He returns his fire on them at

this time Babylon and Juice-Hop are entering the back
of the house. They spots Teeny-Man easily and they
takes cover from the fire.

"Stay back!" Teeny-Man yells to them while
motioning them with his hand they adhere. Teeny-Man
start his charge and Babylon and Juice-Hop covers him.
As he runs and shoots, he misses everything, Babylon
and Juice-Hop doesn't.

It seems that the people who are in the house are
trying to get to the back of the house for some
reason. Teeny-Man sees this and goes right at them and
starts if off.

He see one of them hiding behind a pillar, and
starts shooting at him. A piece of the plaster get's
in his eye. He jumps out from behind the pillar and
Teeny-Man takes full advantage of it. He shoots him
center mass as the man falls, Teeny-Man quickly runs
over top of him and empty his gun into him.

He is right over him and the bullets goes through
the man and strikes the marble underneath him. Looking
around for some more he sees no body else. Babylon
locks on to one that's using a couch for cover.

The young man with both big guns in his hands
starts to chew up the couch. "Oooowwwwwww!" The man
behind the couch yells out in pain. Babylon sees that
the man's gun is air borne. "I'm hit, I'm hit in the
foot," the voice behind the couch continues.

"Come out with your hands high," Babylon yells out
to him.

As he comes out slow with both his hands high,
Babylon goes towards him with both guns still pointed
at the man. He can see that the man is telling the
truth, he's shot in the foot or his ankle one.

Babylon calmly walks over to the man and places
his gun in the center of his face, and pulls the
trigger. The splatter of blood that springs forth is
like watching a balloon full of blood burst
everywhere.

Babylon don't even change facial expressions. In
the pantry there are more men planning their assault
on the young men.

***

"**Sir, there's gun** shots being reported coming from inside a house, heavy gunfire I might add," Mrs. Culp informs Jimmy.

"It's them, get a team over there now!" Jimmy orders.

***

The men plan their assault they have all, but miscalculated one thing, they are not alone. They begin their assault they're laying down heavy fire that forces Babylon and Juice-Hop to take cover. Teeny-Man can't advance either, Juice-Hop and Babylon are now pinned down also.

Out from the washing machine box comes Jaquiel Froscois. The rogue agents never sees or hears him with his silenced forty fives.

"Pssshhh, pssshhh, pssshhh, pssshhh," he guns them down before they knew what was happening. All is heard is the dropping of shell casings hitting the floor. They all takes their places together and surveys the house.

The house is indeed emptied they look pleased at their work. Teeny-Man is looking very seriously afterwards as they all start to reload.

"I'm not finished yet," he tells them. Right at that moment agents come from the back of the house. The shooting resumes, it's the most fire of the day. The agents brings heavy fire at them. Jaquiel Froscois, Teeny-Man, Juice-Hop and Babylon are not giving an inch, they're locked in a gun battle like no other.

***

Twenty minutes later vehicles pulls up to the dwelling and teams enter from different entry points. Jimmy's personal teams are on the scene. They see all the dead bodies lying around. It's a few lying on the floor barely alive, and some in severe pain. They walk over to one of the agents who's alive.

"Where are the youths?" One team member asks.

The Georgetown Heist

"They did this," he answers him.

"Where are they now?"

"They, they, ahh," is all that he can say. One of the team members picks up a gun off the floor and puts him out his misery with a bullet to his head. As the team takes a look around one of them yells out: "Over here, over here."

They all come over quickly they see that its Juice-Hop, he's covered in blood and lying on his back with his eyes wide open.

"Get the cams over here," the team leader yells out. One of the team members is already linked by way of his cell phone and beats the rest over. The entire command room can see it all as the team member slowly scans the entire room for them. They now can see Juice-Hop lying on his back. They split up and search the house with different cams.

"Go to the tile set up on the screen, I want to see all that they see when they see it," Jimmy tells the command room. The jumbo screen has just split into six different screens that's following six different people in the house.

The command room is a little bit down do to the fact that one of the young men is dead. They all have done to adore them especially Babylon, so they just continue to watch the jumbo screen. "We got another one over here," another team member yells.

As they get closer to the corpse they see that it's Teeny-Man's body and the command room is too quiet at this time.

"We found another one over here at the bottom of the stairs," another team member yells out. "It's him, I think it's him over here. As they all gather around the corpse of Babylon Jimmy breaks his silence.

"Let me see him, I want to see him face to face."

"You should have taken your ass in the field, if you wanted to see him face to face," Mrs. Culp says under her breath.

"Get a little closer I want to see the features of his face. That's it, he's not much to look at once he's been killed," Jimmy says.

It's truly over for the young men and the command

room employees are sad for them all. So young, they had their entire lives ahead of them.

"Do I sense a little mourning in here?" Jimmy asks with sarcasm in his voice. "Search them and search every last one of them," he now orders. As they search the young men they just finds some money on them. They search Teeny-Man and takes his ejaculent pills from him.

"He won't be needing these where he's going." One of the team members tells another. The same treatment is applied to Juice-Hop and Babylon. The command room employees are looking at this act in pure disgust.

"Strip them all out, and then perform cavity searches, find my weapons now!" Jimmy yells.

One of the team members places his headset down beside Babylon while he begins to strip the corpse out its clothes. The camera is facing the team member as he start taking off the dead youth's clothes the team member sighs.

"Huh, ahhhh! Um Sir," he whispers over the headset to Jimmy.

"What is it?"

"He's not dead Sir."

"Good then, before he dies off ask him where are my weapons?"

"Um Sir, he's not going to answer any questions right now." With the entire command room watching the team member's face on the screen. They just think the team member has never been around a dead body this long or never been close to one.

"And why won't he answer any questions?" Jimmy asks the team member tiresomely.

"Because he has my gun pointed at my head, Sir." Before Jimmy can yell out his mouth its too late. Babylon fires the gun twice and takes off the back of the man's head, from the front. The command room see this happen right before their eyes. Most of the women can't hold their stomachs.

Others can't watch it no longer Mrs. Gulp has gotten a new zest of life in her. Now all the young men takes action, and their assault on the team with Jaquiel Froscios coming out the empty box once

222

again surprising the team members who now don't stand a chance.

With his silenced forty fives blasting away the Frenchman catches them off balanced and off guard. Before Babylon can get off the floor he has hit four more team members, just wounding them. But once he's up he now goes over the top of every last one of them and places a bullet in their heads.

With the headset turned side ways by mistake. The entire command room, all whom wanted to see it, saw it. They sees how he walks up to each one of them and kills them one by one. The blood just burst into the air with each one head jerking violently with deathness.

Teeny-Man has had to shoot through one just to hit another, but it works. Juice-Hop finishes with his, so is the Frenchman. Only Teeny-Man has a team member left. They all begins to chase him around the back towards the man made pond.

None of them sees the sign that reads: "NO SWIMMING ALLIGATOR!" They all hops over the bricked barrier, onto the pond's bank as they take aim. Jaquiel sees the team member running towards it.

Teeny-Man pays none of it no mind, and continues to chase after him. The team member tries to jump over the alligator, but misses terribly and now the alligator has a hold of him.

"Ahhhhh! Get if off me," the team member screams

out loud. Teeny-Man who never stopped chasing him is right on the scene. And sees that the alligator has him. Teeny-Man is trying to get a good shot off, but the team member is yelling and screaming for his life.

"Boom, boom, boom, boom!" Teeny-Man puts four slugs into the alligator and it releases the man right in front of him. The alligator is not moving at all, but its eyes are blinking.

"Ahhhh, thank you," he cries out to Teeny-Man. Teeny-Man now puts his gun to the man's forehead and squeezes the trigger twice, forcing two slugs through the man's skull, his body falls on top of the alligator's.

"Vut twhy?" The Frenchman asks.

"I wasn't about to let some mother fucken alligator take my fucking kill from me," he answers.

They all return back inside the house to get their money back from the dead team members. Babylon goes up stairs and takes a minute to return. Now as they all are going back to the cars. Jaquiel Froscios is looking inside the black BMW, he sees how her wrist has a line tied around it.

And that line runs up through the safety belt hoop to the back seat. Now he knows how she waved to the man at the gate.

"Enfants perdus," ("Soldiers sent to a dangerous post,") the Frenchman says to himself. As they get into their cars the Frenchman waves to them to follow him. "How dzid Tzeeny-Mon getz thzee womond tzoo dzive thzee car?" He asks himself out loud.

***

As the women looks at each other, one decides to break the silence.

"You know they escaped a trap, and guess by who?" Tonya asks.

"By who?"

"None other than the Butcher himself."

"They'll be dead for sure before the night is over with, messing with that mad man."

"The intel states that the young boys went on the

offensive against some rogue agents and killed them
all. And they also wiped out all of Jimmy's personal
men, he's my man."

"Well I wish you luck Tonya, I have work to do
before I leave." The two women exchanges looks at one
another and LaShonne leaves out.

***

They are now at another one of the Frenchman's safe
houses. The young men already thanked him for his aid
to them.

"Hey Frenchy, look we got to try this one more
time. You don't have to go we can handle it
ourselves," Babylon tells him.

"L'union fait la force," ("Union makes force,") he
tells Babylon.

"Well look I got my gear out in the car my ammo
and stuff. I didn't even get a chance to use the M-
16," Babylon states.

The Frenchman watches them with delight, just the
though of friends going against the world gets his
honorable respect. The odds they have against them and
will face. The above average men would have turned and
ran if th government was after them.

But not these young men and Jaquiel know that he
can not tell his story without the mentioning of his
assisting them with their fight.

"We are going to leave now," says Babylon.

"Tout a vous," ('Wholly yours, at your service,")
he responds to Babylon. Jaquiel makes a phone call to
place a special order.

***

"**This is command**, come in team leaders, is anybody
copying this? Can anyone hear me?" Jimmy asks over the
com.

The command room employees looks at each other.
They know that the young men have killed all his team
members.

"Assemble H-S-F-1," Jimmy orders.

"Sir with all due respect Homeland Strike Force One is a seek and destroy unit, who's sole purpose is to locate and terminate on sight. They do not negotiate, talk nor take any prisoners.

"I really don't think its a good idea to release them on American soil maybe you should deploy another one of our teams," Mrs. Culp asks of him.

"The next time they surface, Homeland Strike Force One will be sent, activate them now. Their mission, to recover the football along with the weapons and terminate all involved," Jimmy orders Mrs. Culp.

***

Jaquiel is just getting back from somewhere and he calls the young men to come and help him get something out the car.

"What's up Frenchy?" Babylon asks him.

"Szurprize I hozz." After bringing in the crates they just watch Jaquiel.

"What's this?" Juice-Hop asks.

"Ammo."

"We got plenty ammo French man," Teeny-Man informs him.

"Thziz iz special ammo mi comradez."

"What's so damn special about your ammo?" Teeny-Man asks.

"Vecause minez arz anti-terrorizt."

"What kind of shit you're on French man?" Teeny-Man asks rudely.

"No T, they are supposed to explode when they hit their targets," Babylon explains to him. "And only governments are supposed to have them." he continues.

"Bullets that explode, yeah we're most definitely passed the life section of the sentencing guideline table chart," he tells them all.

Jaquiel Froscios gives out the ammo to the young men. They are not one hundred percent sold on the exploding bullet thing. At lease not Teeny-Man and Juice-Hop.

"Hey Bab, how do you know these things will blow up?" Teeny-Man asks him.

The Georgetown Heist

"Man I don't know for a fact, but I have read about them in gun magazines before when I was down Oak Hill."

"So it's no telling what the fuck we have, and there's no proven fact that they will explode?"

"Well slim I read that they did and only governments would have access to them. And they were invented strictly for terrorists. So I believe that they will work or explode one."

Jaquiel takes Teeny-Man objection as an objection towards him. Something that he's been feeling since he first encountered the young men. As he looks the young men get their kind of the anti-terrorism ammo, as does Teeny-Man. They take all that they can, filling every magazine they have. Babylon takes out all his ammo and replaces everything with the new ammo. Jaquiel also got some 308's for Babylon's M-16.

He reloads his one hundred round drums with the new ammo also. It's now late the young men as well as Jaquiel are now tired.

"Frenchy we are going to go. But tomorrow right after lunch we're going, so you go ahead and get some rest we'll be here tomorrow." Babylon tells him.

"Pleaze comradez you can stzay thzee night here vith mi, yez?"

"Mistafullah!" Teeny-Man says while tuning around looking strangely at Babylon and Juice-Hop. "I knew it, Frenchy is on that mother fucken hizzamma," he continues.

"Are you sure Frenchy, because we can just come back right after lunch?" Babylon informs him.

"Mi Bab-bu-lawn, you all can stzay thzee night vith mi. It'z thzee leaze I can dzoo forz yooh allz. And alvayz vemembah, people protect thzat vhich thzey hozz an interezt in," he tells them all. And then goes and show them their rooms. "Bonne nuit," ("Good night,") he tells them.

***

The next day comes late for them all nobody wakes up early. This is unusual for Babylon, and especially for

Jaquiel Froscios.

"Bon jour," ("Good morning,") he cheerfully tells the three of them as he brings them coffee.

"Frenchy slim, we don't drink coffee. We ain't been down Lorton," Babylon tells him.

"And we most definitely ain't been is the Feds, but are on our way," Teeny-Man adds.

"Vee vill go out tzoo eat, yez?" Jaquiel tells them.

"That's cool Frenchy," Babylon tells him. Juice-Hop keeps going into the bathroom and they all notices it.

"Juice, what's up with you slim?" Teeny-Man asks him. But still watching him he continues. "You got the shits or something? Hey slim, please don't blow the man shit up with that foolishness."

At the same time Teeny-Man reaches out to him pushing him in the stomach. He grunts from the push its not the kind of grunt that comes from one having bowel problems. So Babylon gets up to see what's wrong with him.

"Hey slim, what's really going on with you, are you alright?" He asks his friend with concern in his voice. Babylon goes to him and lifts up his shirt, and sees that Juice-Hop has been shot. He now looks at Teeny-Man and Jaquiel.

"Juice, you're a cripple slim you can't help us any more. You're going to slow us down, you're going to have to sit this one out."

Juice-Hop looks like the world has just come to an end. He wants so badly to go and do his part, and carry his weight.

"Can you work with it Juice?" Teeny-Man asks him.

"Yeah slim, I can still work," he answers.

"You are wounded Juice, and I know about it. That will make me look for you instead of going forward." Babylon tells him.

"I can carry my weight Bab, you don't have to worry about me if I get crushed it comes with the job."

"Au pays des aveugles les gorgne sont rios."("In the country of the blind, the one eyed men are kings.")

The Georgetown Heist

Jaquiel tells them, they all look at Jaquiel for the moment.

"Zoos-Szop, let'z mi szee it mi comrade." As Jaquiel examines it he sees that it's not that bad at all. Juice-Hop has a deep scrape that's all, right on his abdmonial. Jaquiel goes to get his first aid kit. Now he and Juice-Hop heads for the bathroom. He cleans him up and places stitches in his wound.

Now back in the living room area of the house, they all are watching Babylon knowing that he will have the finale say about it.

"Hey slim, I'm straight, Frenchy patched me up and put his mojo on me," Juice-Hop informs Babylon.

"Okay Juice, I'm not going to get in your way about it, let's go."

They goes straight for a little diner Jaquiel likes. At the diner Teeny-Man and Juice-Hop eat hardy meals as Babylon and Jaquiel has very small portions. After seeing the similarities, Jaquiel Froscios glows.

"He vould make an excellent understzudy," Jaquiel says to himself about Babylon. They finish up with their eating and head out to their cars.

"Follow us Frenchy." Babylon tells him. They drive a good ways from the diner that they had just left. As they pull up to their destination, Teeny-Man is elated he's never been in a casino before.

"Is this the spot B?" he asks Babylon.

"Yeah, this is the spot." he answers him. "The Seminole Hard Rock Cafe Hotel and Casino." he finishes. They all get out and take a good look around. The Frenchman can't believe that the young man has chosen this place to do battle.

"Arz yooh szure comrade zabout thziz plaze? It's not thzat good of a fightzing advantage forz uz."

"It'z perfect for us Frenchy, if you don't feel comfortable please sit this one out. You have done more than I would have asked for." Babylon tells him.

"Yooh walkz thrzoo life vith blinderz on?"

"No, I walk backwards, I don't care where I'm going. I just want to see where I've been." Babylon tells him.

Now Babylon gives them their assignments. All of

them are just waiting for the moment now he Jaquiel
wishes to say something to the young men before they
start.

He will take his time so that they all can hear
him clearly. "The trick is to find out how much sin
you can live with or how much you live with before it
eats you to death and or drive you mad."

Only Babylon truly get what the Frenchman said to
them. After that Jaquiel takes a step backwards, and
Babylon now steps up and pulls out the cell phone and
places a call.

"Everybody get a corner of the building and we
will divide up the floors. Juice-Hop you got the first
and second. Teeny-Man you got the third and fourth.
Frenchy you got the fifth through seventh. And I got
the the rest of it, plus the rooftop." Babylon tell
them.

They are waiting to hear what he says next to
whomever it is on the phone, but he hands it to Teeny-
Man. "Teeny-Man here," he says as he hands him the
phone while pointing out instructions to him.

"Yeah! Who's this? I wish to speak to who's ever
in charge," Teeny-Man tells the woman on the other
end. Babylon now goes and watches the scene to see if
anyone is entering the hotel.

***

"**Sir, it's for** you," Mrs. Culp informs Jimmy.

"Who is it?"

"It's them, Sir."

"Them who, damn it?" Feeling truly disrespected
she puts the call over the intercom, so everyone can
hear it.

"Okay, go ahead Sir," she tells Teeny-Man.

"Hey, I wish to speak to who's ever in charge up
in that bitch." Without the intercom picking him up,
Jimmy gives a hand motion, and writes H-S-F-1 in the
air with his finger. Mrs. Culp is now alerting the
dangerous team.

"I'm in charge, to whom am I speaking with?" Jimmy
ask.

The Georgetown Heist

"Yeah, you're in charge because you're good-n-
stupid. Government supervisors are always stupid. How
in the hell you don't know who I am-"
"You're Nimrod, Babylon!"
"Like I said you are in charge, dummy. You an
idiot. Put the nice lady back on the phone."
"But I'm the one you asked for."
"You're too much of an idiot put the nice lady
back on phone or I'm gone." with a nod of his head
Mrs. Culp answers Teeny-Man.
"Yes." Mrs. Culp answers him.
"And how are you doing today Miss lady?"
"I'm fine."
"I know that's right, you know you didn't have to
wait for that idiot to tell you to get on the phone?
You could have just gotten on."
"He's my boss."
"And not a good one either, let me ask you a
question. Why do the government always have stupid
people in charge of shit?" The entire command room is
trying to hold back their laughter, but he hears one.
"Oh! I hear that, so I'm right he's an idiot. I'm
going to write a book for y'all in there and
everywhere else. It's going to be called "When idiot
bosses happens to good work places." The room is
trying to hold it together they all are laughing now.
"Look I don't like to be disrespectful, so I wish
to know your name so that I may address you properly?"
"My name is Miss Sinclair."
"Well you must be a looker because you're a
terrible liar. You paused and your voice changed, then
you told me your name. So you lied to me knowing that
this might be the last time we'll ever speak to each
other.
"That's sad you know there's a high chance that
I'll be dead any minute now. And you won't even give
me your real name. I done figured some of it out. I
just haven't figured out the why part. Why chase us so
far and violently, it can't be for the diamonds?
"What have we done to deserve so much attention?
And in the end, you out of all people won't even tell
me your real name. And you know that they're going to

231

try to kill me-"

"No one will kill you, Sir."

"I know they won't, you heard me say try." the command room smiles at his remark.

"If you answered the phone, then you are like a top assistant and I know your pay is shitty. But you know everything, you could have warned us or something. But I guess you can call it doing your job, or y'all jobs. Can I ask one question?"

"Yes."

"Is it too, late to turn myself in? It's a little to much for me, I would like to turn myself in." Jimmy face changes expressions immediately and he's beckoning Mrs. Culp to tell him yes.

"Yes, yes you can, are you sure?"

"Hell nawl, I just wanted y'all in there to see the look on the idiot's face as if he has worn us down. Didn't he get exited?"

"Yeah, he did." the room is all smiles they can't believe his spirits doing a time like this.

"Well I've been talking to long, I am about to leave y'all, and don't bet on the idiot getting us, dead or alive."

"Good bye Mr. Barnes." Mrs. Culp says.

"See, and that's why you should be in charge. And one day when you're hungry I'll take you out to eat."

"Oh no Mr. Barnes, I'm not hungry nor am I starving and I am not an eater," she tells him. He smiles on the other end at her remark.

"Oh yeah! You must be famish," he responds to her in a playful manner. "Anyway play time is over, I've talked to you all long enough and to you all in there listening I know if you all could you would, but to those bad ones, come get us!"

With that he disconnects the phone he's being himself. He sees Babylon wave at him and goes an takes his place. The other two goes to their positions. They are waiting to see if Babylon scheme will work. As Babylon goes to his own position he sees that it worked too, good they're here already.

Babylon takes to walking at a fast pace to get to where he's supposed to be. He's met by a tall thin man

with dark shades on. He's the rogue agent's spotter
who now begins to speak into his thin headset.

Babylon knows this is not the one to waste time
on, so he takes out the spotter immediately. Forcing
the thin man through the door that leads to the
stairs. He takes a look at the man's glasses and sees
nothing, but on the side of the glasses he can now see
a camera, and he's looking directly into it.

"Death, it's the last enemy we'll face," he tells
the camera. He points his gun in the face of the man
and shoots him once. The splatter along with that
blast will signal how the day is going to go for the
people who's coming after the young men.

Babylon see the spark from his shot that hit's the
wall after it passes through the man's face. He can
see the back of the man's head from the front. The
anti-terrorist ammo explodes the inside of the man's
head that showers the young man's face.

He begins running up the stairs he can hear some
shooting off on the first floor. That meant that
Juice-Hop is trying to carry his wieght.

***

As the Frenchman awaits his prey it stills puzzles
him, how did Teeny-Man drive the car with the woman
sitting up front? But now he just shakes it off as he
decides to go into the hallway of the floor. He sees a

man dressed in all black.

He knows that this man is here for the youths. So he walks past him, and with the quickness of a gun fighter pulls out one of his forty fives with the silencer and squeezes twice. The man never sees or hears it coming as his body falls to the ground.

The Frenchman tries to catch him, but he falls to hard. Jaquiel now drags the man's badly injured body back to the stairs. Jaquiel goes back into the hallway. The just dragged man in the stairs is breathing extremely fast he's afraid to die. And in his moment of dying he tells all that can hear.

"I'm shot, I'm in the north stairwell." Everybody inside the resort that can hear him. Are too, busy with their own fighting right now trying not to get their selves shot.

***

"**Storm the resort** now, and don't let them escape this time." Jimmy yells.

***

Teeny-Man's hand is sweaty from having it squeezed so tightly on his gun for so long. He can hear the soft footsteps of someone coming up the stairs he lays down on the next flight of stairs going up.

With his gun cocked he awaits to see how many it will be as they come up the stairs in single formation. He see the first one and is about to take him out. But the first man stops and raises up his arm and balds up his fist and the rest of the men stops.

The first man breaks formation to look out into the hallway. Teeny-Man leaps into action shooting the first man twice in his back. And immediately shooting at the next man in line waiting on the stairs and all the rest of them waiting.

The anti-terrorist ammo did their job. Teeny-Man is missing vital spots, but the ammo is doing the damage for him. The agents lay down rolling around in pure pain. Teeny-Man now walks up on all of them, and

The Georgetown Heist

one by one he puts a bullet in each of their heads.

With the floor covered with blood from the agents heads who just been shot. Most of the men headset camera's are coated with their blood he is finish and the entire command room sees it. And they see first hand that life can be taken in an instant.

***

Walking back and fourth to check on all the exits and elevators on the floor Jaquiel prefers to play the part of the crocodile. They don't hunt for their food, they let it come to them. "Bing!" He hears the elevator opening up.

He get's ready for the doors to come open. It's a family of four, a mother and father along with two little girls. He smiles and nod at them as he turns he sees the white crack of the door becoming black. Somebody is peeping through the stairwell door.

Keeping his cool he gets on the elevator as the doors shuts, he pulls out both his guns and waits for a few seconds. After counting in his head he now presses the open button as he comes out the elevator. His targets are directly in front of him and the deputies can't react in time.

"Psssshhhh, pssssshhhh, pssssshhhh, psssshhhh!" is the sound that cuts through the air. With the brass emptied shells casings hitting each other, as they fall to the carpeted floor. The anti-terrorist ammo are too much for them.

***

He sees that his man count is getting low, for he's watching the death of them. "Call up a Blackhawk and an Apache," Jimmy orders. Mrs. Culp looks at him he looks back at her with an evil convinced look.

"This is going to be bad Sir, and impossible to clean up are you sure about this?" Mrs. Culp asks Jimmy.

"Yeah, you damn right I'm sure, now call it in." Just moments later Mrs. Culp comes back with an answer for him.

"Sir, we have them in Homestead."

"Then what you waiting on?" Jimmy coldly asks her. She places a phone call to Homestead Air Force Base.

"This is Homeland One, requesting chopper assistance. One Blackhawk and one Apache in waiting, you're being sent the coordinates and the intel now. The command room knows that he has gone too far with the air strikes.

***

Babylon has both his guns out creeping on the south side stairs. He's at the very top so that everything coming up will be at a disadvantage.

He sees the shadows moving down below, and above him are the emergency routes to the roof. So he softly goes up to see if he can escape from the roof if he needs to, he see that the door has a latch on it. "I can go," he whispers to himself. As the men approaches the floor they themselves are carefully looking taking calculated steps. At the door one of the men cracks it open to have a look, everything looks well.

The men advances inside but one stays behind. Sensing that it's time Babylon eases his way down the stairs as the man on guard looks in on his team. Babylon with his gun raised goes into action. "Boom, boom!"

Two shots rings so loud inside the empty stairwell that it still echo's while the shots hit's the man in his back.

The ammo is too much to bare, Babylon goes through the door to engage the rest of them. The agents themselves are coming back after hearing the shots. The young man opens up on them with the blasting of both Desert Eagles, that alone makes the guess inside their rooms get down.

Striking only three two hides from the young man. Just around the corner in front of the elevators the two men waits. Babylon turns back to the stairs and runs down to the eighth floor from the ninth.

The Georgetown Heist

Running through the eighth floor and now going
back up the stairs so he can come up behind the two
men. Once at the door behind the men he takes a
breather. Now he strikes with his first shot hitting
the back man in his buttocks, he yells out in pain
while he drops his weapon and grabbing his behind.

The man in the front get's up to fire, but it's
too late. Babylon is firing away at him and shoots him
in his right leg, hip and shin. The wounds makes him
lower his MP-5, but the pain forces him to squeeze his
trigger. And he places over thirty bullets into his
team member lying on the floor already shot in the
rear.

Now lying on the floor, but still squeezing the
trigger of an empty gun. Babylon walks over top of him
and shoots him once in the face and the explosion
paints the baseboard.

Babylon walks off to get back in position and
"Pop, pop, pop, pop, pop,!" is all that he hears he
see the wall paneling coming off the wall. He stays
low while running away. He hits the south stairwell
again with guns drawn and goes back down to the eighth
floor.

They follow him with caution one has his hand on
the door handle while another is ready to enter. The
team leader is giving a silent count, "One, two, go!"
the team leader whispers. They advance but he's
nowhere in sight. They are in single formation walking
in a low squatting form with the raise of a bald fist
from the team leader they stop.

Now shaking his hand and fingers sending two to
the north side of the resort and two to the east and
west sides. With one guard at their entry point. The
north side team are still in single formation as they
scout the wing.

They pass by a meal cart with food still on it.
The back man lifts up a top from one of the big
dishes. He sees the Cornish hen on the tray and puts
his hand over the top of it. Even through his tactical
glove he can still feel the heat from it. The front
man looks back at him.

"What?" the back man says with no sound.

237

"We have to keep moving," the front man says. The back man refuses to leave the hen alone. He takes it, and bites a huge chunk out of it. The front man sees this and shakes his head at he sight.

To clean the grease from his glove he takes the end of the meal cart table clothe. As he brings the table cloth towards his mouth he sees the biggest gun he's ever seen in his life coming from underneath the meal cart. It's pointed upwards on the right bottom side of his chin.

His eyes cut to the front man, but the front man is facing forward. "Boom!" The shot on a diagonal course leaves out the top left of his head. The spillage even wets the face and head of the front man, as well as Babylon's gun and arm.

Two more shots rings out from under the meal cart catching the front man in his back. He immediately goes down while the shots rings out the other teams now converges.

Babylon knowing that somebody is coming spring to his feet looking around he sees only one option. The two from the east wing are the first to the north wing peeping around the corner.

"I have visual they're both down," the new lead man relays through the headset.

"Are they moving?" Jimmy asks.

"Negative."

"Any signs of the targets, do you have a visual on the targets?"

"Negative."

"Proceed with caution, out."

"Roger that," the east wing men now turns the corner to walk on the north wing. "Boom, boom, boom, boom, boom!" five shots rings out. With the first shots hitting the front man directly on top of his shoulder and the second hitting him dead center on the top of his head. With the front man's head exploding, a lot of his blood goes into the eyes of the back man.

The next one misses the back man due to the blood in his eyes making him squirm backwards. The fourth shot strikes him in his left thigh which brings him to one knee and the last shot catches him in his neck.

The Georgetown Heist

They never took the time to look up the young man
had scaled the wall using his back as leverage and
using his feet to walk up the opposite wall of the
hallway. Where he just waited for whoever would be
coming for him.

The last double team comes in to aid, but it's to
late. The front man sees the bodies, but he also sees
a spark. "Boom, boom, boom, boom,!" The four shots is
enough to knock him on his backside and send the back
man further behind the corner.

With all four shots hitting him in his chest. The
threat level five body armor with the trauma plate is
no match for the fifty caliber armor piecing ammo. The
first two shots destroyed the chest plate allowing the
third and fourth to explode in his chest.

"Awwww!" Yells the back man who's in crucial
pain. He knows the team member is not faking it so he
reloads both guns and walks around to the back man and
shoots him in the face. "Ratta, tat, tat, tat, tat!"
He snoozes on the last one left at the south stairs,
but he's not shooting at Babylon he's shooting at the
hallway window.

He throws down his weapon in the middle of the
floor, looks over at what appears to be the wall to
Babylon and reaches for something. He grabs it runs
and jumps out the window. Babylon has to look behind
himself to make sure it wasn't somebody else there.

With a strange look on his face Babylon walks in
the direction of the window only to see that the man
is still hanging on to the hose suspended in the air
six or seven stories up.

While jumping down from the wall, Babylon doesn't
know that he has dropped the cell phone and once it
hit the floor the case came off it.

"We have a read again." Mrs. Culp says.

"Pinpoint the location." Jimmy yells. In what
seems like only seconds Mrs. Culp is answering him.

"It's coming from Florida, its, its, its, its The
Seminole Hard Rock Cafe Hotel and Casino," she informs
him and he looks at her with scorn.

"Is this the best that this country can do?" Jimmy
asks violently. He stares at her crazily now.

239

"Pinpoint that location," he yells at her.

"It's coming from the top floors, um its the eighth floor," she tells him.

"Get to the eighth floor quick," he tells the HSF1 team members along with his own teams and the field agents through the com. With the resort lay out on the jumbo screen the command room employees can see the red circular dot that's blinking. They are looking at a 3-D lay out of the building.

"Get out of there Nimrod," Mrs. Culp says to herself.

***

He's in his hotel room going through some of the information his friend gave him when his phone rings. "Hello?"

'Vic! I think we've got your boys, it's a shoot out at a casino. Eye witnesses says it's three black males from late teens to early twenties. I'm on my way to pick you up." Detective Mercury informs him. Vic gets to his suitcase and pulls out his gun and ammo, and goes out front of his hotel to wait for his friend Joe.

***

After hearing their orders the agents and Homeland Strike Force One, stops shooting at Juice-Hop, as his life has just been saved. Now they head for the upper level floors. "The cops must be coming," a wrong Juice-Hop says to himself.

***

Jaquiel is still firing upon the men he refuses to let them go through the door leading to the stairs. They return fire at the Frenchman. He doesn't retreat knowing that's what they want, so they can go. In his mind to get better leverage on him. He shoots a shot that catches one directly in the knee, he's down crawling on the floor. He is the fifth man to try his

240

hand at going through the door with three more left, one of them has a plan.

"Get up!" He tells the wounded man. "Get up damn it, we'll cover you," the man with the plan whispers to the wounded member.

The wounded man tries to make it to his feet. He has no knee, and the pain is unbearable. On his good leg the man who encouraged him just a second ago. Now gives an order as soon as the wounded man is on his feet. "Go, go , go!" he yells.

The remaining team members jumps towards the injured team member and heads for the door to the stairs making a run for it. Now Jaquiel starts shooting again. What the injured man thought to be an rescue attempt, wasn't nothing more than a ruse for him to be used as a human shield.

Fifteen shots from Jaquiel every last one of them hit the injured man, and the last three men makes it through the door. Jaquiel goes over to the corpse and shakes his head in disgust at what his team members did to him.

***

"**I got you** mother fucker, I got your ass now." Teeny-Man yells at an agent.

As he steps over a dead team member on his side of the building. Bodies lay all through the floor sections north, south, east and west. The hallways are smoky, debris is hovering, lights in the ceiling are hanging and the other ones are shooting sparks from them.

Holes are in all the walls, the young man has been working his tactical shotgun. And with this load, it's the last of his slug rounds. "Come on out bastards, it ain't gonna hurt," he tells them.

They stays behind the wall of another side of the hallway, Teeny-Man start shooting again at them. Placing big holes in the walls trying to hit something, but the team members stay low.

He runs out of slugs, but still has his stash from Tammy's basement, so he reloads his shotgun. Sensing he's reloading the team makes a run for the door to go

241

up stairs Teeny-Man finishes reloading and fires four shells. "Awwww! Ooohhhhh! Shit I'm hit, I'm hit," one of the team members yells out in pain.

The man lays in the middle of the hallway floor. Another is laying out between the door way with the door closed on him. Teeny-Man is trying to figure out what's that noise he was hearing.

So he replaces the six shells and walks towards the men on the floor. He sees that there's a lot of loose change on the carpet and some even stuck in doors and the walls.

As he points the barrel of the shotgun over the man in the hallway. "Hey Teeny, that's you? Come on, they're going up stairs for something," a voice tells him. Teeny-Man looks at the door now he takes a few steps back.

"Teeny-Man, I'm coming in slim," the voice alerts him.

As he comes through the door into the hallway Teeny-Man takes cover behind a corner wall. "Hey slim, it's me, fuck part of the game is this?"

He sees his friend with his gun in his hand walking through the door from the back stairs. And shoots the man in the head who's stuck between the door.

"Shit slim, these mother fuckers work too damn good. They blow up and shit be everywhere," Juice-Hop complains.

The Georgetown Heist

Now walking up on the team member who's lying in the middle of the hallway, Juice-Hop shoots him. Wiping the blood from his face he's also mad again with the splatter of blood everywhere.

"Come on slim, let's go upstairs," Juice-Hop tells Teeny-Man and they walks towards the stairs.

"Nawl, let's take the elevator slim," Teeny-Man recants.

***

After leaving the window Babylon goes two levels up, as soon as his foot touches the eleventh floor carpet he's met with fire. He takes cover back out on the stairs. Babylon now goes to the roof entrance stop and turns around with both guns in his hands.

He sees a shadow moving and readies himself. He sees that its only one person, and he recognizes the frame. "Pss! Pss!" Babylon gets his attention. The man turns quickly with his gun drawn. "Comrade." Jaquiel says to him.

He now goes to join the young man up on the next flight of stairs. "They know I'm here and are on their way." Babylon informs him. "Thzen let'z thzem comez." Jaquiel responds to him. They both can hear the door handle turn and the door crack. The team leader is placing a fiber optic camera through the door. "Bing!" It's the elevator on the eleventh floor opening.

***

"Slim I'm telling you my shit is serious. You see how them mother fuckers got some mother fucken where?" Teeny-Man explains to Juice-Hop as the doors on the elevator are opening up.

They have their guns in their hands already as they step out into the hallway.

"Oh shit!" Teeny-Man yells out and they start shooting at the team members that's at the door to the stairs. They both misses bad only wounding them hitting only in non vital spots. Although the ammo sits them down they're still in it.

243

"Move slim, let me put this shotgun on their ass,"
Teeny-Man asks Juice-Hop.

"Hold on, we might need that mother fucker,"
Juice-Hop replies.

So for now they just take up cover inside the
elevator. Jaquiel and Babylon hears he shooting and
they both can hear something against the door. Babylon
takes aim and starts shooting at the door so does
Jaquiel.

Sensing that he done cleaned up the rest he taps
on the door with his gun. Teeny-Man and Juice-Hop
heard the shooting and they now hears the tapping. And
now slowly opening the door. "Hey T, Juice?" Babylon
whispers in the hallway.

"Bab?" Teeny-Man says in a questionable voice. He
waits for a second before he answers the voice.

"Yeah slim." Babylon answers from the stairs.
Teeny-Man and Juice-Hop peeps out the elevator. Juice-
Hop is watching the back door to the stairs. Once he
sees the door crack open and Babylon sticks his head
out he comes running out the elevator.

In the middle of the hallway floor one of the team
members is crawling on his stomach. They all looks at
him and now Juice-Hop goes over to him and puts him
out his misery. As the flash from the barrel goes so
does them.

Walking quietly through the west wing to the main
hallway all their heads are on a swivel. Just up ahead
a team member is listening in on a conversation from
another agency.

"Yeah, I copy that they have armor piercing ammo."
the voice says. The team member listening to the
conversation reaches down and picks up a shell casing
and he speaks through his headset.

"All team members be advised that the targets have
armor piercing ammunition. Repeat they have armor
piercing ammunition."

That did more harm than good because now every
team member is in fear for his life. Knowing that
nothing can stop the ammunition they feel doomed.

Jaquiel points at the bottom corner of the wall
right at the hallway's intersection. They all ready

themselves, Jaquiel raises his hands and with a voiceless count. "Wunz, twzoo, goh!"

They all begin to fire upon the wall space the team members never stood a chance. As they now carefully goes around to see their results. Five in all are lying on the floor and two are still moving. Babylon is the last one to reload and is walking towards the men lying in the floor. All of a sudden they hear movement around the corner. "Go, I'll finish this," Babylon tells them.

The other three bends the corner firing away hitting everything in sight. The walls, doors, windows and a exit sign. The team members scatters for their lives. One of them is being chased by Teeny-Man who's laying down heavy fire.

Afraid of the armor piercing bullets the man without hesitation runs into a side room. With Teeny-Man dead on his six going through the door. It's still open Teeny-Man following continuously firing at him Teeny-Man takes his aim.

Sensing that the man is trying to jump, but Teeny-Man's wrong judgement costs him one. The man takes and dives through the laundry shute.

"Coward mother fucker!" Teeny-Man yells at the man who's gone down the chute.

"Rather a coward than a dead maaaaaaaan," he says going down the chute.

***

Babylon finishes up shooting the two that were laying down moving. He begins to go and join his friends. Not knowing that they're now chasing team members around he hears the firing.

But continues to walk towards the intersection of the floor before he knows it. "Wham!" One of the running team members runs smack into him. Their bodies goes one way while their weapons go another.

Now the agent goes straight for the young man striking him in the face. Babylon shakes it off and rushes the agent striking him back. Babylon strikes him again this time on the side of his head.

J.J. Honesty-Bey

After his assault on Babylon he now places him in
a tactical hold. He begins to just physically take the
young man to the other end of the hallway.

Babylon goes for his waist to pull out his other
gun. But it's too, big to pull out from his back waist
band especially in the full nelson hold that he's in.
The Desert Eagle falls to the floor and the agent
hears and sees it and kicks it to the other end of the
hallway with the others.

Babylon drops all his weight to the floor. He's
free now the two are standing off both are in an
orthodox stand going through various hand motions of
their own martial arts. The agent shoots a kick with
his left leg.

The young man blocks it with his left hand in a
pushing manner. The man throws a decoy left swing and
now tries to sweep Babylon off his feet with a ground
level round house kick. He fails badly Babylon jumps
up and comes down on the man's ankle. "Ahhh!" he yells
out in pain.

He jumps up in a rage and begins an all out
assault on the young man. Swinging wildly striking
Babylon everywhere. Still in his stance Babylon
catches him with an open palm blow to the sternum.

The force from the blow sends him on his rear end.
One of many moves he learned while growing up in the
Nation of Islam. Now Babylon attacks with a flurry of
kicks and blows of his own.

He now tries to make a run for his guns. But its
quickly suppressed when the agent dives on top of him.
Now finally up on his feet and frustrated with his
situation. Babylon looks to his right he sees his
opportunity. He looks to his left and again to his
left to throw off the agent of his intent to go to his
guns at the other end of the hallway.

He fakes his attempt as the man jumps. Babylon
jumps up with an extremely hard kick to the man's mid
section and make a break for the wall while the man is
trying to recover.

As he breaks the entrance glass on the wall case.
The man eyes and mouth becomes wide. The young man has
just taken the fire axe. As he draws it back over his

head to take a swing he accidently hits the water
sprinkler setting off a chain reaction in the hallway.

As the black stuff comes out the sprinklers the
heavy smell of oil is in the air. Now soaked and wet
he takes another aim at the agent. He takes a pull
down swing at him and misses. The alarm is going off
through out the resort constantly ringing.

He draws back like he has a baseball bat and takes
a step into his swing. The swing is a mid body swing,
and the agent squats down as if to duck the swing. The
axe blade scraps his shoulder blade only to end up in
the bottom part of his neck.

Cracking his collarbone with the blade in his neck
on an angle. Babylon draws back once more with more
force over his head and hits something else once more,
but this time the axe is stuck on it. As he turns his
head around he sees that he accidently catches another
team member who was sneaking up on him, in the
forehead with the pointed part of the axe.

With the man still on his feet Babylon swings him
around and yanks the axe out his forehead. Hair,
scalp, blood and brain matter all comes out the man's
forehead with the yank, and his body falls to the
floor.

Now back to the initial man who's still on his
knees. The fear of the axe along with his adrenaline
is causing the bottom of his feet and his scalp to
tingle with sensation. He get's an erection, along
with an orgasm from the lethal swing from the axe.

"Ahhhh!" Escapes from his mouth as he now shivers
onto the other side.

He draws back the axe again and swings through
with a level hit that almost lands in the same
location. His head is hanging off the side of his body
by the little bone and tissue that's left. The
sprinklers are spreading the blood and black oily
smelling settlement everywhere, the carpet is a large
pool of bloody oily water.

***

As the Dade County Special Weapons Attack Team cover

the resort from all sides. People are refusing to leave the area just to catch a look at something.

"Are the shooters in position?" Asks Nigel Thompson the S.W.A.T. supervisor.

"In three mics, Sir." Eric Cooke answers.

"There's a possibility of a fire the sprinkler system has been activated. So visibility may be difficult. But nonetheless your orders are to take out all hostiles," Nigel Thompson informs.

"Roger that."

***

They are running through the hallway and meets back up with Babbylon.

"Hey we got to go I know this bitch is full of bacon." Teeny-Man tells Babylon.

"Bakone?" Jaquiel asks.

"Pigs Frenchy, the police?" Juice-Hop explains.

"Ah yez, I szee." As Jaquiel is looking out the window he sees a reflection of light and shouts out loud. "Franc tireur!" ("Sharp shooters!") he yells and breaks out running.

"Man what the fuck you saying?" Teeny-Man asks him.

"Shzarp shzootas," he repeats in English while pointing towards the window. At this time they all can hear and feel something. The vibrations from it can't be ignored. But they can't make it out so they run to take cover from the snipers.

"Slim, I think it's a earthquake." Teeny-Man suggests.

"Not in Florida." Juice-Hop tells him.

"We had one at home," Teeny-Man continues as the noise is getting louder and louder something is coming for sure.

***

"**What the hell** is that?" S.W.A.T. sniper Tony Joplin asks.

"What's going on up there?" Nigel Thompson asks

his snipers.

"Sir, it's a Blackhawk chopper," another sniper reports to him.

"A Blackhawk? No, that's not right, it's not a Blackha-"

***

The Blackhawk is facing the eleventh floor window on the south side where they all are, and starts to unload the massive sixty millimeter rounds. As the shell casings falls to the ground below it looks like pieces of gold falling out the sky. Inside the projectiles are ripping apart the resort.

The sixty millimeters are going through seven rooms at a time. Debris is flying everywhere doors are coming off hinges. Big holes are in the carpet and even bigger ones are in the concrete under the carpet.

A fire extinguisher just explodes and a white powdery cloud appears. A couple who's been hiding on the floor in the corner of their suite every since the initial shot was fired. Has just run out of luck the sixty millimeter cannons just cuts them in half while they were still in each other arms.

"We can't stay here," Babylon yells out to them.

"Let's go then," Teeny-Man agrees with him.

The war craft stop to take a survey Babylon start shooting at it through the window. He hits the windshield and it cracks. The operator knows from the crack in the windshield that whoever it is shooting has armor piercing ammunition.

They all start shooting at the war craft but mainly hitting it's nose. Another hit cracks the passenger's side windshield and the operator now pulls up and away.

Now making a run for it they all go to the stairwell, but are met by team members. They fire upon them vigorously, but are missing them. With his Desert Eagle in his waist Teeny-Man forces his way to the front of them and fires his shotgun until it empties.

"Gling, gling, gling, gling, gling, gling!" is the

sound that's in the air. Along with the yells, screams and moans from the team members.

The team members are seriously injured they are on the stairs moving around in sheer pain. Jaquiel without hesitation goes and finish them off.

Now they are looking strange at one another. Trying to figure out what that sound was they were hearing. Juice-Hop bends down and picks up a dime, he's holding it between his right thumb and index finger so they all can see it.

They all look around, but all eyes go to the floor and see nothing but dimes and some bent up.

"Hey Teeny-Man, you been shooting these?" Juice-Hop asks. The shotgun shells he'd gotten from Tammy's basement were packed with dimes and that was the sound he couldn't figure out earlier.

"What type of country ass shit is this?" Teeny-Man asks himself out loud.

With the team of agents at bay Babylon goes up stairs to the roof. Right at the door landing there's a lot of black fifty gallon drums that's stacked up with industrial stripper that extremely hard to move.

"We're going to the roof and use the cargo elevator. I brought it up awhile ago and jammed it." Babylon informs them all.

They all start to walk on the roof towards the cargo elevator. Babylon sees that there's still a lot of stripper drums still needs to be brought in that's piled up on the roof.

Almost at the door they all can hear and feel it the Blackhawk is back again. Babylon sees the propeller blades of the war craft over top the fifty gallon drums on the roof.

"Go get in now!" Babylon yells as he pushes everyone inside the cargo elevator and closes the gate.

***

The entire S.W.A.T. team enters each stairwell of the resort. On the south wing they are met my Jimmy's men.

"Sir, it's Dade County's S.W.A.T., awaiting orders?" A team member relays.

"Take out everything in your way," Jimmy orders.

"Roger that, take out everything in our way." Heavy fire from both sides it's the same in every stairwell and most floors. The north wing is having heavy shooting between the rogue agents and the Homeland Security agents.

The west side wing has Homeland Strike Force One, slaughtering the Metro Dade County Police, and everybody else.

***

He still sees the propeller of the assault chopper. But can't see it's body due to the fifty gallon drums that's stacked up on the roof that's hiding him from it, and it from him.

He looks at his friends who are now behind the gated elevator door. He takes aim and start to fire away at it instead of waiting for it.

A brilliant bold move that proves deadly on impact. The first slug to enters a drum ignites it automatically causing an huge bomb like explosion. The impact from the blast knocks him off his feet and carries him over the side of the roof.

His gun goes one way as his body goes another, in what looks like slow motion to his friends.

"Baaaaaaaaaaaab!" Teeny-Man yells out as he's

251

trying to open the gated door. Jaquiel grabs him and the cargo elevator begins to desend.

"Comrade, vee hov tzoo goh he dzid it szo vee can get avay," Jaquiel tells them both. Jaquiel knows its nothing they can do to save the brave young man its a twelve story drop for him. "A bientot comrade," ("So long comrade,") Jaquiel says to himself under his breath in a soft and remorseful voice.

Since the elevator started descending the explosion has had multiple effects. It pours burning furniture stripper onto the Blackhawk. That just completely covers the war craft. Some of it actually gets on both operators inside the chopper. It makes them have to leave the scene.

The chopper is a flying ball of fire going through the air as it goes the sight of it's propeller is a twirling ring of fire. The operator decides to accelerate hoping it will put out the flames.

The S.W.A.T. snipers teams watches it, it's the most eye popping thing they ever encountered on the job. The operator is forced to do an emergency landing. And once the Blackhawk is finally on the ground it's full of flames and one can hear the sound of the fire crackling all over the war craft.

As the craft continues to burn with flames emergency workers clears the path for the fire department, who now comes and put out the flames. The operators are not hurt at all from the fire, but the stripper leaves plenty of burn marks upon their bodies.

The blast bursts open the drums that were on the stairwell causing nearly a ton of furniture stripper to flow down the steps of the stairwell and all over the banister.

The Homeland Strike Force One team, F.B.I., National Guards, Sheriff's Department, State Police, Homeland Security agents, S.W.A.T., Rogue agents and the casino security all are ignoring the burning sensations from the chemical.

But will not ignore what is to come, as the flaming substance from the roof flows. It blankets the entire roof top. Now a back flow builds up and the flames from the roof ignites the stripper inside of the stairs.

The men are fighting hand to hand, shooting, squatting, laying in it, splashing it on each other. The smell from its vapors doesn't effect them. As the fire ignites the substance, the flames races down the steps which occupies the men. With all the turmoil nobody notices the liquid beneath their feet is on fire, nor that the drops are also.

***

"**Lets take the** stairs Joe," Vic tells him.

"Are the stairs secured?" Detective Mercury asks.

"No, they're under fire, all of them," an officer informs them.

"Then lets wait for S.W.A.T. to suppress the situation," Detective Mercury suggests.

***

The cargo elevator reaches the "K" floor in the basement. Jaquiel pulls the gated door open and steps out, after him comes Juice-Hop. Teeny-Man is stuck on the wall inside just staring into time.

"Vee muzt goh comrade," Jaquiel tells Teeny-Man. He doesn't say a word and just stands there motionless and expressionless.

"Hey slim, we got to roll out, them people are all over the place," Juice-Hop pleads with him. Teeny-Man comes off the wall, but is still under a trance. Now they're walking through the kitchen of the resort and see that the kitchen employees are beginning to be evacuated.

***

"**I've found one** of the hostiles, but he's not hostile any more," a voice informs over the radio.

"Where are you officer?" Detective Mercury asks over the radio.

253

"Outside in the parking lot on the south side of the building," he answers.

"Hey Vic, let's go!" They go to view the body of the allege hostile. They will also try to find the identity of the corpse on the ground.

"Sir, this is what's left of the body and over there is a fifty caliber Desert Eagle," he informs Detective Mercury.

Both detectives go to view the body, but its impossible to identify the face the entire head is smashed into a pulp.

"Hey, come run prints on him," Detective Mercury orders. "Vic, you think he's one of your boys?"

"I don't know for sure, but it very well could be. At the diamond bank there were fifty caliber casings found."

***

They have made it out the resort and start to walk towards their cars. They see its a dead issue with the different law enforcement all around. So they goes to the cars just for the ammo and personal effects. Teeny-Man leans over the driver's seat for his things.

He looks in the back seat of the car, it's a blanket folded the long way to cover up Babylon's M-16. "Damn Bab," he sighs to himself. "My mother fucken man, is gone. Bitch ass shit!" he continues in a low voice.

While shaking his head he leaves the M-16 and the fifty caliber ammo its no sense to take it. Juice-Hop goes and gets his ammo and things and now they goes to meet Jaquiel.

"Yeah Frenchy, we um gonna have to steal a car or something," Juice-Hop tells him.

"Let'z mi vent wun instzead comrade," Jaquiel responds.

***

Detective Mercury takes a look up at the resort to try and figure out where the body might have fallen from.

254

And sees what appears to be someone hanging on for
their life.

"Hey! Up there, get help, there's somebody
hanging on a rope," he yells out while pointing up at
the side of the building. Officers are looking up at
the person hanging from the rope and most of them
breaks out running.

"We have a victim hanging from a rope around the
seventh floor, it looks like? Get to the south side of
the building and reel them in." Detective Mercury
orders over the radio.

***

Just minutes later he can feel the breaking of glass
upon his head from above. Whoever it is they're coming
for him. With his legs locked around the hose and his
feet are resting on the brass nozzle that releases the
water.

And his arms and hands are locked around the fire
hose tightly. The officers begin to pull him up he
knows that it's law enforcement so he will meet his
fate. He is now pulled through the window and sees
nothing but heavily armed lawmen.

***

They drive the newly acquired rented tan Chrysler
300m. Jaquiel is behind the wheel and Teeny-Man is
riding shotgun. Teeny-Man turns and looks through the
window to see all the people scattered across the
streets and sidewalks, finally through the checkpoint.

"It was a good move to have us wait until you got
the rental and then meet you with the tools Frenchy,"
Juice-Hop tells him.

Teeny-Man is just looking out the window. He now
locks eyes with a driver of a dark blue Impala. He
turns his head back into the car. On Jaquiel's side a
squad car is in the intersection just watching
traffic.

"Teeny-Man I think its something up with them in
the Impala, because they keep on looking at you and

255

talking to the rest of them in the car," Juice-Hop
alerts him.

Teeny-Man is now turning around to see if the man
is looking at him, Juice-Hop is already on top of it.
The driver of the Impala is reaching for something.
Not taking any chances Juice-Hop begins to fire at the
driver's side of the vehicle.

Jaquiel puts the peddle to the metal and takes off
flying. The Impala gives chase and the squad car puts
out the call over the radio.

"All cars shots fired at the head of ninety five
south bound, suspects are driving a tan Chrysler 300m.
The occupants one Caucasian adult male and three to
four Black males."

"Attention all cars suspects are heading south
bound," the dispatch informs.

***

"**All team get** on ninety five now the targets are
heading south on ninety five. I want all Homeland
Security agents along with Homeland Strike Force One
and my team members to engage them now," Jimmy orders
over the com.

***

"**All S.W.A.T. mobilize** at once and head to
location," Nigel Thompson orders.

***

"**All available officers** pursue suspects be advised
to precede with caution as suspects are armed and
dangerous," State Police dispatches.

***

"**All agents switch** to secure line four. You have
your targets let's not allow these rookies along with
their S.W.A.T. to take down this group of local fire
pots. There will be a joint effort in positioning a

road block at a certain point, if it should come to
it.

"But I know my, agents will not let this go on any
longer than it has to," the Field Operational
Supervisor of the F.B.I. tells his agents.

***

After hearing the call over the radio they immediately
escort him down stairs to the front of the resort.
That's the check point for all law enforcement
officers at the site.

They questions him and he answers with authority.
They take his picture and sends him around to the
casualty and medical collection point.

After a while he gives them the slip and walks out
the resort looking for something or somebody, his
team. He doesn't find them and decides to keep on
moving. A vehicle is what's needed most to make his
escape. So he goes from car to car looking trying door
handle after door handle.

And feeling under bumpers and fenders for car
keys. The few people watching notices him and sees
what he's doing. They know he's trying to steal or rob
something.

So they do what civilians do, go get the police,
and not a one is available he comes across a car and
tries the door handle and it's open. The keys are
still in the ignition. Siting in the driver's seat he
turns around and sees a long blanket on the back seat
covering something.

He picks up the blanket and to his surprise he
sees a M-16, along with some magazines and drums.
Right behind the driver's seat on the floor is a
duffel bag. He reaches back and gets the bag. He has
it resting between the console he unzips it and sees
all the ammo inside it.

***

The back window glass shatters as the bullets go
through it.

"Shit! I heard that bitch go past my ear," Teeny-Man alerts them. He now rolls down his window and begins to fire his gun after having to leave his shotgun in the resort elevator. Juice-Hop follows suit behind the driver's seat. They weave in and out of traffic. Jaquiel is hitting and scrapping cars as he goes.

"Goddamn French man!" Teeny-Man yells at him. "You can't drive worth shit," Teeny-Man continues.

***

He walks from the resort to find another vehicle. In the process he spots an elderly white couple watching the scene at the resort. Behind them are two sets of golf clubs bags with the clubs inside them.

He takes the one behind the old man and hauls tail it out of sight. He heads for the car with the M-16 and the ammo in it. Once at the car he carefully watches his surroundings.

Now he goes into the vehicle and tosses out the duffel bag with the ammo and magazines. With the back door open he leans the golf bag over on to the back seat.

With it halfway in he swipes all the magazines on the back seat into the bag. He takes his time loading the M-16 into the bag. He fully loads up and heads directly across the street walking up to a detail shop that's full of customers and onlookers.

Watching the showmanship cars with all the bells and whistles. He decides to take a look around the back of the place. He knows life, whenever there's a rack of people doing good business out front there's a rack of people out back doing bad business.

In the alley he see only a few cars and a few people talking in different groups. There's a burgundy dodge Magnum with a snake emblem on it sides, and also has the driver's side door open.

The inside is bright white with burgundy piping trim and a chrome steering wheel. The paint job as well as the deep dish hammer rims are shining, a little too much for him.

The Georgetown Heist

The license plate says North Carolina. The Magnum is set to leave in the direction in which he came. As he looks at the Magnum its different from the way he remembers a Magnum, it looks bigger for some reason. Now he walks back to the beginning of the alley to wait on him. The vehicle is now approaching he goes with his first plan. He pulls out a club and props the bag against the wall of a business.

He's in front of the car as it's about to go past him, he takes a swipe like he's practicing his swing. And purposely hits the Magnum at it's base. The car slams on the brakes, and a dark skinned man gets out the wagon. He watches this man getting out the vehicle. He fully hears his voice and pays close attention to his body language.

"What the fuck you do to my car?" the driver asks.

"Please excuse me I was just practicing my swing for the Mike Harper Shoot-Out Classic this weekend," he answers.

The driver now bends down to inspect the damage to his car. He hears a whistling sound that cuts through the air, that just rung his bell. He is hit over the head with a club. It hurts so bad he can't even get the sound out his mouth to let the world know how much it hurts.

Now he's looking around making sure that no one is coming or watching. He takes another swing hitting him on his knee. "This is called the shotgun or the breakdown, it stops you from running away," he explains to the driver.

"I don't know you! What did I do?" the driver asks.

"Right place wrong time," he tells him. The driver now goes into his pocket and throws his money in the direction of him.

"Take it, it's all I have."

"I don't want your money."

"Thank you."

"How fast this thing go?"

"I had it stretched and widen so the V-10 could fit in, and the governor is set at two twenty five."

"I got to get this up off you." Going to the golf

club bag the driver is still on the ground. He sees
the man placing the golf club bag in the back seat.
That's when the driver tries to make a call behind his
back. He sees him, but doesn't let on.

He pulls out the M-16 and places it on the back
seats. He now turns to the man on the ground and pulls
out his gun from his waistline.

"Man please don't kill me," the driver begs.

"I guess you would never call the police huh?"

"Man never," the driver assures him.

"Get away from the car," he's ordered. He begins
to slide away from the car on his backside. He takes a
look everything is clear as he's getting into the car.
Now he places one leg into the vehicle. He starts up
the magnum and he immediately feels the power of it.

He sees the driver still trying to dial behind his
back through the side view mirror. He gets out and
goes over to the driver an points his gun in the face
of the driver.

"You said you wasn't gonna kill me."

"Yeah, but you North Carolina jokers are
terrible."

He fires just one shot at point blank range at the
man's forehead that explodes all over the wall of the
building. His body is already on it's knees he falls
over limp. The man now goes and gets inside the Magnum
and pulls off.

***

The Georgetown Heist

Under heavy fire the Frenchman continues to weave in
and out of traffic. Juice-Hop is firing away, but
notices there are a lot of people shooting all over
the place. Teeny-Man hears the cease of firing from
Juice-Hop.

"Juice, what the fuck you stop shooting for?"

"Look!"

"I know slim, just keep shooting."

"No, look!" Teeny-Man takes a real good look out
the window to see what he's been missing he's stuck
for a moment. "Bab was right the whole time," he tells
the car.

Jaquiel knows that these two are not as sharp and
on the same level as their now deceased friend. He
know that Babylon knew what was going on, but kept the
truth from his friends. Now Teeny-Man sees fully what
Babylon was trying to tell him. Its an all out war
going on outside of their car everybody shooting at
everybody else.

"Comradez, vee muzt keepza fighting, pleaze
shzoot." Jaquiel pleads.

Teeny-Man and Juice-Hop looks at each other with a
looks of uncertainty, but nonetheless they begin to
fire their tails off shooting at everything that
wasn't with them. A squad car pulls up behind them and
rams the back of their car. Jaquiel almost loses
control of the vehilce.

"Push this bitch French man." Teeny-Man yells at
him.

Juice-Hop tries to reach his arm out the window to
shoot at the squad car he misses terribly. And the cop
know he can't shoot, so the cop rams the 300m again.

And this time making the Chrysler do a fishtail,
and Jaquiel lose control of the car. They go into the
guardrail the sparks are flying off the car as they go
sliding down the metal railing. The heat along with
the friction bursts the driver side front tire in to
flames.

The smell of burnt rubber and metal fills the car
as they come to a complete stop. Now they're on the
shoulder of the left side lane. They all immediately
get out and take cover for their lives. They begin to

shoot at everything in their sights.

"Hey we going to have to make a run for it," yells Teeny-Man.

"En garde," ("On guard,") Jaquiel yells back at Teeny-Man.

***

Taking aim, Teeny-Man starts to shoot he misses his intended target and hits a white woman driving a mini van. The van turns and crashes he can see the "World's #1 Soccer Mom." bumper sticker. He just keeps on shooting away.

A Safeway eighteen wheeler is coming down the highway. One of the rogue agents takes out the driver by mistake. The heavy duty truck goes out of control and rolls through the intersection barrier destroying it as it goes through to on coming traffic.

The rig goes head first into the side of a Mazda RX-7 it runs straight over it and never slows down. It now slams into a Jeep Wrangler catching it head on pushing it towards the concrete wall where it pins it between it's self and the wall.

The crash makes the eighteen wheeler looses it's load as the different variety of meat packages fall out on the highway, which looks like it just got through raining meats.

The scrams of the people involved or just watching this horrible sight and the sound of heavy gunfire is what fills the air. With shots hitting the Chrysler 300m., each shot gets closer to them with each blast. A squad car along with two other vehicles are laying down heavy fire on Jaquiel and the other two. They are pinned down with nowhere to run and very little hiding room.

With the shooters still advancing upon them Jaquiel looks around and sees that there's nowhere that they can go for cover.

The driver of the squad car that rammed them off the road is approaching them. Jaquiel takes aim at him and takes him out. His partner goes and immediately tries to pull him to the safety of the

262

car.

Jaquiel isn't having it today, so he continues to take aim and kills off the other cop pulling his partner. Now they both lay out in the middle of the highway Jaquiel puts them both out of their miseries. Everyone involved can hear and feel something, but all are too, busy watching their own battles.

***

This thing can move," he says to himself. The Dodge Magnum is up to one hundred seventy six on the highway, as he races through the traffic like a pro. He has to start slowing down a little do to all the vehicles crashed and sidelined. But the Magnum growls as it passes by them.

***

With more pursuers on their tails and others now setting up positions on them. They try to keep their cover behind the 300m. The S.W.A.T., has their positions and are ready to fire as the other gunfire in non effective to them.

"S.W.A.T. snipers if you can see the question, then you have a go to answer it," Nigel Thompson tells them.

"Roger that, looking for the question now Sir." The sniper is looking for Jaquiel and company. "I see the question, and I have the answer," the sniper informs.

A sniper is about to take out Jaquiel, but one of the rogue agents starts to shooting at everything and one of the shots hits the Chrysler 300m., and makes Jaquiel duck his head. Just as the sniper is pulling his trigger the shot hit's the corner top of the car. Placing a hole in the car that almost bakes Jaquiel's croissant.

"Franc tireur!" ("Sharp shooters!") he yells out to Teeny-Man and Juice-Hop.

"Man what the fuck you saying? Speak english so a mother fucker can understand your mother fucken ass,"

Teeny-Man yells back at him.
"Shzarp shzootaz!" he says in english while pointing upwards towards the bridge.
"Hey Juice, a mother fucker is fucked now huh?" Teeny-Man asks him.
The noise is getting louder and louder along with the feeling of the vibrations. They all look around to see what's making the noise. As it now appears it's bigger than life itself. The Apache assault chopper is just tearing up everything in it's path. It's bombardment reaches the Chysler all three of them makes a run for it.
The bullets just simply shreds the 300m. Once the car ignites the explosion lifts the car twenty feet into the air. The force of the blast throws all three of them in the air and they hit the ground hard.
The war craft now turns it's attention to the Homeland Strike Force One team, F.B.I., the rogue agents, S.W.A.T., Sheriff department, State Troopers the regular police and every body else that follows.
Teeny-Man, Jaquiel and Juice-Hop tries to recover with people still shooting at them they have no choice but to retreat back to the burning car. After firing at everybody they're either hiding, running or dead.
All at once the three hears a vehicle come to a screeching halt, as they all prepare to fire on it.
"Hey, come on y'all get in," a voice invites them. Looking through the fire from the burning 300m. they can see a figure of a man. "Hey! Hey! Come on y'all lets go," he yells once more to them.
They all rise up with caution to see who's this calling them and they can't believe their eyes.
"Ahhhhhhhhhh! Baaaaaaaaab!" Teeny-Man yells out to him extremely loud while running and jumping up and holding him in a bear hug. With Juice-Hop and Jaquiel in tow they all get into the Magnum.
"Juice, Frenchy," he acknowledge them both and the Frenchman can't believe his eyes.
Babylon is in the back seat behind Teeny-Man who's now in the driving seat. Jaquiel is shotgun and Juice-Hop is beside Babylon in the back. They pulls off, but they're not going anywhere, he's just burning rubber

and smoking up the highway.

"Goddamn this bitch is mean," Teeny-Man says about the car.

Upon seeing them pull off everybody who can follow them begins to give chase. The Apache notices the chase also and joins in on it. Now reaching for the volume button he doesn't know about the system that's in the Magnum. Nor did he see the eight twelve inch E.V. competition speakers that's in the back of the car.

Also the two one thousand watt Zeus amplifiers while hauling ass down ninety five. They are just getting off to hit the turnpike and the music is extremely loud.

"Then tell me what it's like?" is the hook being said by Supah Sug while they're looking at their pursuers.

"Comrade, thzee mewzik." Jaquiel tries to beg. The music is too loud and the Frenchman can't take it. They all knows it, but it's funny as hell to see Teeny-Man give Jaquiel that, get the fuck out my face look.

Babylon is the first to start shooting his gun, but after emptying his Desert Eagle. He reloads and switches to his M-16. Now with the big boy in his hands his attitude is that of the weapon.

Taking aim he lets loose on a squad car. The .308 armor piercing ammo is too much. The car swirls off the road hitting the railing. Juice-Hop is firing away but he's missing badly. He hits an elderly man in what seems to be his shoulder. The anti-terrorist ammo has no mercy for the elderly man.

He can see the blood from the wound as he slumps down in his vehicle and turns off on to on coming traffic. He hits a Ford Escort that in turn hit's an old Toyota Supra. The cars crash no one seems to be hurt bad. Babylon is back at it again in his relentless pursuit of just destroying these people.

He take out a drum to reload and catches Jaquiel firing away and actually hitting his targets, so he now starts back shooting.

"That French mother fucker is getten it," Teeny-

Man yells in the car. "Fuck French man, you cold mother fucker. Your new name is Jaq Frozt, you cold mother fucker you," Teeny-Man continues.

The Apache is gaining on them all and Babylon has a better feel with the battle riffle. A Yukon is behind them along with a squad car about twenty feet away.

"Teeny-Man slow down slim," Babylon tells him. Slowing down brings both pursuing vehicles that much closer to them. Babylon has the SUV in his sights and lets it rip from the passenger's side to the driver's side. He hits them pretty good the SUV and everything inside of it he can see where he hit the seats.

Because the anti-terrorist ammo chewed up the headrest. It looks like a pillow fight took place inside there. The Yukon begins going out of control he sees someone comes from the back seat to steer the vehicle. He lets loose once more and this wave is the one that does it. "Goddamn!" Teeny-Man yells out.

Looking in his side view mirror he see the entire windshield go red indication that it was a head shot. Switching drums he readies himself for the squad car. When he hears the shots he turn his head for a second and comes back. It's one of the rogue agents who takes out the squad car.

"Hey, roadblock!" Teeny-Man yells out.

He has to yell extremely loud do to the music being so loud and he still refuses to turn it down. Every vehicle involved takes notice and before anyone knows it. The Apache is back and start firing at everybody involved and at the roadblock just shredding the would be blockage.

The firing of the war craft is like killing an ant with a sludge hammer. It blows the middle of the roadblock to pieces, but only a small path is there. Teeny-Man sees it and goes straight through it as he scrapes two cars very hard going through.

As they go through the roadblock the Apache is on their tails and Babylon nudges Juice-Hop with his elbow. He places his knees up and starts to point at his feet. Juice-Hop agrees, but he doesn't know what Babylon really wants. Babylon places his left hand on

The Georgetown Heist

Teeny-Man left shoulder. "Hit the brakes! Hit the brakes!" Babylon yells.

The Magnum is screeching down the turnpike Babylon has his back to the door and without warning opens it up. Juice-Hop not aware of the move for a second and Babylon almost falls out the car. He uses the stock of the M-16 to save himself from falling out by using it as a prop to push himself up from falling out.

Juice-Hop see the move late, but in response goes for Babylon legs Babylon takes aim at the Apache. The pilots sees him, but laughs at him. The Magnum is now at a full stop and Babylon starts shooting at the war craft.

Sparks fly off the Apache from the bullets. Now a few of the rounds hit's the windshield and cracks it. He just continues to shoot and places five more shots at the windshield. It takes two more to spread the crack in the windshield. It takes only two to break through and the last armor piercing projectile goes up and into the control panel.

The electrical sparks from within the war bird is enough to make the pilot lose control of it. Still hanging out the car, Babylon watches as it goes down and hits the ground.

It crashes to the ground sideways with it's top propeller hitting first. It breaks off in pieces and flies away. It's a vehicle with some rogue agents inside that are at the crash site of the Apache. The rogue agent that's behind the driver tells him:

"Let's go now before it explodes," he says to the driver. But it falls upon death ears he sees this as their chance to escape the war bird's explosion, so now he shakes him.

"Let's get out of here," he says this time with authority in his voice.

The shaking of the driver is all that it takes to make the back agent go pale in the face. Seeing the body of the driver slide off into two pieces, is an frightening sight to him.

In the wake of all the shooting and noise the two back seat passengers never hears the propeller blade from the Apache, enter into the driver's side door, and slice through the bodies of the two men up front and exit out the passenger's door.

Watching the war craft blow up he's still hanging out the door. Now he notices something and turns his head around. He immediately starts waving at Juice-Hop.

"Pull me up! Pull me up Juice," he yells while waving for him.

He throws his riffle into the car and now starts reaching to Juice-Hop for help. Juice-Hop is slow to react. By the time he truly see there's something wrong, Babylon does a full sit up into the car.

Just as he makes eye to eye contact with Juice-Hop. "Wham!" A Chevy Tahoe slams right into the car door taking it completely off and carrying it on down the highway.

"What the fuck?" Teeny-Man says.

"Go get'em!" Babylon tells Teeny-Man.

The Magnum screeches off after the Tahoe. They catches up to the truck and Babylon puts on his seat belt, and Teeny-Man sees it through the rear view mirror.

"You're gonna die now that you put that mother fucker on."

They can see the Magnum pulling along side them. But before they can roll down their windows to get a shot off. Babylon starts firing into the back passenger door along with the front passenger door. He shoots at an angle to get the passenger and the driver.

He gets his wish the driver has been shot. The Tahoe is pulling over Babylon undo his seat belt and reaches over the seat to shake Teeny-Man.

"Pull over, pull over!"

Teeny-Man pulls over carefully following the SUV, Babylon slaps a new one hundred round drum into the M-16.

"Vhat'z gohing on?" Jaquiel asks.

"Bab in his feelings." Teeny-Man tells him.

Babylon jumps out the car and goes over to the driver's side of the SUV firing as he comes, shooting up the door behind the driver. The man never stood a chance as Babylon just chops him to pieces.

He fires once more into the driver's door at a

very low aim. He knows that he had been hit pretty good. Babylon goes and reaches for the handle he turns his head and sees more vehicles on the way.

He now opens up the door and steps up as to get in. He sees that the driver is a white woman and she's looking straight at him.

"Please help me," she begs him with tears in her eyes. Babylon lifts up the riffle to her face.

"Noooooo!" she cries.

He lets off the rest of the magazine into her face. The anti-terrorist ammo takes the woman's entire head off causing her to slip out her seat belt and slide down onto the dead passenger's lap.

He jumps down and goes around to get back into the Magnum. Now back inside he goes into the duffel bag and pulls out five of those one hundred round drums. It is at this time that Jaquiel points towards the spaghetti bowl, the loops of highway.

And Teeny-Man goes in that direction getting off the turnpike. Babylon shakes Teeny-Man once more, as Teeny-Man slow down the Magnum. Babylon gets out and so does everyone else the vehicles continues to come for them. While the other ones are still shooting each other Babylon sees that this is not the time for a standoff.

"Let's bait'em in some more," Babylon tells them. They get's back inside the car and proceed, but Babylon's gut is telling him to do it now. He bangs on the headrest of Teeny-Man's seat and he starts to slow the car down. Now with the car moving slow he jumps out it and smacks the side of the Magnum twice and Teeny-Man pulls off.

He stops the car just a little ways away from Babylon. Teeny-Man looking back at Babylon and sees him pointing to the top of the loop, Teeny-Man drives off. Babylon takes his place and waits on the convoy of vehicles that's coming his way.

He opens fire on them all he's careful not to waste his ammo. So he's aiming with the mind set to kill and or disable. No one to be out done once the shooting begins Teeny-Man drives backwards to where Babylon is at, but he did not get too close to him.

Now all of them are firing their weapons. Babylon digs in and spots a squad car and takes it out. The cop car crashes into a Lincoln Town car that hits two other cars.

The smoke from it begins to rise up he can see good samaritans trying to rescue them. He continues to shoot and watches a motorcycle cop racing through the traffic so he shoots, striking the cop's right thigh. The bike pops a wheely and spins one hundred eighty degrees and throws the cop.

The runaway bike heads for a Greyhound bus. The bus driver tries to swing around the bike, but he can't. The bus catches the bike on it's grill and now runs over it. Some of the bike's parts gets caught up under the bus wheels and causes the bus to start flipping out of control in the air.

With glass and luggage from it's side compartments flying everywhere. The bus finally stops flipping and just slides until it stops, but still leaves room to drive through. Babylon see all the shattered glass and smoke at the scene he just notices Teeny-Man and the other two.

His plan is not working as he had hoped it would. Firing away he hits a black Chevy Blazer that didn't turn over. He know it's bullet proof, but stays firing at it. The Blazer turns off and hits a red Volvo and goes and hit the back of a motorcycle that sends the driver airborne.

The Georgetown Heist

He goes tumbling through he air and ricochetted off an ice cream truck. That knocks him back into the air towards the opposite traffic. Before his body can't land on the ground it is met in the air by the grill of an eighteen wheeler that's keeps him as a passenger on it's grill.

The Volvo is out of control and hits a white Conquest TSI that sends the passenger flying out the car as the multiple collision is occurring. The passenger from the white Conquest gets up from his fall.

Now on his knees he leans back against a previously crashed car. As new cars slams on the brakes and turns the backside of his Fleetwood slams into the passenger of the white Conquest. Pinning him between the two vehicles with nothing but his head is visible.

The Volvo is still tumbling down the highway the windows to the doors all shatters out. An object flies out the Volvo along with the glass and debris.

He can not make it out as the silver Crown Victoria speeds past the scene. It just runs over whatever came flying out the Volvo window. With Teeny-Man and the other two along with Babylon firing. The Crown Victoria has to stop immediately and take some cover from the heavy firing.

Taking cover behind the fatally crashed Volvo they can see a white female head that's stuck through the windshield by her neck with her throat bleeding badly. As they duck from the firing they see that the female is not moving at all.

The first man to the back is the driver of the Crown Victoria. While looking out for his own safety. He sees where the firing is coming from as he continues to scan. He's now in total shock and disbelief of what he's looking at.

He now knows what it was that he ran over while driving. Just staring at it makes him sick to his stomach. The corpse of an infant that has been busted open. From being ran over by the Crown Victoria, it's little body just lies on the pavement like some kind of animal road kill.

With it's eyes popped out from it's little head. It only lies in a small amount of blood because it's little body couldn't produce a lot. More vehicles are beginning to come and Babylon knows that he can't hold them back so he starts to retreat to his friends.

They see him and they know its time to go as he waves them off. They all go back to the car Babylon looks back and can't believe it. "Go, hurry up and get to the loop," he tells Teeny-Man.

The car bends around the ramp he now shakes Teeny-Man seat stopping in the middle of the turn, Babylon runs back down around the bend. He's out of sight and they can hear him shooting at something. All three of them gets out the car, and once their feet touches the pavement: "Kaboom!"

It's a huge explosion that occurs it scares the hell out them all. The pressure from the blast knocks all three of them on their backsides. While still on the ground they can see the fire and smoke from the explosion going into the sky.

With their eyes wide open and not yet fully stable they can see Babylon running towards them. "Let's rock," Babylon tells them. They all are a little slow to their feet. They get up and proceed to the car and take their spots.

And now they go around on the west bound ramp headed for Miami Lakes. The explosion of the gas tanker closes the highway so that nobody can follow them through the ramp.

***

"**Report status?**" **Jimmy** demands.

"Sir, they're getting away," one of his men reports.

"Getting away?" Jimmy repeats while looking around with a disgusting look on his face. "What the hell do you mean, getting away?" he yells.

"Nimrod's last shots blew up a gas tanker Sir, so nobody can follow them. Now that it's on fire in the middle of the highway. No one can follow them due to the ramp being blocked off by the burning tanker Sir,"

The Georgetown Heist

he explains to Jimmy.

***

"Hot damn Nimrod you shaved the tiger," Mrs. Culp mistakenly says out loud.

"Would you like his autograph Mrs. Culp?" Jimmy asks her.

"No, no thank you Sir," she answers and smiles.

***

The phone is now being ignored, but it keeps on ringing, and she finally picks up.

"Hello?"

"You know they escaped again, don't you?"

"And that's why you called me Tonya? They're just street punks on a very lucky streak."

"I'm bringing him in myself, we must have him. I must have him."

"Where are you Tonya?"

"Oh, I'm just so happened to be in Miami on vacation."

"That was your plan the whole time. I don't care what you do I'm finished here," she says as she hangs up the phone.

***

They are driving at a fast pace with the music still loud as hell. Babylon takes his left arm and places it over the shoulder of Teeny-Man. And now is pointing with his left index finger. And Teeny-Man is on point as he accelerates coming upon a lime green car.

Teeny-Man goes and cut's the car off and the car pulls over the side of the road. Babylon gets out the Magnum immediately with the M-16 in his hands. He goes over to the driver's side of the car first. The white geeky looking male is scared out his wits.

"Get out the car," Babylon orders him and the man complies with the demand. The others get out the car and follow suit while Babylon bends over inside the car and sees a white girl with glasses on.

"I need this car, but you stay put for a minute," he tells the young lady. After raising up for a second he lowers his head back into the car.

"And don't get your ass on that phone either," he continues.

"I won't," she replies. Now the rest of them bring their belongings around to the lime green car.

"We have no choice," Babylon tells them.

"The bitch is electric Bab," Teeny-Man informs him.

"It'll get us where we need to go." Babylon tells him.

"Fuck it, lets go then," Teeny-Man gives in.

"Alright then," Babylon agrees. "Hey you, out the car now!" Babylon orders her.

"I'll do whatever you want me to," she tells him.

"I want you to get your funky ass out the mother fucken car," Teeny-Man tells her coldly. She gets out the two door sardine can of a car they all get into the new car except for Babylon.

"Y'all can drive it," Babylon tells the couple about the Magnum. He gets in and they pulls off and leaves the couple. Still heading east bound, Teeny-Man is driving and can't help himself.

"Owwwww! Hey Bab, what did the lion say to the monkey when he had him by the tail?"

"What?" Babylon asks unenthused.

"It won't be long now mother fucker."

Juice-Hop and Jaquiel laughs at Teeny-Man, especially Jaquiel. He seems to have enjoyed it a little more than Juice-Hop and Teeny-Man.

"Hey Bab, it's bad enough this bitch ain't got no mother fucken C.D. player-"

"Thzat'z goodz, yez?" Jaquiel says as he laughs at Teeny-Man.

"Like I was saying before I was rudely interrupted. It's bad enough that this bitch ain't go no mother fucken C.D. player. But slim, a mother fucker can get out and run faster than this bitch here." Jaquiel and Juice-Hop laughs again while Babylon smiles and shakes his head.

The Georgetown Heist

They are a long way from the disaster that they created not long ago. The drive is a nice quiet one. "Hey y'all don't look back it's a cop car behind us," Teeny-Man informs them. Juice-Hop and Jaquiel both turns their heads around to see. "I just told y'all not to turn around and y'all still did it," he continues.

The cop car goes on past without any interference. After Jaquiel gives Teeny-Man the directions they are finally at his house. They pulls into the driveway and cuts off the engine.

"Well I can say this for you French man, I mean Jaq Frozt. You keep a bad mother fucker on deck joe," Teeny-Man compliments him. They all go to the door Jaquiel goes into the mailbox to retrieve the keys to the house. He opens up the door and they all go inside.

"Hey slim, we home free now baby," Teeny-Man tells Babylon.

"No T, not yet we got one more mission to complete," Babylon answers him. Now Teeny-Man is worrying about something.

"Hey B, man look this last one slim was a mother fucker. We almost didn't make it," he tells Babylon in a concern voice.

"Yeah, I can dig it slim, but I got to get rid of this car. And once I get back we can start to get it together," Babylon continues.

"Ay slim, I got something to tell you-"

"Can't it wait until I get back slim?" Babylon asks him. "I have to get this car away from here," he explains.

"Yeah slim, but you know I thought I lost you earlier big boy?" Teeny-Man tells him.

Babylon gets the address from Jaquiel and heads for the door. They all watch him leave out without saying a word to him. He gets into the lime green car and pulls off. After a good thirty minutes of driving he sees a nice patch of woods to ditch the car into. "I hope we can all get this mess over with because I'm tired," Babylon tells himself.

Now he walks back towards the service station that

he passed minutes ago. At the station he calls a cab to come and pick him up. While waiting for his cab to come he goes into the sales part of the station.

Now in he goes straight for the candy section of the store. He's looking for his life source, Twizzlers. He can't find them in the regular candy section.

"Hey, where do you keep the Twizzlers at?" He asks the service attendant.

"Up here under the counter," he answers Babylon. Babylon goes and surveys the goods he knows that some stores don't be rotating their stock properly. He looks down at the assortment of Twizzlers, but all he loves is the regular strawberry flavor.

"Yeah, let me have five of those one pound packs please," he asks.

***

He's on the phone and he is receiving some instructions. "Yez, vhere? Okay thzen I vill get it now," he says and hangs up the house phone.

He now goes up to the master's bedroom and looks through the bottom draws of the dresser. He sees everything that he's looking for. There's two satellite phones and four cell phones also. He feels one of the regular phones vibrate and he answers it.

"Yez! vee vill hov it vardy szoon," he informs the caller. And now he discontinues the call. He gets another caller, but this time it's Ponc'e his assatant.

"Az of vight nowz itz a tzotal of Twzenty wun billion dzarlarz and vizing, in conziteration feez," he informs Jaquiel Froscios.

"Good thzen, vee arz on our vay," Jaquiel replies. Juice-Hop has been in the bathroom for a long time, so Teeny-Man goes back to check on him.

"Hey Juicey, what's up in there? Don't knock the rim off the man's bowl," he tells him.

"I'm straight slim, I just need to get my, shit," He takes a breahter. "A little time to get my shit together that's all," Juice-Hop informs him.

"What you mean, together slim, are you alright in

Chapter 32

in there?" It's still quiet and Juice-Hop has not come out the bathroom as of yet.

"That's it Juice, I'm coming in there," Teeny-Man alerts him. He tries the door handle and it's locked.

"Hey slim, this shit is for the birds," Teeny-Man tells him. Jaquiel hears what's going on and tries to intervene.

"Zooz-Szop openz thzee dzoor," Jaquiel asks him. Juice-Hop opens up and they see the blood. "Oh thzat'z nothzing I can fix thzat," Jaquiel tells him. Jaquiel goes and gets his first aid kit and cleans and disinfect it, and sews him back up and gives him another dose of antibiotics. It's a knock at the door they all looks at each other.

"It's Bab," Teeny-Man tells them both.

"Howz yooh know?" Jaquiel asks.

"His knock." Teeny-Man answers. Jaquiel goes to see with his gun in hand walking slowly on the side of the wall leading up to the door.

"It's me slim, open up," Babylon announces. Jaquiel opens up the and lets him in.

"Yez comrade, howz arz yooh?"

"I'm straight Frenchy." With his friends in plain view of him. "Look its getting close to that time we gonna have to get ready to take care of business," Babylon informs them.

"Slim before you say another word, how did you survive that mother fucken fall from the roof of that hotel?" Teeny-Man asks him.

"Slim, I don't know how it happened myself," he states. "Before y'all came up there with me. I was working and I heard this shooting and turned around and this dude was shooting out the window.

"The next thing I know the dude takes the water hose from the wall and jumps out the window. Next I see y'all and we do what we do and goes to the roof top. When the explosion happen I thought I was gone.

"But the dude who jumped out the window was using his feet pushing off the building. I guess trying to break the glass. I was blown back so far that I should have been dead. But he was swinging to far out that by the time I got to his level he had swung too far.

"I was able to grab a hold to the hose and slide down it and slid into him on the way down and knocked him off the hose. I was hanging on for my life for a good little while I felt the glass over my head break and I knew it was the law.

"They pulled me up with all the acronyms in the country looking at me, and wrapped me up in a blanket. Asked me a lot of questions. They didn't even search me they got a call over the radio saying something about a Chrysler 300m. and a Impala shooting on ninety five.

"They took me to the front part of the resort and took my name and took a picture of me. They all just rolled out of there. They sent me to where all the injured people were at, and I got out of there.

"Found me a lame took his car and rolled out to find you all bullshitting as always, and to make matters worst. You two have taught Jaquiel Froscios A.K.A. Jaq Frozt how to bullshit now," Babylon explains to them all.

"Bravo comrade, bravo," Jaquiel applauds him.

"It's not over y'all we got just one more piece of business to take care of," Babylon informs them.

"Hey slim, I was fucked up about this one. I thought you were gone. I-"

"When I grabbed a hold of the hose, I knew you were going to be acting like some old damn lady," Babylon says to Teeny-Man as he cuts him off from talking. "And I bet you it was Frenchy, who had to bring your butt back to life," he continues.

"Yeah slim, you right about that one Jaq Frozt pulled me through that one. But man I got to get this off my chest," Teeny-Man tells Babylon.

"T, what is it?" Babylon asks.

"Man I don't want to die without telling you the truth. This last one was close as a mother fucker. So I don't know if I will make this next one you're talking about."

"It's not that serious T."

"Bullshit Bab, I can't go to my gave hiding nothing from you. Hey slim, your little brother didn't kill your fish that day.

"I killed your fish by accident slim. I know you remember I was helping you clean your room. Well the screen in your window was too dirty so I went and got some easy-off oven cleaner and sprayed the screen.

"Well some of that foam shit got into the tank and was floating on top of the water, and your fish just started eating the foam. Slim I thought that shit was gangster until they got to shaking and shit then I knew shit was serious. So I scooped them out the tank and they were not moving.

"I was real fucked up about the situation at hand. Slim, I panicked and started to give the fish mouth to mouth-"

"The fish?" Juice-Hop interrupts to ask.

"Fall back Juice, damn!" Teeny-Man snaps. "Slim, I placed one of them between my lips, but it kept slipping out my mouth. So I placed it between my teeth to try to breath life back into it. The easy-off was like smoking the dirt off the dirty screen.

"It was real smoky too, the smoke made me sneeze and I accidently bit the bitch in half. Slim, I hope you can forgive me for that?" Teeny-Man asks in pure sincerely. Babylon looks at him and shakes his head he couldn't care less about some damn fish that died years ago.

"Slim, I lied about something else too," Teeny-Man tells him again.

"Slim, this is not necessary," Babylon tells him.

279

"Yeah it is slim, I got to get right just in case my ticket get punched," he states. Now he continues: "Do you remember Mahogany?" He asks.

"Mahogany who?"

"Pretty ass red Mahogany when you helped me through her window that night?"

"Yeah, I remember that night they moved away right?"

"Yeah, that's the one Bab," he rejoices about Babylon remembering.

"I remember that night Teeny-Man you hit that night," Babylon says with a grin on his face. "Yeah, everybody said she would never give you none," Babylon continues.

"Nawl Bab, I didn't hit the pussy that night."

"Yeah you did, I know for a fact you hit."

"Nawl Bab, look remember I told you I had to go piss-"

"Slim, I remember that night you made me smell your fingers waving them all around my nose," Babylon tries to refresh Teeny-Man's memory.

"No Bab, let me finish. I didn't go to piss, I went back in the hallway and pulled down my pants and shit. I squatted and then I ran my fingertips through my ass. I took my left hand and cracked my ass open, and ran my right hand fingertips all in my ass.

"Then I came out and fanned them under your nose real fast a few times," he confesses to Babylon. Babylon falls silent, and watches Teeny-Man with a puzzled look on his face.

"Hey slim, totally out of pocket for that, I know," Teeny-Man admits to him.

"Slim, you could have kept that to yourself. I wouldn't have held that against you," Babylon assures him.

"Peppy la pew," Jaquiel says, and Juice-Hop is on the floor laughing at Teeny-Man and Babylon. Jaquiel is squeezing his nose with his head upwards.

"Are you finished now?" Babylon asks Teeny-Man. "Because if so we can go on about our business," Babylon continues.

"Big boy, I'm finished," Teeny-Man tells him.

The Georgetown Heist

"We have to be ready for the next phase of our plan. Frenchy be ready for us when we return," Babylon tells him.

"Yez comrade, I vill vee veady vhen yoohz veturnz." They call a cab to come and pick them up, as they waits for the cab the news is on T.V.

"A young female intern has filed an complaint with allegations against Senator Walt James saying that he exposed himself to her and began to masturbate in front of her. She states that he told her that she was famine-"

"What the fuck is famine?" Teeny-Man asks out loud.

"And needed to eat something, and also called her an eater. When asked, the Senator declined comment. The young woman claims to have an eye witness to this act. Another young woman who was allegedly present during the act," the T.V. continues.

Jaquiel Froscios think it's sick, Juice-Hop think its funny and Babylon couldn't care less. Out of nowhere Teeny-Man goes off the handle.

"You mother fucken right the bitch gonna press charges. The bitch is a lioness and you gonna try to feed the bitch with another lioness present? The bitch don't like to share, the bitch do-not-like-to-share! If you know the bitch is hungry, why make her share?

"You disrespected the bitch by giving away her meal, she suppose to hit your mother fucken head. Lames always fucking up shit, if it's two things I hate one, a mother fucker who don't know how to feed a bitch. And two, a mother fucker trying to force feed a bitch.

"If she ain't trying to eat, she's not trying to eat. Mother fuckers just fucks the game up." Teeny-Man says. Nobody in the room knows what he's talking about as their cab pulls up and they depart Jaquiel.

***

"Sir, the football has been found it has been recovered at an lot inside of a trash truck. Checking through the truck's log. It has the route to Elvans

281

Road that's where the Mohammed's live. And also the team has not recovered anything from the Honesty farm. They have finished searching the grounds nothing has been turned up, not even an hit with the hand held survey equipment," Mrs. Culp tells Jimmy.

***

At their hotel Juice-Hop and Teeny-Man goes to their stash spots to retrieve their stones. Now they checks out their merchandise and all is good they heads out to meet Jaquiel.

"Let's hit a store before we head over Jaq Frozt's," Teeny-Man says.

Babylon decides to go and see Tootie before the trip to see Jaquiel, as the cab pulls up in front of the house. He can see his family members all out in the front yard. His family sees them and they goes up to him and his friends.

"Bab, give me some money," a female cousin asks him.

"What you need money for Ki-Ki?"

"I'm trying to go shopping."

"You still trying to go."

"That's fucked up how you do me Cuz."

"I got you before I leave girl." Babylon tells her while looking at Tootie who comes over to him.

"Tootie, I need to see you," Babylon tells him.

"Let's go inside the house," Tootie responds. They go inside and pass everybody going inside to get to his room now inside they get comfortable.

"I need a car," Babylon tells him.

"Shit, that ain't nothing."

"That's good, but I also need for you to start a bank account for my little brothers and sisters." After seeing that Babylon is for real, Tootie nods his head in agreement.

"I need for you to open them with the lease amount and then I will take care of the rest, hear?" Babylon hands his cousin a hand full of money.

"Hey Cuz, what's up you um, hit pay dirt?" Tootie asks him. Juice-Hop and Teeny-Man both looks at him.

The Georgetown Heist

"Damn Cuz, y'all terrible," Tootie tells them.

"Nawl, just a little hungry that's all." Babylon responds.

Tootie get's up and leaves out they go outside with the rest of Babylon's family. A good time has passed and they're still waiting on Tootie to return with the vehicle. He finally shows up in a bright red Dodge Charger.

"Shit, it took your ass long enough," Teeny-Man tells him.

"Ay Cuz, I wanted it to be proper," he tells Babylon.

They get into the car with Babylon getting into the back seat and they pulls off. Teeny-Man is still a little hungry so he pulls into the driveway of a store to put something on his stomach.

They all go inside Babylon goes straight for the candy section for some Twizzlers. The store was kind of huge and they all go their separate ways to get what they each wanted. There is a man watching Babylon from a good distance.

"Oh shit, it's him," the man says to himself. So he's getting closer to Babylon no one else can see him and vice versa. Babylon has no idea that he's being watched and stalked. There's some girls inside the store ordering something that the man behind the counter has just chopped up and placed inside of cups. Juice-Hop over hears the girls when they asked for it. He motions for Teeny-Man to come over to him.

"A slim, what's conk?" Juice-Hop asks.

"Oh that's that classic shit," he replies. The girls are watching them knowing that they are not from around there, and not from Florida, so they just watch the young men.

"Well shit I might as well eat some," Juice-Hop tells him.

"Slim, you can't eat no mother fucken conk are you crazy?"

"That's what they got."

"Juice, let me tell you something. Conk is a mixture of all kinds of shit. I now for a fact one of the things used in it is lye. And—"

283

"Ha-ha-ha-ha-ha!" One of the girls burst out laughing at him. He looks back at the girls with a look of surety on his face.

"Like I said slim conk is a mixture of shit broads put in their hair. It's like the first perm they used to straighten out them nappy as wigs of theirs. It has lye and potatoes in it also and that shit get damn hot on them heifers heads," he explains.

The girls are laughing at his ignorance and he can't seem to know what's the big laughter is for.

"How do you spell it?" One of the girls asks him.

"C-o-n-k," he spells it out.

"Yeah, that's how you spell it, the conk that you are talking about. But that's not the conch that we're eating," she tells him.

"Momma, there's nobody in the world who eat's anything by the name of conk."

"You're right again as far as c-o-n-k." Teeny-Man is thinking he might can get some free sex off, what he thinks to be some country ass Florida girls, so he states a proposal at her.

"Momma I'm a betting man, and I say put your money where your mouth is."

"How much?" she asks.

"I got a grand on it."

"I don't have a stack."

"A stack of what?"

"A thousand stack."

"Oh! Shit, well you got something that you can put up for collateral," Teeny-Man tells her while looking between her legs. "I'll give you an installment plan," he continues while now smiling and nodding at her crotch area.

"I have no problem with that," and now the other girls are talking amongst themselves.

"Bet that up," the rest of the girls tell Teeny-Man.

"What the fuck that mean?" Teeny-Man asks them.

"It means that all us want in on the bet," another girl snaps on him. He think its sweet, and now takes Juice-Hop to the side.

"Juice, I told you these Miami bitches off the

chain slim, they just want to freak off with a mother fucker from D.C." They hear the last part of the conversation.

"We knew y'all were from up North we just didn't know where at," another girl tells them. Teeny-Man think she's lying, in his mind he thinks Florida girls are sweet.

"Hey Poppa," the girl calls the man who had previously served them their food he comes to them.

"Can you tell them what this is inside this cup?" she asks the older man.

"It's conch," he answers her.

"How do you spell it?"

"C-o-n-c-h," he spells it out.

"And what is it, and how do it come?"

"It's a seafood, and it comes in a shell," he says as he looks at Teeny-Man, who's now mad as hell at the Florida girls for this one. The man start to walk away from them.

"You can pay up now," she tells him.

He looks at them in a funny way, but doesn't move a muscle.

"Oh, don't forget we faded your ass too," another girl reminds him. Teeny-Man ends up paying out six grand to the girls.

"Up north mother fuckers are sweet, girl we need to go up there," and Juice-Hop gives in.

"Hey main man, bring me a cup of that shit," Juice-Hop tells him. He pays for it now turns to Teeny-Man. "Slim, you want some? This shit ain't bad," he informs Teeny-Man.

"I don't want none of that country ass shit." He coldly states.

During the course of their education of conch they lost track of Babylon. Teeny-Man spots him talking to some dude. But he can see that Babylon is not himself, so he waves to Juice-Hop and goes the back route to come up behind the man.

So Juice-Hop comes up from behind Babylon and sees that the man is talking about bringing them in. Teeny-Man comes up from behind the man with his gun drawn.

"You got something on your mind, you want on your

ass?" Teeny-Man asks him. The man notices Teeny-Man's gun.

"I'm Detective Vic Williams, I'm from Washington D.C.," he tells them.

"What the fuck you want with us?" Juice-Hop asks.

"I've been tracking you all since you left the city, I left also." That didn't sit well with any of them.

"I say lets pick his pocket and leave him." Juice-Hop suggests.

"I say kill'em him," Teeny-Man suggests.

"Let's pick his pockets then," Babylon says as all the young men have their guns out pointed at Vic. He now sees the Desert Eagles they all have. Vic surrenders and places his hands in the air thinking that the operators of the store will call the authorities.

"We're not going to crush your ass out this time. But the next time you come across out path bullshitting with this cop shit it's your ass," Teeny-Man tells him.

They leave the store with the detective gunless in Florida. The only thing he can do is watch the young men leave him.

"I will not stop, I promise you, I will not stop until I catch you all on my life!" Detective Vic Williams yells his vow to them. They pulls out of sight from the detective. Babylon goes and reaches for his phone and calls Jaquiel Froscios.

"Hey comrade, the tiger is out the cage." Babylon tells him jokingly.

"Thzat'z great Bab-boo-lawn," he replies.

"We're on our way now we'll see you when we get there."

Jaquiel Froscios is just remembering what Babylon said to him about seeing him when he get's there. It's been a good little while since he last talked to Babylon. He's beginning to feel as though something is happening.

He decides to place a call himself to the young man. The phone rings, but Babylon doesn't answers so he hangs up. Now he's pacing his floor wondering where are his young comrades.

He can't take is any longer so he decides to make himself some tea to calm down. In the process of making the tea his phone vibrates he doesn't see it light up or hear it moving on the tabletop.

***

"**Frenchy ain't answering** his phone," Babylon informs the other two.

"Let's wait a minute and then try back," Juice-Hop tells him.

So they all agree on that approach they are enjoying the luxury of the mansion that they just took over. That's located on a secret man made Island off of Biscayne. This is where they want to do business at with Jaquiel Froscois.

***

Jaquiel takes a look at his phone and sees that he has missed two of Babylon's phone calls and breaks his neck to call him back.

"Comez'on comrade pickzup," he says and Babylon answers his phone.

"Yez, comrade hello. Yez okay now thzat vill vee perfect. I knowz howz tzoo get thzere yez. I am leavingz now. I hov everythzing vee need yez. I need a voat?"

***

A short time later Jaquiel is at the address after
getting off his newly took boat. He walks up to the
mansion in a bit of confusion. He do not know who the
young men are with or if they are doing business with
some other people. And just need him to help broker
the deal.

"Jaq Frozt, what's up you cold mother fucker you?"
Teeny-Man yells from the back patio of the mansion
leading to the dock. The Frenchman hasn't a clue, he
knows one thing this is a very expensive mansion that
he's entering. They are at the door waiting on him. He
sees that Teeny-Man has a bottle of Krug, Clos du
Mesnil 1995 that he's drinking from, and Jaquiel knows
that it's something going on here.

"Comradez tells mi vat'z gohing on here?" he asks
them.

"Goddamn Jaq, a black man can't have a good home?
Is that how it is over in France? Oh my bad, I got
money now. You pronounce it Fronce. I most definitely
don't want to go there. A black man don't stand a
chance in France.

"And for your information Jaq Frozt, we actually
are borrowing the place just for this occasion. We got
it from a nice young white couple," Teeny-Man informs
Jaquiel. "Ay Jaq, I just want you to know you ain't
the only one who can um, entertain a mother fucker in
a nice place," Teeny-Man continues.

"It'z nize comradez." Jaquiel wishes to know about
the deal, if it's still on or not? "Arz vee stzill a
goh Bab-boo-lawn?"

"Yeah Jaquiel." Babylon assures him. "They need to
know the layout of the payments or should I say the
methods of payment?" Babylon tells him.

"Comradez thzee procezz vill vee eezy all of thzee
money vill vee vired tzoo thzee accountz in vhich yooh
providez," Jaquiel explains.

"So basically you're saying that you can send the
money anywhere we tell you?" Babylon asks.

"Yez."

"How will we know if the transfers have been

completed?" Teeny-Man asks Jaquiel.

"It vill tzake no longer thzan twzenty minutez tzopz.

"Okay price range Frenchy, what are you willing to pay for them?" Juice-Hop asks him.

"Huh!" Jaquiel sighs. Now looking at Babylon who shakes his head no. "Namez jorw pricez," he tells them.

After all of what Teeny-Man and Juice-Hop went through this should be the easiest part of it, but can't think of what to say. Let alone a price, and Babylon knows it.

"Arz yooh allz in need of a little help in thziz dzepartment comradez?"

"Yeah, but no Jaq," Juice-Hop responds. They all just smile at one another.

"Give mi your namez comradez and I vill tzake care of thzee rezt, yez?" he assures them.

"Maurice Barnes A.K.A. Teeny-Man."

"Neil Green A.K.A. Juice-Hop." A few seconds passes and Babylon still hasn't said a word. Jaquiel takes it the young man knows that he already knows his name.

"Comrade Bab-boo-lawn, arz yooh veady?" Jaquiel asks them.

"No Frenchy, not yet," Babylon answers him. Jaquiel takes out his satellite phone and places a call.

"Ponc'e I needz new accountz szet up now pleaze, and on mi conformation change thzee dzebit cardz over tzoo thzee new namez alzo." Ponc'e is also telling him something on the other end of the phone. "Je suis riche!" ("I'm rich!") He yells out loud out of shock. Now they looks at each other like its their first time ever being alone in a room with a girl.

"Okay Tzeeny-Mon yooh firzt, vut yooh hov szomethzing forz mi, yez?" Teeny-Man digs his hand down in the front of his pants, and pulls out a bag and throws it over to Jaquiel who jumps out of his skin damn near as he catches the bag.

"Ohz shzit comrade!" Jaquiel says in an scared voice.

They all laughs at him, but Jaquiel knows this is no laughing matter. Juice-Hop goes up stairs to get his bag. Now back down stairs he hands his bag over to Jaquiel.

"Here you go Jaq."

"Thzank yooh Zooz-Szop."

Jaquiel Froscios empties both bags on the table in two separate piles and knows immediately what he's looking at. He really don't feel that bad for the young men. Because he knows that they really don't care they just want to get rid of their diamonds.

"Vee arz good comradez, szo pleaze namez jorw pricez?"

They take their time thinking about it since two people already told them that the stones where worthless. Babylon can sense that they are having a hard time. Because of the previous appraisals, so he intervenes on their behalf.

"What did I say that it should be easily worth in the car?" Babylon reminds them both. Teeny-Man thinks about it for a second.

"Ay Jaq Frozt, I'm just trying to get rid of them. Give me fifty million for mines." Teeny-Man tells him.

The Frenchman looks at him for a moment, and then nods in agreement with him.

"I vill give yooh fifty millionm dzarlarz."

"But before you do that I want you to send my mother and father some money first."

"No problem juzt give mi thzee accountz numbahz or I vill give thzem one."

"They got one already, I will get it from them." Teeny-Man goes into the other room by himself. While Teeny-Man is in the other room, Jaquiel turns his attention to Juice-Hop. He is looking at him waiting for an answer from him.

"Ay Jaq, I want the same amount I just want to get this shit over with. Fifty million is more than enough for me," Juice-Hop tells him. He looks and smiles he knows they just want to get rid of them.

"I vill dzoo jorwz alzo," Jaquiel tells him.

***

290

The Georgetown Heist

Teeny-Man is talking to his mother, his father is not home so his mother gives him her account number, but she doesn't knows her husband's. So he goes back to the Frenchman, and gives him the information on his mother.

Babylon calls Tootie for the account numbers for the other family members he requested. Tootie passes the information on to Babylon. He's writing down something, and Jaquiel sees him.

"Ponc'e vee hov a goh," he informs his assistant. Now looking at Teeny-Man. "Tzeeny-Mon, vhere dzoo yooh vant it allz tzoo goh?"

"I want a million each in the accounts that I just gave you, and I want five million in my mother's account," Teeny-Man instructs him.

"Szo plaze wun million dzarlarz each in thzee childzen accountz, and plaze five million dzarlarz in thzee mother'z account," Jaquiel instruct Ponc'e. "Now activate thzee account forz Maurice Barnes A.K.A. Tzeeny-Mon forz forty twzoo million dzarlarz and activate thzee dzevit card." Jaquiel finishes.

They are all looking at the Frenchman. They know that if that money don't show the Frenchman will be a dead man, today.

"Call yoor mothza and hov her tzoo check thzee account, eithza vy phone or computza," Jaquiel asks Teeny-Man.

"Okayz Zooz-Szop, vhere dzoo yooh vant it?"

"Man send two and half to both of them."

"Szend twzoo and a half tzoo both accountz, yez? And activate thzee account forz Neil Green A.K.A. Zooz-Szop forz forty five million dzarlarz and activate thzee dzevit card alzo. Now vee juzt szit bock and szee vhat hoppenz.

The time has gone by now and everybody is still waiting on confirmation. It's been over twenty minutes and they are getting shaky in the room. Teeny-Man gets up to go into the other room to call his mother once more, it's like the fourth time. While he's gone Babylon looks the Jaquiel and smiles.

"I'z hope thzat'z a good smilez Bab-boo-lawn?" He asks.

"It was a good smile Frenchy, I was just thinking about all we've been through in such a short time that's all." Babylon explains to him. "And besides, I don't cross any of my friends for nothing or nobody. Because-"

"Awwwww! It hit, it hit! Slim my mother done fell out in that mother fucker," Teeny-Man runs out and tells everyone as he interrupts Babylon. Jaquiel now turns to Juice-Hop and hands him his international debit card along with Teeny-Man.

"Thzeze arz international dzevit cardz uzed like vegular vank cardz, vut no chargez. Yooh can uze thzem anyvhere in thzee world," he informs them. Juice-Hop gets up and hugs Jaquiel tightly.

"Thank you Jaq."

"Okay Zooz-Szop." Now here comes Teeny-Man following suit behind Juice-Hop. He goes and hugs Jaquiel tightly and Jaquiel pushes Teeny-Man off him.

"Mistafallah! Bahb, Zooz, vhat dzid I tzell yoohz? Tzeeny-Mon iz on thzee hammah, yez?" Jaquiel tells the other two. With Babylon stuck, Juice-Hop burst out laughing at Teeny-Man facial expression.

"What part of the game is this Jaq Frozt? You don't supposed to say no shit like to me dog." Teeny-Man tells him then shakes his head at him.

"I juzt joking Tzeeny-Mon."

"I know that's right, sweet cakes." They all are full of laughter tonight as the Frenchman gets back at Teeny-Man.

"Good mother fucken lookin Jaq Frozt, cold mother fucker you. Any place, any time Jaq Frozt," Teeny-Man tells him.

"Thzank yooh voth, I shzall not forget yooh twzoo." Jaquiel felt Teeny-Man words and felted that the young man was being sincere. They will be forever linked.

"Ay T, you might as well send your girl some money," Babylon tells him.

"I fuck with her like a bear shit's it the woods. In spots, and this is not one of them," Teeny-Man explains to him. "Bab, we made slim," Teeny-Man finishes.

The Georgetown Heist

Teeny-Man and Juice-Hop are getting ready to leave. They stop, now looking at their debit cards and places them inside their pockets. Now their water taxi come and they say their good byes and leave. Now Babylon is alone with Jaquiel and begins to speak his mind.

"Look, I know that these stones are not what we thought they were and I don't care and I don't want to know what they are. Nor how the hell you knew we had them. But I will sell you half of my small ones for this," Babylon tells Jaquiel and now slides him the paper he was writing on.

"I am keeping all the big ones and the rest of the small ones," he continues.

"Oh shzit! Yooh vant'z twzenty five?" Jaquiel is shocked over the price.

"Je pens'ee vou e'tae riche?" ("I thought you were rich?") Babylon asks him. He breaks out smiling at the young man who just spoke French to him. He know its more than meet the eyes when it comes to this you man here.

"I'z hov no problem vith thzee price Bab-boo-lawn." he knows he can't talk the you man down or out of his price, either way it's a steal for him.

"Frenchy, go ahead and get my stuff together so I can be on my merry way." Babylon tells him. He smiles at Babylon.

"Bab-boo-lawn, come vith mi tzoo Fronze," Jaquiel asks him.

"Nawl not yet Frenchy, but I give you my word one day I will be to see you in France. I hope the offer will always be open to me?"

"Alvayz comrade, alvayz." Babylon get's up to leave when Jaquiel stops him in his tracks.

"Bab-boo-lawn, yooh hov a special skill and yooh hov thzat gift, thzat many men vish thzey hod. Dzon't ever looze it mi friend," Jaquiel tells him in his most straighten voice. "I vill tzake care of everythzing Bab-boo-lawn," he assures him.

Babylon leaves to catch his water taxi also, Jaquiel Froscios waits just minutes after. And now he's out the door and also into a water taxi, but

Babylon never sees him leave.

***

Teeny-Man is on cloud nine and this is the best day of
his life. The darkness has gotten darker over the
Biscayne area and he is being followed by someone. But
he don't seem to care about it much not that he can
see the individual anyway.

He walks through an alley way and looks up at the
sky and smiles. He continues to walk and sees a figure
in front of him. He can't quite make it out, but he's
not the lease concern about it and the figure comes
closer towards him.

"Ay! Aaawwwww! Hey B, what's up baby, where the-
"

"Boom, boom, boom, boom!" the shots ring out into
the night and interrupts his words. Teeny-Man's body
hits the ground hard. He gets to his knees struggling
to keep his balance.

"You my man slim," Teeny-Man whispers with
disappointment and sadness in his voice. The person to
whom Teeny-Man just called his man, now places his gun
directly at his face. Teeny-Man shows a bloody smile,
and now he shows some teeth with his smile. The
shooter is disgusted that Teeny-Man isn't begging for
his life.

Now in a rage he shoots Teeny-Man is his face
three times, to watch his blood flow was a sight for
him. He never imagine doing such a thing to him. He
leaves in a hurry to find Juice-Hop.

He's in constant radio contact with someone and
they are trailing Juice-Hop. He's in route to their
location to get Juice-Hop himself.

***

Now at the location he goes straight for his new
accomplices.

"Where is Juice?" he asks.

"He's up in room four fifteen," another man
informs him.

So he goes straight up to the room door and knocks

on it. Juice-Hop carefully comes to the door.
"Yeah, who is it?"
"It's me."
"Who the fuck is me?" Juice-Hop yells back through
the door with gun in hand.
"Why don't you come and see for yourself." Juice-
Hop takes a look through the peephole of the door. His
eyes are big as ever as he rushes to unlock his door,
against his better judgment.
"Oh shit, what's up baby boy I-"
"Boom, boom, boom!" Juice-Hop never stood a chance
he should have kept his first mind and shot through
the door. Just like he done with Teeny-Man, he now
goes through the pockets of Juice-Hop and takes his
debit card also. Juice-Hop and Teeny-Man's friend
get's a call.
"What's your location?"
"We are still in Bascayne about to proceed with
the package," the caller responds.
"Do you have a visual?"
"Yes, he's by himself walking towards the docks at
the shipping yards. He's wearing a white sweat suit."
"Go ahead and get him now."
"Yes Sir, roger that."
"Let me know the exact location once you'd
captured him, out." He drives to the docks on Biscayne
and is awaiting the location of his men. On his way he
knows, that what he's done is wrong. But its the life
that he lives all or nothing. Kill or be killed, he
prefer to kill. His phone vibrates.
"Yeah!"
"We are at pier eleven in front of the Starkiss
warehouse."
"I'm almost there."

***

The man they are after at the docks walks to a
warehouse and goes into a side window of the place and
is met by two men, one white the other black.
"Don't move!" he's told. He looks at the men with
scorn, they have their guns drawn on him, so he won't

Chapter 34

make a move until its time for him to.

"Move over here," he's ordered by the white one, and refuses to do so.

They already knows he's a lot to handle. So they just keeps their guns on him. It's someone coming up from behind them all that's been watching the entire time, so he finally decides to intervene.

The two men never sees him coming because they are too busy keeping an eye on their prisoner.

"Um, um," he clears his throat to announce his presence.

***

Twenty minutes later underneath the warehouse it is dark and the only light is coming from the lonely street pole on the opposite side of the street. He's now pulling up and sees the two figures standing over top of the other two figures lying face down on the ground.

He is getting closer to them all he was told that the prisoner was wearing a white sweat suit. He knows the men with the guns are his, he recognized them by their suits. He can see the white sweat suit on the ground, but he can't understand why it's two people on the ground and then it hits him.

But at this time his men takes a step back into the darkness of the warehouse, as to be getting out his way.

He goes straight for the prisoners and sees the captives have been tied and gagged.

"I'm going to kill your faggot ass first you French whore," he states while he points his gun at the back of the Frenchman's head. "Bye bitch," he tells him and puts three bullets through the man's head.

The two men in the dark look at one another. Now the man moves to the other man on the ground. "Before I kill your black ass, I want you to know that I killed Teeny-Man and Juice-Hop, and it was extremely easy. And I will have all the debit cards to myself. And in the end you're nothing more than a two bit street punk," he continues. He now places two bullets in the back of his head.

The shots ring out into the night. "Now let me see your go hard ass," he says as he begins to turn the body over. Now one of the figures that's in the dark emerges into the light as the man continues to turn over the body and sees the face of the corpse. His eyes gets big his mouth is wide open. He knows it, he's been tricked.

As he tries to cut his eyes as to see behind him. He places his hands in the air, while his Sig Sauer nine millimeter hangs around his right index finger. He hears the "Click!" from the hammer being drawn back. With his arms in the upright position he whispers: "Babylon."

"Boom, boom, boom, boom, boom, boom, boom!" the seven shots empties the fifty caliber Desert Eagle. At point blank range the anti-terrorist ammo makes it, so that Bernard will never be identified by his face.

As Babylon looks at Jaquiel Froscios, and now looks down at himself. He notices that the two dead rogue agent's suits don't look half bad on them.

"How did you find me?"

"I vent bock tzoo thzee vazicz,"

"The Basics?"

"I followed yooh." Babylon gives him a look of appreciation. "Thzee szame vay I found yooh thzey found yooh, thzey had szome help," he says while pointing at the rogue agents.

Babylon finds the debit cards belonging to his friends. "Frenchy divide their money between their families accounts that they gave you." Babylon tells him.

"Yez, I vill dzoo thziz." Now Jaquiel hands Babylon his own debit card. "I tzook thzee libertiez." Babylon takes his card and now starts to walk off.

"Bab-boo-lawn, arz yooh szure yooh von't goh vith mi tzoo Fronze?" He asks once more.

"I'm on my own mission, Frenchy."

'Mi Bab-boo-lawn, in our profession vee keep tzoo thzee shadowz, but vee dzon't hov tzoo keep tzoo thzem vy ourselvez," he tells him.

Babylon looks back and smiles while shaking his head. He just stays walking on in to the night. Jaquiel walks away also he never looks back again. He seems to have just disappeared in the distance.

Babylon is thinking about his friends, for a fact South East D.C.'s finest. He will miss Teeny-Man and Juice-Hop terribly as he walks and thinks about it, he's not even on the planet right now.

***

Walking though the alleyway a dog starts barking. "Shhhh, keepza quiet," the dog continues to bark. "Pssshhh, pssshhh," the silenced bullets fly out. "Arrh." the shot dog cries out from the two shots from the forty five. One in the dog's side the other in it's back.

"Good dzoggy, yez?" He looks around at the house no lights come on. Now he looks down both ways of the alley. He hop's the fence, and goes up to the house and breaks in it. Coming through the back door the locks were just in his way.

Now in the house he looks around in the kitchen the dining room and living room. He sees a picture of Ayatolla Khomeini and Arabic writings all over the place. No one's on the main floor so he takes the stairs and heads to the bedrooms.

The first room is the boys room with bunk beds and

another one going in another direction. Next the oldest, a girl she's knocked out. He slowly turns the knob to the master bedroom, and pushes the door open with slow caution.

He sees that the couple are sound asleep, He closes the door behind him softly. Over at the bed now he snatches the covers off the couple. They don't move an inch. With his gun out and pointed at the bed he kicks the bed.

The both move around squirming and reaching for the covers from each other.

"Je voir que vous pouvoir pas garder un secret," ("I see you can't keep a secret,") The couple is terrified now that they are coming around to what's happening.

"Bizmallah!" the husband says.

"Vhy dzid yooh tzalk?" Jaquiel asks the husband.

"What are you talking about?" The husband frantically asks.

"Thzee ziamondz, I tzold yooh not tzoo szay nothzing zabout thzee ziamondz." Jaquiel refreshes his memory. Jaquiel eyes has adjusted to the dark room he sees the both of them better now.

"They said if I didn't talk they would send me and my wife back to Iran. I told them so be it, but they told me that my children would be leaving with us also. I purposely had children in America to give them a chance at life," the husband explains.

"Szo yooh tzell zabout thzee ziamondz, yez?"

"Yes, because I didn't want my children going back with me." He looks at Jaquiel with a sure look of confidence. "Had it been just my wife and I, I would gladly go," he continues.

"I szend yooh and jorw vife bock tzoo Iran, yez?" With both guns covering both occupants of the bed. He empties both guns into each of them, and reloads and walks over to the head of the bed and put one more in each of their heads and sets the house on fire as he leaves out.

***

J.J. Honesty-Bey

Now as he's driving past the homes all of the porch
lights are on. It's dawn and he decides to wait.
Parking on the corner he's looking in the direction of
the house suddenly the door to the house opens up.

"Ooooh, vight on tzime," he says to himself. A man
appears through the door and begins to run off the
porch and down the steps. He don't stop he turns to
his right and starts jogging. He's on his way past the
Frenchman. Jaquiel ducks down to avoid being seen the
jogger goes past and never sees him.

The jogger is out of sight now and Jaquiel gets
out the car and proceed to the house. He look around
and sees that all the neighbors porch lights are still
on.

It doesn't look like anyone is coming or going
right now. So he goes through with his advance to the
house.

***

As Babylon places an envelope and packages inside the
mail box after leaving the Setai Hotel where he has a
Penthouse for three days. He now turns to walk away
and sees a store. He goes into the store to buy some
Twizzlers. On his way out he begins to think about his
friends again and just drifts off as he walks.

***

As he looks over the entire command room he's totally
upset with everything and everybody. "I can't believe
that damn Tonya!" Jimmy yells out loud. "I'll be glad
once they get rid of her ass and that damn unit she
and that ding bat runs." The command room hasn't a
clue to what he's talking about.

"Sir is there something wrong?" Mrs. Culp asks.

"Yeah, the dinosaur agency that's over due for
extinction. That damn M.O.T.H.E.R.!" He says as they
look at him.

"Is that a real agency?"

"Multi Operational Terrorist and Hostage Emergency
Rescue." Jimmy says.

300

The Georgetown Heist

***

Tired and drenched he walks up the steps to his house he goes in and heads directly to the frig.
"Lee!" A woman calls out to him. He grabs a bottle of water and goes to see her. Going through the dining room to the living room he sees her.
"What is it?" Lee asks. She's silent, but she's looking directly at him.
"Je espoir que eux salair vous bon," ("I hope that they paid you good,") a voice says to him. Lee steps from around the dining room to the living room. He sees the man and he has a gun in his hand.
"What you want?" Lee asks him.
"Yooh," Jaquiel tells him plainly.
"You get the fuck out, before I call police." Jaquiel walks towards the woman and points his gun at her.
"Yooh tzalked, I paid yooh tzoo vee quiet."
"They pay more, you know game." Jaquiel cocks his gun and the woman starts crying. "Get out my house, you not come here no more!" Lee tells Jaquiel as the woman sobs, Lee continues. "He not pull trigger."
"Psshhh, psshhh,"
Of the two shots one enters her forehead and the other enter her eye. The first one exits from the nape of her neck, and the other the middle part of her head. The white wall behind her looks like somebody threw spaghetti on it.
"Ahhhh!" Lee cries out loud and takes off after Jaquiel.
"Pssshhh!" Just one in the gut and Lee goes down on both knees holding his stomach. "It'z szo hard tzoo findz good criminalz thzeze dzays." Jaquiel tells Lee. He's walking over towards Lee and points his gun down at him. "Thzey killed allz vut wun of mi comradez vecauze of yooh."
"Psshhh, pssshhh, pssshhh!"
The first shot hit's the top left of Lee's head leaving out hitting his left shoulder. The second in the left cheek through the teeth and jaw only to end in his chest. The third strikes him in the left

side of his neck and ricocheting off his spinal cord exiting his back.

He falls face first while still on his knees. Jaquiel Froscios turns and walks out the front door.

***

It's dark now and he's about to leave Florida, so he waves down a cab. One stops for him he gets in and closes the door behind him.

"Ay take me all the way to Homestead private strip, I have a private plane to catch." Babylon tells the driver.

They pulls off into the night he just watches the traffic. He notices that it's getting a little darker, where they're going and less street lights.

"Hey, where the hell are we?" Babylon questions the driver.

"It's a short cut," the driver tells him.

"Short cut?" Babylon asks himself. He looks outside it's too dark like the boondocks. "Hey, I'm straight pull over, now." Babylon tells him. The driver sensing the tone in his voice pulls over. Babylon gets out and takes a look around the area.

"This is the boondocks," he tells himself.

"What about my pay?" The driver asks the young man.

Babylon takes a look around and is getting a very bad feeling about this situation. With his back turned to the driver, Babylon follows his gut. And now goes into his waist band and pulls out his gun and quickly shoves it into the cab's window and fires two shots at the driver.

The driver sensing it was rotating backwards as Babylon was turning. Babylon only struck the driver once in the left shoulder and just scrapes his chest. Multiple people are also watching this from far away, with awe.

The cab driver pulls off and grabs his radio and starts talking on it. Babylon starts walking he's lost, but keeps on moving. He can feel it, it's in the air. Two men are approaching him they go past him.

The Georgetown Heist

He figures the vibe came from the two men. Still walking straight ahead looking up at the night skies his mind is back on his dead friends. It's short lived as he can hear the sounds of vehicles coming to a screeching hault.

The vehicles are positioned at an angle on both sides of the street. Now he see a car slowly approaching. He can see it more plainly now. It's dark colored paint shines even in the dead of night from the light of the other vehicles. It's a Maybach that comes to a stop at the end of the other vehicles.

Like clockwork all the vehicles empty out. He's watching this with questionable eyes and mind. "It got to be some Guineas," he tells himself. The driver get's out and goes around and opens the door behind him as he holds the door men runs to the open door. Babylon sees little, next someone is getting out and he sees high heels.

"It's a broad?" He asks himself.

She's fully out the car now. The men makes a complete circle around her. She says something to the men and the circle breaks a path for her. Now she's walking towards him he looks in disbelief at this act of stupidity. She's up on him now and looks him over multiple times.

She's looking around in many directions and takes her flat right hand and swipes it across her throat as to tell someone to kill or kill it.

***

As they lay upon the hill Detectives Mercury and Williams are ready to apprehend their suspect. They have and entire S.W.A.T. team along with their tactical units up on a hill looking down.

As they all hear the sounds from their units none can make it out what's going on. The yells are everywhere, so are the men running getting out of position. And alerting those below to their presence. But the people at the bottom show no care about them.

"I have him," one of the agents reports in his headset. He's talking about Detective Williams and

he's right over top of him. "Put your hands up," he
tells Vic.
"I am Detective Williams, I-"
"I know who you are Vic, don't move and you won't
get killed tonight. I want you to make it home to your
young son and your wife." The man tells him, and with
that Vic goes silent.

***

"**Hey tall dark** and handsome, I see your youth
serving me for the next thirty years. What are you
now, seventeen right?" She asks him.
"I'm not interested in anything you're selling,"
Babylon tells her.
"I can give you the man who kidnapped your
mother."
"I'm straight Momma."
"You're not making this easy for me. Well you
don't suppose to anyway. Well I must tell you, you
don't have many options right now, Nimrod."
"I have enough of them," he tells her while
looking around for possible escape routes using just
his eyes. She knows exactly what he's doing and that's
a sign of a natural.
"I'm here to try to help you that's all I want to
do here."
"You forgot the say, you're from the government."

304

The Georgetown Heist

"Yes I am, but not like you know it."

"Go help the bear." He starts to walk pass the woman and she side steps in front of him, she looks straight in his eyes.

"I can see your soul," she tells him with such enthusiasm as she continues to look him over. "And you are not afraid, I love it."

He cocks back the hammer on the Desert Eagle. She sees and hears it and is unfazed by it. He's rasing it upwards towards her and before he can point it at her.

"Boom!"

"Owwww!" Babylon yells out in pain.

"Oh my, that had to hurt," she playfully says.

Not knowing his determination she allows him to walk up on her. By the time she realizes it, its too late. He has his hands around her throat choking the living life out her. They converge on him, now hitting and kicking him.

"The more you give it to me, the worst she gets it," Babylon yells to them all. "Come on and give me y'all best, so I can give her my best. She will get it way worst than me," he continues.

A woman comes with her weapon he doesn't see her she fires at him. "Arrrrgggghhh!" He bites down on his teeth and grunts. He still doesn't let the woman go. The stun gun has no effect on him. She steps back and adjusts the voltage on the weapon and he takes aim again and fires once more.

"Arrrrrgggghhh!" Babylon growls out loud the stun gun brings him to his knees. But he never lets' go of the woman's throat. A male comes and takes the weapon from the woman and he readjusts the stun gun and fires at him.

The pain is so severe that he let's go of the woman's throat and falls to the ground. The woman now trying to gasp for air her members move in all around them.

The male with the stun gun has it pointed in a downward position. With a quick jolt, Babylon jumps up and takes the weapon from the male. They're all caught off guard and they are amazed at him.

Babylon first fires the weapon at the woman who

first stung him with the weapon. "Aaaahhh!" She
screams out and falls to the ground. Next is the male
who stung him to the ground. "Awww!" He yells out
falling to the ground face first.

As the rest of them run taking cover behind each
other like cowards. Pushing the person closes to them
in front of them. Babylon never sees the man walking
behind him in the dark, and he 's carrying a weapon
himslef.

"Shoooooop!" It cuts through the night air.
Babylon feels something happening to him, but he can't
figure it out just yet. The potency of the
tranquilizer dart totally disarms him. He's going out
now and the first woman has herself together finally.

***

The Operative now sees what's happening down with
Babylon and decides that its time to put Vic to bed.
He himself shoots Vic with a dart that knocks him out
also, and leaves him with the now dead S.W.A.T. and
Tactical teams.

But not before Vic get's a chance to see that
Babylon was confronted and them subdued.

***

So she walks towards him, now over top of him she
begins to talk to her people:

"Look at him!" She yells at them. "Babylon, in a
losing battle he's still defiant to the end. He's
going to do me proud." He's going out now, but she
knows he can still hear her.

"Oh and by the way, my name is Tonya, Tonya Stone
and welcome to **M.O.T.H.E.R.**"

Acknowledgments

Alisha, I got to put her first or I'll never hear the end of it. "I'm your mother's only daughter." Now we have Pam, Bernadette, Marcia and Buttons my sexy sisters. Earnest, Pedro, Terrence and Terrell my brothers. My mother's fine ass sisters aunt Debra and Denise. And the gorgeous Zanobia, love ya Reds! I know I'm going to catch hell for this one Tay, Darrick and Darryl and we have Lil' Darrick, Diamond (my baby), Teia (with your jinxy self), young Tay, Darricia, Darrel and baby Mya. And a big welcome to the family Tiff. Switching lanes my lovely aunts Gloria, Connie and Bunny. And the patriarch of my father's side my uncle Alphonso "Big Teddy" Malone. And a special thanks to Ms. Phylis Copeland for simply being there. The best wrap partner in the world James King, The Notorious Black... Hey slim I know you heard the one about the lion and the monkey's tail before, just to tell you we're on ice that's all. Michael "Mike-Mike" Williams one of those damn Caper's babies. Sean "Big Sean" Belser-Bey, Reginald "Big Reg" Scott-Bey. To the 000's, 007's, 016's and everything up down and in between. All the homies the good, the bad and the ugly. I have no ill will, it's what we do. Now back to me I just tried my hand at something. I look at it just another one of us trying to do something positive. Gerard "Champ" Jordan, you said we're going to be friends forever we won't live forever but I'll take what we have today you're alright Champ got your ways but you're alright. And if by chance that Floyld Mayweather Jr., ever see this or someone that knows him. Tell him to please go to the Maryland prison that Gerard Jordan is in and spar against him, just once please!. My brother, Marlow Bates Sr., better known to the streets as "The Real Marlow Stanfield," I can't wait for your book to drop Marlow. Raqueb "Tic" Wallace it don't get no more real than you homie, and also to the lovely Hope. Hope I'm sending you a sincere get well soon we're all pulling for you. Love Ya! Bernard "Big Dog" Bellamy, David "Big Dave" Potter, Calvin "Poodie" Wilson, Garald "Soldier" Dent, Tracy "Bay Boo" Peterson (The Great Bay Boo), Dwayne "D-Wade" Farmer, Ron "Angola" Brady.

Raymond "Big Head" Pope, Glenn L. Hudson (Big Glen),
Rick Britton from Columbia Maryland, and a young South
East soldier James "Murdah" Miller my young homie.
This is a must here and a rare one Major R.E. Scott,
for the authorization to allow my manuscript to be
sent back in after I typed it up in here in the first
place. And also to Ms. K.A. Robinson and Mr. B Edelen
for allowing me to keep an extra chair in my cell to
use for typing, thank you three. Why is Theodore
"Theo" Johnson from Park Heights in this book? To all
of my Florida family you all have been real good to
old Jive. Football is not the same without you. When I
was leaving Coleman II. Some young boy from North
Carolina told me he's going to be the best linebacker
in the history of the Feds. I told him that was going
to be a challenge. Then he said he can't see why
people called me that and that I don't look like
nothing. I was just an old man that everybody talked
about. He bragged to me telling me that he could read
a running play, any running play while it is going on.
He looked at me and smiled. He asked me could I do it
and I told him no. And he laughed and gave me props
for telling him the truth. After he stopped laughing
at me, I told him that Jive-John can read any running
and any pass play as soon as they break the huddle.
Big Keywest started laughing at him, and told him Jive
ain't no joke at linebacker. Ain't that right David
"Coach" Sears, Big Jit, Biz, T.J., Big Coon (FWB), Lil
Terry? Ain't that right Allenwood Noles, Beaumont
Gators, Pollock Rams and Cowboys? The Badland family I
haven't forgot you. I'll tell the truth that is was in
fact "Mike Harper" who told me to write this book
again. After I told him that I wrote a book years ago.
So he's responsible for this, so if it blows don't be
mad at me be mad at him (Ball). "Chico!" And Plexx I
really didn't want to put you in here because you
killed my man Hump (R.I.P. Hump). And I hope the Feds
come ask you who's Hump and why you kill him? Twin,
Spoon, K-9? I think that's his name it's been awhile.
Hey Boobie, I remember the talks and it was a pleasure
"Black" Note: You know when you've read a good book
when you can remember "Raise you rump and get ready
for the vicious Hump." And I'll take this one to my
grave "Stick the needle in the groove!"

Its seems as though I have to go a little further than expected. The young boy Cornelius "Keady" Johnson, And the (Fruits) Anthony and Dave Mohammed. Old Avon came at me with a little fire in his voice over this, so Avon "The Mayor" McCray, Tarone "Ty" Wilhite, Sandy "P-Nut" Zimmerman shimmy baby. I have to give another special thanks to (Rell) Ben Hood the author of "Halfway To Hell" thanks for the plug Rell. And this old Eastern Shore Bama named Torence "T.J." Smith. And my homie Andre "Pig" Holland. James "Big Cash" Greene-El and pulling up the rear is Quentin "Q" McQueen, oh damn before I forget another special thanks to Sgt. T. Karn, thanks for that helping hand to get me over the hump of getting this book publish. It's hard to believe that you and the other three actually work here, thank you. James and Brian Gibson (Gemo and Knots) be quiet before I put y'all's middle name in here. It took me fifty years to do one thing good huh? I know you two are smiling at me. Look I don't know Granny real name Granny always worked, but I remember Lush? So Rest In Peace Mr. and Mrs. Lush Kelly, Granny always said I was crazy. And this is a must, a heart felt I love you all to everyone who went to Lucy Ellen Moten while I was there, no I take that back let's talk in code. To every one who knows the words to the "Language Art Is Over" song. (Smile) We can always prove if they really, really went there with us can't we? The saddest thing about writing this book is I can't do a special piece for my best friend (and brother) his brother and sister who are my brother and sister. I didn't get their time line dates as I requested along with their full names so I could do a real rest in peace to them and to honor their family which also is my family, so I guess this proves it huh? And especially his mother who took me in when the world was at it's coldest at that time around fifty below "Love ya Ma!" but I don't have your real name, damn it's hurts me. Love me some Miss Betty too, she's just the sweetest woman in the world? I can't forget rest in peace Mrs. Meriam Wilkes, "Big Merm" to her son Tom. Last but not lease my main man Big Bino! Bino I never knew your name, but anyway how you like it? It's pure garbage at its best baby. And by the way this has been a Pure Garbage Production®.

Biography

J.J. Honesty-Bey was born on November the 13th and raised in the small town of South East, right outside of Washington D.C. Which in those days had a population around one hundred twenty five thousand. South East was one of the most beautiful places on Earth to grow up in. He attended Drew, Savoy, Cramer, Wilkerson, Moten, Douglass and Anacostia schools. He also attended the following higher learning schools: The Receiving Home, Cedar Knoll and the prestigious Oak Hill. "Go Tiger!"

This is the worst written book in the history of mankind the sad part is I couldn't put it down.
Earnest "Rat" Ratcliffe R.I.P

This is a classic example of when good stories happens to bad writers.
Anonymous

It was just a simple diamond bank robbery that turned into an double homicide robbery. Now on their way from Washington D.C. to Miami, Florida to sell their precious stones. The diamonds, rubies, sapphires and emeralds are not what they think they are, and the diamond bank itself wasn't what they thought it was. With multiple U.S. agencies including the F.B.I. and Homeland Security, multiple law enforcement, Deputies, Sheriffs, State Troopers, mercenaries and terrorists after them. The youths are running for their lives from people trying to eliminate them. A Frenchman who came to America to rob the same diamond bank only to see it robbed by the youths, he is betrayed by those who employed him for the job. And now he's out on his own looking for the youths. What will happen if he or someone else finds them before the U.S. Government? With the world hot on their heels chasing them to Miami the last thing Juice-Hop, Bernard, Teeny-Man and Babylon needs is for one of them to not be who they supposed to be after pulling off the biggest score the world has ever seen with, The Georgetown Heist.

Printed in the United States
By Bookmasters